The Liberator Saga

* Book 1 *

Dust House and the West Wind

Dalila Caryn

Illustrated by
Yenthe Joline

For my own personal coven: Mom, Alysia and Shani. The magic
is in our love.
~Dalila Caryn

To my amazing siblings:
Elim for unwillingly giving me advice when I ask for it.
Ezra for always making me laugh.
Yerusha for being beautiful and allowing me to take reference
pictures of her.
Chayim for being incredibly smart and sweet.
And Yaakov and Menorah for bothering me while I'm working,
hiding in my room, teasing me, and being cute and funny.
I love you guys so much!
~Yenthe Joline

"After the dust cleared, and all we were left with was wreckage and blood-watering soil, I couldn't help wondering if it wasn't truly us Sarah wanted cursed, and not the town. Her blood, the spring of such sorrows." From the journals of Esther Lynn Franklin, 6th matron of the Women of Terra.

Jemma closed her eyes and rolled onto her back, allowing the sunlight to caress her skin with warmth as the current rolled across her, cooling her in the same instant. No one understood this, the freedom of being one with the cold and the heat and the life of the air. Nothing followed her up here. Not fear, or sadness, or… anything. Here, she was just Jemma. It was like floating in the lake that was the air, and the beat of her wings was like rippling waves.

Throwing her arms wide, Jemma shook out her hair and giggled at the tickling trail of air across her neck. She shut her eyes, tilting her head from side to side to play with the sunlight. She could stay like this forever, peaceful, unfettered hap —

Beep. Beep. Beep.
Beep. Beep. Beep.

Jemma nearly fell from the sky, she was so startled. The alarm on her watch sounded again.

Beep. Beep. Beep.

Jemma rolled over in the air, coming upright with her invisible wings beating. She hovered. Reaching out her right hand, she turned off the alarm and looked down at her dusty husk of a home.

Four walls and a roof, Gran would say. *Can't want for more 'n that.*

The crops looked disgusting. Half were dead and rotting, and the rest looked nearly starved. She ought to do something about that.

The more she looked, the closer it grew. Jemma shut her eyes and filled her entire being with air. She needed to stay airborne long enough to reach the porch or she'd have to walk through that maze of death. Her wings felt heavy just from gazing at the ground. All that soil held was death.

She didn't know how she'd stayed up this long. There were so many chores to do. She couldn't afford to spend all day playing with the wind and the sun.

Jemma opened her eyes, beating her wings with renewed effort towards the plain grayish brown beams of home. When she was nearly on the porch, her hands closed involuntarily into fists, and her teeth clinched up. She'd been doing this for years, but no matter how softly she landed, how much weight she put on her left leg, no matter what, she always felt the impact in her right knee. She felt a crack—as if it would shatter into a thousand pieces again.

Thud.

Jemma clenched her teeth and her eyes, even her hands. She clenched every muscle she could against the pain radiating across her entire right side, but she didn't make a noise. She never made a noise.

And for what? There was no one to hear her any longer.

The pain receded slowly until she only felt it pulsing down from her hip. Jemma opened her eyes and uncurled her fingers. Her right hand felt odd, heavy and sticky. She stared at it uncomprehending for a moment. A pen. An orange, felt-tipped pen was…growing out of her palm like some creepy sixth finger.

Another time, she might not have taken notice; Jemma nearly always had a pen in hand. But this was downright strange. It wasn't her ever-present blue fine-point pen that ink slid from in a smooth soft flow, like paint. Felt-tipped pens were perhaps the least inspiring writing utensil, short of sharpies and lip liner. What could it mean?

Well, clearly there was rain coming.

Orange floods out for attention.

Jemma always saw orange when rain was coming. But usually, the color set the sky on fire, or painted the walls of her home with something other than dirt brown for once. The pen was new.

It was a bad omen.

She'd been careful not to fly any further than the pig farmer's house; everyone knew Earl was a drunk. So, if he saw a nearly fifteen-year-old girl with flaming red hair flying around, who would believe him?

And so what if they did? No one came near this place. *Dust House* they called it. From dust it was made, and to dust it would return.

They hoped.

But what did the pen mean? Jemma's dwindling supply of flying powder was shut up tight in a lockbox, buried beneath Gran in the cellar, so no one could find it. As messages went, this was too vague for Jemma's taste. Couldn't the universe just put a sticky note in her palm with, *You're going to die in a rainstorm,* written across it in big letters.

Written.

Jemma lunged towards the door, her pain forgotten for the mystery of her pen-growing palm. But just one step on her right foot and it all came rushing back. She leaned against the doorjamb for support.

Don't look so weak, girl! Women of Terra don't let pain defeat them.

Jemma straightened and yanked the screen door wide. Without so much as a wince, she forced her feet forward. Left first; her right leg jerked and dragged a little as always, and as always, she pretended not to feel it. Shoving the door in, she walked across the threshold, not even bothering to shut the door as she heard the screen hiss and slam into place. She walked straight to the desk and pulled out a sheet of paper. She leaned over it, her hand poised to write. She wasn't sure she would get answers this way, but putting pen to paper seemed logical.

Gran always said Jemma had the gift of sight. If only she'd let her mind fly the way she did her body. Closing her eyes, Jemma let out a high trilling whistle. Not like a human would, but like a bird with a magnitude of energy in every tiny burst of song.

The sound exploded from Jemma's lips and the air came rushing around her as it did when she flew, quivering like the thrash of a million beating wings. It lifted her hand and the orange pen, protruding from between her bent fingers. It seemed to lift the entire room and set it off on a gentle waft around the nether world, until her consciousness was made up of colorful lights and the distant sound of a woman humming.

Slowly, the lights faded and the room righted itself. When nothing was left of the magic, Jemma stood in her dusty, empty living room once more. Somewhere along the way, she'd stopped whistling, even forgot the pen. Now seeing the plain wood walls of her house, she remembered and looked down.

It worked!

She couldn't believe it, but there before her, written in ugly orange ooze, that looked distinctly like a slug's trail, was the proof. Just two words in block lettering:

HE'S COMING.

There was only one *he* the universe would see fit to warn her about. The curse Gran put on him must be lifting. Time to stock the cellar and prepare for storm weather. Pa was coming home.

"Ruth would be called Sotsona, a name from 'our' people. But Papa's people are ours as well. I bare the name he gave me with pride. I am Sarah Anne Smith, so he will know me on his return." From the journals of Sarah Anne Smith, 2nd matron of the Women of Terra.

As soon as Jemma understood the message, the pen peeled itself out of her skin like a scab and fell to the floor. Jemma stared at it, her mind blank. The pen lay in a pile of goo and the bits of rubbery skin it had claimed. Her hand was covered in the same ugly orange goo as the floor. Pa was coming.

When I die, you'll have to be vigilant. Gran's voice stumbled around the empty space in Jemma's mind.

Absently, Jemma rubbed off the goo on the leg of her jeans. She hadn't been vigilant. Hadn't even been wary. In the three months since she buried Gran in the cellar, Jemma had done almost nothing but fly, write and keep herself and May Bell living. Now she would have to do it all, or as much as she could anyway.

Who knew when he would get here. There might not be time enough to do everything Gran said she should. The cellar had to be stocked, as many crops as could be salvaged should be harvested, and the family stones had to be taken out and buried in a perimeter around the house. Then there was the question of whether to move May Bell into the cellar straight away or hope Pa didn't come home in a temper. And Jemma hadn't looked over one of the family tomes in years, and Gran always insisted that reading the tomes was the most important job of all.

You gotta know your history, girl. Good and bad, or you're just another bee drone goin' about your business without a worthwhile thought in your head.

Jemma still felt the knock of Gran's pointer finger as she tapped Jemma's forehead to drive the point home. Apparently, Jemma had an even harder head than Gran realized.

What if Pa showed up in an hour? There was no way she could be finished with even one of the tasks by then. Of course, that would defeat the purpose of a warning altogether. But maybe it came too late. The universe could screw up, couldn't it? It was vague enough that Jemma might never have understood the message; so clearly, it could screw up. But it didn't matter; she had to do whatever she could.

Family stones were the most important thing on the list, and possibly one of the hardest to do, so Jemma would start there. She headed immediately for the cellar on foot. It wasn't something she'd done much of since Gran died. It was much easier to fly. When Gran was alive, she always made Jemma walk.

You can't always count on magic, Jem Beam. You've got to strengthen that leg of yours.

As she limped over to the cellar door, Jemma realized Gran was right. She was much quicker on foot when she'd been exercising every day. She would have to give up flying for a while. Well…maybe not completely.

The cellar floor was soft earth. The same earth that held all their crops. The same soft earth her great, great gran grew the house out of. People always wondered how it was that their farm was so fertile. The most fertile land in Oklahoma. Whatever was planted in this earth grew; despite drought or time of year, everything grew. People called them lucky, blessed, *witches*. And every once in a while, something worse. But whenever people asked, Gran just shrugged.

"We put everything we love into the earth, so the earth gives us love back," she would say.

And Jemma never said a word. She just stood there smiling secretively at the ground. Gran would turn to Jemma with a bright smile after the people had gone. "It ain't a lie," she'd say before swinging away back into the house.

Gran always seemed to float and sway, like she was dancing when she walked. Or she had, 'til a month before she died; then she started moving slower, haltingly. She'd looked old for the very first time, as if she had simply gone to bed one night vibrant and alive and woken up the next day with one foot in the earth.

Using the stair rail to steady her, Jemma moved between the circle of headstones and sat down on the soft earth before the headstone she'd prepared for Gran.

"It isn't a lie, Gran. I haven't been doing so well with the farm. Not that I was ever much good with that. But I'll do better. You'll see." Jemma looked around the room At the six headstones that stood firm in a circle, all the past matrons of Terra, save one: Sarah, who had died and been buried outside of Oklahoma. "The thing is Gran, Great Gran, Gran Mary, Gran Josephine, Great Aunt Sotsona," Jemma looked cautiously at the oldest of the headstones, the one with the greatest power. "Mother Sisika, seems there's storm weather coming. I'm gonna need a bit of help." Jemma bowed her head for a moment of silence then got to work.

She couldn't move the stones quickly enough without the rest of her flying powder, so leaning forward, she began to dig with her hands. She dug around a spray of pansies that appeared to have sprung up from the ground next to Gran's headstone. After she pulled enough of the dirt away, she ran her fingers under the edge of the flower box planted there and pulled it up. Beneath it, a small tunnel led off, stopping out of sight beneath Gran's grave. A frayed, dirt-crusted rope hung through a small hole in the flower box down into the tunnel. Setting the box aside, Jemma pulled the rope up and out of the tunnel, dragging a corked bottle up along with it.

The bottle was small, fitting into the palm of Jemma's hand. It was made of thick clear glass and had two handles on the sides like a Greek urn. Jemma untied the string from the bottle and ran it back into the tunnel. She replaced the flower box. She may need the hiding place again, so she covered it up just as it had been before.

Once the room was in order, Jemma leaned back and dusted dirt off the bottle. Wouldn't it be wonderful if instead of having to work hard to prepare for the storm, her dusting woke an ancient genie? She dusted a bit harder, rubbed and rubbed and shut her eyes tight, not really believing, but having to at least try.

Nothing happened. Of course not, the *let's make your life easier* sort of magic never did work. Jemma sighed examining the bottle; there wasn't much powder inside, maybe a quarter of a bottle. She would need to make more before long, but it would be enough for what she needed today.

It's not about the magic, Jemma. It's about being weightless as a bubble and open to going where the wind carries you. The magic is what makes you weightless. But the openness — that's all you, Jem Beam…all you.

Jemma shut her eyes against the memory and the tears. She gave herself exactly seven seconds and shook it off. Uncorking the bottle, she tipped it forward onto her tongue and licked up the powder like a sugar stick. Shaking her head at the bitter aftertaste, Jemma set the bottle aside and got to digging around the headstones.

"It sang in my hand when I claimed it — my stone, my place. How can it be called a curse to love this land and this history?" From the journals of May Bell Franklin, 6th generation daughter of Terra.

Jemma found a totem to represent the house, rather than dragging herself and the stones around the whole thing. It was a risk, burying all the stones in one place, but Pa couldn't know about them. It left Jemma with enough energy to grab a bushel of apples from the orchard and set out a sort of alarm system, before pulling out one of Gran's journals and settling in to wait.

Gran always said, "If you don't go out to meet your fate, it'll just kick over the door and come in for you, and that's just one more mess to clean up."

She had been full of those little sayings; usually, Jemma just smiled and filed them away in her head. Taking this one quite literally, Jemma sat on Gran's rocking chair, on the front porch, and waited for her fate to show up.

The sun had been down for over two hours when Jemma decided fate wouldn't be coming today. The only noise inside the house was the see-sawing whine of the floor boards as she walked across them. She hated the silence. It had been like this since Gran had died. In a way, it would be a relief to have Pa home. At least there would be a voice to hear, aside from her own.

Jemma looked around the room for something to do. Nothing. Well, she could read the family tomes like Gran would want, but she couldn't seem to gather enough enthusiasm for that. By and large, they were all just boring stories and Jemma had been reading them since she knew how. She couldn't imagine the secret knowledge she was supposed to have gleaned from them suddenly occurring to her now. On a sigh, she went to the kitchen to make her dinner and realized the one part of the preparations she'd fairly well neglected: food. There was barely anything save for a little bread, a little cheese, and the apples she'd picked.

Well, there was nothing to do about it now. Even if Jemma was willing to go into town, which she wasn't, the market was closed, and she'd have no way to get anything home. She'd pull in more crop tomorrow and hope this didn't turn into a siege. She made herself a grilled cheese and walked to May Bell's room to eat.

She'd forgotten about checking on May Bell in favor of preparing for Pa. Of course, if she hadn't prepared for Pa, May Bell wouldn't stand a chance anyway.

Jemma settled into the stuffed recliner beside May Bell's bed. She almost always sat here when she ate. May Bell couldn't eat, hadn't since the accident, but Allen, May Bell's doctor, said she could smell the food. He told Jemma it would make her happy to know Jemma ate with her. Of course, at the time Jemma was nine, so she believed him. It wasn't until she got older that Jemma realized nothing made May Bell happy, or sad, or anything else for that matter. People in comas didn't know what was going on. How could they possibly be happy? But it didn't matter by then; it was tradition. Jemma had missed days in the past. Once she even decided she wouldn't eat with her anymore, but she always came back.

May Bell lay, eyes closed, her dark hair in two neat braids to protect it from tangles. Her hands lay over one another atop the sheet like a modern-day Snow White awaiting her kiss. For her lack of sun and stress, she still appeared to be in her mid-twenties, but her last birthday left her thirty-four. She was so…sweet looking. Soft and beautiful and innocent. It was impossible to resist coming back. It seemed somehow wrong to abandon her, even though nothing Jemma ever did would wake her.

When she was done eating, Jemma stood up and checked the machines recording everything they said on the clipboard Allen used. She'd watched him do it a million times, or Gran on the days Allen couldn't come by. She took a warm damp cloth and cleaned May Bell's face and the areas around the feeding tube and IV and checked to see if the catheter bag was full. Allen would always talk to May Bell when he did this; he said it was impolite any other way.

Jemma wanted to help for what seemed like forever. She was sure that Gran and Allen felt May Bell responding to them when they cared for her. More than anything else that was what Jemma wanted, to feel or see some kind of response, but she hadn't. Jemma had been caring for all of May Bell's needs since Gran died. It was too much of a risk to keep Allen coming by; he might tell someone about Gran, and then Jemma would be taken out of her home. She wasn't willing to risk it, so she put a spell on him, made him forget he came out to the farm on a near daily basis, and he hadn't been back since.

Jemma tried, since taking over, to always have something to say, about flying or about a book, or the number of clouds in the sky, even about Gran. But now as she moved around the bed, massaging May Bell's arms and legs, stretching and bending them, she could think of only two words. They floated around her brain like the stag on a carousel, always slightly sinister-looking even as it was beautiful. It went around and around, sliding up this time and down the next, on an invisible pole: *he's coming.*

She couldn't bring herself to say that to her mother. What if everyone was right and May Bell heard, but couldn't respond? What would it be like to be trapped inside your head unable to get out, frightened but incapable of saying it? Jemma couldn't do that to her. How could she tell her, the man whose temper had left her in this bed, was coming back, especially when Jemma already felt so helpless to stop him? The longer she went without saying it, the more convinced she became that May Bell knew. She couldn't explain it. Maybe it was May Bell who sent her the message. She just felt that somehow her mother knew.

"The signs say he's coming." Jemma slipped onto the edge of the bed beside her mother's feet, laying down the leg she'd been stretching. "But you don't have to worry." Jemma lifted the next leg and began massaging it from the foot up. "I'll keep you safe. He won't get anywhere near you. I set up an alarm system and the protection circle today. Everything is nice and snug, so you'll be safe." As she spoke, Jemma moved around the bed never looking at her mother's face, keeping all her attention on whichever limb she was holding.

"He's nothing I can't handle," she said with firm confidence, moving to her mother's right arm. "No daughter of yours is so soft she can't withstand a bit of blast and bluster. You'll see. You can rest easy now." Jemma lay her mother's arm down gently and pulled the blanket up over it, smoothing it around her.

"Of course," Jemma muttered, almost to herself, "Gran said when you were little, if you got scared, you couldn't sleep without someone lying beside you." Jemma fiddled with a piece of string that hung down from the blanket, pulling it out as she spoke. "If you want, I'll sleep by you, so you don't get scared."

Jemma stared at her mother's face, searching for some sign that she understood. Nothing happened. She just lay in a peaceful sleep, Snow White in her glass box.

Jemma slipped off her shoes and climbed into the bed on her mother's right side, away from the tubes. She lay on her side, facing her mother, with near a foot of empty space between them, afraid to move and bump her. She sat beside her mother nearly every day, held her hand countless times, and for near three months now, she had massaged her muscles on a daily basis. But she couldn't remember ever lying next to her. She always looked so fragile lying there in the bed all day, so tiny. It seemed strange to lay down beside her, as though she hadn't really been a person until Jemma climbed onto the bed with her.

Jemma didn't know how long she lay on the bed watching her mother. Watching the little puffs and sinks of her breathing. But little by little, the space between them disappeared, until she was curled up at her mother's side. One of Jemma's arms lay over her mother's chest with her hand resting softly on her left shoulder.

"Goodnight, Mama."

Closing her eyes, Jemma heard her mother's voice, as if from the furthest stretches of her memory.

Goodnight, Jemma mine.

Giants Kneel before Him

The town had dirt roads. Not just unpaved or cobblestone but actual bone dry, brown as the ground, fly in your face and make you cough dirt. And Kai knew from the grating in his throat that there was no water nearby. Kai was born in the water, for the water—you could say he was born of the water; there was no surviving here. And Black Boot knew it, even as he pulled Kai by the invisible chain that bound him as a slave, pulling him towards death.

Black Boot dragged gales of wind behind him in his coat, wherever he went. And here—in all this dirt—the winds were sloshing and churning the dry earth, turning the very air brown. Great billowing clouds of dirt formed in front and behind them so the air they walked through was denser than the thickest fog.

There was no escape, no one to help Kai. How could they? No one knew where to find him. No one knew he'd been taken. He couldn't reach his magic. Before long, he'd be an empty thing, serving without any real understanding of what that meant. He'd cease to be.

Kai shook off his defeat, watching the men along the road. They might have been giants before, but they shrunk into their tired brown homes and slammed thirsty wooden doors behind them. Fleeing like so many fish before an attack. They abandoned everything—hulking metal brutes with teeth caked over in dried dirt, animals that knew better then to wait for a rescue and fled off ahead of the rising tide of dust that followed in Black Boot's wake.

Kai should have been as smart when Black Boot's gales descended on his cove. He should have stayed where he was, safe in the caves watching the foam and fist of waves reshape the walls. Then he wouldn't be stuck as he was now, all but swallowed by the dirt that would soon bury him.

That at least was a better fate than an eternity of this. Trudging on, through the town, out of it, along an endless dirt highway. There was nothing, no hope. With every step, Kai dried out more, dying a little. He couldn't take much more of this.

Black Boot stopped suddenly, sending Kai crashing to the ground under the weight of the two bags he carried. He fell on the only patch of green he had seen in days. It wasn't grass but the big bushy leaves of some type of plant. Kai didn't care. Jerking as far forward as his bridle would let him, Kai sunk his teeth into a leaf to break it open, trying to suck out whatever moisture it had. He was completely oblivious to his surroundings as he went from one leaf to another sucking them dry and getting barely a few drops of water.

Screw death and defeat; if he could find water, he could fight.

Kai got through three leaves when Black Boot yanked hard on the bridle, oversetting Kai's balance and sending him face first into the dirt beneath the plants.

"We're not here for breakfast, kelpie," Black Boot said distractedly, his focus off on some spot in the distance. "Get up."

Kai shoved his heavy body from the ground with all the force he could muster. Dirt from his fall was still in his mouth, soaking up the little bit of liquid he'd just found, but he refused to spit it out. Instead he swallowed, hoping to absorb the water again. Bending low to lift the bags, Kai felt his dry body cracking under the strain of his movements. Black Boot gave a light tug on the bridle and Kai lurched forward, barely catching himself in order to keep his feet.

Stretched out in front of them was a seemingly endless field of green. Black Boot stood absolutely still, but the wind rushed on ahead of him, shifting the plants so they bowed in preparation for his arrival. At first glance, the field appeared to be a lush oasis in the middle of this dusty stretch of nothing beyond the town. But as Kai looked closer, he noticed all the plants were poorly kept. Vegetables hung long past ripe on stalks and vines, rotting. The few that were still good looked like they would soon be choked to death by the invading weeds. The land must be abandoned; no one would go to the trouble of planting all this only to watch it go to rot without lifting a hand.

Black Boot had not moved; he stood staring down the path between the crops. He hadn't been this still in the entire time he held Kai captive. His eyes were intent on some shape in the distance. Kai looked but could not distinguish anything from the bleak brown waves that rolled over the fields of crops, but there was a light tinkling music coming from within the cloud of dust.

Kai began to inch towards the taller plants, to his right, keeping his eyes focused on Black Boot's face. His face rarely revealed anything, but as he stared off down the road, his lips curled up into a sneer, showing just a hint of teeth. Kai shuddered, accidentally jiggling the bridle.

"Come on, kelpie. They're playing my song." Black Boot set off towards the sound of the chimes, dragging Kai along in his wake.

Kai stumbled, unable to banish that sneer from his mind. Black Boot had never looked so evil. Kai hoped whoever Black Boot was headed for had seen him coming and had the good sense to run away. Nothing else would save them.

"Orange floods out for attention; Red bleeds, or burns with passions bright;

Green is the face of one who envies; Blue shows tranquility and might;

Grey is the earth, with thirsty pallor; Brown is Terra's healthy hue; Purple

heralds perilous power; Yellow rips a friend from you." From the journals

of Mary Croger, 4th matron of the Women of Terra.

J emma woke to the soft tinkling of the smallest chime she had set out as an alarm system. It was just after dawn, and orange-tinted light slid into the room. Leaning up on one arm, Jemma stared down at her mother. She hadn't moved, of course not, but Jemma thought maybe she saw the beginnings of a smile on her mother's face. Leaning down, she gave her mother a quick kiss on the head and slid off the bed.

"I'll keep you safe." The chimes were growing steadily louder outside. Jemma spared a quick look over her mother's machines and supplies. She would need to order more catheter bags, and—well everything soon. But the supplies should last the week. And if she hadn't gotten rid of Pa by then…

Jemma shook off a shudder and rushed from the room to change. Once she was dressed, Jemma walked outside to meet her fate. The only thing that gave her pause was the sky: not one cloud in sight. She'd been counting on that storm.

In the distance, Jemma saw what looked like a wall of brown smoke, moving in on the farm. On a clear day, she could stand on this porch and see clear across the crops down to the main road into town. Today, all she could see over the tips of the cornfield was the encroaching wall of brown.

Every tiny ting of the wind chimes sent a wave of pain twisting up her bad leg. She hadn't stood still this long since her accident. With every second, the pain grew worse, but somehow, she felt it less. In place of the pain, a vacuum of fear grew outward, knotting up all her muscles so tightly that she could feel the flow of blood as it squeezed its way through her veins. The larger chimes were caught by the wind now, clanging against one another. The clanging of the chimes and the pain of her whole body wound tight into one aching muscle and the invading wall of dust; it was all too much. Her lungs felt empty, as though the air was simply evaporating from within her. All she wanted to do was hide. Let him kill her if that's what he wanted. Let him take the farm, the house, the family tomes, whatever he wanted. Just to lie down and let the dirt fall over her until she blended in so well that she was invisible.

She could run away—well, fly. Who would blame her?

Gran.

Jemma took a step forward and all the pain her fear had hidden came rushing back. She staggered forward and clutched onto one of the porch beams while she regained her balance. Slowly, taking deep breaths with every step, Jemma descended from the porch and into the yard. She walked stretching her leg, shaking off the pain as she walked around to the side of the house where May Bell's room was. She came to a stop a few feet from the window and looked down at the little stump of the old apple tree and the ground around it.

Women of Terra face their fears, Jemma. We don't hide.

Gran had said it a hundred times, seemed to think Jemma was a coward. Maybe she was right. Standing here now, with her feet nearly touching the ground where she had buried Gran's stone, it seemed like Gran was right beside her, trying to pound the fear out of Jemma with a lecture.

"Maybe we should hide," Jemma said aloud, looking at her mother's window. "It's not as though there are many of us left."

"Sure there would be more of us living were we cowards. But that's no life at all, girl. You'll stand firm. It isn't in you to do else."

"Pa hid."

"You're father up and blew away. And you're better for it. But if there's one thing you can be sure of, it's that foul winds and hard times have a habit of blowing back around, Jem Beam. Best to just accept it and buckle down."

"I can't beat him, Gran." Jemma shifted her feet as the pain of standing still crept up her leg again. "I haven't been studying. I don't know what curse you used 'cause you never showed me. And I'm not as strong as you."

"Jemima, did you not listen to a thing I've said? It ain't about beating him." Jemma could feel Gran's hands settle on her shoulders, holding her in place. She could see her deep brown eyes boring into her. *"You are Terra, a daughter of the earth. For you, it's about standing, firm as a rock, shoulders straight, head high, and eyes baring down right at your oppressor. It's about saying, 'I'll not be moved. No matter how high you toss my home, or how low you beat my body, I'll not be moved by anything but death.' Winning's his game, not ours."*

Jemma stared at the empty air in front of her. It had seemed so real, like Gran was there. Gran would definitely blame her if she left. But May Bell wouldn't. She couldn't feel anything so she couldn't blame her. Jemma could mix the flying powder in with the solution in her IV and then, she could carry them both, far away from here. Somewhere safe, where he would never find them.

"There's nowhere the wind can't blow, Jem Beam. Least ways, nowhere you can breathe."

The world in front of Jemma's face flashed a violent purple, and all around her the chimes began clanging loudly.

Purple heralds perilous power.

Too late! Pa was home.

The Ground From Which I Grew

Black Boot would know the way forward with his eyes closed. His feet carried him as though pulled by some invisible force. The ground beckoned him, had for eight long years, and now at last, he was returning to it. Every step infused him with energy.

Eight years. For eight years, he had traveled down this path in his mind, traveled home. And for eight years, he'd been pushed away from what was his. Now he would reclaim it.

He smiled and let the wind paint his teeth with dirt. It didn't matter; he was returning to the ground that made him the master of his own fate. And he had no intention of being driven from this land, or from its power, ever again.

The old witch couldn't keep him away forever. No one was strong enough to hold back the wind.

"Mama makes me read all these stories, of the Women of Terra, all so sad. I can't help thinking their lives would have been better if they'd had fathers like mine. He won't let anything happen to me or Mama." From the journals of May Bell Franklin, 7th generation daughter of Terra.

Brown clouds billowed out around the house in a circle. Leaning on the porch beams, Jemma listened to the fierce whistling of the wind as it beat against the protective shield created by the family stones. It was like standing in the center of a cyclone, untouched. All around her was chaos; dirt, leaves and rocks slammed against each other, the chimes clanged, the wind screamed, and in the midst of it, something metal jangled, maybe chains. But beyond all the chaos, Jemma was sure she heard her mother crying out to her. She sounded just as she had that day: terrified trying to catch Jemma as the storm pulled them apart.

Jemma closed her eyes expecting to relive it all again, as she had a hundred times before. The terror of being yanked into the sky against her will and being spun around like a twig. Her stomach dropping as her mother was yanked up as well, reaching out for her. The dream was the only time Jemma ever heard her mother's voice. But she heard it now, and even though she was thinking about that day, she wasn't feeling it, wasn't reliving it.

Jemma opened her eyes and looked into the wind. Was she out there? Maybe that's why Gran had just given in, because she knew May Bell was trapped in the wind and the chaos that Pa pulled behind him. Maybe…maybe they could be a family again.

For a second, every pore in Jemma's body exploded with hope and excitement. She shifted her weight to both feet, stepping towards the shield, and pain shot up her leg, snapping her back to reality like nothing else could.

Fantasies were for little girls whose fathers didn't cause tornados when they were angry. Jemma lived in reality. And reality was Gran dead from too much work and buried in the cellar. Reality was May Bell in a coma—forever. Reality was months of physical therapy just to learn to stand again and years of it to keep her walking. Reality was that, even if she somehow found her voice, May Bell was broken, body and soul, and she would never get out of that bed.

Standing here between Pa and his goal, waiting to end up a vegetable just like her mother—that was reality too.

The wind died just as fast as it had shown up. The dust that filled the air fell to the ground as though weighted like stones. Out of the clearing air, his two shining black boots stood out against the dust-colored ground. His haggard-looking cloak followed the motion of his legs forward before bumping against his legs and settling back away from his body.

Jemma expected him to seem smaller than he had seemed in her dreams. She'd grown a few feet since he left. But somehow, even standing on the porch above him, he seemed to tower over her, throwing her into the shadow.

His cloak was worn and dusty, like the rest of his clothes. They looked as though he never wore anything else. His denim pants were frayed and faded, and his top was a simple old grey tee. The only interesting part of his attire were the boots, shiny black, with thick soles and braided horsehair for ties; they looked brand new, untouched by the elements. They were the same pair he always wore—the pair that never left his feet.

They stared at each other in silence for a time. Pa's face seemed worn smooth by the dirt he carried around with him. There wasn't a single line on it, but he looked older still. And his shoulder-length hair was matted and dirty. Jemma wondered if he was ever clean. Aside from his boots, which shone immaculately, he looked like he was completely made of dirt, like the terra cotta soldiers she'd seen pictures of in her world history book.

"Been moving tombstones, have you, sweetheart?" Pa said breaking the silence with a sneer. "It's disrespectful."

It hadn't occurred to Jemma that he would know how the shield was created. It unnerved her, watching him pace along the perimeter. Would he know where to look? How to break the spell?

"What should I expect though?" he said as he began to pace along the perimeter. "Your grandmother was a heathen. And she's had you for eight years. What else would you be?"

Jemma nearly snapped that Gran went to church every Sunday, but that would be playing into his hand. And anyway, Jemma didn't go.

The wind didn't follow him as he moved; apparently, the show was over for the time being. But as he moved, Jemma noticed a boy sprawled out on the ground behind her father. He was gasping for air and clinging to something Jemma couldn't see in his right hand. His eyes pled with her, but he seemed unable even to lift his head from the ground.

Jemma had never considered herself a soft touch. She doubted anyone traveling with her father was worth the time or effort of saving. It was probably some sort of trick. But the boy looked near tears, or death, maybe both. And her "heathen" grandmother had raised her to help people in need.

Careful not to put much weight on her right leg, Jemma hurried off across the porch to the old-fashioned water pump. She filled the bucket halfway and started back across the porch. She could feel Pa watching but refused to look his way. Placing the bucket on the inside edge of the shield, Jemma bent over and gave the bucket a good shove, sending it through. It slid to a stop half a foot from the boy's face. He smiled up at her with such gratitude, she nearly smiled in return. But just as the boy was bending his head into the pail, Pa raised his arm into the air and threw it backwards.

The boy flew a few feet into the air knocking the bucket over and landing with a soft thud a few feet away.

"Stop it!" Jemma ordered sharply.

For some reason, Pa obeyed. The boy lunged for the bucket and downed the bit that hadn't spilled out before laying his head against the wet ground as if to absorb the water through his skin.

Pa was looking down at the boy without expression. Jemma wondered if he even cared that the boy was so thirsty he was laying his head in the mud to be close to the water. Who were they to each other? They didn't look alike, but that didn't mean they weren't related. Did he talk to this boy he treated so badly?

It occurred to Jemma, as she stared down at the boy, that the first words she'd said to her father in eight years were "stop it." So much like her last words to him. She wondered if he remembered, if he'd even heard.

No, Pa. Wait. Don't go. Stop. Stop, Pa!

"Do you even know what it is you're helping?" Pa asked, startling Jemma out of the past. He was looking right at her, as though he had been for a while. She would have to pay closer attention. "He's a kelpie. They're thieves, scavengers, and murderers. They carry people off to the bottom of rivers and lakes and eat them."

Jemma said nothing. With her eyes steady on her father, she shot her hand through the shield and yanked the empty pail back against her chest. The boy was still too weak to put up a protest. He fell forward, barely catching himself before his face hit the ground.

"Please…" he wheezed out over his dried-out throat.

Jemma walked back to the pump, filling the pail all the way this time. She'd read about kelpies, she knew the legends. Shape-shifting water creatures that usually appeared in the form of a horse and carried foolish travelers to the bottom of rivers and devoured all but the heart. But legends were built out of fear and imagination, and just a tiny bit of truth. Jemma had no doubt that somewhere, at some time, a kelpie kidnapped a human, but if you judged humans by Ted Bundy, you'd run and hide every time you saw one.

Pa was smiling when Jemma came back with the pail. A real smile, as though she had amused him somehow. It was an expression she remembered well from the "good ole days," as Gran had sarcastically referred to the pre-cyclone days. Jemma could remember nights when she would pull that smile out of her memory and hold onto it, thinking whatever happened after, Pa had loved her once. They had been happy once.

It made her angry now to see it. To have brought the smile with her actions. He wasn't worried about amusing her, making her happy. She didn't want to be the cause of his happiness. But she wouldn't be moved from helping the dying water horse in front of her.

Eyeing her father, Jemma bent down at the edge of the shield and thrust the bucket through, right next to the boy's face, pulling her arm back quickly. She didn't want to give Pa a chance to pull her out, or worse yet, find a way in.

"Not much of a talker, are you, sweetheart? You're mother had spirit like you. Of course, you never could shut her up."

Jemma flinched from inside her soul. It was all she could do not to pick up her own home and hurl it at her father. And she could do it too. Right now, she was capable of anything. She could feel the power pulsing through her, sending off little charges in the air like an electric storm.

Gran tried a hundred times to teach Jemma to move things with her mind, on purpose, but never with much success. But now, right in this moment, Jemma knew she could do it. But she didn't. Pa was the one who lost his temper; Jemma had learned to hold on to hers. She would never be like him.

Turning her attention away from her father, Jemma looked down at the boy. He was beginning to look better. He'd already gulped down well over half the water in the bucket. Jemma thought he might hurl if he didn't slow down, but then if he really was a kelpie he was probably used to a great deal more water. He shifted, setting aside the pail so he could sit up, but leaving one hand wrapped around its edge.

"Thank you!" He sighed out on a clear breath. For the first time, his voice was clear and strong, even a bit musical. "You saved my life."

He began to push to his feet. For the most part, he still looked ashen and dry, but his eyes and his smile had a bit of a sparkle to them that hadn't been there before. Standing, he was at least a half a foot taller than Jemma, and he looked a good deal older than he had on the ground. Originally, she'd thought him her age, maybe younger. But—she looked between him and her father again—he couldn't be a younger brother, but a man who would drop a car on his child probably wouldn't draw the line at an affair. So, he could be an older brother.

Inside and out of the shield, the wind picked up, the chimes rang out. Pa was through being ignored.

"This is all very adorable. Damsel thanking his white knight and all, but I'm tired. Open the shield, sweetie. You know you can't keep me out forever with children's magic."

"No." Jemma turned around to head back into the house. He was right; she couldn't keep him out forever. So, she should work on a plan for when he got in.

"Where did you bury your mother's stone?" he asked, halting Jemma in her tracks.

He didn't know? She couldn't move. How was it he didn't know? She had always assumed he realized that May Bell wasn't dead. He'd had her in his arms. But he thought Ma was dead. Maybe he'd meant her to be. Meant them all to be, but Gran was too strong for him.

"I need to see it. To pay my respects to May Bell. To your mother. Please." His voice was so pathetic and broken, you wouldn't know this was the man who had pulled a boy through the air to keep him from getting what he needed to survive. Or taunted her desire to help. He sounded remorseful and guilty.

Jemma turned to face her father, eight years' worth of anger ripping at her, trying to escape.

"You'll never see her again," she whispered, too angry to do anything else. "Any part of her."

He laughed. Actually threw his head back and laughed, so hard the clouds of dust shook the air. Who was this man? He was nothing like the father she remembered.

"And how are you going to stop me, little Jem?" he asked, walking up to the shield. "If you knew how to keep me away, you'd have done it before now. If you knew how to kill me, I've no doubt I'd be lying here on the ground dead. Do you think I don't know all the poison your grandmother's been feeding you? But she didn't give you what you really wanted, did she? She didn't show you how to beat me. How to get your revenge."

Jemma could see it too, her father spread out on the ground, bleeding and begging her for help. Pathetic, helpless and for once, full of regret. It was so vivid she had to remind herself it wasn't real.

Her father thought she would kill him if she could. Right now, she wanted to. He thought she hated him enough to kill him. He thought he had killed his wife. And all of them just danced around each other like duelists exchanging thrusts waiting for someone to bleed. There was something deeply wrong with her family.

Jemma looked at the boy again.

"Who are you?" she demanded suddenly, needing to know. "Why are you with him?"

"I'm Kai. He stole me from my home and bound me to him as a slave. And I am not what he says."

"Not a kelpie? Are you…related?"

"No! I am a kelpie, but I'm not a scavenger or a murderer. And I am no relation of his."

Jemma shrugged. So she was wrong. She didn't particularly care if he stole, and she knew dead people well enough to know they didn't care about the things they left behind. As for a murderer—well, there seemed to be plenty of those around here, so she couldn't very well judge, could she?

"I couldn't have bound him if he wasn't doing something wrong," Pa said coming to stand beside the boy.

Now that wasn't even slightly true. There were hundreds of ways to bind magical creatures. Folklore was full of them. What, Jemma wondered, did he hope to gain by convincing her that the boy was bad? What was he afraid of? Jemma smiled remembering something about kelpies, about all magical creatures. She looked away from her father, facing the boy.

In the Twist of Her Smile

The smile the girl wore was hideous. It twisted her sweet face into a monstrous copy of Black Boot's sneer.

Kai looked between the two, father and daughter, and began to back away. He'd been inclined to trust the girl; she had saved him after all. And she clearly had no great love for her father. But seeing her now, how twisted her smile had become, he had to wonder if she was any better than Black Boot. The look on her face said no. It said she had found a way to thwart Black Boot, and whatever way it was, Kai was going to be its agent.

"Let him go," the girl said, her eyes fixed on her father, who likewise was intent on her. She held her chin in the air with a look of such smug satisfaction that Kai backed away further.

For all the notice they paid his movements, he might as well not have been there. Kai wished with all that was in him that it were true, that he was at home, and this dry dead place was a dream. It changed nothing. He was still bound, his shoulders were still weighed down by Black Boot's bags.

"He stays with me," Black Boot said with that now familiar sneer. "He likes it here."

Kai could feel all the water he'd swallowed beginning to evaporate within him. There was no moisture in the air here. He needed more. If an opportunity came, to run or to fight, he would be useless as he was now.

"There is more than one way to bind a magical creature. In fact, there are several. Since he is a kelpie, I'm guessing you stole or tricked him out of his bridle."

"Such interest in my life, Jemma. I'm touched." Black Boot sounded surprised and oddly pleased. They were a strange family.

"Let him go. He's mine." The girl ignored her father.

"I saw him first," Black Boot taunted.

"Boy. Uh, Kai?" The girl turned his way, startling him. "I saved your life. It belongs to me now."

Kai stared at her in absolute horror. How could he possibly have been so stupid as to not see this coming? Crap! He'd even told her.

"Very good, dear," Black Boot chuckled windily. "I see your grandmother taught you something useful after all."

Kai ignored the byplay, absolutely horrified. Already, the weight of the bags was slipping from his shoulders and the bridle loosening. Life debts trumped all other types of binding. Good magic over trickery was how most people explained it. Most people weren't being tossed about like a pawn though. There was no physical binding involved in a life debt, and it was so much worse for it, because there was always a choice. He could deny the claim; if he ran away, he might even make it somewhere safe. But he would be cursed. Everything he touched would rot as evidence to the world of his rotten soul. He would become one of the unwanted, the placeless. No better than Black Boot.

Choking on the dry air that would kill Kai quickly enough, if one of these two didn't, Kai nodded his head once to indicate he understood.

"Come stand beside me." She smiled up at him, as though to reassure him that she was kind. Kai did as he was commanded, ignoring her reassurance.

Black Boot moved forward, to grab Kai back, or to follow him through the shield, he was not sure which. But it didn't matter. His daughter was too fast for him. There was a plonk, like the sound of a foot striking the bucket, but she hadn't moved. Still, the bucket jumped from the ground and connected with her father's hand, knocking him away.

Kai moved through the shield. It was a strange feeling; the air grew suddenly cold and hands, so many hands, reached out and pulled him through.

On the other side, it was as though he had imagined the feeling. The air was dry and hot, and the ground beneath his feet was firm. Kai glanced at Black Boot sputtering on the other side of the shield. A shield he could not see. Did the same hands that had pulled Kai through reach up and bar Black Boot's path? This was new magic to Kai, interesting magic. He should learn more.

He glanced at the girl beside him—at the twisted smile marring her otherwise sweet face. He would have to learn a great deal, if he was to survive. If he was to escape.

The Pride of My Heart

Black Boot peered at his daughter across the invisible barrier that separated them. Always something separated them. Things with her were not going as smoothly as he'd hoped, not that he even deserved to hope. But it didn't matter; he was here to stay, and this was his little girl.

She used to smile up at him as though he were her whole world, his little Jem. She wouldn't be able to hold onto her grandmother's hatred for long. Even as she was fighting with him, taking away the boy, he could see bits of his little girl. She always wanted to impress him, had nearly smiled as he congratulated her.

This would work. He could have everything he wanted, and that old hag would truly lose. He would have the power, the land, and his little girl. They would be a family once more, and May Bell would finally be at peace.

"Well?" Black Boot said with a broad smile. "You've barred me from the house and stolen my help. What's next in this grand plan of yours?"

Jemma's eyes widened just enough for him to know she had no idea what came next. But she rallied fast, like her grandmother, staring him down. She glanced from Black Boot to the boy and back, clearly deep in thought.

"Lunch, I suppose." She shrugged disinterestedly. "Drop by again sometime, Pa. We really must catch up," she said over her shoulder, as she limped slowly away.

Black Boot watched his daughter's right leg as she walked. It did not look so much like limping, he supposed; more like pulling, as if her foot were constantly caught on something just a step behind her. How much did it hurt her? Every day, every minute, more? Did she think of him every time it ached? She must resent him for that. But he would fix it. He would make it up to her.

He couldn't let her think of him in that moment for the rest of her life. That one moment, he could see it in her eyes when he looked at her. But he would take the memory away…from both of them. They would forget it had ever happened. They would be happy again.

"Happy. Ha," he scoffed at himself as Jemma and the boy disappeared into the house. When had he ever been allowed to be happy for more than a moment, without someone dying?

He should have seen it coming.

"Just go then," May Bell shouted waving him off angrily. The wind was never calm enough to just talk anymore.

What had he said to make her angry this time? He couldn't even remember. But he was angry too. So angry, he could feel it beating against his chest to get out, like the wind beat at everything in its reach.

He had stayed for her, broken the rules for her; but she thought she had a right to be angry with him.

"Maybe I will," he snapped, the wind flying out with his words and knocking May Bell back a step. He should have worried then. Maybe he did, a little, but not enough. Never enough to cool his temper. "And maybe I'll take Jemma with me."

"Never!" May Bell yelled and shoved back against the wind with a mighty strength all her own.

"She's mine," he said with deadly quiet, and the wind grew rabid around them, snapping at their skin. "You and your whole horde of harpies can't keep me from what's mine." Things began to move with his rage.

"We're keeping you here. We can banish you just as easily." May Bell's eyes flashed with magic, golden lights dancing in her deep brown eyes.

Without warning, the wind swarmed around them, circling, and one great windy hand reached out and shoved May Bell off her feet, sucking her towards the funnel behind them. He lunged out to rescue her, but May Bell managed to anchor herself to the earth.

Then he heard the worst sound of his entire life.

"Mama!"

Not once as they fought had he wondered where his daughter was. At her shriek, he spun to stop her before the cyclone could claim her, but her tear-soaked cheeks halted him. He'd done that to his little girl.

As if suddenly struck by lightning, the cyclone doubled in size, lifting everything from the ground that wasn't planted in it, shuddering and shifting the walls of the house. He couldn't move, couldn't think, couldn't do a thing as the wind reached out and yanked his little girl into the air. She flew up, passing the rocking chair from the corner of the porch, and the tools that leaned against the side of the shed, and the truck they used to carry the harvest into town. And when May saw it, she released her power and let herself be sucked up into the funnel as well, reaching out for Jemma.

Everything he loved was sucked up, dragged farther and farther from him and from the earth, all because of his rage.

He could hear them both over the screech of wood panels pulling free of the roof, over the pounding of his heart beat in his ears. Could see them reaching towards each other, crying one another's names. Then came the words that stopped his heart in his chest.

"Papa, stop!" Jemma wailed, and her tears struck his face.

And it stopped. Everything at once, the circling, the sounds, the wind, and his heart. He wasn't even alive as everything the wind carried plummeted back towards the hard ground. He didn't have time to move before his little girl struck the earth, and the truck landed just barely on her right leg, but enough to pin her fully to the ground and rip a blood-curdling scream from her lungs.

He ran for her, ignoring the stabs and strikes of falling debris pounding against him.

"Jemma, baby. Jemma," he shouted, shoving at the truck with everything that was within him. It shouldn't move. He knew it wouldn't, but she made a noise, no more than a squeak really, and as he shoved, he had more force than just his own, and it toppled off her.

Falling to the ground beside her, he yanked his daughter into his arms, cradling her. He ran a hand across her face, dragging away the dirt that wanted to cling to her damp cheeks.

"It's okay. It's okay, baby. Daddy's here." She didn't respond, didn't move, so he searched frantically for help. That's when he saw May Bell. His fiery, vibrant, May Bell, lying still as stone in a pile of cornstalks beside the tractor, with her body bent in odd angles and blood running from her temple.

He sobbed, loud wracking sobs that shook the earth. Oblivious to all but his pain, he pulled Jemma to his chest tightly. She woke crying out in pain, her eyes drenched with accusation and fear, as if he were a monster.

Jemma had all but disappeared into the house now, and Black Boot clung to the last dragging step as though it would be his last sight of her. He could feel her confusion, her reluctance to leave. He would show her, make her understand that he wasn't a monster. That he loved her. Then everything would be better. They would be a family again.

"When my father left us in a one-room home, with a stove indoors, and a plot of land to till, he thought certain Mama would be happy. 'Twas such luxury. But to be forever near her people but never among them was torture for her." From the journal of Sisika, 1ˢᵗ matron of the Women of Terra, as penned by Sarah, her daughter.

Jemma had no idea what to do now, but she wasn't about to let Pa know that. He hadn't been able to get past the shield, but he would eventually. Better he think she had some grand plan for everything.

Jemma heard the screen door bang shut behind the boy she rescued and wondered what she was meant to do with him. She was near certain he was a victim, but what if it was a trick? Jemma glanced at the boy; already, the sparkle was fading from his eyes. He looked sickly again. What use could Pa possibly have for him? He'd seemed almost pleased when Jemma outsmarted him. Had that been his plan? What if the boy was a spy?

Jemma glanced at May Bell's room. Closed, good. At least he couldn't see her, couldn't tell Pa the woman he thought he'd killed was alive, lying in a bed for eightyears.

Her guest was examining the room like it was a prison. Looking at the house objectively, Jemma realized it probably seemed precisely like a prison to him.

Utilitarian was the only way to describe Gran's choice in furniture. There were two wooden benches and a few wood chairs Gran carved herself scattered about the room, along with two tall bookshelves and the desk. All the same plain oak, same as the floors, and the walls, and every single thing in the house, except the stone fireplace, which was sandstone and not a bit decorative. Even the curtains, which had been white when Gran hung them, were nearly the same color as the walls now—a dusty, sort of soft brown.

When Jemma was little, there had been beautiful things in the house. A lamp with so many colors that Jemma would spend hours just staring at it, tracing it's patterns with her fingers, or watching the light play with all the different shades. There had been pictures on every wall, of happy, smiling family members, or of the lush beauty of the fields stretching on forever. There were happy blue curtains the color of the sky, with little flower cutouts that the light would dance through onto Jemma's blocks as she played.

Then came the storm.

From outside, Jemma heard the smallest chimes tinkling. How long would it be before a storm chased away even this bare, empty space that was her home?

"You live in a coffin," the boy commented. Jemma couldn't help it; she bent over laughing.

He had no idea how right he was. This was the same wood she'd used to build Gran's casket.

Unable to breathe, Jemma collapsed onto the nearest bench and buried her head between her legs. The tears came, the ones she had felt building for weeks now. Burying Gran had been awful. Horrifying, but she just…did it. Like she was one of Sisika's daughters, not a modern girl with proper authorities to call and laws to follow.

There was something very wrong with her. The entire family was wrong. Had been wrong forever. That was the only thing she could find in the family tomes. *They* were the problem. Normal people didn't live on top of their dead matriarchs. Normal people didn't curse everyone who hurt them, or try to contain the wind, or throw trucks onto their daughter's legs, in a fit of temper. And normal girls…if a normal girl found her grandmother dead in her bed, so stiff and frozen she looked almost plastic, she would get to call someone and cry for hours, or lay down beside her and sob. She wouldn't limp out to the barn and build her a casket. Normal girls didn't struggle under their grandmother's weight as they dressed her and pulled her into the casket and arranged her arms, afraid to pull or twist her too far, for fear she'd shatter. They didn't drag caskets into the mausoleum that was the cellar and dig a new plot and carve their grandmother's headstone. There was something very wrong with her.

It took Jemma a minute to calm her breathing and clear away the tears. She looked up and found the boy, Kai, staring at her. Not offering sympathy or apologizing for his stupid mouth, just staring. Wasn't that exactly like a boy? Well, maybe not. He was staring at her still damp cheeks. How long could kelpies survive out of the water? For that matter, what did they eat? Where was she to put him?

She should just absolve him of his debt and release him. But then, what was to stop Pa from capturing him again? Because Pa wasn't going anywhere unless Jemma found a way to make him.

"What do you eat?" Jemma asked in a tone that sounded oddly like Gran's to her own ears, no softness.

"Whatever." The boy shrugged.

"Enlightening." Jemma shoved off the bench and started across the room. "Bathroom's this way."

"I don't need one."

"You look grey," Jemma snapped, unreasonably angry with this boy for being here, for forcing her to worry about him, for making her cry and doing nothing to fix it. "Kelpies, better known as water horses, live near, or in, bodies of fresh water—"

"It doesn't have to be fresh water," Kai interrupted with the beginnings of what looked like a grin. "A lot of us settle near the ocean these days. I live in Malibu."

"Really? Fine, I'll add that to my notes. The point is, you're supposed to sparkle like the water you live in, unless you are violently ill and near death. It's said that the sparkling is what draws travelers to you."

"To be eaten," he said in a low menacing voice like one would use when telling a ghost story.

Jemma was unimpressed; she turned back to the bathroom shoving the door open. "You look like shit. The bathroom, as its name suggests, has a bath, I thought the water might do you some good."

Kai followed silently into the bathroom, tossing one last half grin Jemma's way. She showed him how the spigots worked, then retreated from the room, shoving the door shut behind her. With the door at her back, Jemma let out a puff of breath she hadn't realized she was holding onto.

"Just great." Jemma walked towards the kitchen. "He's probably a spy, and even if he isn't, he's one more person to take care of. Terrific, Jemma, really smart move."

Jemma yanked open one cupboard after another looking for something to eat. "Old Mother Hubbard, went to her cupboard, to fetch her spying water horse some oats, but when she got there, her cupboards were bare," Jemma sighed, "so she lay on the ground and gave up."

She Who Owns Your Life

K ai lay in the tub fully clothed. These were the only clothes he had, and this was the best way he could think of to get them clean without asking the little witch for more help. His skin would absorb most of the moisture anyway. The girl would probably wash them if he asked, but he was already in her debt more than he could afford to repay.

Kai didn't know what to make of his hostess, or captor; it was hard to say which she was. *Just a little girl,* Kai could just hear his father shouting in the back of his head, but he blocked out the words. He didn't need his father to tell him how foolish he'd been this time. But… how many girls in the middle of nowhere knew about kelpies and life debts, and spoke about it all like it was a class she was taking.

He smiled again; she'd gotten a distinctly nerdy look on her face when she began discussing kelpies. It would have looked even more adorable with a pair of glasses to push up the bridge of her nose.

She must be a witch. But not like any Kai had ever known. Her magic seemed very…intellectual. Even when she had thrown that bucket, telekinesis maybe, he *felt* nothing from her. Every witch he'd ever known threw their emotions out with their magic. But not her.

No. She kept her emotions shoved in some hidden corner in this brown box of a home. She kept many things hidden here, if his guess was right.

And Black Boot was her father. That was the oddest part of this whole mess. Black Boot wasn't a man, not really; he was a monster, as bad as, or worse than, any kelpie whispered of in legend. He should not have a family or a home. Not that anyone wanted him here, least of all his daughter. She seemed to enjoy besting him, but she also seemed to enjoy impressing him.

Kai thought of his own father, and the millions of fights they had over the years, but still, they loved to go surfing or to catch a baseball game, and Kai would give anything for him to be impressed just once with something he'd done.

This wouldn't be what impressed him. Caught first by his bridle and now snared in a life debt, to a child.

Kai sunk beneath the water; he had to think of a way out of this. She didn't seem to have any intention of letting him go. He needed his trinkets. If he could get ahold of his magic, maybe he could charm her into letting him go. That shouldn't be so hard; a lonely little girl in the middle of nowhere should be an easy target. She already showed a distinct interest in taking care of him.

And there were the tears; he could use that. Kelpies understood water; it spoke to them. Her tears were full of anguish, and exhaustion, and pain, and confusion and just the tiniest hint of happiness. If he could figure out exactly where each of those feelings came from and fix her problems, she would be so overjoyed she'd have to release him.

Or…be afraid it would all come rushing back when he was gone, and refuse to ever let him go.

Not that any of this mattered. Black Boot still had his trinkets. That was probably why he wasn't upset when the girl bested him; she may have Kai, but the real magic was in the trinkets. Without them, Kai was just a fish out of water.

Maybe he could steal them back. At night, while everyone was sleeping. It would be easier if there was rain. Kai could all but vanish in the rain. But he doubted he could make the weather cooperate. And what would he do once he got them? Run? Or bet on his ability to charm a little girl into releasing him?

Kai scooped up a handful of water and tossed it into the air. The drops danced around his head for a moment before crashing back into the tub. This room was the same plain brown as the others. Did witches hate color?

"Remember when I tucked you into bed with the story of how evil began? Scared you half to death, you were such a curious thing. I saw it right away, how you thought I was chastising you for always wanting to know why. Sorry about that. You see, I'm a proud Gran. When I die, I'll die knowing you'll find a way to care for yourself." From the journals of Esther Lynn Franklin, 6th matron of the Women of Terra.

Jemma was sitting on the bench facing the bathroom when Kai came out. She had a pile of books to one side of her, a pad of paper and a pen on her lap, and a PB&J for Kai on her other side. She would approach this practically. She was stuck with him for a while, and he was stuck with her. They needed to clear the air between them and set up a few ground rules.

Already, he'd been a little bit useful. None of her folklore had ever spoken of water horses being comfortable with salt water. She added it to her notes with a half-smile at the idea of knowing something Gran did not.

Water horses/ Kelpies:
*Water dependent shapeshifters.
*Live in or near bodies of fresh water or <u>salt water.</u>
*Can manipulate water of liquid or vapor form. Many sudden violent storms have been blamed on kelpies having fits of rage.
*Most commonly seen in either horse or human shape, but can assume other forms.
*Tempters: sparkle to draw in travelers with the promise of adventure or some other heart's desire.
*Share tempting traits of other water creatures: mermaids and sirens.

When the door opened, Jemma looked up and stared in absolute shock.

He looked like a different person. When she first saw him outside, his skin was cracked like dirt the sun had baked dry. And his hair had looked as brittle and sad as dead tree bark; even his eyes had seemed like the browning tips of the corn husks, but no more.

"You really do sparkle," she whispered aghast.

Kai's lips slid up at one corner and his eyes only sparkled more.

Shit. She'd said that aloud, hadn't she? And he was getting a real kick out of it, and why not? She'd made a fool of herself. But…she'd never believed it. Gran forced her to read legends about fairies, pixies, elves, water horses, gnomes, and all sorts of others since forever. Every magical creature ever written of or imagined—Jemma had to know all she could about them for Gran to be satisfied. But Jemma had never believed.

But he sparkled. All of him; his hair was a sparkling black with gentle wavelike curls, and his skin—as he moved, the light played across it like it was made up by thousands of individual grains of sand. But his eyes—they were the most devastatingly different. Jemma had a picture of her parents, from when they were first married, on a beach in California, with the ocean stretched out behind; even in the picture, you could tell the water wasn't just one color. It had dark blues, and light greens, and translucent blends of the two. Kai's eyes were like that. Never just one color; so beautiful.

This place must seem so dull to him.

"I thought it was an exaggeration," Jemma muttered and forced her eyes away from him. "Here." She held the sandwich straight out, not looking at him again. "It's PB&J."

"I can see that." There was laughter in his voice.

So, he was a self-satisfied kelpie. Jemma wondered if it was a common personality trait for kelpies, or something all his own.

"I thought we should clear a few things up." Jemma stared at the white legal pad in her lap, as Kai took the bench across from her and dug into his sandwich, but she didn't miss his grin. "If you are a spy for my father, there isn't much for you to tell him, so you might as well tell me now."

Kai hadn't moved much, just continued to chew. It was easier to force her eyes back to him now; this was business, she needed to glare him down. He raised an eyebrow at her as he finished chewing. It was a sarcastic eyebrow, seeming to ask if she really needed a response to that question. But silence didn't intimidate Jemma. She'd barely heard a sound but her own voice for near three months now.

"I'm not a spy," Kai said when he finished chewing.

"Umm." Jemma hadn't really expected him to say anything different, so it did little to assuage her fears. But she nodded and moved on. "It'd be simplest to just release you from your debt, but Pa would still have your bridle, so you won't be any better off."

"I wasn't prepared for him before. I will be this time. He isn't so powerful."

"The last time he was in Oklahoma," Jemma snapped, "the only thing left of this house was a few beams and the cellar. The crops had been ripped out of the earth, the truck was half smashed and upside down, and the rest of the town was worse. If he wants you badly enough, he'll catch you again."

"If he's so all-powerful why don't you just give in and let him have what he wants?"

"I'll find a way to conceal you from him, so you can steal back your bridle. Then I'll release you." She motioned to the books at her side, grinding her teeth at the question.

Just at the moment, giving in felt like the only option, but Jemma was looking for another solution. She'd poured over Gran's spell book for the way to banish him, but she hadn't found anything yet and she was still working, because Gran would want her to, and it was her responsibility. Well…honestly, she was mostly looking because of the boy in front of her and what he represented. It was one thing to give up when it was only her and May Bell who would get hurt, but she couldn't let Pa hurt anyone else.

"I need to know what kind of magic works on kelpies."

Kai shrugged. "Magic is magic; all of it works on us."

"It's not that simple. I'm not naturally magical. I'm guardian to this land. I have to understand the magic I'm doin' to make it work. If there's some magic you have to conceal yourself, I could make it stronger," Jemma offered.

"I can conceal myself, but only in water. If it were to rain…"

"I can't make it rain." Jemma shook her head. The truth was, she should be able to. Gran could, but she couldn't remember the dance, or the offering, and…Jemma had never been able to make it work. "Rain's comin' though, I just don't know how soon."

Kai looked like he would say more but he just lifted the remains of his sandwich and shoved it into his mouth.

"I'm short on food. I need to pull in what's left of the crop. I don't suppose you've ever helped with a harvest."

"Can't say I've had the pleasure," Kai said sarcastically. He leaned against the bench casually—a look that would have been more impressive if these benches were even slightly comfortable.

"I didn't think so," Jemma said condescendingly. "Can you at least cook? I'm awful."

"I guess so," Kai said with a little chuckle. "Is that a chore list you have in front of you? Because that's not exactly how a life debt works. I'm not your eternal slave or anything."

"Actually, you kind of are." Jemma reached out and lifted one of the heavy books onto her lap. "I've been brushing up on life debts. Anything you can do to help your savior, you must do, until your debt is paid in full. Resisting will wear on you and make you a pariah."

Kai's lips were sealed in a thin angry line and his eyes turned dark and stormy. Jemma felt a little bad. She had no intention of making him her slave, but she needed him to understand who was at a disadvantage here.

"Course I've got no intention of forcing you to do anything. I helped you to get as healthy as I could, but I'm not waitin' on you hand and foot."

"If I want to eat, I have to work for it. Is that the game?"

"If you want to eat, you find the food, you prepare it. That's the game." Jemma countered in Gran's voice again. Odd, she'd never thought of herself as being much like Gran, but she did have her finer points. No one messed with Gran. "If you don't want to accept my hospitality, you are welcome to take your chances with my father."

"You sure you know the meaning of hospitality, little girl?"

"That room is off-limits." Jemma ignored the insult pointing to May Bell's room. "So is the cellar."

"Why that room?" he said with a wink Jemma didn't quite follow. He was teasing her again, she was sure, but why?

"It's mine," Jemma lied. She couldn't chance that he was Pa's spy and found out about May Bell. She slept in there most nights anyway.

Usually in the recliner Allen had given her. It was the only comfortable piece of furniture in the whole house.

"Oh, and what about the cellar? You keep your caldron down there?" He looked so smug, like he could see into her mind and knew all her secrets.

"It's where we keep the bodies," Jemma said evenly, looking him dead in the eye.

"Alright," Kai chuckled. "Keep your secrets."

No one ever believed the truth.

I Was Once a Man

Tom Traveler had never been an idle man. When he was young, long before he was given the boots that so defined him now, he had traveled the world, surviving always by a good day's labor. He'd been a cook aboard an ocean freighter, rustled cattle in Texas, worked fishing trawlers in Japan and Alaska, painted houses, landscaped, waited tables, and in more towns and countries than he could remember to count, he had planted and harvested crops of every kind.

Even now, though he dragged the wind behind him, rather than being pushed on by it, Black Boot was not an idle man. He couldn't say when he had come to see himself as Black Boot rather than Tom. Not when he fled the ruins of his home, leaving his sobbing and screaming daughter beside her dead mother, fighting against the pull of every matriarch of Terra, their magic weighing down his steps. No, it happened later, when he no longer remembered the exact shade of his little Jem's eyes, or how those eyes all but disappeared to make room for her smile.

Not that he could see any sign of that now. She had her mother's deep brown eyes, but her smile was such a tiny thing. Tiny and twisted with anger.

Her father's girl then.

Black Boot froze; he had not heard May Bell's voice since they entered Oklahoma. He half worried that just returning her ghost to the lands of her people had laid her spirit to rest. All this time, he had searched for a way to do just that, but a few days without her voice and he ached for her.

He didn't look up to see her ghostly face; he knew what he would see there. Accusation. The same accusation he saw in Jemma's eyes.

Instead, he looked out into the fields that had once been as lush and welcoming as any oasis. He would not want for occupation while he worked to win his daughter's affections.

The fields were rotten from ill use. The few bits of crop that still lived needed harvesting. And the dead plants needed to be pulled before they sucked all the life out of the soil. It was nearly time to sew new crops, and not a single plot had been tilled. Esther, for all her faults as a mother-in-law, or mother, had never failed in her absolute devotion to this patch of earth. So, this was Jemma's doing.

It shouldn't have been such a surprise. She could hardly be expected to harvest and weed and till the whole thing, alone, especially with her bad leg. But he couldn't understand why someone hadn't been hired, or the local grocers offered a discount if they harvested their own product. And he couldn't remember a year when someone did not try and steal right out of the fields. But this…it was as though he was the first person to set foot on the land since the crop sprouted. Something should have been done.

Women of Terra always insisted they were not witches. They picked the name Terra to represent their purpose: to serve the land. When their land flourished amidst the droughts of the Great Depression, they called it merely a reflection of their inner peace and charity. They had appeased the jealous by sharing their harvest freely. But if the bounty of those years was a reflection of their inner peace, that meant this moldering ugly mess was a reflection of his daughter's inner nature, and that did not sit well with him.

Black Boot lifted the heavy bags the kelpie had carried for him and lugged them away from the house to the old barn. Well, new barn; the old one must have been destroyed in the cyclone. He remembered the old one well. He'd been allowed to sleep there while he worked a harvest for the family so he could court May Bell. In the evenings, when her parents would go into town or watch something on the TV, May Bell would climb out her bedroom window and run to the barn to be with him. Esther never liked the idea of a rootless man with her girl.

A thing with no roots has no potential to grow. My girl deserves a man with potential.

The barn had a tiny room with a cot in it, just as the last one had. Black Boot dropped his bags at the foot of it in frustration. Esther's death should have banished her lectures from his mind. But if anything, being here, seeing the crops and his little Jemma, it was only making her voice louder. He could nearly see her standing with one hand on her hip and her eyes full of rage pointing at him and calling him the architect of his daughter's turmoil.

Along one wall were all the tools he would need: hoes, rakes, spades, sickle, knives. The cot lay on the opposite wall. Just beyond a small door was a darker room that held the seeds, bulbs, baskets and wheelbarrow and a small tractor with a wagon hitched to it.

It was the same old tractor, dented in a few places, and a bit dusty, but still good. Esther wasn't the type of woman to throw away a tractor just because it had a few bad memories attached to it. If he shut his eyes, Black Boot could still remember riding through the crops on the tractor with Jemma beside him making up songs to match the hum of the engine. Or see her dragging her little red wagon behind him and May Bell as they harvested the fields; Jemma's eager little hands reaching up to grab vegetables that were just out of her reach, until one of them lifted her up. She was so determined to be a part of everything then. She had loved the land, loved the harvest, loved everything.

Shaking off the memory, Black boot unhitched the wagon, loading it with the tools he would need to go save what he could of the harvest.

Save her.

"Sisika, my mother, loved with all her heart and her pride. She was shunned, but she did not forget her heritage. She told my sister and me that we belonged to the earth, could belong to no other but it, as we buried our brother. Said we were the earth, that we would be stepped upon, and used, rolled across, even moved, but never changed. The earth, she said, can never be completely conquered." From the journals of Sisika, 1st matron of the Women of Terra, as penned by Sarah, her daughter.

Jemma was meant to be reading something. Studying spells or at least the family tomes; it was what she had set Kai up with, despite his protests. But she explained, if he wanted entertainment, he'd better read because there wasn't much else to do here.

It was a lie. She should feel a bit bad for it, but the television was in May Bell's room, and so was her computer. She couldn't get them without risking Kai seeing May Bell. But he was busy consuming every word in the damn histories, while Jemma couldn't bring herself to crack one open.

She sat at her desk staring out the window, tracking Pa and his slow progress through the fields. Not much food had made it into the wagon he dragged behind him with a strap over his shoulder. Most everything was thrown into the pile of stalks he'd chopped down with his sickle to mark his progress.

Jemma drummed her fingers against the desk, annoyed. She would have gotten to it eventually. He had no right to be out their judging her. He had two perfectly good legs, and magical powers, and no wife to take care of, or mother-in-law to bury. Perhaps she should have flown less, and harvested more, but she hadn't seen the point. She couldn't sell any of it in town, since the townies were afraid of her. And even if they would buy from her, it would mean questions, and eventually someone would figure out Gran was dead and come take her away from May Bell. She couldn't put memory hexes on the whole town, as she had Allen, and a few of Gran's friends.

Jemma knew Pa would come eventually. Better she enjoy what was left of her life before her father's temper left her trapped beneath a house instead of the pickup.

But she should have done something. A woman of Terra's first responsibility was to the land, and Jemma just hadn't cared enough to help it. Gran might think they had shared what they loved with the land, but as far as Jemma could see, the land had stolen it. She didn't care to help it. And for that Gran would never forgive her.

Now Pa was doing her work. Thinking she was pathetic and useless. He probably pitied her. She wanted to march outside and tell him to leave her crops the hell alone, but she couldn't. She couldn't risk going through the shield, and he knew it. He was taunting her.

Jemma shoved her eyes away from the window, giving up on any kind of studying. She picked up a pen and did what came natural.

Dear Mama,

He's back. I knew he would be. Gran warned me, but I never did listen. I haven't read the family tomes. I haven't harvested the crop or stocked the cellar. I'm not prepared. All I really did was move the family stones to protect the house. They're working for now, but they won't for long. He knows how the shield works. He wasn't supposed to. Gran said that Terra never share the old family secrets, but you must have. Did you tell him how to get in?

Pa had a boy with him. A water horse; he was near death from being so dry. I saved him, because Gran would have, and you would have. But I wonder if it wasn't some kind of trick. He's in here with me now, and I have to be doubly cautious.

Can't we just leave? I know we're the guardians, and that the land will call to us wherever we go…but it's what he wants. Can't we just let him have it and fly away somewhere safe? I could put a memory hex on him, make him forget he ever knew us. I'm really good at that spell.

Is it really so important that we stand firm? Shouldn't living be more important?

Within Her Tears

Kai hated histories, and that's what she had given him to work with, family histories. He'd read perhaps three pages in total from the first heavy tome. The girl's great, great, great (whatever) grandmother was the world's dullest author. Every page full of boring information about potential husbands, or children's names, crop planning, rain cycles, and troop movement. This person settled here, that person killed them, then they died of yellow fever… Really, couldn't she just skip to the last man standing and save them all some intense boredom?

The next great (something) grandmother was no better; in fact, she was worse. Because she felt a need to discuss her poor mother's life in great detail, nearly all of which had been covered in the previous tome. If this was all the people of Oklahoma did for fun, it was no wonder no one lived here. For the life of him, Kai could not understand why a girl her age, magical or not, would live in a home with no TV, unless she was Amish, which she really didn't seem to be.

Kai lay the book aside and stared over at his captor. She was crying again. Not sobs like before; he couldn't see or hear it. But he could feel the tears trickling out. Sorrow and defeat this time.

Maybe the best way to repay his debt would be to kidnap her and take her far away from this place. Somewhere with a TV and some color. The beach would do her a world of good. But he doubted she would allow that to happen.

Even as she cried, she sat with her shoulders back and her head high, gazing out the window. Her red hair caught the light like a beacon. It was the only color in this dull world. She must stand out for miles. He wondered why she didn't collapse or slump. For someone who felt so defeated, she certainly didn't look it.

Stubborn, he supposed.

Poesy would have given up already if something wore on her that way. She wasn't much of a fighter. But this girl…hell. Kai got the sorrow. He'd only been in this house a few hours, and he was beginning to feel like crying too.

"You have any paint?" Kai asked, tossing aside the riveting tale of pig genealogy he'd been reading and coming to his feet.

The girl looked up slowly, apparently oblivious to the tears on her cheeks and nodded, as though she didn't quite understand him. She probably didn't, but she would.

"I got the hell out of Oklahoma when I was sixteen, and I thought sure I'd never go back. But lord, Jemma, that soil is a powerful magnet. I felt it pulling me home, every step I took away. And when I came home, well, I never wanted to leave again." From the journals of Esther Lynn Franklin, 6th matron of the Women of Terra.

There were five cans of paint under a tarp in the cellar. They were old, at least five years. Jemma doubted they were any good now, but if it kept her guest busy, she didn't much care. It was past time to check on May Bell's machines.

Every can was a different color. Allen had insisted Gran buy them for Jemma after her second surgery. It was a few weeks after Jemma had learned to stand again. She couldn't walk much at all. It took four surgeries to fix Jemma's leg as well as it was now. The doctors wanted to amputate and give her a prosthetic but Gran refused.

Once Jemma was allowed out of bed, she had planted herself in a chair beside her mother's bed and waited for her to wake up. Everyone insisted she needed to get up, go outside and play, but Jemma wouldn't move. The very idea was nonsense; she had always played with Ma and Pa, so who was she to play with now? How was she even to try?

"Damn it, Jemma," Gran yelled, after a week of Jemma refusing to move. "I always insisted you were too clever by half to go to school with the fool children of this town, but if you don't get up and do something, I'll put you in that school and just see how you like it."

Allen rolled his eyes. He did that a lot when Gran talked. Jemma was fairly certain he did it this time because he thought Jemma would like public school just fine. Showed what he knew.

"But Gran…"

"No buts, Jemma. You will leave this room and set about fixing that leg like a real woman of Terra." Gran was not a soft woman, no coddling, or consoling; she ordered and you obeyed.

Allen wasn't like that. "What's worrying you, Miss Jemma?" He always called her Miss Jemma, as if she was already a lady, and he listened, as if her thoughts mattered.

"What if she wakes up and no one's here? You said she can't move. What if she wakes up and can't move and gets scared? She'll think we don't love her." It had burst out of Jemma in a rush along with a fresh wave of tears.

"Nonsense." Gran shouted only to be cut off by a sharp look from Allen. He was the only person Jemma had ever met who didn't seem at least a little afraid of Gran. That was one thing Jemma never could explain. Gran wouldn't let anyone else treat her that way; why did she allow it from Allen?

"We don't want her to wake up sad," Allen agreed. "What if we pinned up some of your old pictures? We can put them up all over the room so she'll know you're thinking about her."

"But her head is looking up."

"We'll put some on the ceiling," he insisted.

"I want to make a new one," Jemma said feeling excited for the first time since the cyclone. "The whole ceiling."

Both Allen and Gran were very opposed to the idea at first; it was a lot of work for a girl who barely moved. But Allen said Jemma would have to leave the house and come pick the paint herself. When Jemma agreed, everyone got on board with the idea.

Allen painted the ceiling cornflower blue, then a few hours a day, Jemma painted her decorations onto a special sort of sticky paper that he applied later. Huge lopsided hearts, silly little flowers with smiling faces, and a clumsy self-portrait with "I love you" written next to it.

By the time it was finished, Jemma had been leaving her mother's side for a few hours every day, so it was much easier for Gran to pry Jemma away for her physical therapy and for some of her lessons, though most of her lessons she took at her mother's side. A few months later, she was leaving the room for several hours every day, then half the day. By the time a year had passed and nothing changed, Jemma was almost never in her mother's room.

That had been the plan, but no one was satisfied with it any longer, least of all Jemma. She'd wanted to go back, but whenever she did, she would look up at that silly, childish, hopeful ceiling, and have a violent urge to just throw a can of black paint over it. Her mother was never going to see it, never going to wake up. And when she saw the painting, it was all she could think of.

No point cryin' over things you can't change.

"Sure thing, Gran," Jemma spoke to the spray of pansies that marked her grandmother's resting place. Resolutely ignoring the past, she lifted the paint cans two per-hand and made her way back up the cellar stairs to the kitchen.

She left them on the kitchen floor and went back down for the last cans and the few paint brushes she had. Only once the cellar door was shut did Jemma call out for Kai to come and take what he wanted.

"Golden locks," Kai nodded, reading the labels on the cans. "Cornflower blue, apple green, hot pink…"

There was a half smile on his face as he spoke. Jemma couldn't tear her eyes away from it, but it made her want to smack him. Laugh at her, would he?

"These are great!" He smiled so brightly that Jemma momentarily forgot what they were talking about. "I can't believe you haven't used these before." He lifted three cans and walked off, nodding to the others.

Clearly, he expected her to carry them. Jemma seriously considered leaving them there and returning to her spot at the desk. But then he would come back for them alone, which would put him near the cellar unsupervised. Jemma didn't trust him there.

She lifted the cans and followed him from the kitchen.

"Aren't you even curious what I want these for?" he asked with his back to her. He pried the lid off one can.

"Assumed it was for painting," Jemma said sarcastically.

"And you don't care what I do?" He threw a casual smile over his shoulder for Jemma.

"No." Jemma set the other cans down and started out the bathroom. "Just stay out of the rooms that are off-limits."

She settled back down at her desk and stared out the window, pointedly ignoring her guest and his unsettling grin. Pa was still hard at work clearing the fields. He seemed to have picked up speed as he went along. There probably wasn't much worth saving. Jemma had cleared most of the back plot for herself and even left some baskets on the road for the neighbors to take weeks ago.

Pa would be working for hours yet, if he meant to make much of a dent. And Kai had shut the bathroom door looking very focused. She could leave. Sneak out and go flying. If she left from the back porch, Pa wouldn't even notice. Jemma hadn't been inside this long since Gran died. She had not walked or stood on her bad leg this long in months. She was bored, her muscles ached, and the longer she sat, the more she felt like crying or never getting up again. She would like nothing better than to sneak out of the house and be one with the sky, leave the whole rotten, messy world behind for a while.

But that would mean leaving May Bell unprotected, something she could not do. With a wary eye on the bathroom, Jemma checked on May Bell's machines. Made her notes and slipped back out. Now there was nothing to do. Nothing but study the tomes like she was supposed to.

With a sigh, Jemma walked to one of the bookshelves that stood beside her mother's door. She reached out for one of the heavy tomes but hesitated, her fingers slipping over a simple red leather journal instead. It had a twisted knot of a heart embossed on the cover and a crinkly spine from being opened so often. Settling none to comfortably on the bench, Jemma rubbed her leg and lay the journal in her lap, allowing it to fall open to her favorite page of its own accord.

I'm pregnant! I will be a mother soon. I haven't been to a doctor yet, but I swear I can feel her heart beating. Mother swears it will be a girl.

I'd be happy either way, but she feels like a girl to me. Tom is so happy. I do not think I have ever seen him so, even at our wedding. He will have a family now, we will be a family, it is all he has ever wanted. He was so worried that children would be denied him, because of his pact with the wind. He calls us his miracle: me and our baby. I have not told him, but I feel the same. He and our baby are my miracle. Before, I went about my life with one day leading to another, and even though I had plans, there was no real future for me, no heart. Now my baby will come, and I will hold her up in my arms, watch her grow and my world will know purpose. I am pregnant. Those are the loveliest words I have ever written.

To See Her Face

It was near dusk when Black Boot gave up on harvesting for the day. He'd cleared near a quarter of the corn field before moving on to the potatoes and carrots. He thought more than one vegetable would do his Jemma's diet good. She looked too thin; not sickly, but not well fed.

It bothered him thinking of her here, day in and out, alone. She was only fourteen, fifteen in a few weeks. Did she even know how to cook? Esther had never been a careless woman; why wasn't Jemma provided for?

And how was it she had ignored him all day long? He'd seen her glance his way only once, though she'd rarely left the living room window. She should be yelling at him, or cursing him, or hugging him, *something*. But ignoring him didn't suit the little girl he'd known. What had she done all day?

When she was little, she was made up of smiles and energy. She was never still. Even when she slept, she would kick at the covers and roll over, so he had to wake up all night and check on her in the winter, to be sure she had blankets tucked around her.

She was so different now. All made up of anger and seriousness. No real smiles, just sneers. Was it only because he was here? Did she have friends she laughed with? He hoped so, but for some reason, he doubted it.

Looking at Jemma was like looking at himself before he met her mother, when he was Tom Traveler, the boy with no home and no hope. Apart from the world because he could not forgive it. He never wanted that for his girl.

Black Boot was suddenly glad he'd kidnapped the kelpie and that Jemma had stolen him. Kelpies were overly cheerful creatures. Bright and hard to break, and very social. He took the boy because he wanted his magic, but he had felt a need to have that specific kelpie, which he didn't understand at the time. Now he thought maybe it was fate. His Jemma could use a cheerful friend.

Black Boot walked to the edge of the shield dragging the wagon. He knew he couldn't make it through, but he thought the matrons would allow him to tip the vegetables into the protective circle.

"Jemma," he shouted. "Jemma."

It would be simple enough to just leave them and go back to the cot in the barn. But he wanted to see his girl once more today. He wanted her to see him. He had missed the sight of her and he would not be denied it now. He stood there shouting her name again and again until he heard her dragging steps on the floorboards inside.

She looked annoyed and was limping worse than earlier. Was it purposeful? To make him feel guilty? Or was it really paining her worse? Either way, he winced every time she did. She dragged her leg right to the edge of the shield and stared at him, waiting to hear what he wanted.

Just this. To see her. That was all he wanted.

"Did you have parents?" she demanded suddenly. Black Boot nearly smiled; she was interested in him. Then she opened her mouth again, "Because if you did, they did a shitty job of teaching you manners."

A chuckle punched Black Boot's breath from his chest. "Very good, little Jem," Black Boot replied with a broad smile. "Though I don't know what I should have expected, what with you being raised by Esther. She always kept a man in his place."

"Not all of them," Jemma muttered under her breath, and from the way her cheeks turned pink, she hadn't meant to say it at all.

"Oh? Did she take a lover then?" It probably was not the sort of thing to ask your fourteen-year-old daughter, but she was here, and he only wanted to prolong the conversation.

Jemma's mouth fell open in shock, and her eyes went wide. Definitely the wrong thing to say. Then her eyes narrowed, and he could tell she was considering the idea. His Jemma was an open book.

"I hadn't thought…I guess he could have—" she looked up suddenly and every visible emotion shut down, as she remembered she hated him.

Black Boot sighed. "At any rate, I'm glad you have her quick wit. It's a fine thing for a woman to have."

"What did you want?" Jemma demanded.

"Can you cook?"

"If you think I'm cookin' for you…"

"No, no," he replied, with a little laugh and a broad smile. "I've been cooking for myself since I was twelve, just two years—" He paused, his hand itching to raise up and brush her cheek. "*Three* years younger than you'll be in a few weeks."

"You remember my birthday?" Jemma said with wide eyes and a shocked expression, but Black Boot knew her game now and only smiled. "I'm so touched. I should give you a father-of-the-year award."

Black Boot smiled at the ground for a moment, nodding. She had a right to her anger. "I'm a fair cook. I had to be, on my own. I was twelve when my parents died; did you know that?" She didn't say a word. Whether she was curious or not, she should know something of his side of the family. "I did have parents, and they did their best to teach me manners. I was always a bit bullheaded though. When they died, in a fire…well, I couldn't wait around for the comfort people said would come in time. I followed the wind, let it brush aside my pain, with adventure. I have a picture of your grandparents. It's in one of my bags. I'll show it to you sometime."

She was still silent. Not that he had expected her to jump for joy or throw herself into his arms. It was a good sign though that she had not simply walked away.

"I'd only meant to ask if I should cook for you," Black Boot went on, when it became clear she would not speak again.

"Like I'd trust anything you cooked." The words were cruel, but there was none of her earlier heat behind them.

"There's that tongue again." Black Boot sighed. "Whatever else you think, or worry about, in your heart, you know I am not here to hurt you, Jem Beam. Good night."

He turned and walked away then. He knew she would not apologize for her words. She had no reason to. So he spared them both the discomfort and walked back to the barn where he would sleep.

Taking a seat on the cot, Black Boot pulled over the lighter of the two packs. He dug through the clothes and other odds and ends until he found his grandfather's ancient pocket watch. Nothing fancy, just a brass watch with the curling pattern engraved on the front. Tucked in the door of the watch was a picture of him and his parents. His father had an arm wrapped tight around his wife, holding her to his side as though he would never let her go, and her hand rested over his hand on her shoulder, gripping him as well, her free hand ruffling Tom's hair.

He hadn't looked at this picture in years, hadn't even thought about it.

After the fire, he had been so angry, hated the whole world. He'd followed the wind, wishing he had its power, wishing he could sweep the world clean of people. Then he met May Bell, and she had this way of smiling. Every time just a bit different, as though each new smile was the first time. He couldn't imagine a world without those smiles. So, he'd thought the anger had died, but he was wrong. It was only hidden. All it took was a bit of rough weather and how easily it all came rushing back to the surface.

Outside the wind picked up, beating against the walls of the shed; it wanted in. He heard her then, inside the wind, but she would not show herself.

"Help her!" she screeched, desperate and high, grating at the walls of the shed, at his ears, even at the air. It was her voice, but it was so different, scarred.

"I'm trying," he whispered aloud. "She's so angry."

"Like you," she sobbed. "Save her."

'I will."

Cradling the watch in his hands, Black Boot shut the front cover and flipped open the back. May Bell's shining, sweaty, exhausted face greeted him, May Bell with Jemma held gently against her cheek, the day she was born. Black Boot ran a finger over wife and child.

"I will, I promise."

"There are so many places of wonder beyond ours. I never knew, but Mama did. How can she stay in a corner, knowing how wide the world is?" From the journals of May Bell Franklin, 7th generation daughter of Terra.

Jemma woke before dawn the next morning. Her leg was aching too much to continue sleeping. She had not slept well; her muscles were so tight it felt like her whole leg was one twisting, burning knot. No matter which way she lay, she found no relief. There was a bottle of pills on May Bell's bedside table. They were Jemma's, but she had only taken them a few times.

They made her groggy, but her leg felt beautiful after taking them. Gran hadn't approved.

We don't hide from our pain; we embrace it, and it makes us stronger.

Jemma hurled the bottle across the room and held perfectly still. Nothing moved.

"Of course not," Jemma muttered angrily and dragged her leg over the side of the bed to sit up. "Nothing ever moves in this tomb."

Jemma laughed weakly as she rubbed her leg, starting at her thigh and trying to push the knot back down to her knee where it began. She refused to look behind her. Her mother lay as still as ever, despite Jemma's desperate need for her. The first time she lay with May Bell, it had been so comforting. As if her mother had been holding her. But last night, Jemma lay there confused, frightened and in more pain than she'd had in years. She clung to her mother's arm and she felt—nothing. May Bell wasn't in there. She was never going to wake up.

It had been one thing for her mother to sleep when Gran was around, and Allen; when Pa wasn't home. But Jemma needed guidance. She needed someone to take her side. She held herself perfectly still, because just at this moment, she wanted to grab her mother by the shoulders and shake with all her might.

"Why won't you wake up?" Jemma didn't look her mother's way as the words slipped out, quiet at first but growing in volume with her anger. "We aren't babies, Women of Terra. We don't let little things like being thrown by a tornado hold us down. Wake up. Wake up, damn it!" She wasn't quiet, her shout echoing around the room.

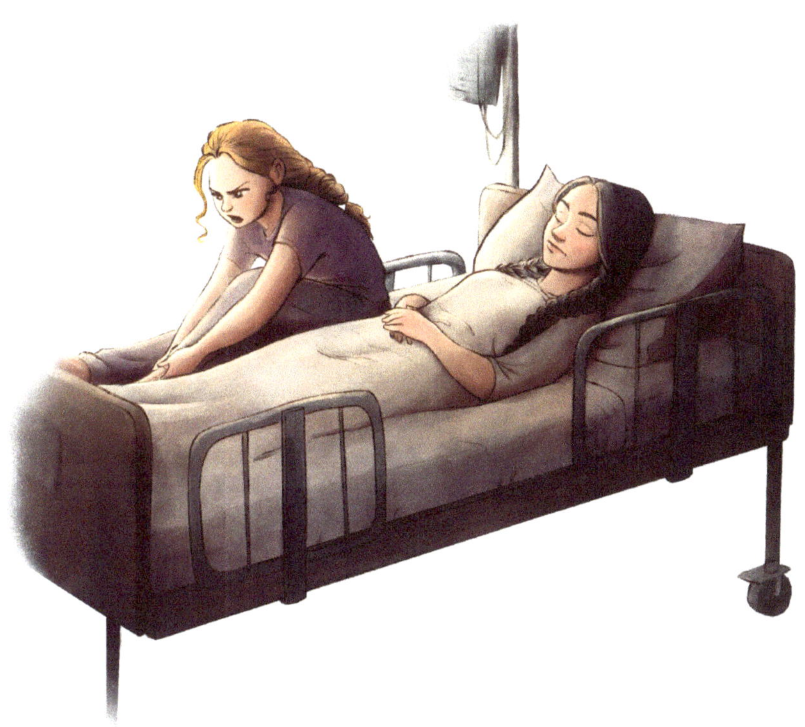

But as the echoes died away, the house was silent. Nothing ever changed. Jemma shut her eyes and counted to ten. When that didn't work, she started over, counting to twenty this time. When Jemma was calm enough to stand, she drug herself across the room to the tiny master bathroom. It was only a shower and toilet. A bath was better for soothing her leg, but she had the distinct impression her houseguest intended to sleep in the tub, and any hot water was bound to help.

Jemma took a long shower but it was just barely six o'clock when she got out. She pulled her hair back into a ponytail, braiding it to keep it out of her way, and dressed in a pair of overalls and a tee-shirt. She left the room, without looking at her mother.

"It's not as if you know anyway," she muttered.

In the kitchen, she stared at the meager bag of bread for a full minute before she realized she was too tired even to make toast. Yanking up an apple, Jemma returned to the main room and settled herself on a bench.

Jemma took a bite of the apple and hefted one of the family tomes that still lay on the bench. Unwilling, or unable to come up with something better to do, Jemma read, searching for some answer for what to do about Pa.

What Steals her Smiles

Kai didn't sneak out in the night as planned. Not only was there no rain to conceal him, but by the time he finished painting the bathroom, he was too tired. It was nearly morning when he finished. Simply rinsing out his clothes and laying them over the curtain rod to dry was enough to have his eyes drifting shut.

He first woke this morning to the sound of something slamming against the wall, and Jemma yelling. He'd nearly run to check on her, but hers was the only voice in the house, the only sound of any kind. It was clear she wasn't happy, but Kai decided to allow her space, and he drifted back to sleep for a few more hours.

Now that he was awake and seeing the room in the light of day, he was even more pleased with his work. He couldn't wait to see Jemma's reaction. He had a feeling this room would drive away whatever was making her angry, at least for a short time.

She was an odd girl. Quiet and angry, but nice. Why was she so alone? Kai had been protector of his little cove for a very short time, but even during his test, he was never alone. Every animal he defended was his friend and the water his closest confidant and partner in crime. He doubted little fire-head Jemma had any friends at all. And she walked around on that clearly painful leg like she was punishing herself. How could people abandon a girl so young and so clearly hungry for love?

He'd known the second he walked out of her bathroom yesterday that he could easily charm her into giving him whatever he wanted. Not just because she found him attractive, or funny, and not just because he could make himself near irresistible if he had his trinkets. It was the sandwich. And how hard she clearly had to work not to be nice to him. He could feel her eyes on him as they sat in near silence. She wanted badly to break it, but because she wanted it, she sat all the firmer. She had even caved and made dinner for both of them. He bet it was just killing her that she hadn't taken any to Black Boot. She was a born caretaker.

Oh, he could charm her. A few smiles, this room, listening to her a little bit, and she would be his. But…Kai wasn't sure he should. He'd started out painting as he always did, because he saw a beautiful sleeping space crying out to be brought to life, but halfway through, it wasn't enough to set the space free. He needed it to speak to that one girl. She must never have seen anything as alive and colorful as these walls; if she had, she couldn't stay here in this flat, nearly-dead land.

He needed to show her life and beauty. Not trick her. He just couldn't stand the idea of the girl who had saved his life, and so casually, being slowly drained of her own life.

Kai dressed in his still very damp clothes and went to wake his captor, as he would a blank canvas. She was stretched out on one of the benches, rubbing her leg with a tiny frown on her face. He doubted she even knew what she was doing. She had one of those ridiculous family histories cracked open on her lap.

"How can you read those?" Kai asked leaning against the back of the bench across from her.

"Know your past to protect your future."

Jemma repeated words she must have heard a thousand times, without looking up. Kai smiled at her bent head. He knew little sayings like that; his father was full of them, but Kai made a point of never repeating them.

Kai bent over more, crossing his arms and leaning his head on them, so if she would only look up, their eyes would be level. He grinned.

"How does knowing which pig begat which pig protect your future?"

That got her attention. She looked up with a bright smile. It was actually rather pretty, nothing like the twisted smirk she wore as she stole him from Black Boot.

"I take it you read some of Sarah's contribution."

"If you want to call it that," Kai said good-naturedly embracing the opportunity to draw her out. "What exactly is the benefit of holding onto her book?"

"Clearly, you didn't get very far. You see, she was in love with Gil Jessup, the pig farmer. He's the great great..." She looked at the ceiling clearly trying to calculate something. "I don't remember how many greats; anyway, he's Earl's great uncle a couple times removed."

"Fascinating."

Jemma laughed. "That's not the good part; it's just where the story gets interesting."

"Impossible. Love of a pig farmer is hardly entertainment."

"Well, Gil was married, to the local pastor's daughter."

"Ahhhh." Kai leapt over the bench, landing on it almost noiselessly. He saw the way Jemma's eyes widened; he imagined it was more to do with jealousy than her being impressed. "So," Kai prompted, "was it war with the witch and the pastor's daughter?"

"Basically. Sarah and Julia hated each other to begin with. Then Sarah and Gil had an affair, and Sarah got pregnant. She wasn't married, and it wouldn't have been particularly hard for people to put two and two together. She spent all her time at the pig farm, learning the art."

"Art?"

Jemma shrugged. "As I understand it, it's your basic art of getting a bunch of pigs of opposite genders, feeding them, and letting them handle the rest."

Kai chuckled stretching his arms out across the bench behind him. She was kind of funny, when the mood took her.

"Anyway, the sisters were already sort of...disliked. This is before Oklahoma was even a state, and white people weren't really allowed to settle here, but this was a missionary *camp*. And Sarah and Ruth, and their brother Daniel, who was dead by then, were the children of a married soldier and his Petowapee mistress."

"Petao—what?" Kai asked.

"Petowapee, It's a tribe," she snapped. "The reservation is just outside town."

"Never heard of them." Kai shrugged.

Jemma wore a look that said plainly she didn't care which tribe names Kai knew. He wanted to laugh, but just waved her on.

"Anyway, the honorable Captain Andrew Milton Smith dumped his second family here when his wife found out. He gave them a little parcel of land and asked the pastor to see to it that his children were 'educated properly.' They weren't allowed to forget, you know. Sarah didn't want her baby to have the same stigma. Clearly, not badly enough not to have the affair, but badly enough to have a plan."

"Kill the pig farmer's wife and run away to Sweden with him?"

Jemma shifted her legs to the ground, rubbing the right, but there was a bright smile on her face as she leaned forward. "Not that good. Her sister, Ruth, was married to a boy who had gone off to join the war. He was Petowapee; she connected more with that part of her heritage, and even changed her name to Sotsona. But Sarah…honestly, I think Sarah was just desperate to belong with the people she'd grown up with. You should read their mother's journal; it was actually written by Sarah later on. Sisika didn't write…" She broke off, blushing. "Different subject, sorry."

Kai was completely captivated, not with the story, but with how caught up she became with all of it. It didn't seem like she found her history quite the chore her earlier tone implied.

"Anyway, Sarah convinces her sister to remain secluded with her for the duration of her pregnancy and to pretend that the baby is hers. Sarah pretended to be caring for her very ill sister, and everything was going along fine, until three months after the baby was born."

"Soldier boy came home?"

"No. He died later, Arkansas post, I think. Unimportant. The baby grew red hair. Every single girl in my family had either black hair or dark brown until that baby. And Sotsona's husband had dark hair as well."

"Gil didn't, I take it?"

She shook her head slowly. "Bright red hair, the color of fire."

"Like yours."

"Yep. It's part of the curse, but I haven't gotten to that part yet."

"Wait! You can't throw around a word like curse and not follow through." Kai was well into the story. Jemma's smile kept on stretching, taking over more and more of her face, until it was as though her eyes just barely sparkled out from behind her cheekbones, giving her the look of a mischievous fairy.

"Patience." She smiled. "Julia knew Gil had an affair, and she was fairly certain she knew with whom. She didn't believe for a second the baby was Ruth's. But she was crafty. She wanted to destroy not just Sarah but our entire family. It wasn't exactly a large settlement to begin with, maybe five families and a few stragglers, and some men were fighting the war. So, the women were running the place, and as the pastor's daughter, Julia was leading them."

Here her smile began to fade. Jemma looked older, as if it had been she who lived through the family's dark days, not her ancestors. "She went from one woman to the next sobbing about how she had been pregnant, and a dark-horned creature had come and stolen the child from her. She said she didn't want to believe it, she wanted to believe that her father had saved Sarah and Ruth's souls, but when she saw the baby, she knew they were still practicing their pagan magic."

"And people believed her?" Kai asked quietly, not really wanting to interrupt, but so horrified the words slipped out.

Jemma shrugged. "Their mother, Sisika, was widely hated when she settled here. She tried to be a part of the community, but she wasn't willing to give up a lot of her traditions, so people called her witch or heathen or savage. It wasn't exactly a time of great trust with the war, rampant racism,—even people on the Union side of the Civil War weren't precisely welcoming of interracial relations. Julia's story…it preyed on the very basic fear of having your children torn from you. It's how fairy tales and urban legends perpetuate themselves, preying on basic, realistic fears, and blowing them out of proportion. So…yeah, they believed her. Or they went along with her."

"To do what?" Kai asked flatly.

"They cornered Sotsona—you know, Ruth," she broke off to explain impatiently. "Out by the old lake, told her they didn't want her kind here, demanded she return the baby and when she refused, they stoned her."

"What the—" Kai cut off his own horrified exclamation with a hand over his mouth, his eyes wide with horror.

"She wasn't dead when Sarah found her," Jemma went on. She looked like she was seeing it all happening before her. Her eyes slowly filling with tears and burning anger.

Kai shuddered.

"Sotsona died in her sister's arms. Sarah was horrified, and frightened, and guilty. She took the baby and ran. That was the only period since this land was first settled that there was not a member of my family here."

"And…the curse?"

"When she held her sister dying, Sarah was filled with a rage that obscured all reason. She made a curse in two parts. She cursed the town, the unforgiven, said they should be punished forever, and all their descendants would be dependent on our family for survival. And that Julia's descendants, the Jessups, should fear all our future generations of women, and serve those of us with red hair. Sarah swore her heir, the redheaded descendant, would bring her revenge to completion, meeting out justice.

"So the lake dried up, within days of Sarah leaving, and the whole valley began dying shortly after."

"Interesting."

"Educational. You see, Sarah had her revenge. The whole town suffered, Julia had three children, and she lived her whole life in fear of Sarah returning, and all her kids had sort of sad lives. But Sarah died only a few years later. She saw it coming too. That's when she wrote her mother's story, so she wouldn't be leaving seven-year-old Josephine without her history. Josephine's life was tortured by the feeling that she was meant to be caring for someone. It wasn't until she and her children returned here that she knew any peace. They came, reclaimed their family land, and began planting, and the valley came slowly back to life. As it did, they bought more and more land, until they got what we have today. But she could never leave. None of us can."

"None of you?"

"Not for long." Jemma shrugged, looking a bit like she was grinding her teeth. "Gran was the first baby born without dark hair. It wasn't precisely red, but it was enough to get people afraid of her. So, she ran away from home when she was sixteen, but no matter where she went, she couldn't escape the need to be here, helping. So, she came home. My mother left for college, but she came back too, after I was born. I called her home, she claimed. I was the only girl in our family, except for Josephine, with truly red hair."

"And everyone is afraid of you," Kai sighed beginning to truly understand this girl. It was so foreign to him, the idea of being crushed under your heritage. He knew his family history; it was sung of by the waves and in the voices of other kelpies. It gave him strength. History gave every kelpie strength. But this girl was suffocating, from the mistakes of people long since dead.

She had no one. Her mother was dead, her father was a monster, and everyone around her thought she brought a curse. Maybe no one would upset her, but they wouldn't befriend her either.

"They're not really afraid of me," Jemma said after a second, shrugging. "There aren't many people who even remember about the curse now. It's just an urban legend people tell kids over camp fires. But strange things happen here, so they're cautious."

Meaning: *Yeah, they're scared to death of me.*

Now more than ever, Kai wanted to do something to help this girl. He understood suddenly why life debts were so much stronger than any other kind of magic. It wasn't good magic trumping all, or even the debt itself. But having her do so great a thing for him, not knowing who he was, or if he would hurt her, especially when she thought it was nothing, his soul couldn't stand the idea of not leaving her better off for knowing him.

"I spoke the curse with Ruth in my arms and your granddaughter on the bloody earth beside me. I spoke the curse on your people, Father. They should have loved me; now, they will never forget." From the journal of Sarah Anne Smith, 2ⁿᵈ matron of the Women of Terra.

They sat in silence for a little while. Jemma couldn't believe her big mouth. Of all the stories to tell, why that one? And to a complete stranger who may yet be a spy? She didn't feel so much worried she'd done the wrong thing, as she felt embarrassed. He might be afraid of her now. Shouldn't that be what she wanted, to have him afraid to offend or cross her? Gran would want that.

It struck Jemma as odd that she never realized before today how very…average she was in the scope of her family's history. May Bell was the odd one. Every other matron of the family had lost her mother at a young age. Gran's mother died a few years after she ran away, and her mother had died when she was eighteen. Of course, Josephine's kids had their mother well into their twenties, but once she found the land, it wasn't long before it claimed her.

All these girls with no mothers, to pay for Sarah's curse. Because there had to be a balance. Would it ever end?

"So, you can't curse people?" Kai said out of nowhere.

Jemma looked up. There was a depth to his gaze she hadn't noticed before. It didn't look entirely at home on his face. It seemed to speak of hidden wells of pain and sympathy. She liked him better as the lighthearted creature, floating on the surface of the water.

"Not without cursing ourselves." Jemma glanced away. She didn't want to know about his depths; she had enough of her own. "It's why Gran's dead. She cursed Pa, said if he set foot in Oklahoma, the ground would rise up and drain the power from him until it swallowed him whole. So, the ground got harder to care for, and help was harder to find until running the farm took all her energy, and she died one night in her sleep. Then I dug her a plot, and the earth swallowed her up."

Kai was staring at her with an open mouth when Jemma glanced over. Served him right for not believing about the bodies in the cellar.

"You're real chipper, do you know that?" Kai said dryly.

Jemma giggled in shock. She covered her mouth and gave herself over to the hilarity that was her life.

"You aren't the first person to mention it," Jemma teased when she had the giggles in hand.

"Come on." Kai stood and held out his hand to her. "Let me show you my handiwork and you can decide if you want the full treatment."

Jemma hadn't wanted to admit she was dying of curiosity about what he was doing with her bathroom. And his outstretched hand offered her the perfect opportunity to find out without asking. She let him lead her to the bathroom; trying to stifle the bubbling excitement in her stomach.

"Close your eyes," he said, blocking the door with his body.

Jemma said nothing raising an eyebrow.

"Close your eyes, little girl, or I'll cover them myself," he said playfully. "Trust me, it's a good surprise."

Jemma rolled her eyes for good measure before she shut them obediently. She wouldn't put it past him to reach up and cover her eyes, and for some reason, that idea made her distinctly uncomfortable. The prospect of this being some kind of trap hadn't even occurred to her, until he mentioned it. But she dismissed the idea at once. Kelpies may be deceivers and murderers, or they might just be another misunderstood species, but Kai was a creature without guile; he wasn't trying to hurt her.

With her eyes shut, Jemma still felt the radiance of his smile. What must it be like to have such happiness inside of you?

She heard the door handle turning and felt the waft of air as he pushed it wide. There was an overpowering smell of paint; she couldn't believe he slept in there. Maybe it wasn't happiness he was effervescing. Maybe he was just high.

Jemma coughed.

"I'll air it out later," Kai said as if reproaching her for the cough. He led her into the room by the hand. "Just give it a chance, okay. Open up."

Jemma opened her eyes, and the boy before her seemed to vanish amidst the wonder of the room. She let his hand fall and walked around him staring at the walls in awe.

"Is it even the same house?" she whispered breathlessly.

Kai chuckled, so he must have heard her. But there was more joy in his laugh than amusement at her, so she let it go. Not that she could seem to hold onto any thought but pure wonder for this room.

"It's like being inside a mother of pearl shell," she breathed, fascinated by the way the colors seemed to move with her, and the sparkling surface of the wall.

Somehow, he had blended her pink, green, and blue paints together in such a way that they seemed to move like the ocean. "How did you make it sparkle?"

He leaned over her shoulder so his face was next to hers and whispered, "Magic."

The word rushed over Jemma with his breath, eliciting a shiver. She stiffened and cast a look over her shoulder, making sure he saw her roll her eyes. But still the word danced inside her.

Kai smiled. "You're an awfully skeptical witch."

"Yeah, Gran mentioned it a time or two." Jemma turned away to continue examining the walls. "But this is amazing."

At first glance, it had seemed he did nothing more than blend the different colors together in a wavy sort of magical pattern. But the closer she looked, the more she saw. There were little figures in the shifting colors. Here, an otter or a jellyfish, a ray, a starfish, a dolphin, even a mermaid. It was an oddly less pornographic mermaid than Jemma had ever seen; instead of just shells, she seemed also to be wearing a seaweed sort of shawl draped from one shoulder to beneath the other arm. Jemma smiled at her, wondering if he had done it on purpose, because he knew Jemma would like it, or if he knew mermaids that dressed that way.

She didn't believe mermaids existed until she met him. Now, it seemed impossible that they did not.

"How did you even imagine something so…alive?"

"It's what I see when I close my eyes," he said with an easy smile, but Jemma could tell he had liked the compliment.

"I'd never have them open." Jemma smiled wide, oddly excited to have pleased him.

"Then, why don't you leave?"

Jemma sighed, heavily. "I already told you, I can't."

"It's not as if you care about the people here, and they aren't taking the time to know you. Let them take care of themselves."

Jemma turned back to the walls. For a while, as she told him her family story, it had seemed like he understood. But he hadn't really been listening. He only heard the bad. Well, to be fair, he did not know her biggest reason for staying. Jemma almost did it, almost opened her mouth and told him about her mother, trapped in her own body a room away. She would have loved this room.

But what if he was a spy? What if this magical room was a trick and not a marvelous gift? What if she was as much a fool as Sarah who thought Gil would protect her?

"How did you make the paint sparkle?" Jemma asked again to change the subject, and to remind herself he wasn't someone she should trust.

Kai shook his head a little, but he pulled a tiny bag out of his pocket and spilled a pile of sand into his cupped palm. "I dust it with sand as it dries; the sand catches the light and sparkles." He poured the sand back into the bag, almost sadly. "Now you know my secret."

Jemma forced a smile and turned away. Why did she have to do that? Was it so bad that he wanted to pretend it was all magic? Why did she constantly have to go around making things real? Gran used to say the only magic Jemma accepted without a fight was flying. It was probably why she wasn't precisely talented at the rest of it.

"So, you would be willing to paint the rest of the house like this?" Jemma asked to fill the silence. And just when, she wondered, had she grown uncomfortable with silence?

"Not exactly like this; you want some variety. But it will all be as good."

"I ought to pay you…but you can probably see I didn't make much profit off the crop this season."

"It's something to do," Kai said shrugging when Jemma finally decided to look at him again. "And anyway, you're feeding me."

Impossible Dreams

It was near noon when Black Boot took his first break of the day. He longed to stand at the edge of the shield screaming for Jemma's attention the moment the sun was up, but something held him back. He wanted to earn back her love, and the only way he knew to do that was to get the magic necessary to free her from the pain of her leg. And that started with properly claiming this land.

So, he worked. The land needed to be cleared and cared for. He'd cleared three-quarters of the cornfields now and was exhausted. He could pretend that the state of the farm was making for more work than he had done in earlier years, but that simply wasn't true. Somewhere along the way, he'd grown lazy. He'd become too busy tricking magical creatures out of their magic, and buying spells, to do a full day's labor.

But no matter how hard his daughter and the land fought him, no matter how out of shape he'd grown, he would do what he set out to. He needed this land. Even dead and rotting, the plants that came out of this soil were magical.

"It's blessed soil," May Bell had said the first night Black Boot set foot on the land. When he was still Tom, the lovesick boy who followed her across the country, even as the wind urged him to go the other way.

They snuck out into the night and ran to the site of the old dried-up lake. There they lay together under the stars speaking of the past, and of magic, and all the powers in the world that brought them together.

She lifted the soil in her hand softly, uncurling her fingers so half of it escaped into the air and fell back to the earth, then she made a fist around the rest. Her grip was so tight, she looked like another woman.

"Mama says the soil is cursed. Says the town is cursed to depend on us, as we are curse-bound to this land. But the truth is, what we put into it of love and passion is returned to us a hundred fold in bounty." Her eyes came alive as she spoke, lighting up the night with her passion. And in that moment, he loved her more than he ever thought possible. "This land could cure the world of hunger if we let it."

May Bell always did have impossible dreams. Black Boot doubted the land could cure hunger, but what it had, without a doubt, was power. Great power, and he needed it. He would have it. Black Boot knew if he could only harness enough power, he could control the fate that had taken so much from him; he could at last command the wind. Halt it if he wanted to, or send it off without him and call it back when *he* needed. He may drag it behind him now, but he never fully controlled it, and that cost him his wife and his daughter. It cost him the life he should have had.

Sitting in the sliver of shade cast by the barn, he looked out across the land that would soon be his. The land Esther had cursed him with. He carried that curse with him, and judging by the state of the land, and how young she died, Esther carried the curse with her as well.

She'd not even called him by his name. Of all things Esther had ever done, treating him like a thing as she cast him out, that was what stung the most.

The screen slammed open. Black Boot looked up excitedly, nearly dropping the raw potato he was munching on. She was coming to him.

No.

It was just the boy, dragging a bench out of the house. He didn't seem to have much muscle, that boy. A bit more time hefting Black Boot's bags would probably do him good.

Black Boot snarled at him across the wide distance. Where was Jemma? Was she punishing him? Denying him the chance to look on her? He stared at the boy, at the carved bench he was dragging around heavily. Was that Esther's work? She used to do lovely woodwork. But it looked…useful, nothing beautiful, or soft, more like a coffin.

Who made Esther's coffin? The battle-axe probably made her own before she died.

But who had buried her? Jemma? Why was she even still here? Shouldn't someone have come for her? Esther's brother Joseph? Or child services? It wasn't like Esther to have left her uncared for, but Black Boot saw nothing to imply Jemma had a guardian of any kind.

He stared off at the living room window. Jemma wasn't there, hadn't been in a while. Did she attend school? Had she ever left this place? Why was she so alone?

"Wasn't a body who knew your mother, who didn't love her. She was such a happy child, wore her heart on her sleeve. But you, Jemma, you wear it in secret. Let it out once in a while; it could use the sunshine. And you'll be surprised how easily you're loved too." From the journals of Esther Lynn Franklin, 6ᵗʰ matron of the Women of Terra.

Jemma was disturbed to find the only thing she could come up with to make for lunch was stew. She was officially out of bread, had no rice or noodles, and while she could just bake the potatoes, she had no butter for them, and that sounded too dull for her. All things considered, she should be happy that she had the ingredients for stew. Gran had forced her to learn how to make it, finally relenting on the idea of Jemma making it from scratch and getting her a mix for the seasoning.

The trouble was stew was bound to make the room stuffy and humid. Not a combination Jemma looked forward to in the middle of this summer heat. Then there was the stew pot; it was large, heavy, and shoved onto the top shelf. Jemma wasn't precisely short, but she wasn't comically tall like Gran either, and there was no stepping stool in here. So getting it would mean standing on her toes; with her leg as bad as it already was, that was going to kill her.

Jemma stared up at the pot, debating the merits of calling for Kai to get it. On the one hand, it would be simple enough for him to get it, and she was cooking for him, which she had never agreed to do. On the other hand, she would look like a wimp, and he might laugh. Even if he didn't, he might pity her. And the Women of Terra weren't wimps.

"It's only as strong as you make it," Jemma echoed the Gran living in her head aloud.

Taking a deep breath, she lifted her right leg just slightly so she wouldn't be standing on it. Even with that, shot pain up her leg, but it was better than it would be if her weight was on it. Braced against the counter, she pushed onto her left toes, stretching her arm high above her, just barely reaching the handle of the pan. She slid it from its perch with her pointer finger managing to catch it in her grip as it slid completely off the shelf.

Jemma settled the pan on the counter and was just settling back onto her foot when the screen door slammed. She startled so much that she landed with most of her weight on her right leg and nearly collapsed. She leaned against the counter, panting through her nose, as she fought a scream by the force of her teeth clamped hard around her bottom lip.

Kai came rushing in excitedly behind her. "Black Boot lef –" He cut himself off, apparently having caught the pathetic sight of her near tears. "Hey, are you alright?"

"Damned peachy!" Jemma snarled between her teeth, dangerously close to tears. "What do you want?"

Kai came around the counter and took Jemma's arm gently. "Maybe you should sit down. Do you have like a cane, or something to take some of your weight?"

"I think I can manage it," she snarled between clenched teeth, shoving off his hand. She didn't want to, but she hobbled her way over to the table and fell into a chair. She stretched her leg out in front of her very carefully, avoiding Kai's gaze. There were a few traitorous tears slipping down her cheeks.

"What did you come crashing in here for?" Jemma demanded. She hated that she could feel the pity in his gaze.

"Umm. Oh yeah, Black Boot's gone," he said, sounding less excited this time.

"What?" Pa's boots were gone? That didn't make any sense; he never took them off.

"I was outside. I saw him pick up and leave," Kai explained.

Jemma scoffed. "You call him Black Boot? Fits. He never does take them off. Did he take his bags?"

"No." Kai grinned excitedly. "I thought at first he was just going further into the fields, but he went all the way out to the road."

Jemma couldn't see what was so exciting. He was definitely coming back. Not that she had thought he would give up so easily. But where would he go? It wasn't like he had friends.

What, like you do?

"Can I get through the shield?" Kai asked urgently.

"Oh," Jemma felt like crying again for no good reason. She didn't even trust him really, but it had been nice having someone to talk with. Now she would be all alone with Pa, with Black Boot. It really was a better name for him. She should make a point of thinking of him that way. "Yeah, of course." Jemma forced the words out. "It's meant to keep him out, not keep us in."

"Great." He was already racing out of the room, not even really waiting for her to finish.

"Bye," Jemma muttered. How well did stew keep? She had already started cutting the vegetables, and it was too much for just her. Maybe she should offer some to Black Boot.

Jemma leaned back in the chair and shut her eyes. She thought she might stay this way forever. She supposed she could pull out the flying powder and use it around the house without worry, now Kai was gone. But she didn't feel much like moving. The only thing that kept her moving after Gran died was caring for May Bell, and oddly, she felt almost more devastated now. It was as though knowing what she was going back to made it all so much worse. And she would have that one room reminding her of just how dead her world really was.

The screen door slammed again, and Jemma bolted up straight in the chair. Kai came in hefting Pa's bags with him.

"What? Why?" Jemma couldn't form complete thoughts, she was so happy to see he hadn't left.

Uh-oh. Careful Jemma, you get attached to people and what happens? They die, they leave, they never wake up, or best of all, you have to send them away with a spell.

"I needed to get my bridle back," Kai said oblivious to her dilemma.

"Why didn't you just escape?"

"I owe you a life debt," Kai said, with his head still buried in the bag.

"Don't be silly, I gave you a bit of water."

Kai looked up at her with a raised eyebrow, clearly thinking she was an idiot. Well, she felt like one, so that was no surprise. But…it might have been better if he had escaped.

"Well, now you have it, you should probably go." He didn't respond, busily rummaging through the bags. "That's all yours?" Jemma asked in disbelief. "You must have a lot of careless people in your neck of the woods."

"I didn't steal any of this!" Kai snapped. "Most of this is Black Boot's. I thought it might level the playing field a bit. Because, I'm not leaving." Kai said the last three words with great precision making sure to hold Jemma's eyes.

"Well," Jemma began, uncomfortable with the feeling that he wanted an apology, and might actually be owed one. "You did steal something then," she pointed out halfway to a joke.

"I am not a thief. Kelpies are not scavengers or grave robbers." He was clearly still offended.

"What's the big deal?" Jemma said defensively, shrugging her shoulders and unconsciously rubbing her knee. "It's not as if dead people can use any of the things you might take off them."

They glared at one another over the bags. Jemma couldn't seem to stop offending him. Maybe if she kept it up, he'd change his mind about staying. Maybe he'd take his things and get somewhere safe.

Kai shifted higher on his knees and leaned in so his face was just inches from Jemma's. So close she could see his eyes darken and shift like a storm. Damn, he was beautiful.

"So. If I'd come across your Gran's dead body, clutching her journal, and I'd stolen that, there would be nothing wrong with it? Cause she can't use it, right?"

Jemma shifted farther back into her chair and looked at her lap. She said nothing but it was clear he'd made his point.

"I take things that people leave behind. Things they won't be coming back for, that nevertheless hold magic, from the unfinished stories that surround them." Kai shifted back as he spoke, his tone growing friendlier.

Jemma stared at Kai at a loss for how to apologize. She hadn't meant to hurt him, or maybe she had. It was just that everything hurt so much. Not just her leg, or her body, but everything. Moving, thinking, existing—everything hurt. And he could just run around, jump, heft these bags and all without a moment's pain. He could close his eyes and see the most beautiful things imaginable.

When Jemma closed her eyes, all she saw was Gran. Lying on her bed stiff and cold, and…empty.

Or May Bell still and beautiful like Snow White, and just as useless.

All she had wanted to do was scare him away before Pa crushed him under a house or made him a slave again, or did something worse, like stole the beautiful things in his head. She just wanted him gone before she got attached to him, and Pa ruined Jemma again, by destroying anything in her life that was beautiful.

Unfinished Magic

She wasn't talking again. Kai didn't understand this girl; maybe she was crazy. This place would do it. But he didn't think that was it, so at least she wasn't completely crazy. One minute she was sweet and kind of funny, in a sad way, and the next second she was biting your head off and insulting everything. She wouldn't accept help, even though it was obvious the pain was getting to her and she was frightened. And worst of all, she could just sit there without talking, for hours.

Kai had never known another person like her, and he wasn't sure he wanted to either. Half the time, he liked her, but…

He watched the way she rubbed her knee, squeezed it really, like she wanted to break it off. And her eyes had that faraway look she got when she was looking into those deep dark places inside her. Like the cellar where the bodies were buried. Literally.

He still couldn't fathom that. It wasn't so much the action of burying her own grandmother that startled him, but the way she'd said it. So matter-of-factly, but you could almost see it happening inside her eyes, as though the curse held her in its thrall and the earth would swallow her up as well.

Generally, Kai avoided the deep dark inside. But not Jemma; she went there at least once an hour. But maybe it was because she didn't know how to do anything else.

Kai fumbled around in Black Boot's bag until he found his trinkets, his bridle. It was the old way of explaining it. Like he was literally a horse that could be broken by controlling the magic he spent his life collecting. Until he felt it happen for himself, he had never truly understood how tied he was to his trinkets. They were things he collected because he saw their beauty, but he didn't realize they held him as much as he held them.

The second his fingers touched the bag of trinkets, Kai felt a wave of energy crash against him, and at once, a soothing lap of calm. He was safe. He was home.

Kai felt Jemma's eyes on him. Apparently, the change was not just something he felt, but a visible thing. All at once, he was not so confused or angry with his savior. Kai smiled at Jemma; he lifted his bag of trinkets free.

Without a word, he upended it on the table and nodded his head for Jemma to have a look. He felt certain she would understand once she saw. He needed her to understand, oddly more than he had ever needed understanding from anyone.

She shifted one piece at a time not saying a word. Her silence was a siren song. Drawing him in, starving him so he was desperate to know her mind.

Kai nearly laughed aloud at his own silliness. She was just a little girl, a sad, lonely, but oddly open little girl. It must be something to do with the life debt, because nothing else could explain his intense need to understand her, to help her, to have her understand him, and most of all, to make her smile.

Her fingers brushed a scrap of torn paper; it was bumpy from the combination of damp sea air and warm sun, and had a little doodle of a shark attacking a stick figure surfer. She ran a finger over it, and a light smile played across her face before she replaced it and moved on, to a bent ticket stub for *The Avengers*. Then she was playing with the broken purple shoelace with the frayed end, and with a disgusted face, poking at the broken half of a used popsicle stick until she noticed the partial phone number scribbled on it, then she really did smile.

Imagining the boy frantically searching the beach for that phone number, Kai wondered. Or was it a girl in her head? Breaking the stick in half and tossing it aside because she wasn't interested.

That was where the magic came from: the possibilities. The bent pocketknife she was playing with now, or the one hoop earring beside it, might be trash to someone else, but to Kai, they were stories. The only thing that could limit their worth was his own imagination.

Kai could tell the second she found the centerpiece of his collection. Her face took on an adorably disapproving expression and with only the tips of her thumb and pointer finger, she lifted the bikini top into the air. She stared at Kai with an eyebrow up and her nose stuck out as though it was drenched in something foul.

"Best night of my life," Kai lied with a broad smile. He laughed as she dropped the bikini back on the table and leaned back in her chair.

"Boys are so gross." She barely managed to restrain her smile.

"It was your mind that went there," Kai pointed out, having fun with her again. "For all you know, it belongs to my sister, and I stole it because I don't want her going to the beach dressed that way. Or maybe I wear it."

Jemma rolled her eyes rather than speaking her skepticism, but Kai smiled anyway.

"It's a nice collection," Jemma said at last, as Kai began stuffing the objects back in the bag. Another time, he'd get her to come up with stories about one of them and sketch her story. He and Poesy did that once in a while, on a warm night as they watched the sun setting and the breeze off the ocean cooled the air. Poesy loved the game; he'd bet Jemma would as well.

"I mean it," Jemma said into the quiet that followed her comment, as though the quiet worried her, made her wonder if he was still angry.

"Thanks."

"I'm…sorry about before." Jemma shifted uncomfortably.

"It's cool. Wanna see what else he's got?"

Her face said no, but she nodded. "Yeah, okay."

What would this girl leave behind? Was there anything she didn't finish?

"Mama will be furious. She doesn't like Tom, but we're soul mates. The psychic said we would remake the world together. We will be married tomorrow, and tell Mama and Pop when we pass through Oklahoma, this spring." From the journals of May Bell Franklin, 7th generation daughter of Terra.

Honestly, Jemma wasn't at all sure she wanted to see what was in Pa's bags. No, Black Boot's bags. Maybe it would be easier that way; she was just looking at the bags of the monster trying to blow down her door and steal the land she was meant to protect. It would be a good advantage, knowing what he carried around with him. Or it should be, if he was only Black Boot. But part of him was still Pa; seeing his things could make that harder to ignore.

What if she didn't like what she saw? How would she handle it? Worse, what if she did like it? What if it made him…human? What if it made her miss him? What if she wanted him to stay, and hold her, and *be* Pa? What if it made her weak?

Kai was staring at her expectantly. She wished he would just open it if he wanted to; she didn't want to be the one. But she had a feeling, basically calling him a thief earlier, was going to make him stubborn.

"Maybe I should finish lunch first," Jemma blurted out.

"He'll be back soon."

And, what? He planned to just give him the bags back? Jemma doubted that.

With a sigh, Jemma reached out to pull the open bag onto the seat beside her. Kai lifted it from beneath to help her, then settled back to let her do the searching.

The first things to come out were clothes. Dusty, dirty, musty clothes. Jemma tossed them aside in disgust.

"He must have passed a laundromat somewhere."

Kai didn't reply. Reaching in again, Jemma found a pair of binoculars and several road maps. When she found his cell phone, she couldn't help but flip though the contacts. The farm's number was in it, but she doubted he'd ever called.

She tossed it aside and reached in again. Purple flickered at the edge of her vision as she retrieved a journal. She flipped it open, trying to appear casual as she reached out to see what her father thought about. Before she had read more than a line on the first page, Jemma sat straighter in her chair, and her hands clenched around the journal.

"Spells," she bit out, flipping from page to page, wanting to rip them out and shout at the top of her lungs. Would he never learn? Would she? Of course it was spells; it was always spells. "He's collecting magic."

"But he didn't write them." Kai leaned over Jemma's shoulder to peer into the book. She'd forgotten he was even there. But she looked closer, and he was right. Every spell was in a different hand.

"To control currents. To alter courses. To contain something invisible…harnessing spells." Jemma fell silent reading the pages more carefully, despite the purple haze before her eyes. "He wouldn't be able to write these. He may not even be able to read them."

"Why not?"

"Well, he's a wind guardian. When you become a guardian, you swear to serve and protect your charge, without controlling it. All these spells could be used to control the wind."

"Doesn't he do that already?"

"Yes, and no. Honestly, I'm not exactly sure." Jemma shrugged. "It's like the wind is tied to him, his moods effect it, but…"

"If he can't use them, why is he collecting them?" Kai interrupted.

"I'm not sure. They aren't written as though they're for the wind." She studied the spells one at a time, trying to reason out her father's thought process. "Maybe he thinks if they aren't written for the wind, he can speak the spells and change them, to use on the wind. Or maybe…he always wanted power; maybe now he wants power over more than just the wind. Either way, we cannot let him have that back."

Carefully, Jemma set the journal aside and reached into the bag again. It was easier this time. Easier to distance herself from who they were to each other and simply search for a way to defeat him.

There was nothing more of interest in the bag. A tube of toothpaste, a tooth brush, and five greasy bottles of lotion.

"Well, he would need it, wouldn't he." Jemma tossed aside a bottle of lotion. She didn't want to know that he had dry skin or brushed his teeth. It was all too normal for her to stomach. She needed him to remain something less than human.

The second bag was much heavier and a bit cumbersome. It kept slipping around on the chair she and Kai lifted it onto. Holding onto the bag with one hand, he moved around and shoved another chair under it to hold it up.

Jemma opened the bag with slow precision, afraid—of what she couldn't say, but there was something wrong with this bag. It sent tingles down her spine just touching it. Banishing the feeling, Jemma reached in blindly and pulled out a glass jar.

Her breath caught as soon as she had it in the light, and it slipped from her hold. Kai barely snagged it in time to keep it from shattering on the ground. They stared at each other with near identical looks of horror. Then their eyes returned magnetically to the jar.

They Will Remember My Name

The town looked as tired and dead as the farm. More like the set of so many ghost movies than the quiet but thriving town Black Boot recalled. No one was on the street in the middle of the afternoon on a Wednesday. There were maybe three cars, none looked new, two were so dirty one could imagine the owners had given up on ever cleaning them. Even the church had boarded windows. The only businesses without boarded windows were the grocery store, and the diner across the street, where all three cars were parked.

As he drew closer, Black Boot got a good look at the cars. He froze in the middle of the street, seeing the past. The dusty green truck, bent in on the side from where it struck his little girl. He could almost feel the pinch of the chipped paint biting into his hand as he shoved it off Jemma's body.

This was the place to find his answers. Esther wouldn't have just given that truck away. She would stare at it every day, to grow her hatred of him, to feed her curse and keep him as far away from his girl as she could.

Shuddering, Black Boot stepped onto the sidewalk and marched straight into the diner.

An angry wind swept in with him, upsetting all the napkins and sending the bell on the door ringing wildly. Around the room, the patrons looked up, startled as the hair was lifted off their necks and their menus were tugged at by the wind. The door shut behind him, cutting off most of the wind, and Black Boot watched the napkins flutter to the ground, as if to hide. He looked up then, returning the stares of all ten occupants of the restaurant.

None of the faces jumped out at him as especially familiar, but it had been eight years, and the only people he ever cared about were either dead—or Jemma.

No one spoke up, staring as if he was about to pull a gun and slaughter them. He hated townies, always had. One man came to his feet. His stare was different from the rest, shifting back and forth, from confusion to comprehension. He was near Black Boot's age, in his mid-thirties, and tall. From the way several eyes shot to him, looking for guidance, Black Boot would lay good money he was important in town. A sheriff maybe; he didn't have the look of a pastor or mayor.

Black Boot looked the man straight in the eye, as he addressed the whole of the diner. "I need information about the farm up the highway twenty miles or so outside town. About the family that lives there."

"Avoid them," the waitress said under her breath. She was standing at one of the tables, menus in hand, but when Black Boot's eyes shifted to her, she looked away.

Behind the counter, the cook went back to his stove, as if this settled the matter, but the rest of the room remained absorbed in Black Boot's presence.

The sheriff-looking man had a dawning look that was all too familiar. He was reaching for a memory he knew he should have but just couldn't find. Someone had bamboozled him. Black Boot had a fair idea who.

"What did they do to you?" a young woman asked. She was maybe twenty, had her feet up on the opposite seat and a bite of cake on her waiting fork.

"Nothing." He wasn't here to give information; he wanted to get it. "I saw only a child. Do any adults live there?"

"The witch, Esther," the girl said snidely. "She'd just assume curse you as greet you."

She was warming to the subject, and but for the bamboozled man , the other patrons were settling down and returning to their meals. Black Boot snagged the arm of the waitress as she passed.

"Hun, I'm gonna' need four burgers, a bunch of fries, a salad and a few pieces of your best fruit pie to go in a hurry."

She nodded none to comfortably and pulled her arm away. Sidestepping him, she returned to the kitchen.

"Come to think of it, the old crone hasn't been around in a while," the girl was going on, undaunted by her less than enthusiastic audience. "Course, it's the little one you should really avoid. She sits there guarding h–"

"Shut it, Clarissa," the man snapped, cutting the girl off mid tirade. But his eyes remained on Black Boot. Had the girl been about to say something? Something this man wanted secret? Wasn't that interesting. Even bamboozled, he was trying to protect the family secret. Who was he?

With a bitter glare, the girl slid the fork into her mouth and turned away in a snit.

"What is it you want with them?" the man asked Black Boot, shaking his head as if to clear it.

"Something of mine is there. I want to see it's cared for." Black Boot stepped up closer to the man, taking his measure. "You in charge here?"

"Not likely," Clarissa scoffed under her breath, but there was a hesitance in her gaze as it passed the man, belying her arrogance.

"I'm the local physician. Allen Brickman. And you are?"

"Tom Traveler."

A chill passed through the diner at that announcement. All eyes returned to him. Good; if they knew his name, they knew to fear him.

Clarissa dropped her cake and sat up straight, as if struck by lightning.

"May Bell's hus –" A woman in the back booth slammed her own palm over her lips, as Black Boot's eyes fell on her.

"But…she killed you." Clarissa was too stupid to shut her mouth.

Black Boot eyed her oddly. Esther, kill him? She didn't have it in her, much though she'd have liked to. But by far, the reaction that was most profound was Allen's. His head snapped around as if just waking up in a foreign land. His eyes latched onto the waitress, behind the counter.

"What's the date today?"

"July twentieth. Lord, but you are acting strange lately."

"I'll kill her," Allen said making to leave, but Black Boot snagged his arm holding him in place.

"Just a minute, friend."

"I am not your friend. You shouldn't have come back." Allen held Black Boot's eyes, unafraid it seemed.

"That may be, but since I'm thinking it's my daughter your talkin' 'bout, I'm gonna insist you wait."

"A daughter you *abandoned*. She's not yours any longer."

"No?" Black Boot snarled, and the wind shoved at the door of the diner, upsetting the pile of napkins again and eliciting several gasps from the patrons. "Is she yours, then? Is that why she's alone, and underfed, on a dying farm?"

Allen shook his head. "No, that's her bull head, that she likely gets from you."

"Ha. Did you not know Esther?"

"Here!" the waitress interrupted, before Allen could reply. She shoved two bags into Black Boot's arms, forcing him to release Allen. "On the house, if you leave."

Allen was already out the door. Black Boot nodded genially, undisturbed by the fear. Fear meant they would leave him be. With the bags in his arms, he followed the *doctor*, who'd threatened his daughter, from the restaurant.

He was climbing into Esther's old truck. Black Boot was half tempted to sweep out his hand and send the truck flying into one of the boarded-up shops. He didn't want it anywhere near his Jemma, especially not when she was already so angry with him. It was so like Esther, leaving his daughter always with a reminder of what must be the worst day of her life.

"Those for Jemma?" Allen asked, startling Black Boot.

He nodded.

"I suppose you want to come along. Get in then," Allen said and ducked into the cab of the truck. When Black Boot was sitting beside him, he turned towards him boldly, "Don't interfere with me and Jemma. We have things to say to one another that haven't got a thing to do with you."

Black Boot made no move to reply. It was taking all that was in him not to simply kill this man. He thought he had the right to make such demands of Black Boot. Who was he to Jemma? Did she love him?

The wind picked up outside the truck, shaking it. He heard laughter. May Bell's bitter laughter beat at the truck as they set off out of town.

It's nothing you don't deserve.

"History is full of them, Jem, people who hold to the belief that they know better than others, or that others' lives are covetable. Be better than the rest of us. Want what you are, and nothing more. Please." From the journals of Esther Lynn Franklin, 6th matron of the Women of Terra.

"I t's a pixie," Jemma breathed, pulling the jar from Kai's hands and cradling it in her own reverently.

Kai stared after it, equally mesmerized. "He captured a pixie," he said in disbelief.

Jemma had never seen anything so amazing—and awful. The pixie was constantly in motion, one moment a ball of light, the next a spear ramming against the lid of the jar. It shoved against the lid, seeming to explode into a million little flecks of light, before reforming into a ball.

"This is no ordinary jar, if it can hold a pixie. Where would he even get such a thing?" Jemma said gingerly setting the jar on the table, to examine it more closely.

"There are places." Kai's tone was almost hesitant. Jemma glanced his way; his eyes were looking off deeply. Was he worried about telling her the sort of places her father must frequent, to get such horrid things? Or to tell her he frequented them himself?

Jemma turned back to the jar; it seemed so ordinary. She lifted a hand to the lid, intending to test it, see if she could set the pixie free, but Kai dropped a hand over hers.

"No, Jemma." He shook his head very firmly, suddenly more serious than he had been since she rescued him.

"It's a captive, like you were. We have to release it."

"He shouldn't have caught it; it's wrong. But you can't be the one to let it out either," he said in a rush imploring her to understand. "Think about it, pixies aren't known for their agreeable natures or patience. What if it thinks you were the one who trapped it?"

"That's a risk I'll just have to take. I can no more leave it in there, than I could leave you on the ground dying."

The Door to the Deep Dark

Kai wasn't about to move his hand. There was soft hearted, and softheaded, and at the moment, Jemma was being softheaded. Pixies were considered the second-most deadly type of fairy, and the single-most powerful, and she wanted to unleash one for no good reason.

"I can't repay my debt if you die at the hands of a fairy."

"Then you'll just have to save me." Jemma shoved at his hand uselessly. He was stronger than he looked.

"I don't have anything to fight pixie magic, Jemma."

"This is hardly the desperate situation you're making it out to be." Jemma shrugged nonchalantly.

"You've read about kelpies, so surely you've read about pixies as well."

"Of course." Almost as though he wasn't there, Jemma bent her head around his arm, so her face was pressed up to the jar, and he saw it in her eyes: the wonder that tempted people to their doom. That was how pixies killed. They drew you in with their beauty, and their seeming innocence; once they had lured you away from everything that could protect you, they turned.

"They're tiny because they have such great power," Jemma said absently. "If they were larger, their power and size would unbalance the universe. They are made up of light and energy, like tiny conscious stars. They can take any shape they like, so long as they appear no larger than a few inches."

"And what about the bad, Jemma?" He could almost hear his father, the way he had taken Lypsy by the arm and led her away from the dark market the first time. How he had pled with her to see the truth. "What about leading people into the darkest corners of the woods, to torture and eat them? What about stealing magic, and turning people about, so they cannot remember who they are or where they are going, so they wander in circles, lost to the world?"

Jemma looked at him with an oddly disappointed expression. "What, like kelpies are thieves and scavengers? Like you prey on the desires of those who seek adventure, and feed their hearts into the waters of the world?"

Kai drew back startled. But still, he didn't move his hand. "These aren't just made up stories, Jemma. I've seen it."

She nodded. "I'm sure there are bad pixies. And I'm sure there are kelpies who kill too. But...I didn't know you weren't one of the bad ones when I helped you. I can't do differently here just 'cause it is you warning me, and not Pa."

Kai slid his hand slowly away from the bottle, holding his breath. She was intrigued by the pixie, but she wasn't captivated. She wasn't Lypsy, in love with the adventure of it all. Jemma was a warrior, protecting everyone or everything within her reach.

And Kai wasn't his father. If this pixie was a bad one, Kai would protect Jemma, or die trying.

Jemma unscrewed the lid. As soon as it was loose, the pixie did the rest, bursting free and sending the lid flying against the wall. It darted around the room. It moved so quickly, Kai almost couldn't keep track of it, but he forced himself to. It burst over and over into little showers of light, before reforming into one tight little ball of amber light.

"It's like fireworks!" Utter delight filled Jemma's voice. Kai took his eyes from the pixie, seeking Jemma. Her face was alight with wonder and happiness, and for the moment at least, no pain at all. She looked, free.

"Beautiful," Kai agreed without moving his eyes.

Suddenly, the pixie darted between them to hover over the bag, in the shape of a hummingbird. It stared at Jemma expectantly. Now the bad would come, Kai thought and tightened his grip around his trinkets.

The pixie shifted suddenly into the shape of an arrow aimed right for the bag.

"There must be more of them," Jemma exclaimed lunging for the bag. This was going to be bad. One pixie he might be able to help her escape, but several?

Kai was clenching up for a fight when he heard the distinct sound of breaks screeching outside the house. Jemma's hand froze over the bag, and the joy that painted her only moments ago dripped away. She looked frightened and anguished once again. There was a loud screech of a rusty car door opening and slamming, and through it all, she held careful breath. Who the hell had shown up now?

"Jemima Tulip Franklin, get out here this instant!" a man yelled.

Jemima Tulip? Who named their child something that terrible?

"Shit." Jemma whispered releasing a breath, her whole being sinking away with the air, and she pulled her arm slowly away from the duffle.

"I will be Smith no longer, nor will my daughter bare her father's name. She is Terra, its daughter and its keeper, no other shall hold her." From the journals of Sarah Anne Smith, 2nd matron of the Women of Terra.

"Traveler." Pa's voice was the first thing Jemma heard as the screen door screeched behind her. "Her name is Traveler."

It was on the tip of her tongue to tell him she had changed it last year, as a birthday present, taking her grandfather's name instead. But her eyes fell on Allen. He paid Pa no mind, staring instead at Jemma, and though he looked heartily angry, there was more of sadness and disappointment in his eyes. He must know about Gran. What was she to say? She could barely feel the pain in her leg, she hurt so badly just looking at Allen.

All she wanted to do was throw her arms around him and hold on. She wanted to let go of everything holding her up and let him take care of things like family was supposed to. She had missed him so much more than she'd expected when she cast her spell.

It had just all been *too much.* She had been terrified of losing everything at once, so she cast a spell to make him forget, expecting it to make everything simpler. After all nothing ever changed with Mama, and Jemma had stopped needing help with her leg a long time ago. As her doctor Allen didn't really need to come by much, but looking at him now, with half of her heart wanting to cry and half of it wanting to laugh, because she was so happy he was here, she realized somewhere over the years they'd all become family. Jemma, Gran, and Allen were a family. So in sending him away Jemma had lost everything anyway. It was almost worse than if she'd let someone take her away from May Bell, because she knew Allen was going along with his life never remembering their family.

Every day had felt longer and emptier than the last. It was just her and her comatose mother. The more days that passed alone with May

Bell the less May Bell seemed to be Mama, and the more she was just, Jemma's patient: May Bell Traveler.

But now—Jemma walked to the edge of the shield. It was keeping Allen out as well as Pa, so he must be very angry. She stood just in front of him, with her heart weighing her down, waiting for the worst.

Somehow Allen had broken free of her spell and come home, but the shield was keeping him out. It didn't know if he was a friend or a foe now. Jemma could barely breathe. What if he didn't want to be family now that Gran was gone? Now that Jemma had cursed him? What if the last three months was what the rest of her life would look like? Why did it hurt so much more to see him locked out by the shield than it had to send him away?

"Where is your grandmother, Jemima?" He never called her Jemima, knew she hated that name.

"In the cellar." That sounded so stupid. He must know the truth, and there was no way to avoid it, but she tried all the same. She heard a startled guffaw from her left, only then realizing Kai had followed her out.

"Alive?" Allen asked, recalling Jemma's attention.

Jemma shook her head, looking down at her feet, and her throat began to burn.

"How long?"

"Three months," she whispered, tears forming behind her eyes, as she saw it all over again. But she fought the tears; she didn't want anyone to see her cry.

"And why didn't I know this? Why haven't I been coming by, Jemima? Do you honestly think you have a right to keep this from me?"

She Might Never Smile Again

"That's enough." Kai walked in front of Jemma, shielding her. Not two minutes ago, she had been smiling, thrilled to be setting fairy free, and he had been terrified for her, but this was somehow worse. Shouldn't someone just give the girl a hug?

"Clearly, she's sorry. Just give her a break, will you?" Kai faced off with the stranger. The man looked near Black Boot's age, and clearly he was close to Jemma, but who he was Kai couldn't tell, an uncle maybe.

"Who the hell are you?" the man demanded, looking much more the picture of the angry father than Black Boot ever did, or had a right to. And it was clear which man she held in esteem, which only made his treatment of her worse.

Jemma pushed Kai gently aside and stood facing the man.

"I'm sorry, Allen. I shouldn't have put a spell on you, but I didn't know what else to do. I couldn't let you take me away from—" she cut herself off, glancing at Black Boot. "Away from here; it's my home."

Then there were the bodies in the cellar; wouldn't want to leave those either. Kai nearly laughed. *This place is so bizarre.*

"Is that what you think of me, Jemma? Am I so awful?"

Her tears fell, despite the great effort he felt her put into holding them back. Grief, pain, regret. She certainly carried a lot of regret around for such a small girl.

"No. But you can't control everything. Gran didn't leave a will, and Mrs. Hamish wants…"

"The property, so she can sell it to Agracorp, I know. But you don't know everything either, Jemma. Esther left a will; it's in town with her attorney. This is why you need to come to me, to trust me. We have to do things together."

"I'm sorry," she wailed and covered her face with her hands, her tears running freely now.

Kai started forward to comfort her, as it appeared no one else would, but the man, Allen, beat him to it. He stepped through the shield, apparently no longer impeded, and wrapped Jemma tight in his arms.

Black Boot lunged at the hugging pair, but the shield held him back. Kai could almost see the imprint of hands on Black Boot's shirt where he was restrained, and smiled. He shouldn't; it was wrong to delight in other people's suffering. But it was nothing Black Boot didn't deserve—being forced to watch his daughter turn to someone else for comfort.

The Unforgiven

lack Boot was consumed by a swirling hungry rage, and so was the wind. It whipped around the house, setting the chimes off in a mad song, and rocking the chair wildly. It yanked up the dead earth, sloshing it around the house, like the contents of a blender.

First, that man felt the right to chastise his daughter, and then—then, she fell into his arms and let him hold her.

The wind blew harder, upsetting the smallest of the chimes so they flew off their nail and clattered against a porch beam. The wind shoved at the man with his arms around Black Boot's girl forcing him back a few steps. He had everyone's attention now.

Jemma acknowledged his presence for the first time since sun-up. Her eyes were pink and puffy from her tears; she clung tightly to the arm of the man who made her cry.

Her father she fought with and scoffed at and ignored, but this man—he could have no idea that Jemma's eyes had been purple until she was three, or that she was deathly afraid of rabbits until May Bell gave her one to raise. This man, who could be *nothing* to her, she clung to and apologized to. She wanted his approval, and Black Boot would not tolerate that.

She could see it; he let her see it. She knew Black Boot could take the man away if he decided to.

Jemma pushed the man's arm aside slowly and stepped forward. The braid of her ponytail spun around in the wind like a pinwheel as she came closer to the shield. Her eyes held his quietly, not threatening or frightened, just questioning.

"What are you going to do, Pa?" she asked sadly, casually. "Drop the same old truck on him, just 'cause he's my friend?"

The wind rushed up around Black Boot, stronger than he had ever felt it, and shoved him like two gigantic fists in the chest. He stumbled into the truck. And all the wind fell away, leaving only silence between him and his girl.

"That was an accident," he choked over his sudden hoarseness. "I never meant to—"

She cut him off. "An accident? Slamming a door on someone's finger is an accident, breaking a vase is an accident. Throwing your wife fifty feet in the air and crushing your daughter's legs beneath a truck because you lose your temper is not a *damned accident!*" She waved her arms around wildly, seeming suddenly full of all the rage and passion that had so characterized her mother. So unlike the silent girl he met yesterday. "I don't even think there's a word for that. But I can tell you what it's not, and that's forgivable."

"I never meant to hurt you."

"You did," she said flatly, shrugging her shoulders, as if it was nothing. As if finding him unforgivable was nothing. "You more than hurt me, you…broke me. Broke our whole family."

"I wanted to stay," Black Boot said knowing in his heart that it should make a difference, hoping it would. "I wanted to take care of you and to fix it."

"But you didn't. You chose the wind and the power." She shrugged again and turned around. She walked away without so much as a glance behind her, and the man followed her into the house.

"I'm going to fix it," he called after her.

The boy stayed behind, looking at Black Boot almost pityingly. In that moment, he wanted nothing so much as to pick up the wind like a cloak of strength and strangle the boy with it. He dared to pity Black Boot.

But no matter how he wished it, now, when he wanted to control the wind, it deserted him. Just as it always did when he needed to control it.

Slowly, the boy followed Jemma into the house.

"I'll fix it, you'll see!"

Black Boot stared at the ground before him. The ground that held the family stones. There had to be a way for him to break through the shield, to go after his girl. From the corner of his eye, Black Boot saw a scuff, such a little thing, at the tip of his right boot, but it stood out like a beacon. It was a streak, like a splatter of mud.

He knelt down mechanically, nothing but that scuff able to intrude on his consciousness. He brushed at the mark. Nothing happened. He scrubbed harder and harder, frantic now. But it was no use; his boot was scuffed.

His boots couldn't be scuffed; it was impossible? Esther had made them indestructible. Completely indestructible. Her curse couldn't be taking him so quickly?

A breeze so soft it was nearly imperceptible grazed Black Boot's forehead, brushing aside a tiny tuft of hair.

Choose better this time.

"I'd never thought of leaving the land in any permanent way. I love it, unlike the rest of my family. But I have always believed it would be me to break the curse, and Tom thinks the only way to do that is to leave and never look back. Maybe he's right." From the journals of May Bell Franklin-Traveler, 7th generation daughter of Terra.

"Well?" Allen demanded the moment the screen shut behind Kai. "Who is this and why is he wearing my clothes?"

"His clothes were dirty." Jemma shrugged. "That reminds me, I need to do some laundry."

"Jemima," Allen growled. Jemma glared at the use of her full name but said nothing.

Now that the initial emotional meeting was behind them, Jemma found herself a little bit mad at Allen. He was acting like her parent, something he'd never done before, using her full name, which he knew she hated, and worst of all, acting like he had a right to be angry, when being bamboozled was mostly his own fault.

Kai stepped forward, breaking up the staring contest. He looked at Allen distrustfully, but he didn't look ready to attack him as he had outside.

"Kai Micah Shoal," he said holding out his hand. "Jemma saved my life."

Allen raised an eyebrow, looking over Kai's shoulder to Jemma, even as he shook Kai's hand.

Jemma wanted to laugh at the question she saw in Allen's gaze. Kai was not interested in her. When had Jemma ever attracted *that* kind of attention from a boy? Never, that's when. Jemma felt suddenly very tired. The pain in her leg was back, and now she had a headache to go along with it, and she was hungry. All she really wanted to do was go to her own room and cry for a few days.

"Not again, Jemma." Kai startled her, turning her way his concerned expression, contradicting his exasperated tone.

"What?" she demanded, at a loss.

"The crying. Enough already; he isn't worth it."

"How do you know?" she demanded in a watery voice. Feeling even tearier. And which "he" wasn't worth her tears? Because at the moment, she couldn't say who the source of her tears was.

"Water," Kai replied, waving his sparkling arm as if it should be obvious.

And Jemma felt foolish, because it should be. If kelpies could control water they must be able to feel it.

"I always know when you're going to cry. I can feel it."

Allen was staring between them with avid curiosity. And Jemma couldn't sort one emotion from another. She opened her mouth to apologize to Kai for the tears but froze.

"So ignore it if it bothers you. Or go back to Pa." She threw an arm out angrily. "I bet he never cries. I'll cry if I want to."

Kai smiled then, and his eyes sparkled even more than when he'd found his trinkets. "It's your party, huh?"

Jemma gave a watery laugh as her cheeks flushed. He had his way; she didn't feel a bit like crying anymore.

"Adorable," Allen drawled. "As thrilled as I am to know Jemma saved your life, that still doesn't explain why you're here."

"I owe her a life debt," Kai said, as if Allen should know this.

"And you mean to repay this how?" His tone was about as menacing as Jemma had ever heard it.

"Painting," she blurted out. There was no point trying to explain to Allen that Kai intended to stay here until he had saved her life as well. He would never understand. He wasn't magical, and at the moment, he wasn't even the fun friendly Allen he'd been since her second surgery. "You should see what he's done with the bathroom already."

Allen looked skeptical, and she felt Kai smiling at her incredulously, but he didn't know that Allen wasn't magical.

"He's amazing."

"I really am," Kai said as if teasing, but Jemma was sure he must know how good he was. Allen narrowed his eyes, staring Kai down; he only smiled in return.

Shit, this wasn't helping.

"Just go look."

Allen walked around them.

"Quit encouraging him." Jemma punched Kai in the shoulder lightly.

"Why? It's kind of fun." Kai laughed.

"He doesn't get it, he's not magical," Jemma sighed. It was such a long story, and she didn't particularly care to tell it just now. She looked back and forth between the bench and the entrance to the kitchen, not sure which she wanted more: food for her stomach or rest for her leg.

"She's right," Allen said coming out of the bathroom. "You do excellent work. You could make good money at it."

Translation: get lost.

Kai smiled at Allen. "Thanks, one day maybe. Once I've repaid my debt."

"I'm hungry," Jemma blurted into the tension.

Allen looked at her despairingly; he was always worried about her eating habits. "Your father bought you food from Millie's; I'll get it from the truck."

Jemma didn't say anything. She couldn't.

Your father bought you food.

I can tell you what it's not, and that's forgivable.

Your father.

Black Boot.

Your father.

Only You

She was crying again, but Kai didn't try to stop her. He felt the magnitude of her pain as her tears slipped silently down her cheeks, so utterly confused. Kai wished there was some spell he could do to let her father feel half of this. He'd dropped a car on his own daughter and abandoned her. What kind of father could even continue living after doing something so horrible?

She looked so alone standing in the middle of this empty room as she cried. He should go to her, hug her. But he couldn't. Kai avoided the deep dark for good reasons. Already, she had taken him there once today, reminding him of his missing cousin. And the life debt was affecting him in ways he wouldn't have imagined possible. He felt like they were bound together —forever. If he held her, let her cry on him, her tears would crawl inside him, and he might never be able to avoid the deep dark again.

The screen door slammed behind Allen, catching her attention and saving Kai. Or so he thought. Jemma looked up at him with watery eyes, piercing his soul. She knew he'd watched her cry and offered no comfort. She seemed even to know why. But that wasn't what pierced him. It was the quiet understanding, as if she simply accepted that he couldn't be the kind of man who comforted her, and she didn't think any less of him.

It only made him think less of himself.

They gazed at each other silently for a moment as Allen came back in toting two bags.

"Clearly, you were more of an eater when you were a child. He got way too much food. He's off clearing the fields." Allen shook his head as he spoke setting the food on the bench. "Your gran would have something to say about the state of the farm, Jemma."

"Would, if she were alive," Jemma agreed walking towards the food as if magnetized.

"It isn't funny."

"Am I laughing?" Jemma returned.

Every time this man spoke to Jemma, Kai had the urge to hit him. Couldn't he see how much she was hurting? His tone reminded Kai of his father in all their worst moments. It made Kai edgy. He had to take that kind of crap from his father, because he was his father, and they loved each other. But whatever this Allen guy was to Jemma, he wasn't her father.

"Who's been feeding you, Jemma? Clearly, no one's been looking after the farm. And what about May Bell?"

Jemma's eyes shot to Kai full of sudden fear. What was that about?

"I'm talking to you, Jemma," Allen snapped. "I love you, kid. I'm sorry that you're hurting, but…what possessed you to think you could do this all on your own? You should have called me."

"I did!" she bellowed, slamming her fisted hands against her sides. "I called you, as soon as I found her, but you were away for your weekend with Maggie. I got your voicemail," she said in an injured snarl, and Kai saw before she finished the sentence that Allen understood why.

"Do you know what it said?" Jemma's voice sounded venomous, as she answered for him. *"Jemma, if this is you, give me a break kid. Only emergencies okay? We really need to get you some friends."*

"Wow." Kai shook his head aghast.

"Jemma, it was a joke. I … and Esther dying clearly qualifies as an emergency."

"Not really," Jemma replied. "I left her right where she was for hours, while I got things ready for her. Didn't bother anyone but me, so it couldn't have been very important."

"I'm sorry."

Jemma shrugged. Kai wanted to shake her; why did she just let everyone get away with treating her like crap?

"Come eat, Jemma. How long has it been, a week?"

"I was making lunch when you showed up, but I found…oh!" Jemma spun to face Kai suddenly, too suddenly. She must have turned her leg wrong because she gave an involuntary shout and pitched forward.

Kai dove to catch her, pulling her up against his chest and holding her tight. He could feel her clench every muscle. Her hands balled into fists as she fought against the pain, against letting it show. Kai shook his head and bent down further. Lifting her off both feet, he carried her over to the bench. She wasn't very heavy, as if her bones were somehow lighter than a normal person.

Allen shoved everything aside as Kai came over. Once she was settled, Allen pushed Kai away, crouching in front of Jemma and rolling up her loose pant leg to examine her knee.

"You haven't been taking your medicine, have you?"

"She has medicine?" Kai all but shouted, pacing behind the couch. "You have medicine and you walk around like some kind of martyr, hurting yourself worse?"

Allen smirked approvingly, massaging Jemma's knee. Kai hadn't seen it before; there were so many scars on it, and the skin around it looked stretched and twisted. Jemma's hand shot out, blocking her knee from view. She glared up at Kai, but the tears running from her eyes ruined the effect.

"It makes me woozy and Gran said –"

"Jemima Tulip, don't make me yell at you for a third time in one day," Allen interrupted. "Your gran never had pain like yours. Hers was all in her soul. That sort of pain you power through, there's nothing else to do with it. But physical ailments you treat, or you make them worse."

"Quit calling me that," Jemma whispered, looking away.

"Where is the medicine? I'll get it."

Kai felt Jemma's humiliation in her continuing tears. He felt bad about that. She had nothing to be ashamed of, but he couldn't fix that now. Just the medicine, but she wouldn't look at him.

Shaking his head, he crossed to her room; the pills were probably there. He'd lay good money they were what hit the wall this morning. He was starting to know this girl too well.

"NO!" Jemma's shout had Kai jerking around, even as he opened the door to her room.

No. Not her room after all. Kai's gaze shot to Jemma angrily; without a word, he slipped into the room to look for her pills. He found them laying in the far corner and bent to retrieve them. As he stood, his eyes drifted to the woman on the bed. The woman she was hiding from him, as if he was the monster her father accused him of being.

She had an IV and other tubes, but she seemed to breathe on her own, slow even breaths, like low tide.

Kai knew that face.

Only you can save her.

It sang, the wind, in a woman's voice. Only you. Kai knew better than to listen, he was safe in the caves, had gotten as many sea skippers and foam fairies into the safety of the sunning rocks as he could, and a few animals as well. They were safe here, and here they should stay.

Kai was familiar with such enticements.

Only you can save her.

Like mermaids beckoning from rocks, or sirens lamenting into the breeze, they were words that drew a man to his doom. Still, Kai's feet brushed through the rising tide, the lap of waves urging him back into the cave, to safety. But she needed him.

The wind screamed through the mouth of the cave, stirring up a spray of waves so he couldn't tell sky from ocean, or sea from shore. All he could make out in the clash of air was the woman, fighting against a mighty arm of wind.

Only you can save me.

Hell. Was that her mother? She'd helped Black Boot capture him.

She'd stood in the middle of what looked like the ocean, shoving urgently at the wind. And Kai was the protector of this stretch of beach, during his trial at any rate. He glanced back, hesitating. He'd saved magical and sea creature alike from this unnatural storm, and now there was one more, calling out.

He could almost see his father's raised eyebrow, his disappointment that Kai wasn't up to the task. "This isn't like your art, Kai, or chasing after your treasures or some camping expedition. This is responsibility. Something you've never taken. I don't want to come home and find a shore littered with dead things, and you with five new paintings."

Shying away from his father's voice, Kai had inched forward; she needed him.

Only you can save me.

Maybe she wasn't bad, maybe —

Kai turned suddenly from the room, shutting the door carefully behind him. He walked silently over to Jemma.

Her eyes were full and large, overwhelmed with regret. "I'm sorry. You could have been…"

"A spy." Kai nodded, holding out the pills. Once she took them, he turned, walking out to the porch, back to his project. Back to something that made sense, because nothing else did. Not even the girl who'd saved his life.

"Why did Papa leave us here, so close to him, and to our mother's people, but so far away from everyone? No one wants us. No one wants me, none but Gil, and he only wants me in secret. Why can my name not be shouted in the town square, or my hand held at the pulpit? What is so wrong with me?" From the journals of Sarah Anne Smith, 2ⁿᵈ matron of the Women of Terra.

Jemma watched Kai disappear onto the porch; she felt like sobbing more than ever. She was utterly humiliated from having to be carried, then he got mad at her for being in pain, like it was her fault. And he knew when she cried, which considering the number of times she had done that in the…*day* she had known him, humiliated her even more. And he'd seen her leg. No one but Allen ever saw her leg, not even Gran, since Jemma's last surgery. Jemma saw to that.

She couldn't walk, couldn't cook without injuring herself. And now she wasn't even being allowed to make her own decisions. Then he found Mama, and his eyes had looked at her the way Pa did, when she said he was unforgivable.

She was the worst person in the world. All Jemma wanted to do was vanish into oblivion. Things would probably be better for everyone that way.

"Long day, Miss Jemima?" Allen asked gently, sounding like the old Allen, her friend.

"Please stop calling me that."

"Finally got yourself a conquest, I see."

"No." Jemma shook her head morosely. "He already thought I was weird, and now he knows I'm pathetic and a liar. He probably feels vindicated for not trusting me."

"If he doesn't trust you, he has no reason to be upset that you don't trust him," Allen pointed out. Then her friend vanished, and he was parental Allen again. "I suppose it's too much to hope that he is actually leaving."

"I don't think he will," Jemma said hoping she was right. Hoping she had a chance to make him understand. "He left his bag behind."

"Alright. You eat. I need to check on your mother, but I'll get you some water first, so you can take some of these."

"I can't be groggy now," Jemma argued. "Pa is here, and he's angry."

"You're taking them. Two of them. You don't take care of yourself. I only hope you did better with your mother. I can't believe you kept me away from her for so long."

Jemma shoved a handful of fries into her mouth to avoid biting Allen's head off. She wished he would just go away, like everyone else. But she couldn't say it; she'd said it to Gran.

"Three months. Do you have any idea what could have happened?"

"The same as happens every other three months. Not a damned thing. I change the tubes, clean around them, change her catheter, and her saline bag, give her massages, and do the physical therapy. I take care of her."

"I know you care for her, but there are things you wouldn't know to check. Or even understand if you had. Do you think I keep all those records for my own amusement? They help us know what she can't tell us, help us to make sure she doesn't get an infection or have organs shut down."

Allen was still on the ground beside Jemma, massaging her knee. She lifted her own hand and pulled his away.

"I'll get you some water."

He walked away leaving Jemma alone, as she wanted to be, but only for a moment. He was back with the glass of water, watching her down her two pills, but neither of them spoke. Jemma wondered what it would be like to control the wind the way Pa did. Allen would likely be in the air, yanked around and crying out for help right now if she did. Maybe she should cut Pa some slack.

"I'll check on May Bell." But he didn't move; he stared down at her silently. "We all love you, you know?"

"Whose we?" Jemma asked bitterly waving her arm at the empty room.

"I love you, your gran loved you. Your mother loves—"

"My mother doesn't know she exists, much less me."

"Esther would have slapped you for a comment like that."

Jemma raised her chin, all but daring him to do it. "Wouldn't have made it any less true."

Allen turned on his heel and left the room. As soon as Ma's door shut behind him, Jemma buried her head in her hands and began sobbing. She didn't mean it, didn't mean any of it. But it just made her so angry, so enraged that she couldn't see or think or do anything but lash out.

How did they know what May Bell felt? Jemma didn't. But Gran and Allen seemed full of her mother's secret musings. What made them so much more connected to her?

Jemma just wanted to curl up in a ball and die. She was the worst person in the world.

A bright ball of light darted from over Jemma's shoulder and blinked loudly before her. She saw the light between her fingers and pulled them away.

"How long have you been back there?" Jemma asked the pixie.

It danced around before her, shifting shapes so quickly that Jemma had no idea what to make of it all. Then suddenly, she knew what it meant. She might not be the worst person in the world after all, because she was going to rescue all his victims. Wincing at the effort, Jemma shoved her leg off the bench and stood, following the pixie into the kitchen.

She Speaks with the Voice of the Wind

Black Boot tore through the fields, tearing down stalks and ripping root vegetables out of the ground. He was a man on a mission. Something was happening to him and it wasn't good. The boots were scuffed, he couldn't call the wind, and he was beginning to feel weak. Weak, sorry and pathetic. He needed strength for what he planned to do.

Today the wind had pushed him. That hadn't happened in years, not since he first put on the boots. If the wind could push him around, then anything could. He wouldn't allow that to happen. A father, a leader needed to be strong.

"Go against the wind and it pushes you back; go along with it and it carries you." May Bell appeared in front of him in the wind. "You taught me that."

"Damn it, May Bell, I can't be everywhere at once!" Black Boot shouted, yanking at the air wanting to strangle it, but he couldn't catch hold. It was as if he was losing himself, becoming just another bit of dust in the wind. "It's easy for you." He jerked away from her returning to his work. "You can be anywhere you want. If I go along with the wind, I won't be *with* her. I'll never be able to make it up to her."

The wind rushed up across Black Boot in a screaming slice of cold.

"I'm never with her! She doesn't hear me. But you can reach her. You have to do it, Tom. You have to."

"She said I was unforgivable." He dropped the head of the sickle into the dirt, seeming to sink with it.

May Bell and the wind swept around him, until she stood like a misty cloud of earth before him. The sun burned through her eyes.

"You aren't here to be forgiven. You're here for her. Or at least, you should be."

"Of course I am."

"Then show me. If you fail us again, I will make sure you never know peace."

Smoother Edges

Kai didn't know exactly what made him angry. It wasn't as if she didn't have a right to her secrets. A right to protect her mother as no one was protecting her. And it wasn't as if he'd told her everything about his life either.

Kai sanded the rougher edges of the bench, preparing it to be painted, and tried to figure out why it was that he was suddenly so angry. He wasn't even sure much of his anger was directed at Jemma. Certainly, the secret bothered him, but more the way she'd reacted to his discovery, as if she still thought of him as her father's spy. She should know him better than that.

After one day?

Kai shook his head and sanded the bench harder. He knew *her* better than that after one day. Of course he did have the benefit of having her family history laid out at his feet and her tears as a guide to her deeper sadness.

He supposed if he looked at it from her perspective, if half of what he heard or interpreted this afternoon was true, he could understand why she wouldn't trust him. He probably wouldn't trust anyone. Kai had experienced his fair share of knockdown battles with his father over the years, but none of them resulted in him being pinned beneath anything. And there were the bodies in the cellar, which he'd first taken for a joke. They were real. And she had buried one of them. Then there was this man, whose relationship Kai had yet to ferret out. Who was apparently a friend, but didn't put much effort into being kind to her.

And she'd been here, alone, but for her comatose mother, since her grandmother died. All things considered, she seemed fairly sane. Well-adjusted even.

Kai finished the sanding and stood staring at the bench. He rubbed the sand paper between his fingers, feeling it crumple back into the magic sands he made it from. It didn't really matter what he painted on the bench; it would be just as uncomfortable for her.

The wind brushed over Kai's face gently, and he heard her voice again.

Only you can save her.

Kai looked around, expecting to see her ghostly form again. But there was nothing but empty space.

What was he to do about that? Jemma's mother helped Black Boot capture him, and apparently, she expected him to save her daughter somehow. Should he tell Jemma?

Tell her what? *I think I saw your mother's spirit dragged around in the flaps of your father's coat. The reason she can't speak to you, is because she's with him. She may be just as bad as he is.*

No, he couldn't do that to her.

But what if she wasn't bad? What if she was just as trapped as every other magical being Black Boot came across? Jemma would want her set free at the very least. What if Kai could reunite her spirit with her body? Would that even be a good thing?

From across the porch, Kai heard a window screeching slowly open. Kai spun towards the sound and watched a pair of tiny hands lifting the window. Was that a leaf elf?

Apparently, Jemma had finished setting Black Boot's captives free. A ball of flame shot out right at the leaf elf, making her jump; even Kai jumped back reflexively, as the elf shoved the window up with sudden force. She spun around, glowering.

"Nona!" Jemma shouted. "No fire."

The flames vanished, and Kai couldn't help laughing. A leaf elf, a fire imp, a pixie and Jemma—she was something else.

Kai looked down at the bench and an idea struck him. He ran back into the house to scavenge for what he needed, like a good kelpie.

"Can't say who was first to decide the curse needed breaking; could have been Josephine, the first to be called Terra. She read her mother's journals, followed them home, but she never showed signs of trying to exact revenge. But best as I can tell, the undoing is a matter of repaying the costs ourselves." From the journals of Esther Lynn Franklin, 6th matron of the Women of Terra.

Jemma had the windows open. She hovered around the kitchen starting a load of laundry with Kai's damp clothes and her father's disgusting ones. Nona, the fire imp, had insisted Jemma use her flying powder until the medicine took effect. It really did help; there wasn't any pressure put on her knee. There was still a dull sort of ache in her leg but it was nowhere near as bad as it would be if she were standing.

Jemma had set all her father's captives free, and it left her more confused than ever. On the one hand, he was a monster who had stolen all these beautiful creatures from their homes and families. He had a fire imp, a leaf elf, a gripie, and a pixie, and Kai, a kelpie. It was such an odd bunch. Fire imps only lived near active volcanoes; gripies were highland creatures that lived underground; a leaf elf, on the other hand, could be found just about anywhere with foliage, but were incredibly hard to find, because they were so fast and could become invisible; and pixies lived somewhere between the visible human reality and a mysterious fairy land.

Then there was Kai. Jemma always thought kelpies lived in fresh water, but apparently, he was from a beach somewhere. Maybe none of her information about magical beings was accurate. How had Pa even found them all? It should disgust her. It did, she supposed, but it more intrigued her and frightened her a little. So much power to capture them, so much power wielded with them. What were they all for? She couldn't think of a single magical ability they had in common or a spell that required such oddities.

Jemma wanted to hold onto the anger and the disgust and let everything else go. She wanted to see him not as Pa, but as Black Boot, but something wouldn't let her. He worried about her enough to bring her food and Allen, though he clearly hadn't been happy about it. And Jemma understood what it was to lose your temper, so it was becoming harder and harder to blame him for her leg. Especially when he was standing in front of her, the only family she had left to speak to. He was clearing the fields for her, hadn't even said a word about how poorly she was caring for it. Worst of all was the way he had looked when she called him unforgivable.

Jemma felt all twisted up inside when she said it, in her soul. But in her mind, it felt right, felt like a relief. He should hear the words. Gran would probably think Jemma was right to say it.

Truth don't always smell good. But if it's truth, it's truth.

The trouble was, Jemma wasn't so certain it was the truth. It was what the truth should be. She shouldn't be able to forgive him. He shouldn't just walk away without a scratch on him, and with everyone's love still intact, when he had destroyed their lives. But when the wind rushed up and shoved him, and his eyes seemed so frightened and lost, Jemma wanted to run to him, to hug him and take it all back. Even as she felt happy for saying it.

What would Mama think of what she'd said? Everyone else seemed able to divine her feelings; why couldn't Jemma?

She took a bite of the pie Pa brought her. She was nearly done with the third slice, hadn't saved a bit of pie for anyone else. She should feel bad, but she lifted the last bite into her mouth and closed her lips around it with a smile. She hadn't had pie in so long. A breeze swept in through the open window and Jemma's eyes drifted shut, letting the cool air carry her away.

"Jemma.

"Jemma mine. Look at Mama," Jemma felt a giggle inside herself but kept her eyes shut tight. They were spinning in a circle. Mama held her by the hands and Jemma's feet were off the ground, just brushing the wheat stalks as she spun around again and again.

"Just let go, honey. Let go and you can fly anywhere you want."

"No." Jemma opened her eyes and stared up at her mother, frightened. "I wanna stay with you."

Mama smiled her quiet "I love you" smile: no teeth, just shining eyes and curled lips. Then she gave Jemma's arms a little tug, lifting her through the empty space and pulling her close.

"Alright, Jemma mine. We'll stay right here, together."

But they weren't really together, were they? Jemma opened her eyes as the wind drifted away and stared out the window after it. Pa was clearing fields like a mad man, barely even pausing. They weren't together either, not really.

Jemma felt eyes on her and shifted. On the table beside her right hand was one of Pa's captives, the gripie. He glared at Jemma's hand.

"Where I come from, a hostess feeds her guests first."

Jemma snorted.

The Man Who Guards Her

Kai was just snagging a burger from the bag left on the bench when Allen came out of Jemma's room. Well, her mother's room. Kai had already taken most of the supplies he needed outside and had just come back in for the paint. The man hadn't noticed him yet, so Kai just took a bite of the burger and watched him. He looked thoughtful.

"How are you connected to this family exactly?" Kai asked, drawing the man's attention. He took another bite.

"How's that your business?" Allen asked.

Kai shrugged.

"I'm their doctor. I've been coming here to keep an eye on May Bell for years now."

"But not from the beginning, I think." Kai reached out to his left, to rummage around for some of the cold fries; food was food.

"No. I didn't live here then. I met Jemma after her second surgery. I was working at the hospital in the city, when she had it."

"Second surgery?"

"She's had four. Her leg keeps growing and every once in a while, we have to operate to keep it as straight as possible."

Kai nodded taking everything in; it still didn't explain what brought the man here. He was a piece that didn't quite fit, and in Kai's experience, that spelled trouble. His eyes drifted past the man to the door he'd come out of, the off-limits room.

"What's wrong with her mother?"

Allen let out a huff of air looking oddly heartbroken over a woman he couldn't possibly have known before. "Well, she's in a coma. She was lifted by a tornado, and then dropped from fifty feet in the air onto a tractor. I don't know why she's still alive, honestly. She has spine damage, and probably brain damage, although it's impossible to say how much, but she's special, something is keeping her alive."

Kai nodded, his mind stuck on all the damage. "How bad is the spine injury?"

"She'd likely be paraplegic, if she was awake. Why so interested?"

Kai shrugged, weighing the risks and the benefits. What if he could put her mother's spirit back in her body? She would never walk. But that wasn't such a big deal was it? She would be alive after all. But then there was the brain damage. What if he put her back and she couldn't speak, couldn't remember her daughter, or herself?

"Gotta get to work," Kai said rather than answer. He wasn't about to tell this man that he knew where to find the woman's spirit.

"Wait a second." Allen laid his hand on Kai's arm to stop him passing. "Since it seems like it would be difficult to get rid of you, I'm leaving you be for the moment. But you should know, I'm here to protect this family. You don't have any right to get angry with Jemma, and the second I see you risking her happiness, or safety, you can bet your ass, magic or no, I'll find a way to get rid of you."

Kai smiled. Shrugging off the man's hand, he lifted the paint cans and walked out the front door. Honestly, the threat was the first thing the man had done of which Kai completely approved.

"Sy would have been a pastor were it not for me. He gave his sermons to his last day though, in fields or around dinner tables. He just couldn't quite reckon how a man could preach under God's roof while married to a witch. He teased that he was sent to save me. I can't but believe it was true." From the journals of Esther Lynn Franklin, 6ᵗʰ matron of the Women of Terra.

J emma was hovering over the pot, stirring the mix in with the onions and potatoes. After having her hostessing faults pointed out by Woolworth, the gripie, Jemma had made each a snack from the remains of the lunch Pa brought, but it was getting late, and stew took a while, so she decided to work on it for dinner. The pills had taken effect now, and her leg felt wonderful, but she enjoyed flying, and since hovering was the closest she was likely to get today, she was embracing the fun of it.

Jemma's initial anger at finding all her father's captives had worn off as the hours passed. Now she was excited for the company and charmed by the experience. Even though she hadn't precisely believed in the magical creatures Gran forced her to read about, she always wanted to see them. All she ever did was read about things. Not anymore. She had five magical creatures as houseguests, and she could ask them anything she wanted, get to know their customs, and opinions, get to know them.

Woolworth was her favorite so far. He was older than the others, cantankerous, didn't approve of a single thing Jemma did; he reminded Jemma of Gran. He looked exactly like a tooth with arms, legs, and a face, so it was hard for Jemma to look at him without smiling, but she was resisting making any toothache jokes.

Whenever he talked, Jemma wondered what it would have been like to have him and Gran in the house at the same time. Would having someone so similar around make them more or less disagreeable? Gran would have had fun fighting with him, Jemma imagined. He was the only male in the room and had taken it upon himself to try and direct them all. It wasn't going well for him.

Nona, the fire imp, or smelting as they were better known to witches, was unsurprisingly short-tempered. It was mostly directed at Woolworth, in the form of tiny little flying balls of fire, which seemed to have no effect on him whatsoever. Jemma wanted to ask what his skin was made of but was worried he would take offense. Nona looked like a cartoon rain cloud most times: charcoal grey with puffy little features, but when she got mad, she would glow red and seem to smolder. She also got annoyed with Hippa pretty often.

Hippa was the pixie, a baby apparently. She couldn't keep still for a moment, which seemed to drive Nona crazy. Hippa's voice was too soft for Jemma to hear, but she was beginning to understand her little shape shifts, and the others helped when Jemma got lost.

The last creature, and so far the quietest, was Tangerine, a leaf elf. She looked by far the most human of any of the creatures. Just very small and able to camouflage her skin. Aside from her name, all Jemma had discovered of Tangerine was that she considered herself a master chef and that she was a bit bossy. She was not at all pleased with Jemma's stew mix, but when she saw the state of her spice rack, she relented and "allowed" Jemma to use the mix, insisting that Jemma get better supplies immediately.

Woolworth and Nona were slicing vegetables, a little smaller than Jemma would have, for stew, but she didn't complain. None of these guests were bigger than her hand, so she supposed smaller sizes were all they could handle.

"These should go in now," Jemma said reaching out with her left hand for the vegetables. Tangerine was standing on Jemma's right hand seasoning the stew with what few herbs she had found.

"Should have been in already," Woolworth snapped, glaring at Nona.

"Oh no," Jemma said in mock horror. "You should have said something."

Woolworth growled.

"Something smells good." Allen's voice preceded him into the kitchen. His eyes widened as he rounded the corner and he gaped around the room.

"You aren't at all surprised by curses, but magical creatures leave you speechless," Jemma remarked dryly, her defenses rising at the sight of him.

"Well, you know it's not every day I see them."

"How often do you get yourself cursed?"

"Around here?" Allen said in a teasing voice. He walked around the kitchen counter and leaned in over the pan, taking a long sniff. "Smells terrific."

"Thank you." Tangerine sighed and Jemma realized suddenly where she got her name; blushes made this elf turn completely orange.

Tangerine nudged Jemma's hand, and then kicked it. She barely felt either, but she saw it and smiled.

"Allen, this is Tangerine." With her free hand, she pointed to the counter where the others were. "And Woolworth and Nona. And somewhere under my hair is Hippa."

Hippa was in love with Jemma's hair. She had unwound it from its braid and gotten rid of the ponytail. Now she was pulling each individual hair apart so they curled loosely around her face, like a cloud. Jemma could barely feel it, so she didn't mind, and anyway, the pixie was just a year old and had been kidnapped; if it gave her joy, Jemma didn't see any reason to stop her.

"Wow," Allen said at last. "Where did you find all your friends?"

"In those jars. He was holding them hostage." Jemma nodded out the window.

"That boy!" Allen shouted making Jemma laugh.

"No. Black Boot. Kai was a captive as well. He's a kelpie. Haven't you noticed how he sparkles?"

"Can't say I have," Allen said slowly. Jemma got the distinct impression he wanted to ask something else. "I shouldn't have yelled at you," Allen said after a second. "Your mother was being well cared for; your notes were very thorough."

"It's cool." Jemma shrugged, borrowing a phrase from Kai. "You're right, I'm not qualified. You spending the night?"

"Obviously," Allen snapped. "I'm not leaving you alone with that boy. I don't care how much he shines."

"Sparkles," Jemma corrected.

Hippa burst suddenly out from under Jemma's hair and darted in front of Allen, shifting into a little star that glinted as it rolled around. Then she popped into a tiny little sun radiating light.

"That's Hippa. She's illustrating the difference between sparkling and shining."

"Clearly," Allen said taken aback. "Ummm, is there anything I can do to help in here?"

"No. Out, out, out," Woolworth snapped. "Too many cooks."

"Really, Woolworth, manners," Jemma said lightly. She kind of liked him picking on Allen. With one more nod for the room in general, Allen left. Jemma watched him go; she was still angry with him, but there was no point saying it.

"We need bread," Jemma insisted suddenly.

"Ha," Woolworth scoffed, jumping up and down on the counter. "And what do these look like?"

Jemma glanced at the tiny rolls he was pounding out, and her lips curled wickedly. "Croutons."

Witch or Goddess

Kai was an eavesdropper by nature, plucking great knowledge out of the little shared moments with strangers. Threads of random conversation had nearly as much power as any trinket he'd ever collected, but of a different kind. Eavesdropping didn't inspire his imagination; it expanded his understanding, of other people, of the world, and occasionally of himself. That was the reason he so appreciated Jemma's open kitchen window as he worked.

He was used to painting with his headphones on, tuning out the real world for the one inside his mind. But he thought this might be better. Jemma's new friends were entertaining, to say the least. They fought over everything from how the food should be prepared, to who had suffered the most from captivity, but most of all, they fought over Jemma, struggling for proximity to her, as if she was some sort of deity. He wondered if she realized she had just formed herself a little army, and without even trying. He doubted it. She wouldn't understand that to these creatures, simply the act of setting them free was as powerful as the life debt Kai owed her.

She might not be a deity, but she was something special. So, as he painted, instead of trying to make Jemma a new world, he found himself trying to awaken the beauty she couldn't see in the world around her. Because for all her laughter and joking, Kai heard a great deal of sadness in her voice, and he wanted more than anything to take that away.

He finished putting the first coat of paint on and was just waiting for it to dry so he could start the real work, the detail work. He was going to run out of paint soon. Not with the bench, he had enough for that, and maybe one or two small things after. But all that would be left soon was the barely-touched gold, and tiny amounts of purple and white. He had too many grand plans for the empty canvas that was her house to stop after this, so he needed to get more.

Kai wandered across the porch to peek in the window at Jemma and her companions; he nearly laughed aloud. It was the single-most vibrant, colorful thing he had seen since he set foot in Oklahoma. Jemma was hovering a few feet off the ground, another trick she had kept secret from him, and her hair was billowing around her like fiery red clouds as she stirred the steaming pot, with an over-long ladle. The pixie was resting on Jemma's shoulder in the shape of a little hummingbird again. There was an elf on Jemma's hand moving her arm around to direct Jemma's stirring, as if she was a puppet master. And off to her right, a gripie and a fire imp were fighting with knives twice the length of their bodies.

She really ought to stop reading other people's, less-than-accurate magical books and write one of her own.

Kai tilted his head to the side, leaning back against the porch rail, struck by the idea. *Jemma's Guide to Magical Creatures.* Kai knew just how to make her do it.

As quietly as he was able, Kai snuck back into the house. He heard Allen in another room, on the phone. Kai snuck straight up to the giant bookshelf that held all the family tomes, and pulled out one after another, until he found a blank one. It had a boring brown leather cover and a leather strap, just like the house. It was perfect. Kai snuck out with the tome, stopping on the porch to grab a few paint buckets. He went out to the dirt just past the porch. He could see in the window from here, but with the growing darkness, he doubted anyone saw him.

Kai sat and reached into his pouch of sand. He pulled out two little grains between his thumb and pointer finger. He rubbed the sand together, allowing the moisture from his hands to grow the sand, until it was a little ball, then he rolled it between his palms. When he pulled his palms apart, Kai had a long, pointed cylinder, similar to a pencil. He pulled the paint buckets closer and flipped open the journal.

He started with the background. He was tempted to sketch her in the deep dark of a forest, or at the edge of a cliff, something suitably mystical for so special a girl. But Jemma didn't quite belong there. She was a witch to be sure, and one as interesting as any a novel could create, but still she was very much a creature of reality. So, he drew a kitchen, only not with the shelves and a microwave behind her; instead, he drew a wide open window with neatly-tied purple curtains, and a green and golden corn field stretched out behind, in the beginnings of a starry night.

The pot had to go as well; it didn't suit her clouds of hair, or the steam rushing up around her face. No, she needed something deep and wide, cast iron, with just a hint of something sinister, bubbling at its rim.

"My Jemma has such a bright smile, everyone wants a peek when I take her out. I love showing her off, and Tom just beams like the sun." From the journals of May Bell Franklin-Traveler, 7th generation daughter of Terra.

When the stew was ready, Jemma sent Hippa through the window for Kai, and Tangerine off in search of Allen, while she, Woolworth, and Nona set the table. It was a little embarrassing for Jemma that she couldn't think of anything better to serve her smaller guests with but measuring cups. She had nearly put down a tablespoon but worried someone would find it offensive.

"I'm sorry we don't have anything more appropriate to serve you with," Jemma mumbled, fighting to hide her blush. She could feel someone behind her, probably Allen, but she didn't turn. "We don't really entertain very often. Not at all, really."

"It's fine," Nona assured her, but Woolworth continued grumbling.

"Bet you had something to serve the kelpie with."

Jemma shrugged. "I gave him a PB&J. Wasn't sure what kelpies eat."

"Their young."

Jemma chuckled in spite of herself. "Well, he is young yet. I'm not sure he has any."

"Course he does," Woolworth sniped. "Prolific, all of them. Watch out for that one."

Jemma shook her head, blushing for a whole new reason.

"And me without even one child." Kai's musical voice floated in from the doorway. Jemma glanced around to see him; he was probably offended again. But when she caught his eye, Kai just winked.

Winked. As though they were in on a joke together, as though nothing had happened earlier. Jemma didn't know what to do, she just stared. Were all boys like that? She had noticed with Allen, when he was mad, if she just left him alone for a while, he would come back acting like nothing ever happened. But she'd assumed it was just him.

"I've shamed the entire kelpie breed, I suppose," Kai went on with his little joke, but he didn't look at Woolworth once; his eyes stayed with Jemma, making her all kinds of uncomfortable.

What was he waiting for?

"Just see you don't try and redeem yourself here," Allen snapped, and Jemma jumped. She hadn't even seen him standing behind Kai.

All at once, the hilarity of the situation hit Jemma and she cracked up. Bending forward, she covered her face and giggled. As if someone like Kai would even look at her that way.

"I don't think you're his type," Jemma said to Allen, between giggles.

Both Kai and Allen watched her carefully, as if there must be something wrong with her. It only made Jemma giggle more. It was their own fault; they had forced the pills down her, and she couldn't quite grip onto her sanity with them taking effect.

"Enough!" Woolworth shouted, jumping up and down on the table to get attention. "Eat."

Without a word, everyone took their places around the table.

Poking the Dark

Kai watched Jemma carefully as they ate. There was something different about her, maybe it was just the medicine making her smile and giggle and blush, but he didn't think so. She was enjoying her guests. He wasn't especially used to apologizing for things, though he imagined if he was home, his mother or his sister would have made him apologize for storming out, as he did earlier. But not Jemma. All he had to do was smile, and she was happy with him again.

The girl was too easy. He needed to do something about that before he left.

Jemma was talking almost constantly, asking all her guests questions about where they lived and what sort of magic they had. She hadn't gotten around to the bad yet, like how her father had captured them, or what they intended to do to him for revenge. But it didn't show on her face, like Kai would have expected. She usually wore the bad on her face, but now, she looked like a fantasy geek at Magicon. Nothing dimmed her light as one question led to the next, and the next.

"Do you ever feel cold, or hot, or are you always the same temperature?" she asked Nona. Her spoon was poised halfway to her mouth; it had been that way almost since the start of the meal. Kai thought he'd seen her take maybe two bites.

"I get hotter when I throw fire," Nona said with a sort of evil glee. "But to me, hot is good."

"But can you get cold? I mean, if you went to Antarctica, say — would you still be warm, or do external temperatures effect you?"

"If I can keep moving, I can keep living," Nona said evasively, then she shuddered. "I've been cold before, and it's as though it slows me down and drains away my magic."

"Where were you?"

Nona stared at Jemma sadly; her cloud face seemed to droop and she took on a dingy grey color. It wasn't clear if she would answer. "In the jar."

Jemma leaned back nodding. "Oh."

"Never been to Antarctica," Nona said in a more cheerful voice. "But I bet if I were free, I would be plenty hot, even there." She winked at Jemma.

Jemma smiled, but not quite as brightly. Her eyes drifted past her guests, out the open window. "I wonder what sort of magic is in the jars. They don't feel especially powerful, but they must be."

"Dark magic," Woolworth snapped. "From the dark markets, where fey creatures sell their own secrets for a bit of coin."

Kai stiffened at the mention of the dark market, and as if she could feel it, Jemma's eyes moved over him sympathetically.

"It's probably for more than just coins," Jemma said as if she was puzzling something out. Kai didn't like it that her eyes stayed on him as she spoke. "I mean, what secret wouldn't you sell to save someone you loved? That's how these things always start: one person has something the other wants, and before they've really considered it," her eyes drifted off Kai's face and out the window, "they've made a deal they cannot come back from."

"Well, I've five children," Tangerine put in firmly. "And every one of them knows nothing you can get in the dark market is ever worth the cost."

Kai didn't say anything, but he knew there was a difference between knowing something and believing it when the night was long and you were missing the ones you needed most.

"Five children?" Jemma asked, devastated. "How old?"

"My girls are my oldest, ten, thirteen, and fifteen; my boys are seven, twins."

"Wow. Do they have a father?"

"Of course they do," Tangerine said shaking her head. "But they will be missing me."

"Of course." All Jemma's earlier enthusiasm evaporated at the mention of Tangerine's family. "Do you have children, Nona?"

"One. A daughter, eight. She was with her cousins at the zoo when…. She loves the panda bears."

"Woolworth?" she asked flatly.

"Two, both grown, strong boys like their father. I have seven grandchildren too. And some nephews and nieces, and a few great nieces. "

"And you say kelpies are prolific," Kai mumbled sarcastically.

"What about you?" Jemma demanded of Kai, suddenly intensely agitated. "Where is your family? Why haven't you asked to call them or anything?"

"They probably don't even know I'm missing yet," Kai shrugged. There was no way he was calling his father for help unless he was bleeding to death on the ground.

"Not know your missing? How would they not know?"

"They were away when Black Boot took me; they should still be away."

"They left you alone? And they don't even call to check on you?" She was on her feet now and leaning across the table.

Kai felt oddly defensive, wanted to jump to his feet and yell back that his parents had never dropped cars on him, but he stayed seated. He planted his feet flat on the ground, and moved his hands to the back of his legs, simply holding Jemma's eyes with his own. She had nothing to be so crazy about. His parents were the good ones.

"It was a sort of test, a rite of passage. My father didn't even want me to do it, but I insisted. I'm seventeen, not ten. I was left to defend the cove for two weeks."

"A test!"

"Yes." Kai was very aware of the eyes of everyone in the room, though clearly Jemma was not. He sat perfectly still, and his voice was infused with studied calm. "One I clearly failed."

"Of course you failed!" she shouted, waving her arms wildly. "You weren't ready for him. What sort of parent abandons their child that way?"

All at once, Kai felt an unsettling rush of warmth towards the wildly screaming girl in front of him. He didn't like it at all. Sure it was great to have someone worry for him, and completely absolve him of fault for getting caught. But at the same time, what the hell! He shouldn't feel like hugging a fourteen-year-old, fire-headed hick.

Kai pushed his seat back calmly and stood, so she wasn't glaring down at him.

"They didn't know he was coming, Jemma. It's tradition."

"They didn't know he wasn't coming. They should at least be checking on you."

"Good point," Woolworth interrupted sagely. "Heartless. Kelpies eat their young, you know."

"When he left, my father gave mother a choice: stay with us and let us be raised as Christian children, or return to her people, without us. She stayed, always outside both worlds." From the journals of Sisika, 1ˢᵗ matron of the Women of Terra, penned by Sarah, her daughter.

At Woolworth's voice, Jemma realized suddenly that she was leaning across the table, shouting at Kai for no good reason. And what was worse, he looked so cold, shut down. He didn't look like himself, and she had done that. He must be really hurt.

"Heartless, kelpies eat their young, you know," Woolworth said.

It should be funny. He didn't really mean it, she knew. But just at the moment, the comment made Jemma want to cry more than anything.

Kai was seventeen, so maybe it wasn't so strange for his parents to leave him alone. But all of a sudden, she had seen him as a person, instead of as her magical guest, and people, other people were supposed to have parents who didn't let them out of their sight. Other people were supposed to go on picnics and visit Disneyland or museums. They were supposed to have someone there for them, all the time.

Jemma liked that fantasy; she liked to imagine what her life would have been like if her father didn't carry the wind in his coat and her mother wasn't in a coma. She didn't like to imagine a world just as screwed up as hers.

Jemma settled back into her seat without a word, looking away. But she saw him take a seat out of the corner of her eye. Her gaze went to Allen, just for a place to look, but he took this as a cue to change the subject.

"How will we work out the sleeping arrangements?" he asked with an intensity that did nothing for Jemma's mood. She was tempted to shove him face first into his bowl.

"*We* won't work anything out. I will."

"How?"

"Easily."

"Jemma."

"Allen."

All her guests were amused now. Even Kai was cracking a smile. But Jemma was not amused, and neither was Allen.

Still, it seemed to settle the room. No one spoke again until they were through eating. Jemma didn't have much of an appetite. Her mind kept wondering over all the families her father had broken apart and how she could repair them. Because she had to repair them. As much as she would like to keep her new friends here forever, they all needed to go home. She couldn't be selfish like the rest of her family.

If there was one piece of heritage she wanted to shake off, it was that. Every one of her ancestors' stupid mistakes had been ones of selfishness. Curses, affairs, cheating the wind, all for their own selfish reasons. Jemma meant to undo as much of that as she could, before she gave in to Pa and there was nothing else she could do.

When dinner was over, the pot wasn't quite empty. Jemma was tempted to just throw it away; it was only really enough for one person. And lately, she had been feeling especially lazy. It was easier to throw away.

Tangerine hopped up onto Jemma's hand on the rim of the pot. She pinched it for attention.

"You can be better than bad and still not be good," she said looking Jemma steadily in the eye.

"What makes you think I want to be good?" Jemma challenged, knowing perfectly well what the elf thought she should do.

"Your hesitation," she said with a soft smile, a mothering smile. Jemma had been missing those. "Goodness doesn't come easily. That's why good people take so long with everything."

Jemma sighed. Leaving the pot on the table, she walked to the cupboard for another bowl.

The Offering

*B*lack Boot watched the little dinner party with mixed emotions. It looked something like the feasts Jemma used to have with her stuffed animals. It was such an odd group. At one seat, she would have Jemima Puddle Duck; at another, her stuffed dragon, Cuddles; and another, her stuffed rainbow fish, Angel; and last of all, the soft doll her grandparents had brought back with them from a vacation, in New Orleans.

It was the ugliest doll Black Boot had ever seen. It looked like nothing so much as a voodoo doll, and from the look Esther gave him as she handed it to Jemma, he would bet it was one. It had triangle-shaped, painted on, yellow eyes, and a little line for a mouth, and it was made out of what looked like a mishmash of old curtains, but Jemma loved the thing like nothing else. She called it her baby sister and named her Kadawada. She wouldn't go anywhere without that doll.

He could just picture her, sitting in the dust, at the stump she used for a table, with her little stolen harvest piled high. She explained to her stuffed animals that the harvest had been bountiful, because they had given the land their love.

She practically had her grandmother's speech memorized, and she would recite it to her little friends with her head high in the air and a bright smile on her face.

"Papa, Papa, come quick."

"What's the matter, Jem Beam? Need more food?"

"No. Cuddles has never met a human man before; she is very intrigued to meet you."

"Oh." Tom chuckled and threw himself into the dirt with his daughter. "Is that so? Well, I have never met a dragon before. I heard they eat people."

"Eat people?" Jemma fell backwards laughing. "Don't be silly, Papa, everybody knows they only eat leaves."

"Only leaves, my goodness me, aren't they terrible hungry then?"

"No, they just eat lots and lots."

"Oh, I see. Papa has to get back to work now." He leaned over and pulled Jemma's head to his lips for a quick kiss. "Save me some of the feast."

"Papa, give Kadawada a kiss."

"Oh, I nearly forgot. Mmmmwa. There, a kiss for both of my girls. Love you."

"Love you, Papa," her words sang after him, and he smiled, but he didn't look back.

He never looked back.

Jemma had an even odder mishmash of guests now. He should have known better than to leave the bags unattended. It shouldn't surprise him to see Jemma surrounded by the creatures he captured, as though she was their queen, but it did. Her mother had been like that, pulling everyone to her, like a magnet, and making them shine with her energy. It should be good to see Jemma that way, but all he could think was how many dark things she would draw in.

May Bell was more equipped for the darkness; no one but Black Boot knew the darker side she hid. She wasn't just soft smiles and easy belief, his May Bell; she was secretly sinister. Jemma, for all her coldness and smart mouth, was an innocent. You could see it in the way she helped the kelpie and in the way her eyes found the ground when she was ashamed. Dark things would destroy Jemma.

He could tell her he had captured the creatures only for her. But he doubted she would believe him. Unforgivable. That's what she called him, and she certainly had reason to think so now. He knew what was said of people who captured the fey folk and held them in jars like moths. It was said that nature would turn against them. But he didn't care. All he knew, coming home, was that Jemma was alive. But he had no idea how he would find her. She might have been in a wheelchair, unable even to stand. He brought the creatures for her, to heal her, and to help him free her from the land.

Black Boot turned away from the house, walking out towards the wheat fields, the only crop he'd made no progress on. He hadn't had a dinner like that one, full of laughter and conversation, since the cyclone. Even May Bell's ghost, in all the years of following him, rarely sat with him as he dined or shared a conversation. She could hold a grudge like no other.

He was an excellent cook, had been one in several towns. But nothing he cooked now could compare to May Bell's burnt grilled cheese and watery potato salad.

Black Boot walked between the wheat stalks, running his hand across their hard dry surfaces. He would find a way to make Jemma forgive him. There had to be a way. He couldn't spend the rest of his life watching his girl love everyone but him.

Behind him, Black Boot heard the crunch of gravel on the path from the house. He spun around, expecting to see the man Jemma protected from his wrath earlier. He froze.

"Jemma." He started forward happily. She had come to him, yards away from the shield that would protect her. She thrust out her arms, sloshing a little liquid over the rim of the steaming bowl she held out.

"We had extra," she said, nothing more.

"Did you find them, or that kelpie thief?" Black Boot nodded to the pixie at Jemma's ear and the elf on her shoulder. He made no move to take the bowl. He wanted to talk to her, and this was the only way he could think of to prolong her stay.

"You say thief like it's a bad thing. As a kidnapper, I'd think you would admire it."

"Him then." Black Boot chuckled. He could see straight through her bravado. "Well, he didn't get this." He pulled the pocket watch from his pants pocket and held it out to Jemma.

When she made no move to take it, he lifted the bowl from her hands and left the watch in its place.

"It has that picture I told you about," Black Boot went on, taking a sip of the stew. "And one of you, with your mother."

That was the ticket. Her fingers closed over the watch hungrily.

"It's from the day you were born."

Jemma didn't open the watch, she just stared up at him a moment longer. She turned away and walked back towards the house.

"Goodnight," she called over her shoulder.

"Thanks for the stew."

She didn't respond. But maybe, just maybe he wasn't so unforgivable after all.

In Another World

Kai and Woolworth were stuck with the dishes. Kai didn't mind the chore, but he could have done without the company. The gripie never stopped complaining. To distract himself, Kai spent his time contemplating whether the word gripe came from the creature or if they were named that because it was all they ever did.

Kai hadn't seen Jemma since dinner. She walked out with a bowl of stew and ordered him to do the dishes. He supposed she was in the room with her mother, not that she could possibly eat the food, but maybe the smell helped her somehow. Or maybe she had some other sick relative hidden in the attic. Kai nearly laughed at the idea before it occurred to him it could be true.

Her "friend" Allen wasn't lifting a finger to help, Kai noticed. Instead, he was leaning against the doorjamb blabbering on his cell phone. To a girlfriend, Kai guessed from the tone. If the man said "it's just for tonight" one more time, Kai might just yank the phone out of his hand and tell the girl to get a life.

Why hadn't he asked to call his parents?

Kai couldn't seem to stop thinking about what Jemma screamed at him over the table. She thought he had bad parents. He didn't, she just didn't understand. Of course, if Poesy had asked to have two weeks alone to prove herself, even if she was seventeen, Kai would have fought it. She needed protecting. But it wasn't the same with him, was it?

"Course it is, you idiot." Woolworth splashed the soapy water up into Kai's face. "That's why you're here. So she can save you."

"I …what? How did you…"

"Gripie," Woolworth said, as though this explained everything. "Hear thoughts."

"I've never heard that."

"Course not," he griped. "Tallies never listen to anything they don't say."

"Sorry." Kai wasn't precisely sure what he was apologizing for, but he knew the gripie expected an apology. "We don't eat our young, you know."

"Eh! Almost no one does. Should've watched you closer though, but that's why you're here."

"I asked them to go. I wanted to prove I was trustworthy."

"Isn't about trust or ability. You watch what you love." Woolworth sat down on the edge of the sink, sounding deeply serious, and stared into his empty hands. "Even if it doesn't need protecting."

"Well…" Kai wanted to defend his parents one more time, but he was caught by the faraway look of the gripie. Who hadn't been watching him? And what did he mean "so she can save you"? Kai was supposed to be saving Jemma, not the other way around, right?

The screen door banged, and Kai set off running for the other room. He didn't know who was coming or going, but he didn't want Jemma to see his surprise before it was ready. Jemma was standing just inside the doorway with her right hand fisted, staring off across the room in a sort of daze.

"Where is the other bench?" she asked at last. "Has it been gone all day?"

"Where were you?" Kai demanded.

Jemma turned to face Kai, slipping her right hand into the pocket of her overalls. She just stared. Kai knew this game; you couldn't grow up with two girls and not know the staring game. He simply returned her look.

She moved so suddenly, he never saw it coming. Lurching forward, she yanked out a chunk of Kai's hair.

"Ouch. Jemma! What was that for?"

"A spell," she said rubbing the hairs apart between her fingers, as though looking for something.

"You're putting a spell on me? Are you okay? Did you talk to Black Boot? What did he say to you?"

"I'm not putting a spell on you," Jemma said after letting him run down his list of questions. She had such a quiet way about her; it was unsettling for any living being to be so quiet all the time. "I'm putting one around you. I'm real tired; think I'll turn in now."

"It's barely seven," Kai said, flummoxed.

"Where is he sleeping?" Allen interrupted.

"Oh, will you give it a rest, perv," Kai yelled, just as Jemma was replying, much more calmly than she had the rest of the day.

"In the bathroom, Allen. He's a kelpie, they need the water."

"So, you always sleep in the water?" he asked with a disgusted expression.

"No. At home, there is moisture in the air. There isn't here."

"So, a humidifier would work?"

Kai shrugged, noticing that Jemma was ignoring them now and walking off in the direction of her mother's room.

"You can sleep in Gran's bed, Allen." She called over her shoulder. "I changed the sheets of course, but it is the same bed, so be careful not to roll onto her ghost."

With that marvelous exit line, she shut her mother's door, in both their faces. Kai smiled after her, rubbing his head absently where she had yanked out the hair.

"She's still upset."

Kai only smiled; she sure knew how to put this guy in his place. "Maybe if you'd quit acting as if you don't trust her, she wouldn't be."

"I trust her. It's teenage boys I don't trust. She's especially vulnerable right now."

"Yeah, and she's my sister's age. And when she isn't crying or talking about the earth swallowing her grandmother whole, she sort of reminds me of my sister." Not really, but that was neither here nor there; he wasn't interested in her. "You've got nothing to worry about."

"Then why are you still here? What exactly are your intentions?"

"Wow, this place is backwards. Intentions? I'm here to help, however I can, until the opportunity to save her life presents itself."

"How are you helping her?"

Kai sighed. He didn't like this guy, or trust him, but Jemma did. "Come on, I'll show you."

"Found where I was birthed. Bit of a hovel. Not that I've had much better. Rest better now, no more blood behind my sleepin' eyes." From the journals of Josephine Ness, 3rd matron of the Women of Terra.

Jemma sat on the edge of her recliner staring down at the hair in her hands. Pa's watch weighed heavy in her pocket, but she didn't take it out. She would need to be alone for that, and just now, Hippa and Tangerine were sitting with her silently.

It didn't even occur to her until she sat down that the pain was gone, had been for a while now. She barely felt her leg at all. Across the room on May Bell's dresser was a photo of the three of them: Jemma, May Bell, and Gran. It had been taken just before the cyclone, professionally, as a gift for Gran. It was one of the few photos to survive, probably because it was still in the city at the photographer's shop. They looked like a different family. Every one of them. Gran looked somehow softer and happier.

Jemma was sorry to be disappointing her, but she liked having the pain gone. She had walked out into the fields and back, without even noticing her leg. She could help harvest, she could do all kinds of things. Was that really so bad? Would the woman in that picture have been disappointed, or just the woman after, who didn't take pictures, or buy nice things, or…or ever get over her pain? Was it just that woman who would mind?

"Are you doing a protection spell?" Tangerine asked hesitantly, calling Jemma back to the moment.

Shaking her head, she looked down at the hair between her fingers.

"I hadn't thought to. But I suppose I have enough hair. I didn't mean to hurt him."

"Nothing he didn't deserve," Tangerine said primly.

"What for?"

Hippa burst out of Jemma's hair and shifted into the shape of the jar she had been stored in, and Kai's hand on top of it. Then into a shape like a screen door striking the frame; all the while, Tangerine prattled on about how he had been rude to that nice man Allen.

Jemma smiled vaguely.

"I need Nona for the spell," Jemma said to change the subject. "Do you think you could find her, Tangerine? And maybe something from each of you for a spell?"

Tangerine nodded. Without another coherent word, she hopped off the arm of the chair, disappearing from the room in a streak of light. Jemma shook her head after the elf and turned to her mother's dresser; she pulled out a pad of paper. It was where she kept those records Allen berated her about earlier. All she really did was write down the things he used to write and compared the numbers. As long as they stayed about the same, she didn't worry. But it wasn't as though she would know what they meant beyond that.

Jemma tore off a blank sheet and ripped it, slightly lopsidedly, in half. She closed her eyes searching for the right words. She wasn't especially used to making up spells, but she knew what she wanted, and Gran always said that was the first step.

Identify a problem or objective.

Plan a solution.

Exert your will.

Gran liked to speak her spells. She liked the old ways best, the telling of tales instead of reading them. But she gave in and wrote most of her stories and spells because *this generation* couldn't be trusted to keep oral traditions alive. Jemma liked to point out that even Gran's generation couldn't be trusted, but Gran only scoffed. Still, Jemma knew Gran liked it when Jemma challenged her.

Jemma preferred writing her spells and burning them. She liked the feeling that the flames carried her words out into the world on wisps of smoke—actual, tangible things her words.

On one half, she wrote the protection spell. That was basic enough; there was only so much protection you could ever give a person. But she made sure Pa couldn't touch Kai, or her other friends, to harm them.

The other spell gave her pause. She knew what she wanted, and she knew how to get it. What gave her pause was whether or not she should.

Jemma felt the comforting flap of Hippa's hummingbird wings, and made up her mind. In a rush, she scratched the words onto the page and rolled up little bits of his hair into it. She dropped the rest of the hair onto the first page and waited for Nona.

Would she be as decisive once she found a way to return Hippa and the others to their families?

Jemma rubbed her knee absently.

"Here you are," Tangerine said, depositing a wiry green hair that must be her own; a bit of fluff that was oddly coarse like wool, from Nona; and a bit of white skin from Woolworth, which felt exactly like chipped stone, into Jemma's hand.

"You need me?" Nona floated up before Jemma's face.

"Yes." Jemma took all the contributions and added them to Kai's hair on the first paper. Hippa fluttered over, and a bead of light flew off of her onto the page. Jemma rolled it up into a scroll like the other. "Would you burn these please?"

"My pleasure."

The scrolls burst into bright flames on the dresser, but the flames touched nothing else. In only a few seconds, the scrolls were gone, and nothing was left to show they had been there but the threads of smoke in the air.

"Two spells. Did you curse him?" Nona asked gleefully.

It was on the tip of Jemma's tongue to ask what she had against Kai, but she just shook her head. She didn't care.

"Thank you for your help. I think I'll go to sleep now."

"Okay, don't worry about us," Nona said and sped off towards the door.

"I think Hippa wants to stay with you," Tangerine said quietly.

"That's fine." Jemma yawned.

Tangerine flashed out the door, somehow managing to flip the light switch on her way. Jemma pulled up the leg rest of the recliner, and stretched backwards, shutting her eyes. Hippa perched herself at the top of the head rest, with her little hummingbird wings beating constantly. Jemma vaguely wondered if she was even able to be still, or if like the bird she so favored, her heart would give out if she rested too long.

Jemma's hand slipped into her pocket and closed over the watch. She wasn't ready to see what was inside, but it felt good to hold it.

Testing the Waters

"You padded the bench." Allen walked around Kai's work, inspecting it. Kai found himself just a little edgy.

He'd made it for Jemma—a man might not understand. It was too soft, too feminine. Men carved their place in the earth, like the waves, beating it down until the shape suited them. They didn't sit around doodling flowers and trying to please other people. Men had better things to do, like protecting the cove.

Kai nearly scoffed. Wouldn't Dad be exstatic to know just how right he was about Kai? That he wasn't ready. That he wasn't man enough to handle the task.

"Jemma is going to be thrilled," Allen said after completing his fourth circuit of the bench. "She loves wild flowers. Did she tell you irises are her favorite?"

"No. I'm glad. They just seemed to suit her." He crouched down beside the bench and ran a hand along one of the little clusters of flowers, looking for things to improve. "Quiet flowers, not as flashy as the others, but more interesting. And she tends to favor purple. I've known her two days and she was wearing purple both days."

Allen just nodded, watching Kai.

"Of course it's not finished yet. I've got to add her friends."

"You do excellent work. I was serious when I said it could make money."

"It's not about that." Kai turned away. No one seemed to understand. It wasn't something he did for money, or even for the praise. Painting was like the water for him; he died a little every time he was away from it. If he stopped painting, he would go insane.

"You aren't keeping up the ocean theme."

"Nope. Different theme for every room. That way she has some options of scenery when she gets bored of all this brown."

Allen laughed as though it had never occurred to him just how monochromatic Jemma's life was.

"Well, she's just going to love you tomorrow," Allen said snidely. "Too bad I can't claim it as mine. Then maybe she'd cut me some slack." He rubbed a hand over his face sighing. "I shouldn't have questioned her care of May Bell."

"You didn't," Kai said shocked. It was a little weird that the man was talking to him about this. But it was completely unbelievable that he would doubt Jemma's devotion to her mother.

"I beg your pardon."

"Like I said, I've known her two days now, and I already know she'd turn the world inside out to help someone she loved. Her mother was never in any danger with her. You know it. I know it. You were worried about you."

"Is that so?"

"Yep. For three months, she got along without you. You don't want that to happen again." Kai studied the man before him, as he would a portrait subject. Most people didn't realize how much they revealed with their facial expressions. "It was a good way to make her feel useless, like she needed you. But it was a stupid way to make her *want* you around, which any fool can see, she already did. Which brings me to a question. What exactly are your intentions here?"

Allen scoffed and straightened to his full height, as if to intimidate Kai. "Mine? I've known Jemma since she was nine. I've been coming by here for years, Jemma's like my niece. I'm here to see she's happy and cared for."

"You could take care of her without making her feel dependent on you. Why do you need to be inside that house so badly? What is it about this place that makes it so coveted?"

"I need to be near Jemma to care for her." Allen side-stepped the question and he wasn't even subtle about it.

Kai had no way to prove the man was lying. But his instincts told him Allen was hiding something. It all came back to this house. Kai turned back to the bench.

"I need to finish this. Then I'm making an ottoman from the rest of the pillows."

"You're going to a lot of trouble for someone you've only known two days."

"She saved my life! Had no reason to, even made sure I was freed. What about this don't you understand? There is no such thing as too much trouble to go to for someone like that."

Allen sighed. "Got any particular design in mind for the ottoman?"

Kai nodded and showed the man his sketch. Allen wore a distinctly amused expression as he looked at the design. But after a minute, he simply sat down and began trying to make what Kai had drawn.

It didn't take long for the rest of Jemma's guests to come out and start lending a hand. And it was a good thing; Kai only watched Allen out of the corner of his eye, but the man didn't have an artistic bone in his body.

Dreams on Fire

The air was boiling. Steam rose around Black Boot until it pooled into sweat, soaking through his shirt. The smell of smoke and rotting plants thickened the air, suffocating him as he rested against the wall of the shed.

Drops landed on his eyelids shocking them open, but his eyes burned so badly from the smoke, he nearly shut them again. Then he saw it. The barn was gone; he was sitting on the cot, in the middle of the cornfield. Full and tall, the corn stalks reached for the sky, as though he had never cut them. The world surrounding them was ablaze, but the corn stood unaffected, dripping a green oozing mold onto the flames. In the distance, Dust House was all but crumpled from the fire but still burning.

Black Boot could only watch as the house returned to the dust it grew from. He should move. Should rush to save something, anything. But he could only stare. Then something moved in the house.

She walked through smoke and flame unharmed. The light played across her as though they danced together. Her hair hung down to her waist, waving always just beyond the reach of the flames. She wore white, her wedding dress, and for a moment, he was certain he would see her innocent smile when she turned his way. But her face was twisted into a malicious snarl. Eyeing Black Boot in the distance, she raised an arm and pointed behind him.

Black Boot spun around, helpless, to face his own back. He watched himself, arms pumping futilely, swinging the sickle at the stubborn corn. He watched the earth beneath his feet, muddy with the ooze of death, slip around him. Watched as his boots slid across the mud, and his body plummeted towards the yawning earth. The earth opened up to swallow him whole, and Black Boot was no longer watching. He was falling. He felt the earth vanishing beneath him, dragging him down from his core. He swung the sickle out wildly for purchase. It struck stone, and slid screeching away into the mud.

Then May Bell was there, with a sweet smile. She crouched in the ground stretching out a hand. She lifted the stone from the ground, and dusted it lovingly with the hem of her wedding dress, then she turned it around for Black Boot to see. It was a headstone. His headstone, but his name, Thomas Traveler, was scratched out. It read:

~~Thomas Traveler~~ Black Boot

Beloved Husband

Unforgiven Father

One with the earth he coveted

Black Boot came awake with a shout on his lips, a war cry. They would turn on him.

The barn was dark, but he knew at once where he was. The air cooled him in seconds as it rushed across his sweat-soaked clothes, leaving him shivering at the edge of the cot. He stretched his hand out in the darkness reaching for his bag. Nothing.

"Argh!" Black Boot slammed a fist against the wall. They had stolen his things, his magic. His protection. This had to end.

Black Boot charged out into the night. He couldn't even tell what time it was, because he had handed that traitor his watch. It didn't matter; he would never sleep tonight.

May Bell was warning him. She wanted him to move, time was of the essence.

He dragged nearly all the tools with him and marched into the wheat fields. He dropped the tools to the ground, too late remembering his boots. The shovel struck the edge of his right boot just as he was jerking away and slashed a heavy gouge across it.

He bent down franticly, but could not bring himself to touch them, to harm them further. He was half afraid they would crumple away at his touch. Unbidden, May Bell's face floated into his mind, as she had been in the dream, crowing over his suffering. Why? She was still angry. But in her heart of hearts, she still loved him. Why wasn't she protecting him?

Facing the Siren

Kai was outside alone, when Black Boot went storming out of the barn like a man possessed. The bench was finished, and Allen, with Tangerine's help, had finished the ottoman. Allen turned in not long ago. It was only eight-thirty, and in California, it wasn't even that late. Kai wasn't ready for bed, for a lot of reasons.

There was something building in the air, something bad. Kai wasn't much given to intuition, but twice in his life something had warned him of coming danger, and both times, he'd ignored and lived to regret it. He wouldn't make that mistake a third time.

The wind was growing impatient. Just standing here against the wall of the house, it was beating against Kai. The chimes wouldn't stop clanging. One of the smaller ones wasn't even ringing; it just spun around and around on its nail. Kai was tempted to walk over and lift it free, but he didn't. He just stared at it spinning, like his thoughts.

Only you can save her.
That's why you're here, so she can save you.
Of course you failed. You weren't ready for him.
You're too soft.

They were the sort of thoughts he usually painted over, painted away. But even though it had settled him some to paint Jemma's bench, the thoughts hadn't been buried under the paint.

If this were an old movie, he'd be leaning here with a cigarette in his hands, and he got it now. It wasn't about the cigarette actually settling the character; it was so they had something to do. He was standing here, staring into the wind, waiting, because he knew she would come if he waited long enough. But just standing here, with nothing in his hands, nothing to focus his mind on, it ran wild.

He could imagine, with very little effort, Jemma trapped beneath the truck, still parked a few feet away. He could see the woman in the wind, her mother, standing over her sobbing. And Black Boot, a great silhouette against the setting sun walking away. It was a picture of despair and heartache, and he couldn't see that Black Boot coming back had made it any better.

Jemma was a sweet girl, for all her sadness—a bit of an innocent. She deserved fairytales, wonder, and adventure. Not heartache, loneliness and responsibility.

"I stormed out on your daughter earlier." Kai spoke the words so low, he barely heard them, but he knew she would. "But it wasn't her I was angry with. You shouldn't have put me in this position."

"Only you can save her." The woman materialized before him. She was only a little taller than Jemma, with thick straight black hair that hung to her waist. Her eyes were an odd mix of brown and gold, seeming to shift with her expression. She wasn't much like Jemma, except that smile, not so much the shape of it, but the transformative power. One minute she looked sad and lonely, then her lips tilted and she was another woman, happy, or devious, or warm.

Kai doubted he could ever capture a smile like that on canvas. It was a mirage. She tilted her head to the side and raised a brow, as if waiting for a response. Kai didn't know what to say, now that he had her here. He couldn't tell her about her body, could he? He still wasn't sure what side she was on.

He'd been so certain on the beach.

She needed saving, so he pushed aside his fears and his father's voice, left the cave. His feet made their way through the churning waters quickly, like he was just another drop.

The waves that crashed against him only split apart and fell away, as though they were striking rocks, but the wind was another matter. It had a life of its own, a dangerous grip. It yanked at Kai, shoving him back and pulling him forward at once.

He pushed against the wind. Ducking as low as he dared. He couldn't slip into the water for fear the woman would vanish. Sliding a finger over the pouch at his waist, Kai let the magic flow from it into the water, rushing out towards the woman.

She fell still, her hand settling over the arm of wind, almost…lovingly.

Kai paused, not so sure any longer. But his magic was rushing forward; a wave rose like a cupped hand to scoop the woman up and carry her to safety. But it couldn't touch her, not magic, nor water.

She stood untouched, smiling softly.

A great catch of wind threw Kai off his feet. He tumbled backwards.

Only you.

Her whisper floated on every crash or woosh around him. Kai struggled to stand, but his body was no longer his own. His legs folded beneath him, and he reached out desperately for his pouch of trinkets, but it was gone. His lungs locked and little lights popped before his eyes. No. This couldn't be happening.

Kai fell forward on his hands and knees like a supplicant, and two shiny black boots stepped casually into his field of vision.

Standing over Kai, unmoved by the rushing wind, like a giant boulder in the midst of a cyclone, stood a man. In his hand dangled Kai's pouch of treasures.

"I always wondered if that really worked," the man said with a cruel smile in his voice. He threw two large duffel bags at the ground in front of Kai, slipping Kai's treasures into his coat pocket. "Here, my arms need a rest."

On someone else's command, the giant's command, Kai's hands reached out and lifted the heavy bags; he pushed to his feet. The woman slid up beside the giant calmly.

Only you can save her.

"Jemma is the quiet one," she said when Kai continued to stare. "You have me here; talk."

"Did you really bring me to save her? Or were you just helping him?" Kai nodded out towards the field.

The woman didn't even turn. "Only you can—"

"No. Quit that. I'm a kelpie. I know those words, the power of them, that's always what the sirens sing, 'only you.' But it's never true. It's believing it that gets you into trouble."

"Then why are you here?" She laughed.

"Because I'm the idiot who thought you needed help," Kai all but shouted. "But you don't, do you? You like wandering around with him, having a chance to get your revenge for how he hurt you? You like having him need you, love you, hate you. Love him being completely unable to do anything, don't you?"

She shifted back from Kai, the smile drifting off her face, and her eyes grew bright from the glow of her golden flecks.

"None of us chose this life, boy," she snapped.

"Didn't you?" Kai advanced on her, nothing more than air with a shape, and yet she held so much power here. "Why didn't you stay with Jemma?"

"I couldn't."

"I don't believe that."

"It doesn't matter what you believe. It only matters that you save her."

"From what? What is it you have planned? Why are you helping the man who crushed your daughter beneath a truck?"

May Bell straightened. The wind picked up around them, but she was unmoved. The wind lifted leaves and dust from the ground throwing them Kai's way.

"You know nothing," she hissed. "I have seen again and again the women of this family devote everything they have and everything they love to this piece of ground, as though it loved them back. And all it ever does is suck them dry. I won't have that for my girl. This ground is going to give her something for a change. We're going to be a family again. It owes her that."

Kai scoffed, stepping away from the woman. "Everyone keeps saying how they want to be here for Jemma's sake, but it rings false. You just want to be here. And she's in the way."

May Bell looked out onto the land. "We had a good life once. Tom was never perfect, neither was I, but we loved each other. We would have done anything for each other. But this land…it rose up like a wall between us, and the wind tried to drag him away, to drag Jemma away, even as the earth called to her. Do you understand?" She faced Kai again, her eyes imploring. She meant it to look sincere, maybe she thought she was sincere, but all he saw was desperation. "She's a child of two worlds, and they wanted to pull her apart. We broke every rule finding one another."

Her eyes found Black Boot out in the field, and her features softened. She looked young and hopeful. In that moment, Kai saw Jemma in her face, and it horrified him. Would she be like her mother one day, dark and twisted, but unable to see it?

"We broke the rules, and the world wants her to pay the price. She's paid it long enough." May Bell's stance was resolute and calm. "It is time she was paid for her service, time we all were. Once we have control of the land, and Tom can truly command the wind, we can just live. Just be. "

Kai backed up a step, and then another. He turned around and walked across the porch towards the door to the house.

"Only you can save her," she called out in that same soft voice that called him from the safety of his cave and into this maelstrom of darkness and suffering.

Kai threw a glare over his shoulder. "Isn't that a shame."

He pulled open the screen door and rushed into the house, being sure to shut the wooden door behind him. He didn't trust that woman.

"No reason to," Woolworth muttered. Startled, Kai turned to his left. The gripie was sitting at the edge of Jemma's desk watching him. "Helped capture you too, didn't she?"

Kai nodded. He cast a quick glance over his shoulder towards the room where Jemma slept. He was full of nervous energy. He didn't like this place. He didn't like the position Jemma's mother had put him in. He didn't like the idea that only he could save Jemma. He didn't much like the gripie's opinion that he was here to be saved by her either. She'd saved him once already; he wasn't sure he could stand to owe her twice.

There was nothing good to be said of this place. But that intuition Kai worried about was telling him he wouldn't be here long. And he wasn't sure anyone else would be either.

"I can't sleep in a world devoid of color. You wanna help me with some heavy lifting?" Kai asked the gripie and was rewarded with its first genuine smile.

"Jemma had the dream, of blood and soil. I know it. She woke up screaming. She cried all day and still fights against sleeping. We need to get her to Mother's Farm, at least for a while; she needs the land." From the journals of May Bell Franklin-Traveler, 7th generation daughter of Terra.

J emma was wandering through her past. It was a dream, she knew it right away, but it wasn't like any dream she'd had before. She was watching herself, completely separate from the moments and the emotions that came with them. She just floated along beside a warm ball of light, watching events unfold.

It was the morning of the cyclone, but hours earlier. She and Pa were playing hide-and-seek. Pa had his eyes covered, counting;

Two. Three.

The little Jemma on the ground tiptoed over to Pa with a mischievous smile. She had seen Mama do it to Gran once, when they played as a family: tie her shoelaces together, so she went stumbling around the room. Jemma had just learned to tie her own laces; everyone was so proud. She would untie them, and retie them ten times a day to impress everyone. She could make Pa proud and make him hop all at once.

Seven. Eight. Nine.

"Don't," the floating Jemma whispered after her child self, as two little hands stretched gingerly towards Pa's laces.

She had one shoe undone and was just reaching for the second foot when Pa shouted.

"NO!"

He jerked his foot away and Jemma shot into the air, yanked by a sudden burst of wind. Up, up, up, she went, giggling. She didn't know any better. And Pa was on his knees jerking the laces back together.

The gust disappeared and Jemma was falling, without even time to be frightened.

"Jemma!"

Mama came rushing out of the fields and plucked her daughter from the air, just moments before she would have hit the ground. In her mother's arms, little Jemma was too caught up with laughter and adrenaline to notice anything. But floating beside the ball of light, Jemma saw her mother's eyes, full of anger and fear, pierce her father to the ground, where he was bent over his shoes. He hadn't moved at all.

The ball of light beside Jemma flashed bright, blinding her for a moment. When the light cleared, she saw herself sucked up by the cyclone, for the first time in her life terrified of flying. Pa was on the ground, watching. For a moment, it looked as though he would move, would do something, but he didn't. He never did.

In the cyclone, a tiny sobbing Jemma stretched out her hand towards her mother; Mama reached out as well. But they were too far. The little Jemma's voice was ragged from tears and screaming when her eyes fell on Pa, and she begged.

"Papa, stop!"

And it stopped. Everything at once. Jemma was falling; Mama was falling. Straight for the ground.

Beside the ball of light, Jemma turned away; she knew this part. She didn't want to see it. But the ball of light grew warm, rested on Jemma's shoulder like a comforting hand; the light wanted her to see something. She looked up at the sky, watched as her mother fell. But Jemma was closer to the ground, and Mama saw it and her eyes flashed with power as her lips moved rapidly, though Jemma could not hear what she said.

Then Jemma felt it, in her grown-up body, as though she was the one falling, even as she watched. A great hand of earth reached up and wrapped around Jemma, jerking her to the left and softening her fall, as she struck solid ground.

The truck hit a moment later, but not on her chest, as it would have before. And the rest of her body was barely harmed, because her mother had stretched out her magic and cradled her. But she didn't have time to do the same for herself. Jemma saw her strike the back wheel of the upside-down, tractor and flop off it into the dirt. And her breath caught. She reached out for her mother, would have run over, but the ball of light flashed again, and the carnage was gone.

She stood on her porch with the wind chimes clanging, and the dust storm, that was Pa, approaching the house. But her eyes drifted past Pa, into the wind that rode on his coattails, to the figure in the dust. At first, Jemma thought it must be Kai, but the dust shifted, and Jemma saw the long hair pulled off in the wind and the bright shining smile on her face. Mama?

Her smile was so bright it seemed to take up all the space in Jemma's mind; she could barely see the ball of light hovering beside her. Mama rushed at the porch, just as anxious as Jemma to be reunited.

Half asleep in the chair beside her mother's bed, Jemma rolled over and her hand flopped out onto the bed atop her mother's. Her face relaxed into a calm smile and she slept on.

Poisoned

Black Boot worked through the night; he knew from the light across the field that someone in the house did as well. Probably all of them. They could feel him coming. What were they preparing for him? He doubted it was a welcome. It must be a very powerful spell if it kept them up all through the night. And, he had helped them.

They had all sorts of magic at their disposal with the creatures he brought. She would use them against him, unforgivable as he was. It was probably why she brought him the stew.

Black Boot stopped cold, with his foot on the rim of the shovel, digging for the stones. He was a fool. She had come out sweetly, with a bowl of stew, and he was so happy to see her, to have her care for him that he had swallowed the bait whole, without question. It was probably poisoned. How could he be so stupid? She'd all but told him she hated him that morning, then she brought him food. She'd done this to him. The boots were fading, he was losing power, and his own daughter was the key to his demise. His own daughter. He'd not even been angry with her for stealing his insurance policy.

He needed the book back, and the creatures. But she had them all. She was in there with her new friends cursing him.

This had to end. He needed to find the stones. That's what May was telling him with the dream. The stones were buried in the fields. Once he had even one, Jemma's shield would be gone, and they'd see who was more powerful.

He'd take the house. He'd take the land. And the power. And they would all pay. Jemma, his sweet little girl—she would be the one begging for forgiveness.

"Your Grandpa Sy was a joker. Hadn't known me ten minutes when he got on my bad side, accusing me of casting a spell on him. But he made me smile with the same words a hundred times. I miss that." From the journals of Esther Lynn Franklin, 6th matron of the Women of Terra.

The sky was a bright burning orange when Jemma peeked at it through her mother's blinds. It was more orange than Jemma had ever seen all at once. The storm would be here soon, and it was going to be a big one.

Jemma felt her entire body fizzling, as though she had used the flying powder. Her bones felt airy and her blood felt like bubbles jiggling around in her veins. Jemma loved storms. Loved rain, and lightning, and thunder, and a darkened sky. Anything could happen in a rainstorm. It was like living in another world. But she had a feeling the rain wasn't the only thing lightening her.

She woke holding her mother's hand. There was a happy feeling to opening her eyes, as though she would wake surrounded by love.

Jemma was smiling as she dressed, truly looking forward to the day. Perhaps everything wasn't as dire as she made it out to be. Around the time Jemma turned fourteen, she discovered she actually fit some of May Bell's old clothes. Not a lot, but enough that from that time on, she had frequently worn her mother's old clothing. Gran and Allen insisted on buying her clothes of her own, took her all the way to Oklahoma City to go to the nice shops and pick out expensive clothing. But her favorite things were still her mother's.

May Bell had favored purple, she had the coloring for it. Gran liked telling Jemma redheads had no business wearing purple, but it was one of the few arguments with Gran that Jemma always won, simply by continuing to wear purple. She wasn't nutty though; she only wore the darker shades. Lavender made her look like a Power

Puff Girl. She knew there were plenty of people who felt the way Gran did, that purple and red looked bad, but she didn't much care.

There were several things in May Bell's closet Jemma had never worn, mostly because they were too large. But there was one dress that always called to Jemma. It was a long sundress of dark green with an intricate geometric design wandering across it in a deep plumb color, and it had a braided silver belt. It was too long for Jemma and quite a bit baggy in the chest. But today, she didn't care. She wanted to wear something special, something beautiful, and just a bit grown-up.

She bunched the extra length at her waist and tied the belt beneath it, and used safety pins to tighten the straps so her lack of bosom wasn't exactly glaring. She wore her hair loosely around her shoulders as Hippa, who still slept on the back of her chair, liked. Jemma leaned down to kiss her mother's head.

"I love you, Mama." She waited a moment. Today, it felt almost as though she would open her eyes and reply in kind. But nothing happened.

Oddly, it wasn't deflating. Jemma just smiled her goodbye and went to leave the room. She opened the door and froze.

There was a wall of fire blocking her way. She jumped back, breathless, and the fire shifted. Words appeared in the flames.

WATCH YOUR STEP! WET PAINT.

As soon as she read the words, the flames vanished, and she could see the room. Jemma's breath caught; a tiny charmed giggle escaped her.

From her doorway, connecting to every other visible doorway, Kai had painted a path of gold bricks.

He'd painted her a yellow brick road.

She couldn't catch hold of the smile filling her face. She never much cared for *The Wizard of Oz,* but this…it was wonderful, her own little fantasy land.

One of the paths led over to the fireplace where a patch of floor, looking like a large area rug, was painted green. The missing bench was back, but it wasn't the same bench any longer. It was painted with a wilderness of flowers, and it had been padded.

Oooh, and the fireplace, he'd painted the wall leading up to it, and each of the stones. Gone was the boring functional sandstone and the harsh edges of the mantle; it was a rainbow now. Her very own.

To See Her Wonder

Kai had barely slept, maybe an hour all night. But he didn't care, this was the best he ever felt painting. He'd started out angry, restless. Just determined to give Jemma one thing to smile about, but halfway into painting, his mind came alive with ideas. He only wished he'd had enough time and paint to bring them all to life. She deserved a fantasy, and Kai wanted to give it to her.

The idea of the yellow brick road had sprung out of her being crushed beneath a car. He'd just bet she hated the story, a witch smashed under a house after a tornado; it would all hit too close to home. Someone else might have shied away from reminders like that, but Kai liked the idea of remaking them. This wasn't Dorothy's yellow brick road, or Dorothy's Oz. It was Jemma's fantasy domain.

He was resting in the corner between her desk and the wall when she opened the door. She didn't notice him, which suited Kai fine. From here, he could watch the play of emotions run over her face: the surprised delight and wonder, even a bit of amusement. He watched her trace the path with her eyes, saw them widen when she saw the bench and nearly pop when she noticed the rainbow. She was happy.

Kai leaned back, ready to shut his eyes. That was all he'd wanted. It didn't matter if he ever slept again; he'd bet no one had ever made her smile like that.

When she began to whistle and came off the ground a few inches, Kai sat up straighter. For a moment, it looked like she just levitated, had a zero-gravity pack inside her somewhere that she could just switch on and off, with a whistle apparently. But as he looked closer, he saw the air shifting behind her; something was beating a current into it. She had wings, invisible wings.

Butterfly wings would suit her best, Kai decided, and he couldn't help but smile at the image in his mind. Gossamer thin, but complex, like stained glass, and definitely purple. He would have to paint her that way.

She fluttered over to the fireplace and landed standing on the unpainted bench, her eyes following the trail of the rainbow. She giggled looking into the fireplace, and Kai had a desperate desire to know what she was thinking. He hadn't painted inside the fireplace; it seemed like a pretty big fire hazard. What was she looking for in there? Did she think he was silly?

Her eyes shifted to the bench and she crouched to look closer. She winced at the motion, but otherwise seemed not to notice her leg. She was captivated. Her hand stretched out, tracing the shapes of different flowers. Then she caught sight of the foot stool and nearly fell reaching for it.

"Careful." Kai was up and running across the floor to her side. "I wasn't trying to break your head open," he teased reaching out to help her straighten. "This area is dry, I did it first."

"Oh." She seemed to barely notice him, using his steadying hand for balance, she reached for the stool again. She pulled it to her chest, squeezing it experimentally. "It's a fairy stump!"

"Aren't they called toadstools?" Kai asked, charmed by her reaction to the mushroom-shaped ottoman.

"Only the ones that puff up on top. The flat ones are called fairy stumps."

"Very informative." She still wasn't looking his way, busily turning the stool over and over in her hands.

"Did you make this?" she demanded, finally looking his way, with an expression exactly like a five-year-old on Christmas morning.

"Sorry, I only commissioned it. Allen and Tangerine made it, so I could paint."

"It's beautiful. It's all beautiful. Where did you find things to pad the bench?"

"I'm a kelpie. I ran around your house and scavenged for them."

"I don't know what to make of it, and I haven't told anyone. Jemima levitated. I hoped it was a good sign, that she wanted to wander with the wind, like her father, but she still can't sleep through the night without holding the jar of earth Mama sent for her first birthday. The magic may tear her apart." From the journals of May Bell Franklin-Traveler, 7th generation daughter of Terra.

Kai was wearing a sly grin, as though this was just some little trifle he'd handed her. As if he didn't know that this was the most fantastic gift she'd ever been given, maybe the most fantastic gift anyone was ever given. She was torn between a giddy, almost nauseous desire to throw her arms around his neck and kiss him, and the much steadier desire to punch him in the shoulder, for making light of this.

He'd padded the bench; all alone that one gift would have earned him her gratitude, but he hadn't stopped there. He was making her home into a fairyland. Her brain wouldn't work properly, she couldn't focus. He'd scavenged for the padding, he said, and she should hit him for insulting himself. But he was smiling, and she couldn't seem to pull her eyes away from him. He'd made her a yellow brick road, and she loved it. From someone else, she would have thought it was an insult, calling her the Wicked Witch of the East, but from him, she loved it. And he'd given her a rainbow, and a fairy stump and a flower garden. She'd always wanted a flower garden.

Jemma tore her eyes away from him before she did something really stupid, like kiss him or burst into tears. It was all too wonderful.

Shoving the fairy stump into Kai's hands, she nearly knocked him down lunging for the bench.

"It's Hippa!" she exclaimed, oblivious to the twinge in her leg as she crouched before the bench to run her finger along the little painting. She was nearly hidden in the middle of a patch of wild irises. She was in the hummingbird shape she seemed to favor. Jemma would have missed her but for the shimmering quality he'd given to her wings.

Kai was laughing behind her. He even said something about leaving her brainless but Jemma was too thrilled to pay him any mind. She simply leaned in closer examining the rest of the bench carefully.

It had nearly all her favorite flowers, and some others she'd never seen. Most were in different shades of purple. But there was a patch of snapdragons of every color. There was a patch of yellow and white daffodils, and then there was the bouquet, the only group of flowers that did not appear to be growing right out of the bench. They were tulips; there was a dark purple one right in the center then one of every other color they grew. And standing there, tying a tidy little lavender bow around them, was Tangerine.

Jemma giggled. It was the perfect place for her.

"Oh, look at Nona." She was bright red and steaming above a patch of alyssum. "She looks like a fiery cloud raining purple and white snow."

"Sometimes purple and red work," he said casually tugging at the ends of her hair. When she looked over, he just winked, and Jemma couldn't breathe. She barely noticed his hand slipping away from her hair, and into his pocket.

"Where's Woolworth?" Jemma asked just to have something to say. She was having trouble thinking again.

"Right there." Kai pointed to the far corner, at what looked like a purple and white picket fence but was actually a neat little row of Larkspur. At the foot of the stalks, with a hand gripping each one beside him, was Woolworth, shaking the flowers so a soft spray of petals fell around him.

Jemma ran a hand over the back of the couch. This truly was the best gift she'd ever received. She turned and threw her arms around Kai for a quick hug. "Now, even when I find a way to send them safely home, they'll still be here." She couldn't seem to let him go. "Thank you!"

"No sweat." Kai shrugged off Jemma's hug with a carefree smile.

"You're such a boy." Jemma shook her head. He'd gone to all this work, but he was too shy to accept the thanks.

"I kind of thought so." Kai straightened and stretched out a hand to help Jemma stand.

She placed her hand in his and froze. "Wait. Where's your picture?"

Kai's mouth opened and shut several times, and his eyes grew wide.

"You have to give me a painting of you as well."

"I'm not very good at self-portraits."

"Then you'll just have to work on them," Jemma said unimpressed.

She let him help her up; standing was excruciating. It was why she so rarely crouched. It felt like her bone was scraping bone, which it was. So much of her ligaments were gone.

"Have you taken your medicine yet?" Kai snapped.

Jemma glared back. She would never understand that reaction, Allen had it often enough too. She was the one in pain, so she was the one with a right to be angry.

"Haven't had a chance yet, nurse," Jemma said rolling her eyes. Kai helped her sit on the padded couch. It was wonderful, so different from the hard wood.

"I'll get them." Kai said more calmly, but he didn't rush away. Instead, he crouched down in front of her, and lifted her bad leg onto the fairy stump. "How does that feel?"

He looked so hesitant. Jemma couldn't imagine why. Hadn't he just given her the best gift ever? Was it possible he really didn't see that?

"It's wonderful."

Kai nodded and went off to find the pills.

On the Edge of the Coming Storm

"Of course the floor isn't finished yet," Kai spoke with his back to her. He slipped the bit of hair he'd stolen from her head into his bag of trinkets. The first thing he could truly say he'd stolen. It was well worth it.

It was always a relief when someone appreciated his work. It wasn't that he didn't think he was good or didn't know it, but no matter how many times his work was loved, he felt nervous with each new piece. As if this one would be the piece that revealed he wasn't such a great artist.

"What do you mean?" Jemma called after him. "It's beautiful."

"Yeah," Kai agreed searching her desk for the pills. "But the rest of the room just has the yellow brick road and the wood."

"Most people like wood," Jemma pointed out.

"It doesn't go with the esthetic."

"Fairyland," Jemma whispered wondrously.

Kai smiled; she really was too easy. The way she looked at him earlier, as if he was the most amazing person in the world. Kai shuddered; he'd wanted to run away. So he made light of it. An annoyed Jemma was easier to deal with.

"Something like that." Kai stared off around the room; he knew he'd seen the pills somewhere. "I need more paint though."

"Make a list, I'll have Allen get some. Oh, there it is." Jemma pointed across the room to her bookshelf where the pill bottle was sitting. "I'll get it."

"No. Jeez, is it always this hard to help you?"

"Wouldn't know, I don't have any problems with it."

"It's never easy," Allen said from the open doorway. One hand was rubbing the small of his back and the other rubbing over his face. "Wow. When did you do all of this? Why doesn't it smell like paint?"

"One of Woolworth's many talents. He can apparently clean the air. Watch the paint." Kai nodded Allen away from the brick road as he carried the pills to Jemma.

He needed to get a sealer, make sure they couldn't ruin his artwork with foot traffic.

"Clean the air, really?" Jemma asked. "I've never read that."

Kai smirked. "Typical. Tallies never listen to anything they don't say."

"Tallies?" Jemma asked with a smile.

"That's what Woolworth calls anyone taller than him."

Jemma giggled. "Are you making friends then?"

"Guess so. Here, I'll get you some water."

Kai moved off watching from the corner of his eye as Allen very cautiously made his way over to Jemma, looking at the artwork to avoid her gaze.

"Kai's making a list of paints and things he needs from town, and I'll make a list of groceries too. You can get it all after you check on Ma."

"Yes, Miss Jemma. Will you be forgiving me then?"

"I'll think about it."

Kai heard them from inside the kitchen. It reminded him some of how he and Poesy fought. But he still didn't trust Allen. There was something he wasn't telling any of them.

Kai should be exhausted, but something of Jemma's response had exhilarated him. Reawakening the nervous energy that kept him moving through the night. He wanted to get to work on the rest of it, finish it, before something happened. Because something was going to happen. Something bad.

He filled a glass of water in the sink, nodding to Woolworth and Tangerine, who'd been up most of the night with him but were already starting breakfast.

Kai could see the rest of the living room, as it should be, laid out before him as he walked. How characters from books he thought Jemma would like would come to life, stepping off the bookshelves.

How there would be a dark wall, with a haunting forest, and creepy creatures peeking out from the shadows. He'd love to do the ceiling as well: griffins, fairies, dragons, and a few birds, and Jemma with her butterfly wings, flying. But as he looked up at the ceiling, the image wasn't quite so clear. He had a feeling he wouldn't get a chance to make that before whatever terrible fate was coming struck.

Jemma was alone when he came back, leaning to her left to examine every one of the couch cushions in turn. He was half tempted to tell her his plans for the rest of the room. She would like them. But he liked her wonder as he revealed each new piece. She was due some good surprises.

"There are irises on every one of these sections." Jemma stared at the couch, as Kai stopped beside her.

"Yep."

"Most people would have done tulips." She looked up curiously. Seeing the water, she popped open the pill bottle and took one out. She stared at it for a second then broke it in half.

"Because it's your middle name?"

She nodded. Reaching out to take the water, she slipped one half of the pill in her mouth. Kai raised an eyebrow to indicate she should take the rest. She only raised an eyebrow right back. Kai shook his head.

"That's why I made them a bouquet, to set them apart. But I thought irises suited you better."

"They're my favorite." That look was back, as though she had never imagined someone might know her well enough to guess her favorite flower, as though he was amazing and she would love him forever.

Kai didn't know how to respond. How to let her down easy.

"Rain's coming," Jemma said out of nowhere.

"Okay." Kai chuckled. Trust her to save him from the hard stuff.

"I've been seeing orange everywhere. This water's orange."

"No…"

"Not really, I know. But I always see orange before a rainstorm. Orange pours out for attention." Jemma blushed at Kai's raised eyebrow. She spoke into her lap. "It's from an old family poem. I forget how it goes exactly."

No she didn't. He'd bet his right hand, but for some reason, it embarrassed her.

"Anyway, when I woke today, I couldn't see any blue in the sky. It was on fire with orange. There is nothing in the forecast, but a storm's coming, tonight, maybe tomorrow. And it's a big one."

"Sounds good to me. This place could use a bit of rain."

"I still see her when I sleep. Ruth, no, Sotsona —she chose that name. I see her dead and bleeding in my arms. How can you forget such things or forgive them?" From the journals of Sarah Anne Smith, 2nd matron of the Women of Terra.

Just like that, he believed her. So simply, like she'd only said her hair was red or it was a Tuesday. When Gran realized Jemma had the sight, she went into overdrive, convinced Jemma should be studying magic; that she could change the future; that she was immensely powerful.

It was almost scary the things she'd said.

But Kai just believed her. Nothing more, nothing less. Jemma looked away from him, hiding her smile. Today was going to be a good day.

Her eyes fell on the floor he'd painted her. From across the room, it looked like just a patch of green, but there were individual blades of grass. They seemed almost three-dimensional, moving with a breeze that wasn't even in the room. There were little mushrooms scattered around in it, some toadstools and a few more fairy stumps. And wild irises and a tiny patch of clovers, and moss on one side of a little rock.

It was perfect, and it was hers, and he had made it for her. Only her.

"Where's Allen?" Kai asked when Jemma continued looking at the floor.

"In checking on Ma. Look," Jemma said, taking a deep breath. This was going to be hard, but she had to apologize. "I…she's the only thing in the world…"

"Jemma." Kai laid a hand on her shoulder. "I overreacted. You were protecting your family, that's a good thing."

Jemma just stared at him, nodding. She wanted to cry again, but nice tears, happy to have someone around again who just believed her, who forgave her like it was nothing. But she fought them; Kai would know exactly what they meant. And it was one thing for Jemma to realize she loved him and another thing entirely for him to know. She hadn't had someone new to love since Allen came to town. It was a good feeling, full and alive. Like she hadn't felt since Gran died.

But Jemma wasn't stupid, she couldn't let Kai know. He might like her, and he might want to help her, but there was no way someone like him would love someone like her. So, it was best to keep it to herself and save them both the embarrassment.

"I'm gonna go make breakfast." Jemma downed the rest of the water to be sure it wouldn't spill on her beautiful floor.

"Woolworth and Tangerine are already at it."

"Oh. Well, I need to have a look around and see what to put on my grocery list."

"It'd be simpler to just write down what you do have," Kai teased.

"Sure, but then Allen will come back with things he likes or things that are cheap instead of what we need."

Kai smiled. "So go with him."

"I don't go into town." Jemma stood. She could tell Kai wanted her to rest, but she wasn't tired and her leg felt fine.

"Ever?"

"Not for a few years now." Jemma wandered around Kai when he got in her way, and walked alongside her yellow brick road.

"Don't you have any friends there? People you hang out with."

Jemma shook her head, looking over her shoulder at Kai as though he was nutty. Why did he want her out of the house suddenly? To paint her another surprise probably, but he couldn't do that without the paint.

"If there is some other surprise your working on…" Jemma began, only to have him interrupt her.

"I want to know where your friends are?"

"Here." She shrugged.

"Why? You are perfectly capable of making friends. Give them a chance, show them the curse stuff is nutty."

Jemma stopped and stared at him. "No one in town wants me around their children. They're frightened of me."

"What did you do?"

"Survived a fall from inside the tornado that ripped our house away and destroyed the town. The town used to be bigger, a lot bigger. Then Pa had his tantrum, and three farms were obliterated. A lot of homes had major damage, roofs ripped off, things smashed through them. And town was worse. A bunch of buildings had cars thrown through them, or parts of other buildings. When it was over, everyone knew where to look. The tornado's center was right over our house. It came here first, then I guess, when Pa stopped the one that had me and May Bell, a group of tornados flew off across the valley."

"Wow."

"It wasn't the first time a fight here ended in a tornado in town. It happened a lot that summer." Jemma said it flatly, looking off into the past. She'd never had to tell anyone about this before. Never talked about the way her parents fought and fought, so it seemed they might split the world apart, or how their anger and sadness had run off into the world making a mess. She didn't like to think about it. She liked to think about the happy days. Or the way both of them would smile at her, even then.

It was something like being the child of a Greek god, she imagined. All the guilt of having been a part of such selfish, pointless destruction. And both of them guardians. They should have known better. Gran left for one month to visit Grandpa's brother, and while she was gone, her daughter and son-in-law laid waste to the town.

And everyone knew it.

"At first, I think, most people just thought we were having a particularly bad storm season. They didn't bother us. Then, a few days before the big cyclone, I was little, but I remember the mayor coming by. Apparently, people put together a petition to get us off the land. They couldn't do it, but he offered to buy the land. When that didn't work, he looked at me, and then back at them, and said, 'A home this dangerous is no place for a child. Clean up your act, or it won't be her home anymore.'"

Kai gasped.

"Mama didn't look scared," Jemma said looking into her memory. "For the first time, I remember she looked truly angry. But she didn't do anything. After the big storm came, a whole bunch of them came for me."

"A whole bunch?"

"The mayor, the sheriff, a group of women—I don't remember who exactly.

"Gran had just come home, and found us. She cursed Pa and then she sort of went crazy. One minute she'd be holding onto Mama and the next, she was digging through the rubble for a phone. And I was on the ground next to Mama, bleeding, crying, and screaming about…"

"What?"

Jemma looked up. Of all the things to be embarrassed about, she supposed this should be the least of it. She had been seven after all. But she was embarrassed.

"My doll, Kadawada. I thought she was my sister, but in the storm, she'd been ripped apart. Her head was stuck to one blade of the tractor and her body to another, and there was stuffing everywhere. Ma was on the ground right in front of her, bleeding, not moving, and my legs hurt so much, but it was like someone else was feeling them. All I could look at was Kadawada."

She glanced at Kai. He wasn't laughing at her; he looked almost sad, as if he was mourning the doll with her.

"When they came to pull me away from her, I screamed so loud. I can still hear it sometimes. And the earth started shaking, and it got windy again, and Sheriff Hicks, who was reaching out for me, jumped back cradling his arm. I'd broken his wrist."

"Whoa!" Kai's head jerked back a bit, but he didn't run away. Jemma supposed that was a good sign.

"I know I must have done it," Jemma said trying to recall the moment. "But I don't remember feeling any great surge of power. Just scared. They all ran off, terrified. And they started saying I'd brought the storm, left Mama in a coma, and killed Pa."

"Killed him?"

Jemma shrugged. "No one knew where he was. It made sense."

"And…that's when you stopped going into town?"

"No, actually. Gran kept making me go. Even when I had to use a wheel chair or crutches. I stopped when I was twelve, almost thirteen."

"What happened then?"

"Clarissa Hicks." Jemma made a nasty face and spat the girl's name out. "Most people left when their insurance money came, they just picked up and moved away. There are lots of rundown, empty houses off Stonehill Road; it was the worst hit. But Sheriff Hicks and his family stayed. Clarissa was having her driving test. She's awful. She almost hit this kid, he couldn't have been more than three."

"So, why don't they hate her."

"I was stupid. I saw her about to hit him, and I flew over to rescue him."

"That's heroic, not stupid."

"Same thing," Jemma said morosely. "Clarissa saw me fly, but all anyone else saw was her car go careening into Baskin Robins. She said she saw me try and throw the kid into the street, said she'd swerved to avoid him."

"And everyone just believed her?" Kai looked suspicious, like she was making the story up. Jemma had to admit it did sound a bit far-fetched when she said it aloud.

"I don't know." Jemma shrugged. "Probably not everyone."

"And you just gave up and left. Because of some stupid girl."

"She was standing there, basically calling me a murderer, and saying how I'd always had it out for her family, that I was a witch. And I almost cursed her."

"Almost! Curse her if it will make you feel better; she deserves it."

Jemma giggled. It was just the sort of thinking she couldn't afford to start, but it was nice to hear.

"I would have, but the kid I saved, he ran up and wrapped his arms around my legs, he called me an angel, asked me to show him how to fly. I was bending down to pick him up when people started shrieking. So, I walked to Gran's car to wait for her. When she came out of the library, we went home. I never went back. I didn't tell her, but someone else probably did, because she never asked me to go again."

Kai just stared at her for a moment. He was leaning back on his heels like he was trying to put space between them. But his eyes never left her face.

Then he opened his mouth. "That's really sad and hick-townish. And I get why they aren't your favorite people, but if you're telling me you sat here for two years pouting, I'm going to lose all respect for you."

Jemma burst out laughing, grabbing onto Kai's shoulder to hold herself up. She'd always thought friends would be sympathetic and have her side in everything. But this was so much better. He made her laugh at herself, all the time.

Jemma looked into his sparkling eyes, half mesmerized, and made a joke of her own. "Can you blame me? They never rebuilt the Baskin Robins."

Kai chuckled. "Well, that's another story."

It wasn't until a few minutes later, when Jemma had her note pad and was off to the kitchen to make her list, that it hit her. He was going to leave. They all were, and things would go back to the way they were before, only worse. She'd have five more people to miss.

Maybe she and Ma should leave. Let Pa have the house and wander off, ignoring the call of the land. And go where, Jemma? A woman in a coma, and a teenager who could see the future and fly but had no marketable skills.

The circus?

Ghost of What Never Could Have Been

*B*lack Boot collapsed against the barn. He had no energy left, but the wind could do the rest for him now. It swept across the field of downed stalks and ripped out roots carrying it away from the house. The farm was a mess. What was wrong with that girl? This place was always an oasis in the past, lush and beautiful. When he worked its fields, he'd never been alone. Esther and May Bell worked the land beside him.

Their entire history of harpies had worked the land through pain and heartache. So what if she did have a limp. Did that give her an excuse to abandon her birthright? She should at least have pride enough to find workers.

"Why does it bother you?" May asked materializing in the glint of light and bits of dust on the wind. "It suits your purposes well enough."

"Our purposes," Black Boot snapped then dragged his eyes away from his wife. "I don't know what to do with a daughter whose abandoned her pride."

"Why should she take pride in the land that's taken everything from her?" May Bell's voice was bitter. She was in a bad mood again. Her moods had been so erratic since they returned here; he almost regretted coming.

"This is her birthright, her responsibility. Plenty of people in the world are born without this sort of heritage. They fight for the right to have this. I won't have a lazy daughter."

"I never worked this land because it was my birthright." May paced away with the wind. "I took care of it, because I loved it, because I was the fool who thought if I gave it my love, it would give me everything. What's it ever given her?"

"What's she given it? That's how it works, May. If she wants something from it, she has to work for it. Just sitting around here letting it rot and wanting something from it, is laziness."

"She isn't lazy!" May Bell spun on him screaming with tears glinting in her eyes. "She's lonely. And she knows just where to place the blame: you, and this…" She kicked uselessly at the ground. "This stupid patch of leeching earth."

"Stupid? Leeching?" Black Boot came to his feet as the wind picked up around him; he nearly shuddered. He wasn't the only one commanding the wind any longer. "This land gave you your magic, kept your family alive and thriving for generations, while the rest of the world *suffered*. It gave me power over the wind. And it's going to make her whole again. Make us whole." He advanced on her; she was the one who'd made him believe it. She needed to believe or she wouldn't help him. "I'll have its magic, and when I do, I'll have the power I need to care for Jemma. To protect her from the rest of the world. She'll never be dependent on other's whims again. People will come to us. Fear *us*!"

May Bell stared at him, and he could see in her eyes that she was as torn as she had been when she had first trailed after him. Uncertainty made her dangerous.

"You don't need the power," she said quietly, her voice quivered. He hated it when she spoke like that, low as if to calm him and quivering with fear. What did she have to be afraid of anymore? "It was never meant to give you power over the wind. We broke the rules and look where it led. All we ever wanted was to give you power over yourself. But you can't handle that. You never could control yourself."

"That's not true!" He shouted and little whirlwinds appeared in the fields, lifting dirt into the air. "I've always taken responsibility for myself."

"Yourself maybe, but never your destruction. You did this, not her. You!" She vanished, and Black Boot was left staring into the fields at the tiny whirlwinds. As small as they were they still threatened everyone's safety. With great effort, Black Boot calmed his racing heart. He drew in a deep breath, held it. Robbed of air, the whirlwinds vanished, leaving little holes in the earth to betray their existence.

Black Boot stormed off towards one of the holes. He knew May Bell wasn't far behind; she was never far behind him. Even before he dragged her ghost in the wind, she followed him everywhere. Left school for him, left home, disobeyed her parents and her heritage to travel before the wind. As he did. Until Jemma was born. She ignored the call of the land for him, but when it began calling to Jemma as well, when Jemma couldn't sleep for the dreams, they both returned to the land. For Jemma.

And look what came of it: Jemma crippled and angry, the land all but destroyed, and May…May was dead.

He hadn't even realized she was dead, not when he was sitting beside her, trying to drag her body to him, along with Jemma's. Then her ghost appeared beside him, screaming and crying, telling him to put Jemma down, saying he'd no right to hold her after all he'd done. Calling him a monster.

It was madness that day, not just the storm. But Jemma, sobbing in his arms, bleeding, in and out of consciousness, and May Bell bellowing in his ear to the point he didn't even hear Esther drive up. Didn't realize she was there until she stood over them and the earth set to shaking. The air filled up with the voices of her ancestor witches.

He'd looked up, met her gaze, and Esther was a different woman. As tattered and rickety as her home, and possessed of a power she'd never wielded before. She cursed him.

Black Boots, scourge upon our lands, blight on our name, leave this place and never return, or the earth will open wide to swallow you whole.

May Bell just stood there, sobbing, torn between her mother and her husband. She shook her head no, begged her mother not to, when only moments before, she had been beating at his eardrums with her threats. He lay his Jemma on the ground, and rose. Already he felt the boots threatening to slip away, the wind threatening to drag him along, forcing him instead of being led by him.

His eyes found May Bell's ghost. *"I'm so sorry, May."*

Her eyes swollen with tears, she walked to him, as she always did, as she had on their wedding day. She always came when he called. She'd reached out to touch him, but her hand fell through him.

He couldn't stand there a moment longer, in the wake of his temper. So he fled, even as Jemma woke again, and shouted out for him to return, begged him to stay.

He walked and walked, and only when he was half a mile from the farm did he hear May Bell's voice, sobbing.

"Bring Jemma. Please, bring Jemma. She needs you."

He saw her then, trailing him in the wind, with tears in her eyes and slumped shoulders. She was trapped—with him. And it was too late. He couldn't go back, and she couldn't choose Jemma over him. They were stuck together, as they had been since their eyes first met across the beach on a cool summer evening.

She was his fate. Good or bad, and today it seemed she meant to make it bad. Just like everyone else, she was turning against him.

Black Boot stared into the hole. It must go two feet deep, empty, but it gave him an idea.

If he could only claim the land in time. If he could only take the place of the matron, as May said he could. Before the boots vanished, before Jemma figured out how to destroy the boots and any chance of happiness they still had. If he could convince Jemma of all the land had cost her, if she truly turned her back on it, then anyone could claim it. And Black Boot knew just what to do with it.

He could fix Jemma, bring May's spirit back to his side. He could have the power, and his family, and no one would ever hurt them again.

The wind rose up around him, and little whirlwinds danced off to do his bidding.

More Than Meets the Eye

Kai went looking for Allen after he left Jemma to her list making. He was in her mother's room; Kai leaned against the door frame looking in. He hadn't noticed the painting on the ceiling before, too caught up with the woman in the bed. It was sweet, childish. He knew intellectually how long Jemma had been without parents, but seeing it so clearly illustrated was a bit staggering.

"Jemma did it a long time ago. Back when she thought her mother would wake up," Allen said, startling Kai.

"And you've just let her sit around here moping since?" Kai walked into the room, to the opposite side of the bed, to look at Jemma's mother.

"Is that what she told you?" Allen scoffed. "No, we don't let her just sit around here and mope. She goes out, couple times a month. And every year for her birthday, she and Esther take four- or five-day trips places. She was going to take a college course online, wrote to the professor who runs it and asked for permission to take it as a senior-year elective."

"Online courses? Wait! Senior year?" Kai asked startled. "How old is she?"

"Fourteen," Allen sighed as though the idea bothered him too. "Esther home-schooled her, and she doesn't really stop in the summer, so she's starting her senior year."

"She really is nuts. But I guess it fits. She gets very brainy and geeky about things."

"You mean intellectual and analytical," Allen offered sarcastically. Kai just ignored him. He knew the words, he just didn't think they made the point any more clearly than his had. "She even has pen pals," Allen went on. "They're mostly her cousins but…"

"She has cousins?"

"Yeah. Well, second cousins. Esther's brother's grandkids. She visits them in Texas once in a while."

"I didn't even know there could be male members in this family."

"Sure. They just aren't *bound*," Allen said, making little air quotes, "by the curse."

"You don't believe in the curse?"

Allen shrugged. He stared at Jemma's mother rather intently for a minute, like he was fighting something. There was less certainty in his voice when he spoke. "I believe in the power of suggestion."

"Oh, and I suppose that's how Jemma kept you away for months: suggestion."

"You misunderstand," Allen said his eyes finding Kai's. "I'm not sure I believe in the old curse. I'm not sure I believe there is anything binding the women of this family to the land. Or that they cursed this valley and the Jessup line." Allen shook his head looking equal parts doubtful and annoyed—nearly angry. "But Jemma has always been something special. I don't know if I'd call it magic, but she has power over people. She doesn't use all her senses the way other people do. She uses her brain like it's another sense, no, a tool. Like she can use it tangibly in the physical world." Allen's eyes took on a sort of glazed, almost frightened quality. Kai wondered just what it was about the word *magic* that disturbed "normal" people to the point they needed to explain it away.

"All I know is if Jemma wants something, and sets her mind to it, she usually gets it."

"Except her," Kai pointed out looking down at Jemma's mother again. He should tell her he'd seen her mother's spirit, been captured by it. Maybe she could find a way to reunite soul and body if he did. But…wouldn't it make it so much worse if she couldn't?

"Except that," Allen agreed and his hand drifted through the air to gently brush a few loose strands of hair off her face. "Why so curious?"

Kai shrugged. "It just doesn't make sense that she has no friends. It's so easy to make her happy. But she's all sadness and anger."

Allen went back to checking the machines. "Three months is a long time for someone like Jemma, someone so serious, to be alone with their thoughts. And my guess is, if she spelled me to stay away, she spelled her relatives not to wonder after her."

Kai nodded.

"And she's grieving. Her grandmother was basically the only family she had and now she's gone."

"I suppose. She didn't seem to have liked her much."

At this, Allen actually laughed. "Jemma's fond of sharing the bad. Esther wasn't cuddly. But she loved Jemma desperately. And Jemma loved her, they had fun together. Had little private jokes, and loved to prank me. Trust me, Jemma's missing her grandmother."

"I want to go into town with you," Kai said after a moment.

"Don't have to ask me twice," Allen replied genially.

"No. I didn't think you'd mind." Kai nodded slyly and walked towards the door.

"What do you want in town?"

With his back to the man, Kai smirked. Was he worried the water horse would lead everyone to their doom to avenge Jemma? It wasn't a bad idea, but Kai was a little more farsighted than that.

"Paint." Kai threw a smirk over his shoulder. "Mostly. I like to make my own selections."

"What else?" Allen seemed to be trying to stare Kai down, but Allen didn't have the hang of that yet. If he meant to take on the role of Jemma's father, he might try asking her real one for tips on intimidation.

"Not much. I'm gonna shower. Wouldn't want to go into town wearing your clothes and all this paint."

"It's about standing firm, tough as the earth, as you face off with life. I put a lot on you, Jem, but not because you are Sarah's heir. Because when you were in so much pain that another person would've folded, you stared your father down and demanded your due. He was the failure, and me, never you." From the journals of Esther Lynn Franklin, 6th matron of the Women of Terra.

Jemma was all but kicked out of the kitchen. Tangerine and Woolworth insisted on making the list, because Jemma's culinary pallet was lacking. Since the biscuits were already in the oven, there wasn't a thing for her to do but set the table. She should be offended. In the past two days, she'd been all but accused of being a know-nothing Okie. But she was actually kind of amused by it. Pa, and Kai, and even Nona and Woolworth might think her unsophisticated, and worry that Dust House was all she knew of the world; but Jemma knew differently.

She could see where they had gotten that impression. She wasn't exactly bubbly, or forthcoming, and in the last three months, she'd begun to feel sort of…absent. As though everything before Gran's death, the good and the bad, were a dream, like stupid Dorothy, and this sepia world was all she would ever know. In those months, she hadn't been entirely sure that she'd ever left this house either. They seemed tied together, her and the empty house, as if they both came into existence in the same moment and nothing before even existed.

She was just glad everyone had come along and put her life back in technicolor. She stared at the yellow brick road as she set out little teaspoons of jam for her smaller visitors. She needed to find a way to be happy with the time they were with her and not try and trap them here, trap the color, as she knew she could so easily be tempted to do.

Hippa was awake now and playing in Jemma's hair again. It tickled a little, all her fluttering around under there, and it gave her a vague feeling of déjà vu.

"Where is Nona?" Jemma asked Tangerine and Woolworth, who were busily scribbling with their heads together. Jemma felt sure she heard the word Haggis tossed around, and since she actually knew what that was, she rather hoped Tangerine won the debate. Sheep guts didn't appeal to her.

"We made a truce," Woolworth answered, looking away from the list annoyed. He was already slightly miffed with Jemma because she forced him to concede and put about three weeks' worth of canned food on the list. She needed to stock the cellar, but he didn't like her pessimistic attitude. "Nona is not allowed in the kitchen while I am here, so I don't kill her."

Jemma chuckled. "You two really hate each other. How did you manage stuck in that bag together for so long?"

"That was different," he said flatly and turned away.

"I'm so sorry, Woolworth." Jemma rushed over to the counter. "That was insensitive. Please forgive me."

"Not your doing." Woolworth stared up at Jemma fiercely. "You don't apologize for him, *ever*."

Jemma nodded. "Just for what I said."

The gripie shrugged. "It was only a question. Take out the biscuits."

Jemma went to the stove following directions. Never apologize for Pa—it was an odd notion. All morning, she'd heard the chimes clanging but forced herself to ignore them, when all she wanted to do was run into town and warn everyone. She'd felt bad about that last summer, for so long. About the storms one after another that tore the valley apart, and that last destructive cyclone. So many people thought she was to blame for it; it was hard to disagree. But Woolworth said she wasn't to apologize for him, ever.

Jemma lay the cookie sheet on the stove top, wondering how exactly the tiny creatures put it in, in the first place, even as her mind pondered Woolworth's words. She looked up, out the window and her breath caught. There were whirlwinds, almost tiny tornados, all over the wheat field, and holes, so many holes.

She hadn't been paying attention. Was so caught up with her happy feelings, and her fairyland, and how much she would miss all her new friends. She had been busy thinking what a good day this would be, and Pa had been setting about to make a fool of her.

He was looking for the stones. And it wouldn't be long before he found them. She needed to get to work. Needed to send her friends away, keep them safe. Then she needed to find a way to safely banish Pa.

Jemma walked out of the kitchen without a word. Careful to avoid the paint, she walked through the living room and down the hall past the bathroom. Someone was showering, probably Allen, but she paid no attention. She went straight to her room. She hadn't been there in days, almost weeks really. Even before her guests arrived, she spent most of her time in May Bell's room.

Jemma opened the door and knew at once that someone had been in here. Probably Kai; several of her throw pillows were missing. He must have used them as stuffing, when he padded the bench. She looked around for anything embarrassing that might be lying out. Not that it mattered. She meant to send him away too, and he wasn't likely ever to come back. So what should she care if he was laughing at her, far away across the world?

Shaking off the worry, Jemma walked over to her bookshelves and began pulling out books. *The Complete History of Spells, Curses, Enchantments and Charms as a Guide to Medieval Perception* by Dr. Ruth Alden. It was one of Jemma's favorites. Professor Alden broke down the basic structures of different kinds of spells, everything from the sleeping and waking spells so common in fairytales, to the curse on Odysseus and the destruction of Sodom and Gomorra. She addressed not so much the magic itself, as what it was that drove the different spells, and what it said about different cultures and ages in history. Jemma loved Dr. Alden, to the point where she found out she was offering a course online, and wrote and wrote until she allowed Jemma into the class, after a permission slip from Gran, because of the adult content addressed.

For some reason, the very analytic approach helped Jemma when she was trying to reason out spells. That book had given her an idea, and since then, nearly all the magical books she used were by academics exploring something other than magic. Jemma grabbed volumes I and VII of *Encyclopedia Mythical: The Definitive Reference on All Creatures of Legend, Myth, and Fantasy,* by Neil Gerrnan, Cornellia Fink, R.J. Took, and C. Lews. Volume I addressed fairy and their kin and volume VII had everything she needed to know about natural force guardians or gods. She wouldn't call Pa a god, and he'd stopped doing much in the way of guarding the wind long ago, but that was how he started out, so that was what she needed.

Gran hated these books. Laymen writing about something they wanted to understand but never would. She never understood why Jemma felt the need to approach magic so intellectually.

Magic isn't something you learn in school, Jem beam. It's either in you or it ain't. It's emotion, pure and powerful, walking out of a body and into the world, makin' it new. You can't get at it in a book.

Jemma would never say this to Gran, but she rather thought that was the problem. Everyone was too emotional about magic. Pure emotion brought the storm and cursed the land. Pure emotion was bad. When Jemma felt herself getting emotional, was when she fought like hell to keep the magic in. So she liked the books, liked to read the way other people thought spells worked, so she could see the deeper pitfalls and avoid them.

She liked to know as much as she possibly could on a subject before she set out to do something. With a little effort, under the weight of the books, by no means small tomes, she went to her desk, and got her favorite blue fine point pen and a white legal pad. Why anyone used yellow pads was beyond her; *yellow rips a friend from you.* She walked back to the kitchen so she could keep an eye on Pa as she worked.

Woolworth and Tangerine eyed her oddly when she came back in and cleared a space. But neither said a word to stop her. After a few moments, they left her alone at the kitchen table.

"My mother never slept through the night before we came here. Then she never smiled through the day. It is hard, so hard to love this land, these people, but I do. They're my people. It's my land, what I will give to my children. I know it is not what Sarah wanted, but I have to help them through this drought; they are part of my love." From the Journal of Mary Croger, 4th matron of the Women of Terra.

"Dill, cumin, fresh rosemary, lemon grass…"Allen read from the list walking into the kitchen, oblivious to Jemma's deep preoccupation. "Do you even know how to use any of this?"

"Tangerine and Woolworth are threatening to teach me to cook," Jemma said absently. She had a feeling they wouldn't have time. "They want to expand my palate."

"Well, good for them," Allen said haltingly.

He wanted to ask about the books, she could tell. He never much liked it when she dug into these books. He had argued with Gran about giving Jemma normal things to do and read. That was when Gran took her side. It was funny to Jemma; they hated the books the same amount, but for completely different reasons. When Allen gave her *Harry Potter*, it only sparked Jemma's curiosity more, and she took the books back out and dragged Gran over for questions. That was when she found Professor Alden's online course on curses and convinced her to let Jemma audit. The spells, the creatures, the very ideas in *Harry Potter* had intrigued her and reawakened her interest in how magic really worked.

"I'm taking your boyfriend with me into town," Allen said, to bait her.

"Oh?"

"He says he likes to pick his own paint."

"Sounds reasonable." One more thing that would come to nothing. Maybe she should tell Allen not to waste the money. But it would be easier to work with both of them gone.

"Seems fishy to me," Allen said, and chuckled at his own joke. He sounded annoyed when he spoke again. "If he's meant to save your life, shouldn't he be here?"

"He isn't tied to my side like a shadow. He can have a few hours away." Or the rest of his life, if what she had planned worked.

Jemma sighed, looking away from the books to the doorway. "He painted me a yellow brick road."

"Yeah." Allen smirked. "Have you told him yet how much you hate *The Wizard of Oz?*"

"I was thinking of reading it again," Jemma lied to annoy him. But the idea had merit. Some things deserved a second chance. "Where is everyone? Food's getting cold," Jemma bellowed in the direction of the door.

Allen shook his head and walked over to the table, taking a seat.

Hippa popped out from under Jemma's hair, startling her; she'd forgotten the pixie was still with her. Nona came flashing into the kitchen and nabbed a seat at the table.

"Tangerine and Woolworth already ate," she said breaking off a bit of biscuit and dunking it in the jam before her.

Hippa hovered over a biscuit tilting her hummingbird head from one side to the other; she seemed unconvinced it was in fact food. After a moment, she flitted away from the biscuit and dipped her beak into the jam all on its own.

Jemma smiled. She would miss Hippa, nearly silent but constantly comforting. Like in her dream…Jemma could just see the edges of it. Hippa had been there, and Mama, but…

"Wow, what's all that?"

Jemma looked up startled. Kai was standing in the doorway with a grin on his face, but he sparkled so much it was hard to see. He had never sparkled so much. He was beautiful, mesmerizing. Jemma knew her mouth was open but couldn't seem to shut it. He looked magical, and in her mind, she could hear a buzzing voice that seemed to promise he sparkled only for her.

Only you.

Only you? Where did she know that from? All of a sudden it struck her: *sirens*. Jemma's mouth closed and her eyes cut across Kai cruelly. He was sparkling alright, had gone to a lot of effort to make sure he did, but it wasn't for her. He wouldn't bother with that for her.

Jemma wasn't so sure she thought he looked good after all. He didn't look like himself any longer. With an offended snort, Jemma turned away, back to her research. She lifted a biscuit to her mouth.

"She's writing a spell," Allen said in a vague, confused voice.

Kai hesitated in the doorway a moment longer, then with his usual ease, he sauntered over to the seat opposite Jemma. He smiled her way, even went so far as to wink.

Jemma was steaming, exerting considerable effort to ignore him.

"Writing a spell, huh. I never knew it took so much…" He spread his hand over her books. "Study."

Jemma only glared, but then she caught sight of his wrist. He wore the purple shoelace tied around it. Curiosity overtook annoyance and she searched his head for the earring. Did he have to wear his trinkets to make them work? Had he been kidding about the bikini top, or did he actually wear it?

As if he could read her mind, Kai smiled all the broader and wiggled his eyebrows at her.

"Jemma likes to research before she casts a spell." Allen tried to turn the conversation his way. When Jemma and Kai only continued to stare at each other, he grew annoyed. "Am I missing something here? Why are you upset with him suddenly?"

"He's off to play siren," Jemma snapped.

She hadn't expected him to like her, or to want to play siren with her, but she particularly disliked the idea of him going into town and calling all of the women to him. It made her angry, made her want to lash out. It was moments like these Jemma had to work her hardest to restrain the magic. Because she could do something really awful like cast a spell to deform his face, make him the most hideous creature to ever walk the earth and just see how he liked the sort of attention he called then.

"Like singing-sailors-to-their-doom sirens? But…they're girls."
Kai laughed.

"You need to read one of the books I gave you. Just one." Jemma snapped at Allen, why was he being so annoying? "Grace Horace's book, for example. I gave it to you months ago. It's all about how so many evil magical creatures are depicted as women tempting men to their doom, all because men did the writing and liked to think of themselves as little victims of evil women and not just faithless assholes."

"Language, Jemma! Your gran would be furious."

"Good thing she isn't here then. Look, if you aren't going to read the book, can I have it back? I really liked that one."

"She actually wrote that men liked to see themselves as 'little victims of evil women and not just faithless assholes'?" Kai asked, amused.

"No," Jemma admitted with a shrug. "She just pointed out that the stories would have been very different if they were written by women and discussed what the male counterpoint would have been. I made that last part up myself."

"Esther was a bad influence on you," Allen sighed under his breath.

"How so?" Jemma demanded, pinning him to his seat with her glare. "You just said she'd be angry about my language."

"Language sure, content no."

"Are you kidding?" Jemma asked seriously. "Gran wouldn't like me calling men assholes. Maybe specific ones, but not the whole bunch. That would include Grandpa. She loved Grandpa." Jemma's voice fell away.

Oh, Jemima. She could just hear Gran's voice as she glared across the table at Allen. Could feel her hand running down her hair and her arm holding Jemma close, as she tried to convince her to go away to summer camp. *There's more to life than this place. I want life for you. Adventure. I want love for you, more than anything. I want you to find friends, and a man to love you so much that he makes you laugh a hundred times as much as he makes you cry. And makes you want to dance when there is no music, and even when you know it will hurt your leg. I want you to love someone so much that even this curse feels like a blessing. But you can't find any of that if you never let yourself leave—not just this house, but the weight of it all here, and go into the world for a time.*

Jemma felt a tear running down her face, and without a word, she stuffed the books under her arms and left the room.

To Their Doom

Kai watched Jemma go. Her tears were mostly sadness, but there was some embarrassment he was sure came from knowing he would feel the tears, and a weighty understanding he couldn't quite explain. He should go after her, explain why he was going out to tempt her townspeople. But he resisted; it was better she hate him but have friends when he left, than understand his reasons and stop him setting the record straight about her.

"So, siren, huh?"

Kai glanced sideways. He knew his own reasons for not chasing Jemma down, but what about Allen who professed to care for her?

"Not exactly," Kai said after a minute. "They're actually like… cousins, I guess. Them and mermaids. But she's right; there are male sirens and mermen. Water horses don't do the whole singing thing."

"And just what exactly do you do?"

"As a species?" Kai asked sarcastically. What did humans do as a species? "Well, the usual: breathe, eat, our young mostly, breed, we do a lot of that."

"Seriously," Allen interjected sharply. "What is it she thinks you are going to do?"

"Water horses sparkle, it's a visual, rather than auditory representation of the magnetic energy we project into the world, like sirens do with song."

"Magnetic energy? To what aim?"

"Depends on the kelpie. Mostly, we're social creatures, but we're sort of homebodies. We project the magnetism to bring new friends to us."

"So, it doesn't just work on the opposite sex?"

"No. Why would it? I'm gorgeous; all sorts of people want to be near me," Kai said and raised a brow at Allen. When he didn't respond, Kai shrugged. "It can work on just about anyone."

"Why don't I notice this incredible magnetism?"

"Hm." Kai leaned back thinking it over. He wasn't exactly trying to attract Allen, but then he wasn't trying to attract Jemma, was he? He'd liked the idea of seeing her reaction, but he wasn't trying to get her to like him. "I don't know. There are always some people it doesn't work on. And it works best at attracting likeminded individuals. Thrill-seekers find thrill-seekers; geeks, geeks. You get the idea."

"And just what exactly are you planning to do with this magnetism?"

Kai shrugged. "That all depends."

"Meaning?"

"Some sirens sing people to their doom. Usually bad people, and not exactly saintly sirens either. But there are others who sing people to their fate, to friends they would never have met otherwise or to incredible adventures. Let's just say what I do in town depends entirely on the responses I get to a few, very pointed questions."

He could tell Allen didn't like the sound of that. But Kai didn't much care. If Allen refused to drive him, he would walk. The townspeople would either find their way around to liking Jemma or they could face the consequences.

Allen left to get his wallet and keys, leaving Kai alone and thoughtful. Was Jemma jealous? Was that why she got angry? It was a funny notion, but it also made Kai a little nervous. He needed to be careful with how much he impressed her.

Mom always said Kai made a habit of sparkling like a beacon when he set out to impress someone, and if he didn't have a care, he'd attract the wrong person. He'd taken that to mean he might attract creeps or something. But maybe she just meant he should care about people's feelings.

He should certainly be careful with Jemma's.

He wasn't sure about leaving like this. What if Black Boot sensed an advantage and tried to attack Jemma? Not that it was his presence here that kept Black Boot out; that was all Jemma's shield. Nevertheless, he would feel better if he was with her, but—

Almost as badly as she needed protection, she needed a friend. Something bad was coming, and he doubted very much he would be around long after it. She needed someone to be here when her life settled.

"I never wanted the love of these people, as Sarah does, but I have wanted Papa's love. I have longed for it, but no more. He did not return when Daniel died, nor Mama. He has no love for us, so I will love him no longer." From the journals of Sotsona, sacrifice of the Women of Terra.

Jemma went to her own room. She needed her head clear, and in May Bell's room, some of her thoughts always strayed to her mother. And she wasn't needed there anymore.

"You didn't put anything fun on the list." Allen entered not even bothering to knock on the door. "Do you want some ice cream or Cheez-Its?"

"Why are you acting like this all of a sudden?" Jemma said morosely, her back to him. "Gran dies and suddenly you want to play step-dad. You aren't my father; I have one. I'm workin' on a spell to banish him."

"I'm not trying to be your father, Jemma, but you need someone to look after you."

"No, I don't. I got by just fine the last three months. Me and May Bell."

"You did better than most fourteen-year-olds; you survived. But you didn't do fine, Jemma. The farm is a mess. You were here all alone, dropping further and further into depression, and that's understandable, but it's not fine. Jemma, you need someone else."

"I liked you as my friend. But you aren't that any more, are you?"

"Jemma…"

"She knew, didn't she?" Jemma interrupted, hoarse with anger and pain. "And so did you."

"What?"

Jemma looked up at him. She knew her eyes were still red from the tears that carried her from the kitchen. And she let him see it. He was a part of this.

"She made a will that you knew about. And she kept on pushing me to go away this summer. Talking to me about colleges and marriage, and all the things she wanted for me. She was trying to get me away so he couldn't hurt me, wasn't she?"

Allen didn't say anything. And that was answer enough.

"What would she have done with May Bell?"

Allen rubbed the back of his neck, walking over to the desk. "Jemma."

"What would she have done with May Bell?" Jemma repeated tightly.

"There's a home in Tulsa that she liked."

"Whose?"

"What?"

"Whose home?"

"It's called Ferndale."

"So, not a home, then; a hospital."

"A permanent care facility. Jemma—"

"Is that what's in Gran's will?" Jemma interrupted demanding the truth.

Allen shook his head. "She didn't specify. But it is what she wanted us to do."

"What do you mean us? You're not family."

"She named me your guardian."

Jemma nodded and turned around. She couldn't look at him, she felt so betrayed. So enraged. He kept this from her. Gran kept this from her. They left her out of her own life. And now she was all alone.

"Did she give you Mother's Farm too, and Dust House?"

"It would be a good idea if we made a date to go to town together and hear the will. You'd understand better I think."

"I understand fine. The man who put my mother in a coma and then abandoned us for eight years is back to decide our fates. You are my guardian. A fact that Pa could easily challenge and maybe even win. You and Gran thought it would be good to hide the fact that she was dying from me. And you thought the middle of this would be a great time to go away for the weekend with your needy girlfriend and leave a sarcastic message on your phone. You came back, no longer my friend but my parent. And we're a *we* now—because you said so. Did I miss anything?"

"You forgot the part where I love you."

"No," Jemma replied coldly. "I just don't believe it."

"Well, I do." Allen bent down to kiss Jemma on the head in fatherly fashion.

Jemma sat stiffly and waited for him to move away. Waited for him to leave. They'd never been very demonstrative before. He was trying too hard. Trying to be what he thought a guardian should be, trying to be a father. Jemma didn't need one.

"Did she leave you the land?" Jemma repeated. "Or was she going to let him just take it?"

"The lands yours, Jemma. She'd planned...to get you away so you'd have more time. He can't claim the land without—" He fumbled around for the words.

"Without the matron," Jemma said flatly. "Unless of course the land is abandoned." Jemma scoffed, focusing on her spell.

"I do love you," Allen said, waiting. When she didn't respond, he left the room. Jemma listened for the sound of the screen door. When she heard it, she nodded at Hippa who sped outside to make sure Pa didn't see Allen and Kai leaving. If he wasn't in a place to spot them, she was to do nothing, but if Pa was near, she was to blind him and come rushing back.

Jemma was taking care of everyone. With a little help when she needed it, but not much. She and May Bell had been *just fine* without Allen, without Pa, without Gran. She didn't need a parent. The more Jemma thought about it, the more merit the idea seemed to have. She should get emancipated; she was only a few months away from getting her GED. That had to count for something. She would need to find a viable job, maybe something online. She was a decent writer; maybe she could be a correspondent for a news site or a magazine.

Hippa flew back into the room and flashed into a thumbs-up sign. Jemma smiled. There were signs everywhere, if she was only looking in the right places.

Holy Ground

*B*lack Boot was halfway through digging up the field with his whirlwinds when he remembered an excellent burial place for the stones. It was a little stretch of field about a half mile from the house that was never planted on. Right beside the old lake that dried up from Sarah's curse.

There was an old grizzled tree there; it hadn't sprouted a leaf in all the time Black Boot had known of it, but it wasn't dead. Every year, it twisted around more, raised higher—a great wizened hand stretching up to the sky. The tree was once surrounded by a low wall. It was there the women of the town cornered Sotsona and stoned her.

Every year on the anniversary of her death, the matriarch of the family would lead the other members in a special memorial service. She would walk to the wall at midnight and place a stone along it—a symbol that the family owed another year of prosperity to the generosity of this, their first sister to die for the family.

When Jemma was born on that anniversary May was beside herself with excitement. She called her mother and swore she could feel the service taking place during her delivery. She said Sotsona was with her, and that it was a sign the curse was breaking. He hadn't minded then, he was too happy. Even when May dragged him back here so Jemma could be part of the ceremony on her first birthday he'd been happy for his daughter to be connected to her heritage. But it wasn't for Jemma. It was all about that ceremony, and it hadn't even changed the curse. He minded now.

Black Boot hated the ceremony. That family dwelled too much on their dead. It seemed as though their living members were less important. Black Boot hated morbidity as a rule. Hated funerals, the process of lowering a casket into the ground and covering it up, as if to say the person never existed. Hated the finality of it.

When this land was his, he would wipe away the wall with a great slash of wind. Rip out the grizzled old tree. He would build a stable here and a pin to exercise horses. He would make it a place of life and activity.

He could just live once he owned the wind, the land—the power. No one would question him, no one would have the power to take from him ever again.

But he had to find the stones, and they weren't here.

Black Boot stood staring into the ground before him; he dug so there were more holes than there were spaces between them, but there was no stone here. It seemed Jemma wasn't much like the rest of her family. It would be the perfect place for Esther, holy ground, as far as she was concerned. But it wasn't here.

What did Jemma consider holy ground?

All around him the earth began to shake and shift, knocking Black Boot back towards the lake. Towards one of the gaping holes in the ground. He felt a hand reach out of the ground and grip onto his coat, yanking down.

He saw himself falling again, swallowed up by the earth and the marker in May Bell's hand. His breath caught in his throat and he set his shoulders forward, against the tilting ground. He took a step to his left, to steady himself, onto a little mound of earth between holes. As soon as he stepped, the hand fell away, the earth stilled. Satisfied.

Then he saw it, his left boot, all but drowning in dirt. He lifted it free and shook with all his might, but the dirt refused to fall away, caking over it so it looked less like a boot and more like a lump of unformed earth.

"Ahhhhhh!" he bellowed towards the sky. Wind swept across the ground shoving the dirt back where it belonged. But it was too late for his boot; the earth was clinging to it. Calling it back.

"You can't have them!" He shouted in the direction of the tree, advancing on it as the wind did his bidding, filling the holes before his feet. It was her hand, Sotsona, the first sacrifice of the family Terra. She was reaching out from beyond the grave to strike down any who threatened her legacy. "You can't have the boots, you can't have the land, or my daughter. And you can't have me."

"Dearest Jemma,"

The Journals of Esther Lynn Franklin, 6th matron of the Women of Terra.

Jemma had several books spread out around the room, even Pa's journal of spells. She'd searched it until she found what must be his plan: a transfer of power. It read oddly like a deed, but for the bleeding into the ground and the magic he would steal from his daughter.

The spell required that Jemma forsake her place as matron and bleed into the ground, giving it over to the Traveler line, as he bled over the same spot. Then came the worst part: he would burn the remains of all the dead matrons, Gran's remains, Sisika's, Great Gran's, every one of them, burnt and folded into the soil, with the boots. The basin, where the lake used to be, would be refilled, ending the curse, and by burying the boots with the remains of Jemma's family, he would simultaneously end Sisika's line and tie the wind to Mother's Farm. Of course, he'd probably change the name.

How he thought he could convince Jemma to do this, she wasn't sure. Maybe he thought, because she'd let the farm fall into disuse for one season, she would be open to giving over the land. Maybe she would have been, yesterday.

But he wanted to *burn Gran* and use Nona to do it, because her fire was pure and would purify the action. He would burn away Jemma's heritage, use the creatures he'd captured, her friends, to bring his plans to fruition. Nona for the fire and Kai to flood the basin. He'd use Tangerine to raise a new crop before the season was out. He'd be like a king, with the kind of power he meant to wield.

Jemma supposed she was meant to be comforted that he would use Hippa to heal her leg. Complemented even, that when planning world domination, he'd paused to consider his daughter. He even meant to use Woolworth to change her memories, but to what? Would she think

214

he had never left? Would she think the land had been his always? That Gran had never existed? Would she be anything that was her?

He called her a heathen, but he meant to do things more disgusting than any spell Jemma's family had ever laid.

Once it was done, she imagined he could read the other spells. He wouldn't be a guardian anymore, or just a man as he'd been born. He'd be a witch. He had spells enough to make him quite a powerful one. She thought of the flash of purple she'd seen when he first arrived, and the little bits that danced in front of her eyes as she read his book of spells—perilous power indeed.

All thoughts of just letting him have what he wanted went away. This wasn't only about her. He had plans for the whole world. As much as it made her determined to fight him, to stop him, it also made her feel small and frightened. So she sought the only comfort she knew: Gran's.

Her journals. She didn't write like the others. They mostly wrote as events were going on, but Gran's journals were a retrospective, written in the form of letters, to Jemma.

I know you never did much like real stories, Jem Beam. Find them depressing, I think. Which is why there's no accounting for your taste in literature: Bridge to Terribithia, Jacob Have I Loved. *Really girl can't, you read just one thing with a happy middle? Well, maybe there are none. Not in books, least ways. But my middle was happy.*

My middle was where I found myself, found my joy, and found your grandpa. My middle was where I had your mother. And where I first dreamed of you. Not like your dreams, of the real future, but wishes. I wished for you.

There were little notes like that scattered throughout. One line she'd be writing about the girls at school throwing dirt clods at her and shouting, "Drown her. Drown her," as they chased her home; then suddenly, she'd be giving Jemma another little piece of advice.

I think all journals should be written years later, Jem, when a body's had a chance to look back and see the good and the stupid and the ugly rolling around together in the mud getting equal parts dirty. I hated those girls, went out of my way to let them know it. And I felt the victim of their prejudice. I was, don't get me wrong, but then I went home. I never once had to worry about a roof over my head or food in my stomach. I never once had to wonder if I was loved. I had a family, a history like none of those girls would ever know. They had fear of me, so they struck out; they had jealousy, so they sought to destroy. But I who had so

much, I showed them up least once a day in school or mocked their clothes. I could have drawn them into our family, made them blessed with me, but I wouldn't.

I won't say they had a right; they didn't. But I was far from perfect.

Jemma much preferred reading the little bits like that to the actual stories. When Gran was alive and saying things like that to her, Jemma would have rolled her eyes or made faces. She should be like that now, but…it was exactly like hearing her voice again. And Jemma wanted that.

But just at the moment, she was focused on other parts of Gran's journal. The part where she cursed Pa. She didn't write down the exact words; she probably didn't remember them. Although how one could forget the words of a curse they'd lain was a bit hard for Jemma to understand.

I told him the boots couldn't set foot in Oklahoma. Told him our earth would swallow him whole if he did. I'm so sorry, Jem, I know you wanted him here, I knew it then, heard it in your cries, but…

Jemma, your mother left for college such a vibrant, strong, faithful child. She believed in the land and her place on it, and she only went into the world to help make it better. I was so proud of her, of the job Sy and I had done. I thought, here was a girl who didn't need to see the world to find herself, here was a girl better than her mother, and all her ancestors combined.

Then she came home, with him on her arm. Even though I saw so much less of who she'd been, I thought it was her who brought him here. But she followed him, everywhere and anywhere. When the wind picked up to leave that summer, so did she, but not back to school as she should have; she followed him. She gave herself over to a belief in him as she had once given herself over to the land. It was only then that I realized she hadn't left home so much sure of herself. She'd left sure of her pa and me, of the lessons we'd taught her and her place here. Soul and all, she loved this place. But she didn't know herself. She knew belief, and it was easily transferred from the land to the man who stole her heart.

Your Pa isn't a terrible man, and though I called him a curse on this family, he wasn't wholly to blame. Not as I was; I knew better. But I watched my daughter vanish into his shadow and wilt for lack of light. It wasn't until you came that she got some of herself back. The day you were born, she felt your place, felt the land calling to you, and saw in you all the strength she lacked. She came back here for you, after a time. And he followed her at first, but the wind, the thrill of nomadic life, it called to him and he was torn in two. It made the monster I cursed, his inability to choose, his divided heart.

I couldn't let him stay, my Jemma. He would have crushed you under your love for him. He would have torn you apart. I know you cannot forgive me, but I did what I did for the love of you. And I would do it again, in a heartbeat. I only wish I had done it after the first time I saw my daughter ripped from the ground by his temper.

Jemma wanted to be angry with Gran. Why couldn't she be more specific? She didn't need apologies, she needed information. But she kept going back and reading the words again and again.

Was May Bell weak? That had never been the impression Gran's stories left. But reading them now, Jemma had to wonder. She only really remembered the one cyclone, she knew there had been several that summer, but she didn't think any of the others had touched their home, their family. Was she wrong? What if she wasn't remembering? What did it change really?

Everything.

I watched my daughter vanish into his shadow and wilt for lack of light.

Jemma remembered her mother as a strong woman, firm and bright and happy. They had been happy, hadn't they?

Sparkling

Kai didn't look left or right as he walked through the general store. *General store*—jeez, this place was so backwoods, it was unreal. It took more effort than it should to sparkle as he walked, but he knew it was working. He could feel the eyes on him, hear the footsteps of those so enthralled they would follow him.

There was only one row of paints, and none of the colors were the ones Jemma had; they must have gone to a real store. The sort of place that wasn't basically a Walmart without the cheap pricing and decent overhead lighting. The sort of place that didn't sell horse feed and human feed within feet of each other, or have a home improvement aisle right next to a clothing aisle.

Kai rather doubted Allen, and Tangerine would have much luck with their list either. When they were about a mile from the house, Tangerine had poked her head out of Allen's pocket; he'd swerved so wildly—if they weren't in the middle of nowhere, there would have been an accident. She insisted on coming along to choose her own ingredients but promised to stay out of sight. Kai doubted she was happy to be here. This wasn't the sort of place to stock wheatgrass, kale, or quinoa.

It wasn't just the seven shades of white paint and only three of blue that were depressing Kai. He couldn't shake the feeling he shouldn't have left Jemma. He didn't think she was in danger, at least not a physical kind. But she was so upset by the sparkling. He didn't get it. Why should it bother her? Ambrosia never got upset when he sparkled, and she'd been his girlfriend off and on for most of their junior year. Why should a little girl he absolutely was not dating, get so angry when he went out to charm people?

"Um, excuse me." It was a shy voice, young too. She was one of the first to start following him, and apparently the first to grow bold enough to speak.

That was part of the trick. You never look at your targets, never give them a sign you know they exist. It has to feel entirely their own idea when they succumb to your spell. Kai didn't move, couldn't. If he turned right now, his face would show his sudden distaste with the whole thing.

"Have a care, Kai," Mom said smacking him in the back of his head. It was Poesy's birthday, and Kai was forced to be at the party with all her friends. He had no idea why; they were going to celebrate as a family later anyway. He'd much prefer to be in his studio painting. But here he was, not bothering anyone and Mom slapped him.

"What did I do?"

She leaned in and her eyes were burning daggers as only she could. "You're already attractive and older, you don't need to sparkle to make your sister vanish, and you look like the New Year ball. Quit it!"

It was nice having everyone look at you like you were something special. He loved the feeling, needed it some days. If he knew all eyes were on him, could feel them, then he was never surprised by them. But…

"Can…can I help you with anything?" the girl behind Kai stuttered.

Kai pasted a smile on his face and faced her. She was probably a few years older than Jemma. She had sharp features and large deep brown eyes; her long black hair was pulled into a tight little ponytail and she wore a white button-up that set her apart as store staff. There was a group of four behind her, staring, completely unabashed.

What would it be like for them later, to wake up and realize they'd trailed a seventeen-year-old stranger around a store gawking? And he wasn't even famous. Would it bother them? Would they feel their wills had been stolen? Their souls? Was that where the legends came from? How was it he had never noticed the sordid nature of it all before?

"Sir?"

"Oh." Kai shook his head, smiling. "Sorry, I was lost in thought. What'd you say?"

"Can I help you find anything?"

"Well," Kai sighed, turning back towards the paint selection with a frown, ignoring for the moment the rest of his admirers. "I'm painting a mural at this house outside of town, but there isn't a lot of selection here, is there?"

"Oh…are you an artist?" The girl said stepping between Kai and the paints, she kept her back to him, straightening the cans, but kept throwing looks over her shoulder.

"Yep."

"Wow. Would I have seen any of your work?"

"Oh, not yet. But I'll tell you what, if you help me find some brighter paint, I'll let you be the first to see the house when it's finished."

"Really? Ummm. Well," she leaned in towards Kai, imparting a secret. "If you're wanting to stay in town, the best place would be Link Groover's Hardware Store on Deertail Road."

"Link Groover's Hardware Store." Kai nodded. He was going to punch Allen; he'd implied this was the best he could do.

"Yeah, I could make you a map."

"I'll show him," a woman behind them offered, stepping forward. Kai shifted his attention her way. She was around Allen's age, mid-thirties, and she looked distinctly like the sort of person who would be a lifelong waitress. "It's the oddest thing," she said tilting her head from side to side. "You seem to sparkle?"

"Ohhh!" The young girl next to Kai practically shouted, jumping. "Wait right here. I'll be right back." She ran off in the opposite direction. A few feet from him she stopped and threw a look his way. "You won't go, will you?"

"Of course not," Kai assured her, watching her run away like a lunatic.

"That's Fern, we call her Owly. She has this tendency to look at everything wide-eyed. She's either the dimmest girl in town or the most easily impressed."

The woman in front of Kai was already trying to turn him off to the competition. This was sordid. Did he really want to get Jemma a friend this way? Certainly not that woman.

"Whose house are you painting?" another of his admirers called, a man this time. A bit old for Jemma, somewhere in his twenties, Kai would guess, and he didn't look like a man with any goals for the future. He wouldn't do either.

"Jemma…Traveler, or…"

"Franklin," a woman corrected from off to his right.

"Dust House," a pretty brunette, at the back of his gathering, said in tingly whisper.

"Clarissa," the woman to Kai's right, the newcomer who knew Jemma's name, spoke up in a mothering tone. She was shaking her head back and forth when Kai looked over. "Who are you?" she asked Kai, looking intrigued, but not nearly as enthralled as the rest of his crowd.

She looked to be in her late thirties maybe early forties, and the food in her cart, like the tone of her voice, marked her as a mother. She raised an eyebrow as Kai studied her.

"Kai Shoal. I'm a friend of Jemma's."

"Ha. A captive more likely. She's a witch, you know," Clarissa called out, distracting Kai momentarily.

"Shouldn't you be at community service, Clarissa?" the mother inquired, none too politely. "Those seniors aren't going to clean their own bed pans."

Kai laughed. This was probably the Clarissa from Jemma's story. He was pleased to see she wasn't quite as loved as Jemma might think. Kai focused on the girl for a moment, driving her off. It was another trick of the kelpie, the sparkling that attracted admirers could turn harsh and repulse. *Usually.*

The girl humphed and flounced away, and Kai felt a little better. This may be sordid, but it had its uses.

"Esther's letting you stay in the house?" the mother asked skeptically, looking Kai up and down. "With Jemma?"

"I found it!" Fern came rushing over, saving Kai from answering. "It was in the back. We sold most of them ages ago, but we had three left." She was waving a tee-shirt around and her eyes were indeed so wide he could understand the nickname. "They're all smalls, I'm not sure it will fit you. Not that you're too big or anything. You're a really nice –"

"Fern!" the mother shouted, and Kai nearly laughed. He guessed she wasn't just anyone's mother. "Don't you dare finish that sentence. Come here now."

"Mom! But…I just want to…"

Kai decided to save her. "So, you know Jemma?" Kai said to the mother. "Who are you, if you don't mind my asking?"

She shook her head, rolling her eyes at Kai. "I'm Doe Little."

Kai bit his cheek to keep from grinning. But the woman did it for him.

"I know. I nearly refused to marry my husband, even he makes the jokes. So, why is Esther letting you around her little girl? She hides her away like a treasure. And just what exactly are you looking for here?"

Kai smiled, looking at the pair of them, mother and daughter. They would do just fine.

"I'll tell you, if you'll tell me what the whole 'Dust House' thing is about."

Torture

Black Boot tore up every piece of ground he could think of. Where had she buried the stones? They weren't anywhere near the barn. Or the wheat fields where Jemma used to play hide-and-seek. They weren't at the little creek where she pretended to fish with him, splashing her toes in the water more than anything else. They weren't anywhere near the five apple trees the family called an orchard.

It made no sense. They had to be somewhere.

"I only need to find one to break the circle. Why can't I find them?"

"If they were easy to find, the spell would never work," May Bell said in a low angry voice. She had been pouting all day, staring off into the distance and muttering little insults.

He didn't know what was wrong with her, but he didn't like it. It felt like the first days. As her silent spirit trailed him in the wind, pulled away from her precious land. She would glare at him, but never speak, smile when he was hurt, or sway in front of him until his mind was full of her and only her, then vanish, to torture him.

"I wish I'd never brought you here," she whispered.

"You and me both," Black Boot muttered. But he meant it. He hated this land as much as he needed it. Hated who it made him, what it made him: Black Boot. Not a person, a thing. Now being that *thing* bound him as much as it freed him. "I was better off before I knew you."

He didn't look at her, but she was so much a part of him now that he felt the words pierce her. Felt them pierce his own heart and harden hers. The boots grew heavy, slowing his steps, dragging him inch by inch into the ground.

"*You* were better off?" she snarled. "Which one of us is *dead* because of your temper? Whose mother is dead from banishing you? Whose child is destroyed because of you?"

"Mine! Jemma is my child. You're dead, remember? She only belongs to one of us now."

The ground rolled, her eyes flashed and as she walked towards him, Black Boot wished, just this once, he could touch her. Wrap his hands around her arms and pull her to him.

It was torture, this existence—never without her, but never with her. They always fought before, but then…they could touch, and it had nearly made the fighting beautiful. There was only ugliness now.

When she was just before him, when he could see the burning in her eyes for what it was—anguish, and rage, the same as his—Black Boot dropped his head. It fell forward and hung just a breath away from hers. So close it nearly shredded his soul.

"Oh, May. I don't know how much more I can take. She isn't mine. You aren't. What did I do to us?"

The earth stilled, and the flash of May Bell's eyes receded into a pale glow. On a shuddering sigh, she let her tears free and reached out for her husband, knowing she could never touch him.

"Tom can't stay much longer, but Jemma can't be gone more than a month without the nightmares, even with the jar of earth. Mama says there's no way to keep him. Plenty of couples are separated part of the year, but he'd be gone so much more than he's here. Pa says Tom must choose, us or the wind, but he can't, and we love each other too much to be separated. This land can do anything, it must have a way to help us."

From the journals of May Bell Franklin-Traveler, 7th generation daughter of Terra.

Jemma had seven spells on the kitchen table. She left her room a while ago, realizing she liked the noise the house was filled with lately. She forced Nona and Woolworth into the same room simply for the fighting it brought.

It had cleared her head; the spells just came.

One each for her friends to send them home. And one to banish Pa for good. There was even one for Allen and the town. Why bother being emancipated by legal means, when you could just hex people into thinking you were eighteen?

She had it all. Everything she needed. But Jemma hesitated. A stronger person would just work the spell for Pa—using her magic to cast the boots apart, tying his power into one of the magic jars, thus barring him from gaining other magical powers, and then banishing him from Mother's Farm, never to enter her sight again. But Jemma couldn't bring herself to do it. She wanted to say goodbye. She wanted to ask him what Gran meant, about May Bell disappearing in his shadow.

She wanted…to keep him.

Gran was right, Jemma wanted to keep him, to have him here with her.

Woolworth and Nona were making such a loud fuss over nothing at all that Jemma rather wondered if they did it for effect. To help her. And Hippa was just fluttering by Jemma's face, rubbing her warm little hummingbird head against Jemma's cheek over and over again. It was similar to Gran's hand soothing back her hair. The feeling just sunk into Jemma, and she wanted not to feel another thing.

"It will be so quiet when you're gone," Jemma whispered.

Hippa never spoke loud enough for Jemma to hear, but she meant her as well. This home would be like before: a tomb, with Jemma and May Bell locked inside, waiting to die.

Hippa fluttered away so fast Jemma almost cried at the loss of her, but she fluttered back moments later and something bronze went falling through the air.

Jemma caught the watch just in time. She still hadn't opened it. Hadn't looked.

The room had fallen silent. Jemma looked up and found Nona and Woolworth on the table before her, just nodding. Jemma pressed the little knob on the top of the watch, and two doors sprung open on either side.

Slowly, reverently, Jemma pulled back the first door. It was the picture of her and Mama. Mama looked tired. There were a few hairs plastered to her face, soaked with sweat it seemed, and she was slumped against the pillow, but her smile was so large, the rest of it seemed unimportant. She was staring down at the baby in her arms, chubby, with eyes so puffy they almost looked closed, but for a little sliver of white, and there were exactly two curling red hairs on her head. It was perfect.

Jemma sighed and turned the watch over. The other picture: her grandparents and her father standing together next to a sold sign with a large house behind them. They were tall people. No surprise there, Pa was a tall man. And they all three looked so happy. Her grandfather had an arm slung around both his wife and son, and they were all grinning. Pa looked so young, her age he'd said. He was thin, like a pole, and geeky, with his braces and lopsided smile. You would never know they were only months away from being murdered in their sleep with a house fire. A fire everyone thought Pa started.

The parallels in their lives didn't escape Jemma. She found herself wondering what she had never wondered before. She knew the story, knew he was suspected, but never once, even after the cyclone, had Jemma believed he was capable of killing his parents. But now, after he'd kidnapped these wonderful beings and come here with a spell to steal Jemma's magic and her heritage. Now she couldn't help but wonder.

They looked so happy. Like the picture of Mama, Gran, and Jemma, before the storm. Had they been happy?

Jemma shoved away from the table, absently following her yellow brick road to her mother's door. She hesitated there a moment, her eyes locked on the family in the picture. With a snap, she shut both sides of the watch and stormed into the room.

"Nothing makes sense anymore." She walked to her mother as though this, her anger, could wake her mother where her love never had. "Were we happy? Were we ever happy? Were you happy before me? Before I brought you back here?"

Nothing happened. Jemma began pacing. She slammed her feet on the ground as she walked, comforted by the returning pain. Pain made sense. It shot up her leg, reverberating like striking metal. At last something familiar, something certain.

"Gran wanted me to go away, to give in. All this time, I thought she was pushing me to be ready to fight him, because she thought I'd break the curse. But she was doing it because I wouldn't leave. Because she didn't want me to end up like you." Jemma spat the words at her eternally silent mother.

"I shouldn't be angry at you. You can't help it, but dammit! Wake up! We are Terra! We've been walked on for centuries, picked up and shoved aside, ground up and plowed over, but we don't give up! I need you." Jemma let out a startled sob and collapsed on the bed beside her mother.

"When we would fight, Gran and me. When I got angry and she watched me, said 'You gotta control that temper, Jem. Don't want to end up like your father.' I would hate her so much. I would think, maybe I do want to be like him. At least he got away. But…I couldn't say it. I couldn't say anything. It was like I was you, trapped, just not in my body. I was trapped because she was the only one who loved me. Loved me enough to stay when I was hateful, or dangerous, when I lost my temper, or refused to work in the fields. She kept loving me anyways, and if I left, I wouldn't have that anymore."

Jemma rubbed her thumb over the back of the watch. It was smooth and warm from being against her skin.

"She told me stories about you. About how amazing you were, strong and proud; told 'em to make me feel guilty, so I'd want to be like you. You were Santa Claus or God. A fantasy she pulled out to keep me in line or reward me. But Pa's real. She's gone, Allen's not my friend anymore, and you're just as imaginary as ever. But he's here. And he smiled like he wanted to know me, like he could love me. I'm trying to send him away because that's what everyone else thinks is right." Jemma dropped the watch on the bed and stood, pacing again. "So what if he is bad. I can stop him when he loses control. And even if he's mostly here for the earth, I don't care. I never wanted it; I just want someone to stay," she whispered, staring at her mother for the longest time, as the words faded from the room. She sighed, "And it makes me just as selfish as the rest of you. You wanted him, he wanted power, and Gran wanted you happy. She knew it was wrong to make the boots, it says so in her journals. She said she knew, and she said she told you. But you didn't care. And she always gave you what you wanted."

Jemma scoffed, oblivious to the tears running down her face. Her leg ached, pulsing, like a flashing reminder. May Bell lay, just like always. Her hair was getting long; it needed a trim before it was difficult to brush. Jemma glanced at the saline bag. Allen must have changed it before he left, it was almost full.

"They were going to put you in one of those places. Didn't even ask me. Why am I the only one who doesn't get to have what they want?" Shaking her head, Jemma walked out of the room, shutting the door gently behind her.

She needed to send her friends safely home, put May Bell in the cellar, shut the storm door, and say goodbye to Pa. There was a storm coming. And this one was all Jemma's making.

Family Secrets

*T*here was a much better selection at the hardware store, and by the time Kai had his paint, he had all kinds of information about Jemma. It seemed she'd been holding out on him. There were at least three magical incidents described by the locals that Jemma had failed to mention. The one with the flying root vegetable bullets was his favorite.

She said she wasn't naturally magical, but if even one of the stories were true, she absolutely was. If she got mad or scared, or if someone was in danger, the magic came out; that made it instinctual. So it had to be in her. The question was, why didn't she believe that?

He had collected a different sort of crowd at the hardware store: older people, intent on story telling. The Little family, who were apparently relatives of the boy Jemma rescued from Clarissa's driving test, had been invited over for tomorrow. Now all Kai needed was a few more likely friend candidates, so Jemma could have her pick. He rather thought she'd like Fern. He already liked her, and he loved the tee-shirt. He was going to give it to Jemma and watch her expression.

"Can't see Esther paying to have that house painted. Calls herself a minimalist now." Mrs. Berttie, was an older woman, apparently a good friend of Jemma's grandmother. It bothered Kai, not telling these people the woman was dead, but it really wasn't his place. Jemma must have her reasons for keeping them in the dark. "Course, if you ask me, she's still just too angry about everything they lost in the tornado. Doesn't want to bring in more she can lose."

The woman was probably right. Kai had now been in every room in "Dust House." It was a rather apt name, and the only ones with any color or signs of life were Jemma's and her mother's. Jemma's room wasn't what he'd call pretty, but it had a certain Jemma flair: books everywhere, a laptop she'd apparently been hiding from him, and a wall completely covered with a tacked up breakdown of magical creatures. She was trying to sort them into kingdom, phylum, class, genus, species (was that how it went?), like she was a biologist.

Kai wouldn't have painted her room, even if he thought he had the time. Well, maybe her ceiling. Something soft and girly, like a bunch of fairies waving tulips. She needed softening.

"How'd you say she found out about you?"

"I didn't," Kai said and put extra effort into sparkling. In his experience, people forgot to wonder about him if he sparkled enough. They didn't really believe he was real, so what was there to worry about?

"You think you're a sly one, don't you?" she asked with a grin. "Alright then, give me a hint. What's that house going to look like?"

"Well, I have this plan for the living room, where storybook characters or places are on all of the different walls."

"Gonna put in Jemima Puddle Duck?" The woman laughed with a sort of evil expression, but at once joyful. "It's Jemma's namesake."

"You're kidding?"

"She's not," Allen said, walking up behind Kai with a woman at his side whom Kai recognized from the general store, the one who'd tried to make him dislike Fern. In Allen's breast pocket Tangerine's little head was poking out and glaring at Allen's companion. "I wouldn't suggest painting that duck. Jemma hates the story."

"Now, of course. She's a teenager, they're all contrary," Mrs. Berttie threw out. "But when she was little, she dragged the stuffed duck everywhere. You didn't know her then."

"What was she like?" Kai leaned in towards the woman, older than his grandmother, and stared up at her as if enraptured.

She chuckled. "Boy you'd best not be looking at Jemma that way. Esther will kill you."

Kai only flashed her a broad grin. Behind him, Kai noticed Allen stiffen as if he would say something, but he didn't speak up. Curious.

"Well, she was a sweet thing, little Jemma, such a peacemaker with her parents. Everyone waited for the day she would do it."

"What?"

"No one's told you about the curse?"

"Jemma did. But she didn't say she was supposed to do anything. Just that her hair is some big reminder of it."

"Ha!" She smiled broadly and leaned in close to Kai, speaking with a voice full of mystery and dark glee. "It's not just the hair. She was born on the memorial of Ruth's death. One hundred and thirty-five years to the day."

"Damn," Kai whispered. He didn't know much about witches, but symmetry like that tended to lend one to a significant role.

"Her next birthday will make it a nice round one hundred and fifty years since Ruth died and the curse was laid. As far as I've pieced together Sarah never made specific reference to that year, but some of the locals have it in their heads that Jemma's fifteenth birthday would be when…" Mrs. Berttie shrugged, seeking the right words.

Kai was riveted. He'd known magic all his life, but this was different. Magic was part of Kai's life. But it consumed Jemma's. She would never be allowed to just be her own person, would she?

"Well, when *justice* gets *met out*, as the curse says. It didn't hurt Jemma's myth any that she'd already found Gil and Julia's only direct descendant." Mrs. Berttie waved over at Allen. "And all but dragged him back to town with her. Everyone used to think she would break the curse. But at this point, what with her father coming home so close to the anniversary and the little troubles she's had with locals the last few years, it seems more likely that she'll curse us worse, and get Sarah's revenge."

"Jemma doesn't curse people," Kai snapped. But his attention was all on Allen, who still wasn't speaking. "Does she know who you are?"

"Of course," Mrs. Berttie said, even as Allen was shaking his head.

"Esther knew. But…we never told Jemma."

"No." Kai shook his head. So that was why he wanted in the house. It was all a part of the curse. "No, I just bet you didn't."

"The boys have off and gone. They get no dreams of blood. But my daughter has the affliction. How many more? Will she never be satisfied?"

From the journals of Josephine Ness, 3ʳᵈ matron of the Women of Terra.

Jemma moved May and all her machines into the cellar with the help of her guests. She also moved a few essentials down with her: the family tomes, the rest of May's medical supplies, and Jemma's camera. She, Woolworth, Nona and Hippa sat together for a picture, and she took one with each of them individually. She would have liked to get one of Kai and Tangerine as well, but to be on the safe side, everything went into the cellar and the storm door was shut.

If the house was destroyed, the cellar would be safe, Mama would be safe. And even if Jemma herself did not survive, someone was bound to find May Bell and care for her.

She could barely breathe as she walked out of the cellar, leaving her mother alone with nothing but the bones of her ancestors to protect her. Her steps felt weighted; something was fighting to pull her back. Back to the soft earth, to the crypt, back to the voices. She could hear them all today, their voices, their cries. But she couldn't make out their words, only their sadness and fear. Only their anger.

And all of them calling to her.

When the heavy storm door at last shuddered the boards, falling into place, and Hippa had used her magic to seal it from within and rejoin them in the main house, Jemma could breathe again.

"Are you alright? Jemma?" Nona hovered before her face, but Jemma barely noticed her. Her head was swimming.

The winds had picked up a while ago, and the sky was darkened with clouds. Out the window, Jemma watched as two of the small whirlwinds fused and tore off in the direction of the old lake.

There wasn't time to wait any longer. So far, nothing was headed for town, but she felt Pa's growing impatience. She could sense his anger and the wind struggling to use that to destroy him. It was unsettling, feeling his inner maelstrom. Jemma couldn't shake her unease—the feeling that her mind needed to be gone and her body wouldn't let it go. The orange was so bright it was sickening, and it didn't just fill the sky and bits of water any longer; the whole world was made up of different orange shades.

Jemma limped heavily over to the kitchen table for her spells. Her leg hurt so much worse, and her head was heavy. She felt…torn.

"Jemma?" Woolworth now, hopped into the air and landed on the table before her. "What is it dear?"

Jemma shook her head as though through a fog. She collapsed into a chair. The voices were back, screaming so loud, louder than the orange, attacking her. But not loud enough to drown out the piercing whistle that drilled at her eardrums.

There was a pen in her hand again, as if from nowhere, like the day of the warning.

Tears slipped unnoticed from Jemma's eyes, and she lifted the pen and narrowed her lips. A high shrill whistle exploded from Jemma and her eyes slammed shut.

The pen moved as furiously as the wildly careening world. Nothing would be still or quiet, and everything yanked at her, calling out for her attention. It was so much. Too much. Her leg ached as never before, as if something had crawled inside it and would rip it apart one sliver of muscle or chunk of bone at a time.

Jemma let out a sob and collapsed onto the table.

"Shit! Woolworth, what do we do?"

Jemma heard them from far away, but couldn't open her eyes. Everything hurt too much.

"I don't know. I don't know. What was that?"

"Jemma?" Nona's voice was so quiet and hesitant, but even it grated across the raw surface of Jemma's mind.

A bright light flashed behind her eyelids. Then, slowly, as if it was taking her a great effort, Jemma felt Gran's hand sooth down the back of her hair. Warmth followed along behind it and spread out through her body. It was as if she and Gran were floating in the sky, letting the sun sooth them and the air caress them.

"It's alright, Jemima my love. You just rest here a while. Ain't your doin'. And not a bit of it's yours to fix, if you don't want."

"Gran?" Jemma croaked, her lungs burning. "Gran I'm sorry. I miss you so much."

"I know. And I miss my Jem beam."

"What do they all want, Gran? They're all so loud, and so lost. I can't make it out."

"Sure you can. You were always something special. 'Member when you started calculus? I couldn't make heads or tails of it to help you, and you hated it so much that it made your head hurt, and you wanted to quit school."

Jemma nodded and felt the scratched surface of the wood beneath her face, but ignored it. She was with Gran, that was all she wanted.

"How'd you make it through?" Gran asked. Jemma shrugged, and she could almost feel Gran laughing against her. "One step at a time. You gotta open your eyes."

"I don't want you to go away."

"Oh," Gran choked out. Her tears struck Jemma on the hand, little drops of warm rain. "My Jemma. I will always love you."

Jemma shuddered in Gran's arms. She knew, knew Gran couldn't stay, but couldn't she just this once have lied to her about the hopeful things?

"Would you hate me if I didn't send him away?" Jemma whispered, so low she wasn't even sure Gran could hear her.

"Never. You do what you can with what you've been given, and I'll be proud. No matter what it is you do. I love you more than the earth, more than my calling, more than life. Don't you be forgettin' it."

The warmth, and the light, and the weight of Gran's hand faded away. As Jemma opened her eyes, she saw it was her own tears that had struck her hand. Gran was where she'd been for months now: in the ground that made her.

"Jemma, are you alright?" Nona demanded.

Slowly, Jemma nodded her head. Her eyes swept across the table. It wasn't a pen in her hand, but a penknife, and with it, she'd scratched out the words of her vision.

In all different hands, the words were gouged into the table.

"What was that?" Woolworth demanded. "You didn't talk or see us."

"Couldn't. That's what it's like when I let out the sight, can't see another thing." Jemma let her eyes run over the words, so many demands, and pleas, and from so many people.

Loose the wind.
Save them.
Set us free.
End this.
Banish him.
Save him.
Claim your place.
Claim your stone.
End this.
Loose the wind.

Over and over, those last two demands were repeated. *Loose the wind,* was written in at least three different hands. But there was one carving, in the center of the table, in larger letters than the rest. It was written only once, but once was all it took.

FREE ME, OR DOOM YOUR MOTHER.

"Are you sure, Jemma? Foresight isn't meant to be painful."

"There's more than one kind of sight," Jemma said vaguely. She couldn't tear her eyes away from the threat.

The wind picked up outside to tell her who had made it. But if the wind knew Mama was alive, how did Pa not know?

"What sort of sight do you have?" Woolworth demanded, angrily.

He was worried for her, they both were. On her shoulder, Jemma felt Hippa's warm head rubbing against her cheek. Jemma glanced aside at Hippa. Had she helped Jemma see Gran? Jemma rather thought so. They regarded each other in silence. After a moment, Jemma sighed and looked at her other guests.

Her leg still ached, like it was splintering, and her head

pounded, but the whistling had receded, and the orange was a quite glow, rather than a bright attacker.

One step at a time.

"I have all kinds of sight," Jemma said to Woolworth slowly, leaning her head closer to the table where he was. "I'm sorry I frightened you. I don't like to look, but sometimes the universe insists. This was sight of the spirits; living or dead, all things of spirit form can reach out to me. They took over because they had a message for me, and I was ignoring."

Woolworth looked at the scratching on the table, stiffly. Jemma wondered if he had been hurt during her vision. He'd been on the table.

"Are you –"

"How can we help?" Woolworth interrupted.

Jemma shook her head. "I need to get you safe."

"No you don't," Nona insisted. "Dear, there's sight, and there's reason, you're better with reason, I think. Aren't four heads better than one?"

"But…your families."

Hippa burst off Jemma's shoulder and shifted rapidly from one shape to the next. She became everything from the jars, to the creatures in them, to Jemma, and the dinner they'd shared, and her head rubbing Jemma's cheek. Jemma was near tears again and smiling before Hippa got to the end of her tirade, popping into the shape of a tiny girl, Thumbelina-sized, wrapped in Jemma's arms.

Jemma nodded. "I love you too, Hippa."

"There are as many types of family as there are of sight," Woolworth snapped. "We're staying to save this family, then we'll go home to our other families."

Jemma nodded as the tears slipped out.

"I have to banish Pa, but I have to make sure the town is safe first. When the wind is loosed, after so long in captivity…"

"It might destroy everything," Nona finished for her, and Woolworth nodded.

"How do we protect you and your home?" Woolworth asked.

"We don't," Jemma said staring at the repeated words: *End this.* It didn't just mean the mess with Pa.

That was Sotsona's hand, Jemma knew it well. The hand of the first sacrifice. Every girl in this family knew that hand. She meant that Jemma should end the curse, end the fighting, end the selfishness. There was only one way to do that: Jemma had to put the others first. Had to save the ones who would likely never thank her or even welcome her help.

"I have to put others first or the curse will never be lifted. And there is one more person I have to help, the only way I can, before I banish him."

Woolworth and Nona exchanged glances, and it seemed Nona was elected to do the talking. "Are you sure? It might make it harder to send your father away if he knows your mother is alive."

Jemma nodded. "You can be better than bad and still not be good."

"And you fancy yourself a good witch," Woolworth scoffed.

"No. A good person."

Chaos

"May! May Bell!" Black Boot shouted her name again and again, rushing off across the fields.

One moment he was standing with her, mere inches from her and wishing with everything he had that he could feel her once more, then she was gone. Just gone.

He couldn't feel her in the wind. Couldn't see her before him, and she didn't answer his call. This never happened before. In all the years of dragging her along in the wind, she had never been more than a few feet away from him. Now he couldn't find her.

It couldn't happen this way. She couldn't pass on without him getting a chance to say goodbye. He'd said such things to her, like before, like the day of the cyclone. She couldn't just leave again. He wouldn't let her.

The winds picked up with his fear. The tiny twisters he had used to search the ground returned and grouped into one large tornado.

"May!" He charged across the land, the tornado at his back pushing him forward all the faster. He didn't even notice the tools he'd left out fly up into the cyclone. They spun around the funnel higher and higher, faster and faster, until they struck, and the hoe went hurtling off towards the house.

The shock of glass shattering and the clank of something striking the ground in the living room brought Jemma to her feet and spinning around. She'd been making plans for how to protect the town, but as the wind swept in through the broken window, papers flew into the air, and all Jemma noticed was the hoe. In the middle of her beautiful yellow brick road, scratching through the fantasy. Bringing bad luck.

From the corner of her eye, she saw the tornado in the distance and wanted to cower, but she couldn't look away from the hoe. It was a bad omen. There were tornados after Pa left, natural ones and Jemma had been scared, like any one would be, but not debilitatingly. But this one was headed right towards them, and this one was unnatural, and Jemma — couldn't move.

She swallowed hard staring at the rip in her fantasyland, and trying to find her strength.

"I'm not afraid of storms," she whispered to herself. Hippa dove for cover under the shelter of Jemma's hair.

"Why the hell not?" Nona shouted, her voice quivering. "I'm afraid of storms like this."

"I'm not afraid," Jemma repeated and took a step forward. She had to stop the storm, she didn't have a choice. Hippa was here, and Nona, and Woolworth, and Ma. She had to save them. She took another step. "I'm not afraid."

Black Boot saw the hoe careen through the window of the house, but it barely registered. May Bell was standing, beyond the shield that kept him from the house, crouched in the dirt. Her hand descended towards the ground, bent into a scoop and rose up — empty.

A shovel went hurtling out of the twister straight for May Bell.

"May," he shouted a warning, forgetting she was a spirit. As the shovel slammed right through her and into the porch steps, she stood slowly, distracted, and walked towards him.

"I could almost feel it," she said softly, as though unaware of the twister. The wind was yanking up and throwing anything not planted in the ground, everything but the two of them. There were buckets and tools, and even the wheelbarrow flying around in the wind, but she walked towards him slowly, oblivious.

"The earth. I can smell it, Tom. Feel it calling to me, and I hear the voices, all my ancestors."

"Fight it," he ordered, and for once, it was Tom who asked. Young and desperately lonely. She had called for Tom and found him. "You can't pass on, May. I need you. I'm sorry about before, I didn't mean it."

"Tom, everything dies."

"No." He lunged forward to grab her, but found only empty air. "No. Not this time."

"Maybe it isn't so bad," May whispered. "This doesn't feel bad, it feels like coming to life. I'm tingling all over, and for just the slightest moment, I think I reached Jemma. I heard her crying out for me, so scared, and...resentful." A wind chime whipped by them, with loud clanging racket and crashed into one of the porch beams, denting a chime before it flew off again. "I heard her voice, but I couldn't make out her words. I tried and tried to go to her."

"To Jemma," he whispered, half thrilled for her—she had wanted that for so long—and half terrified. Losing her to Jemma would be nearly as bad as losing her to death. This life may be torture, but at least she was here.

"Yes, then I smelled the earth, and I heard the voices, and they were reaching out for Jemma, so I reached out with them, and I think she heard, I think she has the sight."

"But...then you'll have to pass, to reach her. Don't do it, May. We'll find another way."

"Did you even hear me? She's angry, she resents me, and you. And she has a right. I have to do what I can."

"Not that. Help me find the stones and we'll all be together," he shouted, truly frightened. "Once I have power over the wind, we can all be together. We can be happy."

"How? I'm dead! She never sees me. How will that work, Tom? You have to let me go."

"Never!" he bellowed. The twister grew again. Shrubs planted around the porch were yanked out by their roots and flew up into the air. There was a loud creaking sound as the slats of the roof began to fly off.

"I knew there had to be a reason beyond Jemma that you wanted to be in that house." Kai said shaking his head.

Kai, Allen, and Tangerine were on their way back to the farm. They drove with the windows down to flush out the heat of the car.

"I don't *want* to be there," Allen shouted over the loud flapping of the wind through the windows. "I *need* to. For Jemma."

"And because you're cursed to serve her family." Kai said angrily. Poor Jemma, she thought this guy was her friend, but he was only there because a hundred year old curse was forcing him to be.

"I don't believe in the curse," Allen said between his teeth.

That sounded more like an angry desire than an actual statement of truth to Kai.

"So why not tell Jemma the truth?" Kai challenged.

There was a long silent stretch. Allen looked straight ahead as they drove down the empty road. Then at last he sighed and looked askance at Kai.

"Because Jemma believes," Allen whispered.

There wasn't much to say to that. Kai knew it would break her heart if she knew. So they drove on in silence.

The closer they drew to the farm, the less they felt the heat. A few miles away yet and the sky was growing darker and the wind damp. But it wasn't regular rain. The wind was growing heavier—throwing someone's tears at them. *Black Boot's*.

Already Allen was driving eighty miles an hour, but Kai didn't think that would be enough.

"Drive faster." There was so much pain at the farm, so much fear. He could barely feel Jemma in the mess of swirling emotions, but what he felt from her wasn't good.

Tears were drying on her face—heavy tears of grief, and responsibility, and fear, and determination.

"Something's wrong with Jemma."

Allen pushed the gas pedal to the floor.

Kai felt Black Boot's tears, something he didn't want to feel. It was much easier to wait for his chance to kill the man when he could think of him only as a monster. But he felt him, felt his all-encompassing terror. Fear of death, fear of his power, fear of life without it, fear of Jemma and fear for her. Fear. Fear. Fear. It was nearly all there was to the man, fear and regret. The closer they drew, the more Black Boot's fears seeped into Kai and mixed in with his own.

Frantically, Kai rolled up the crank for the window. He couldn't let them touch him. The tears were confusing him. Kai saw things he shouldn't be able to: Jemma lying trapped beneath the truck, blood on her face and her leg, and pain on her face, even when unconscious; Jemma's mother bent at awkward angles, looking completely empty. He heard Jemma, in a child's voice, raw with pain, cry out for her father to stay.

It pulled him away, the sound, into the deep dark.

"Lypsy please, let's go home." Kai was eight, standing next to his fifteen-year-old cousin as she examined the trade. "This isn't fun anymore."

"Just a minute, Kai." Her voice was already miles away though she stood before him.

They were in the dark market, past the pleasant magic, the temptations that drew you in: fire dancers, lightning wands, wood fairies dancing on spider silk, and the orbs that held the vibrant beating heart of the sea and whispered of adventure. They were even past the dimming magic, sinister and intriguing, hexes, and enchantments to make you powerful, gold that could never be diminished no matter how you spent it, and spells to capture any creature in the world. They had ventured all the way into the darkness, where there were no lights, except those illuminating the goods for sale. You couldn't even make out the faces of the vendors, so forbidden was the magic sold here. There were unicorn horns, mermaid tales, and the dust of a fairy's last breath, but worst of all were the creatures: slaves captured for their magic and sold to the highest bidder. Fairies, sea creatures, dragons, leprechauns, elves, nymphs, two headed dogs, werewolves—every creature imaginable, even kelpies.

It seemed like a good idea when he thought of it. An adventure he would never forget, to visit the dark market with his cousin and see all the forbidden things his father thought him too young and too soft to understand. But now, Lypsy gazed into the pixie cage, and Kai felt the darkness closing in around him. He fought hard not to sparkle and prayed Lypsy had the good sense to do the same. They needed to leave. For once he was in complete agreement with his father. This was a bad place.

"Lypsy?"

"How much for the pixie?" she whispered.

"Nothing you've got. Why don't you stick to things your kind can use, like a cockleshell necklace. Put it around the neck of a would-be lover and he will be your willing slave."

"I want the pixie."

"But, Lypsy, Dad said they're evil. Come on, let's go find Dad."

"Yeah, Lypsy," a dark voice teased from inside the booth. But Kai felt the eyes on him, not his cousin. "Better run along home, unless you have something of value to offer. Daddy's waiting."

"What do you want for it? I'm only half mermaid, the other half water horse. You want the call, my sparkle?"

A laugh came from in the booth. "Well, we're getting closer to my price. What about him? Throw in a slave and you got yourself a deal."

Lypsy wavered. Her eyes moved towards Kai, but even as she turned, it grew so dark between them. Kai couldn't see her face, and he was certain she couldn't see his.

"For how long?" Lypsy asked. Kai shuddered, nearly ran, nearly left her.

"Lypsy? It's not worth it. Come on." He reached out for her hand but couldn't find it. She was moving away, so Kai did the only thing he could think of: he sparkled. Brighter and brighter, to draw her eyes to him. "Calypso! Dad will get you whatever you want, just come home."

"He can't give me what I want," she said flatly and her voice turned away from him, turned towards the pixie. "He isn't my father."

"Well, well. Sounds like your willing to bargain after all."

"How long?" her voice was sharp, like rocks too long beaten down by the waves.

"I usually want for life."

"Then you won't need my magic, will you?" Lypsy countered, coldly. "You see the way he sparkles, son of royalty."

"Truly?"

Kai inched away, as the man's voice grew closer.

"Just look at him," she said, in a voice like silk, soft and enticing. It commanded the trader, as she inched away.

The man grew closer, and Lypsy grew farther away. Then suddenly, chaos broke out. A cage holding a phoenix burst open, and the phoenix flopped out as though woozy. Without warning, it jumped up into the darkness and a scream split the night.

"Run, Kai," Lypsy yelled. He turned to obey, but she wasn't following. It took Kai only seconds to miss her; he turned around searching for her.

"Lypsy," he called into the darkness, seeking her with his magic instead of his eyes. But he couldn't find her, and the pixie's cage was gone as well. "Lypsy? Don't go!" There were voices closing in around Kai, with dark intent all but falling off them. They would capture him, make him a slave like the other *creatures, punish him for her theft. But Kai couldn't move. "Lypsy! Don't leave me here."*

Kai's breathing grew heavy as the house came slowly into view, as the tornado came into view. Allen slammed hard on the breaks. But Kai couldn't sit still. He charged out of the truck, straight for the house. He would not lose one more person

Pa was standing before Dust House, yelling at the wind like a mad man. Jemma was almost to the door with the hoe in her hand. She had to get it outside or the bad luck would stay forever. She forced her feet forward as the tractor was lifted off the ground and pulled towards the tornado. Her knee gave a great tearing shudder, as if of its own mind, trying to pull her backwards, towards the storm cellar.

She was panting, and there were tears on her face, but she forced herself forward, against the pain and against the fear. Using the hoe like a cane, one step at a time.

Jemma made it out onto the porch by sheer force of will with her friends on her heels. Her teeth would be ground into dust soon, and she wasn't sure her leg would ever stop hurting, but she took a step and then another.

"Pa," Jemma whispered. "Pa, I need to tell you something," she said a little louder. But he didn't look over.

"Aaa!" Jemma screamed, and stumbled forward as the hoe flew out of her hand, yanked back to the twister. "Pa!"

"I'm going to fix things. You'll see," Pa shouted at no one, ignoring Jemma.

"Please stop," Jemma shouted, but her voice quivered with fear. She shouldn't be afraid. She couldn't afford to be afraid. But every time the tractor went around in the tornado, Jemma saw its blades flying through the air, and blood, and stuffing, and death. She was so tired of death.

"No one is going to die!" Pa shouted and the wind grew.

Jemma was clinging to a post to keep from being dragged off by the wind, and she felt Nona and Woolworth clinging to her ankles in a similar fashion. But at Pa's words, the chaos in her mind stilled.

All those times Gran would tell Jemma she didn't want to turn into Pa, it was his temper Gran had worried about. But what if it was his fears that should have given her pause?

"Papa, stop," Jemma ordered and just as in the past, all at once the wind fell still, tossing aside the odds and ends it had collected. And Jemma only had time to throw Hippa towards the house before the tractor came hurtling towards them.

My Heart Stops

"Jemma!" Two voices rose up in the silence of the absent wind, racing towards the barrier.

Kai was running as fast as he could, saw the tractor go hurtling towards Jemma. He screamed out her name and lunged forward, but a hand reached out and grabbed Kai, throwing him through the air, away from Jemma.

"Stay away from her," Black Boot snarled and charged for the barrier, but he couldn't get through. He pounded on the invisible shield shouting her name. All that could be seen was the tractor with the thick layer of mud on its wheels and blades.

"Jemma! Jemma answer me, baby."

Kai was battered but he jumped back to his feet. Black Boot and her mother were at the barrier, held out by the family witches. Kai ran, as fast as he could, ignoring her parents and paying no mind to the barrier. It wouldn't keep him out, couldn't. He had to get to her. He had to save her.

He was nearly there when the wind picked up, knocking him back several steps. And Black Boot was before him.

"I said stay away!" He reached out and wrapped his hands around Kai's throat. "She's mine, do you understand? You can't turn her against me."

"Look at her," Kai said as Black Boot squeezed his throat. Kai searched the porch, looking for Jemma, listening for her breath, but there was no sign of her. "I don't need to turn her. You're killing her all on your own."

Black Boot only squeezed harder.

"Let the boy go," Allen ordered, coming up behind Black Boot with a bat.

Kai shook his head as best he could. "Get Jemma," he choked out nearly crying. He should have stayed, he should have protected her.

"No!" Black Boot shouted, twisting his fingers tighter.

Kai could barely see, there was a bright light before his eyes, and the world seemed to swim. All he could think of was how badly he'd failed her. Then suddenly, Black Boot dropped him, cradling his right hand, screaming.

Kai fell to the ground blinking back the angry darkness before his eyes. Then he heard Jemma's voice. "Allen, Kai, get inside the shield."

He looked up at her from the ground and a wave of relief rushed through him for half a second. She was well, she was safe, she was... completely unharmed and unconcerned. Her eyes were all for her father.

She was just like Lypsy, so self-assured and selfish. Did she even see anyone else?

"Mama did it! She took a mound of clay and molded it with her hands. She has such a way with her hands. A pair of black boots were made, from the earth, to cling and tread upon it, so wind may no more pull away what Terra wills be with her." From the journals of May Bell Franklin-Traveler, 7th generation daughter of Terra.

J emma wasn't exactly sure how they'd done it. But as she was falling to the ground, to avoid the tractor, and realizing the hoe had flown back inside, thinking how her luck would always be bad now and how odd it would be to die under the machine that had killed her sister and left her mother comatose, the smoldering warmth of Nona's fire eased her to the ground, cushioning her. Woolworth held the tractor, just a foot from her, with the power of his mind, until Jemma could gather herself enough to roll away.

Hippa was back, hiding again under Jemma's hair. As she walked down the porch steps, all she could think of was how much she really did hate *The Wizard of Oz*, and every other book, movie or television show that made tornados look not-so-terrible, almost fun. Tornados were ugly destructive forces that moved across the earth like the hand of an angry god, knocking aside a board game he was losing. It would be wonderful to live somewhere that never, not ever in the entire history of the world, had a tornado.

She saw Pa whip out and grab Kai around the throat, but she wasn't worried. Her spell would stop him. When Pa started screaming for dear life and dropped Kai, to wrap his unmarred hand around his burning blistering one, Jemma just nodded at Kai and Allen.

"Allen, Kai, get inside the shield," she said calmly. Something had flattened inside of her when the tractor failed to flatten her body. She wasn't afraid anymore. She was just tired.

There was something wrong with Kai as he stood. Gone was the sparkling, easy smiling boy she met two days ago. And in his place was a dark, angry creature. His eyes bit into Jemma as he walked heavily through the shield, as if it was fighting against him.

Jemma nearly stepped back, he looked so angry. But when Allen came through as well, she heard Pa's whimpering and her eyes were pulled to him.

He looked pathetic, scared and small and not unlike Kai when she first saw him. Jemma wanted to look away, wanted to just walk into the house. He'd walked away, as she lay bleeding and crying and her entire world was torn apart. But he whimpered, and the sound shuddered across Jemma's nerves.

She couldn't look at his face without reaching out to help him. Her eyes fell on his boots. Not so black any longer.

She'd never seen them any less than pristine. The earth couldn't crust around them as it did regular shoes. Nothing could touch them, nothing could scuff them. You could drop an anvil on one and it would not so much as bend. But not so now. The earth was rising up around them. They barely looked like boots anymore. They were returning to the ground.

Pa was losing the boots, and with it, his temper. Of course. It always came back to the boots. She took a step towards Pa but a hand shot out to stop her.

The Walking Darkness

"What do you think you're doing?" Kai demanded, yanking Jemma back.

Jemma let out a little involuntary yelp as he yanked her around and stared up at Kai shocked, but he barely noticed.

"He nearly killed you! You aren't invincible. Stop giving him chances."

"He doesn't want to kill me," Jemma said twisting her arm to get away from him.

Kai felt it this time, saw the pain on her face, but he couldn't let her go. He couldn't shake all the swirling emotions. He felt Black Boot's desperate desire to shove his daughter away, where she would be safe; felt his heavy guilt for how much he'd already hurt her and the gaping longing for her love. Worse, he couldn't stop seeing Lypsy's face when he looked at Jemma, the way Lypsy had looked just before she'd given in completely to the emptiness of grief and betrayed everyone who loved her.

"Really, Jemma? How many times does he have to try and crush you before you get it through your thick head? He doesn't want you around." Kai snapped the words and watched her cringe. He wanted to call them back, but he couldn't, and he couldn't stop.

"He wants the land, and you're in his way. And you just keep letting him trick you, like that girl in town, what was her name? Minnie? Be honest, you knew she wasn't your friend, just like you know he doesn't want you. But he's not some idiot townie you can frighten with flying vegetables. He knows what he's doing."

Kai saw the moment his insults struck, but she wasn't backing down. Her eyes flashed and the light caught her hair. The magic all but exploded from her; this was a new Jemma altogether.

"I will always regret that I wasn't stronger. That I did not know how to say <u>no</u> to one I loved so much." From the journals of Esther Lynn Franklin, 6ᵗʰ matron of the Women of Terra.

Jemma stiffened, but for once, she managed not to feel even a bit like crying as her heart broke. He'd been gathering gossip in town. Heard their stories and come back looking at her differently. Like she was pathetic, like she didn't know exactly why Pa had come home.

Jemma had to admit, half of her fear this morning, as he left the house sparkling, was that they would change the way he looked at her. That they would take away her friend. Or maybe he was like Minnie, only pretending until he could get what he wanted.

"I know what I'm doing." Jemma yanked her arm free and started for the shield, but his words halted her.

"What's that, Jemma?" Kai demanded. "Trying to trap yourself friends with life debts because you can't make any on your own?"

Jemma turned her head slowly towards Kai. Pa's whimpers seemed to match the tingling rage that skidded across her skin. She felt electric, an exposed wire. All it would take was one little brush against her and she would release a torrent of lightning on the earth. Already she let off little sparks. At Kai's feet, the earth leapt up, crawling all the way to his knees, and holding him in place. It hardened into impacted rock, making him cringe from the pressure.

"If I wanted to keep you here," she whispered, "I wouldn't require your constant need of rescuing to help me." She walked slowly forward. "But I wouldn't keep you if my life depended on it," she snarled, stopping just before him. Her eyes were about level with his nose but it didn't matter, they both knew who was more powerful.

"I don't have room in my life for a shallow little water pony." The earth around his legs burst apart at her words and sent Kai tumbling to the ground.

Allen was behind him, with the baseball bat in the air. He stared at Jemma dumbfounded. She eyed the bat and looked back at him with a raised brow.

"Still think I need you?" Jemma asked bitterly and turned away, walking casually out of the shield.

She walked straight up to her father. He was barely even aware of her as she took his hand into her own. She reached into the pockets of the dress and removed the watch he had given her. Very gently she lowered it into his palm and closed his fingers around it.

She heard him sigh in relief, immediately, but he didn't look up.

"I put a spell around him, around all of them. You can't harm them without harming yourself." She thought of what he shouted into the storm, thought of the fear they seemed to share. "Everybody dies, Pa. But it doesn't have to be your fault."

He raised his eyes to meet hers, and there were tears in them. Jemma almost stepped back from him. It didn't feel nearly as good as she had imagined, seeing him at a loss for sadness.

"You didn't kill Mama," she said at last, but he only continued to stare. "She's in a coma, but she isn't dead. And I'll let you see her. When I get back."

Jemma stepped away. She didn't know what she had been waiting for: a hug, an apology, a promise never to hurt her again or tears of joy. It didn't matter; she clearly wasn't going to get it. She looked down at Nona and Woolworth who stood inside the edge of the shield.

"You know what to do. I'll be back soon. Oh, and there's a spell in the kitchen to send Kai home. Either of you should be able to work it. Get rid of him."

Jemma didn't even look his way, didn't look at Allen. She simply threw back her head and let out a piercing screech like a hawk and shot straight into the air. She had a town to protect.

The Dust Settles

"**I**'m not dead," May Bell said, awed, staring not after their vanishing daughter, but into the house.

Black Boot couldn't think, couldn't seem to move. Jemma had held his hand and tried to comfort him. And she'd been wearing May's dress, from so long ago. She looked so like her mother for a moment, but at once so sad. May had never really looked sad, even as she trailed him in the wind.

"Why doesn't she want you here?" Black Boot asked the boy he'd nearly killed, wrapping his hand tight around the watch. *Everybody dies Pa, but it doesn't have to be your fault.*

"Tom, I'm alive," May Bell whispered again, but his mind hadn't quite worked its way around to that yet. He ignored her.

The kelpie didn't answer. He had a hollow look on his face, a look of failure and fear and deep, unconquerable shame. Black Boot knew that look.

"Fix it," he muttered to Kai. "I'd like to say fix it or leave, but…" he rubbed the back of the watch, still warm from her hand. She needed friends. "Just fix it."

He turned away and began walking towards the barn.

"Tom, I'm alive. Didn't you hear me?"

"Yes," he replied, not sure how that could be a good thing.

She was in a coma, and he'd dragged her spirit after him. So what if she was alive? She might never wake.

"Did you see her?" he asked quietly, and his voice took on some of its old, softer innocence. May noticed. She stopped in her tracks, just before him, and looked up into his eyes gently. "She looked like you. She's fourteen, nearly fifteen. I kept picturing her five, the way she would jump into my arms and smile at me like I was magic."

"You were to her."

"Not anymore."

"We'll fix it, Tom."

"How?" He ran his hand over the back of the watch. Maybe she could forgive him, maybe not. But he would never be her hero again. She was nearly a woman, and he could tell from the sadness of her eyes she barely believed in magic. She'd never give over her land to him. No matter how much it cost her. He'd been wrong to see the farm's state as a lack in pride. She had pride, power, and enough anger to fight him — forever.

May's face dipped down before his, so his eyes stared into hers. "I'm *alive*. Don't you see what that means?"

He shook his head slowly, and May drifted to the ground in front of him. "I'm alive," she said with a wide smile and she stretched out her hand towards the boots. "We don't need her to give in. I'm matron now." Her hand, little more than air, slipped out across the crust of earth around his boots and dust fell off into the wind. In less than a moment, she had them wiped totally clean, shining bright.

Black Boot gasped, his eyes riveted on his shoes as May Bell returned to her feet. "I can make us a family again. I can fix it all."

Shallow

Kai sat in the dirt. He still felt it all rolling around inside of him: Black Boot's pain and fear; Jemma's sadness, anger, and pain; and things he'd kept shut down tight for years. Lypsy. Every single bit of fear he'd ever felt for her, mixed in with his anger towards her, and worst of all the guilt. Most of all guilt.

What the hell was wrong with him? On a loop, he heard them: Lypsy offering to sell him or Jemma's scream for her father to stay. But all he saw before him was the moment yesterday when he'd watched Jemma cry, knowing all she really needed was a hug, but unable to reach down and offer the comfort she needed.

He'd been so afraid of letting her in, of finding the deep dark so crowded that it spilled over into the carefully crafted and maintained pleasantness of his life. Nothing ever scratched his surface. And now it had, and another girl had run away.

I don't have room in my life for a shallow little water pony.

His failure to offer her comfort felt so much worse than what he'd said. But both things were unforgivable. How would he ever make her understand?

Silence descended as Black Boot walked away. Kai heard the ping of Allen dropping the bat to the ground. Kai didn't even look. Hippa was right in front of him, floating in the shape of a single, glaring eye. Another time it might be funny, but he felt the piercing of the eye straight through to his soul.

"I'll get the spell," Nona snarled, but Woolworth halted her.

"Wait."

Kai looked up and met the gripie's stare.

"You know what you did wrong?" he asked. Kai only nodded. "Then you'll stay and make it right."

"You aren't the one to decide that," Allen said.

Slowly, Kai pushed to his feet, watching the staring contest between Woolworth and Allen.

"And I suppose you will? With what magic?" Woolworth challenged.

"Doesn't it disturb you at all that her father wants him here?" Allen demanded. He had a point. What if Black Boot wanted him around not for Jemma, but because he had something planned for him.

Woolworth looked off in the direction of Black Boot's retreating form and very slowly shook his head. "I think, for once, he was thinking only as a father."

"If I was thinking only as a father, after what he said to Jemma, I'd want to kick his ass and never see him again," Allen snarled.

Kai glanced his way, nodding. Tangerine was hanging out of the pocket staring at Kai silently, but after a moment, she laid a hand on Allen's chest, patting him.

"That would give her what she wants in the moment," Tangerine said. "And satisfy a thirst for vengeance, as leaving now, without fulfilling his debt, would curse the boy. But what Jemma needs is for someone to stay. Stay and fight for her friendship."

"For the murder of my sister, I demand retribution: Waters of the valley, desert those who spilled her blood. Earth of my family, turn stone beneath their hoes. Let them shrink in the shadows of those they would destroy. May they toil on these lands in everlasting shame and never know joy." From the journals of Sarah Anne Smith, 2nd Matron of the Women of Terra.

J emma had flown during storms before, but this was different. She had to work harder than ever before to stay on course, as she flew towards town. It was as if the storm was at war with itself. Hot winds bashed against freezing ones, and wet clouds met dry air; this couldn't all be Pa.

Jemma had a feeling the rain clouds had to do with that first spell she'd done with Kai's hair, but that didn't explain the rest. Something unnatural was coming.

Loose the wind.

The words beat at Jemma. The clouds were so dense, Jemma had to risk flying closer to the ground in order to see where she was going. It wasn't so much that she feared what would happen in town. If she had to make them all forget, or if she had to run away, she would do it. But if someone from out of town saw her, someone just driving along Highway 20, that might cause problems. It might cause an accident, and Jemma didn't want to be responsible for that.

She avoided thinking of anything but her goal and the weather as she flew. She didn't want to think about what Kai said. She didn't want to see Allen, frozen with that bat in the air, or hear Pa's whimpers. She didn't even want to think of the words scratched into the table. She just wanted to protect the town, get as many people as she could away.

They would all see. She wasn't some little child in need of protecting, or some weakling who couldn't do what was required. She would save the town, she would save her friends, and she would banish Pa, and when it was all over, they would know how powerful Sarah's heir was.

Jemma landed in the center of Main street. She wanted people to see her, to fear her, or at the very least, point and stare. But there was almost no one around, and the people who did see her, just nodded her way and walked on. As if every single one of them went around flying.

It pissed her off.

Jemma stomped, as best as she was able with her leg aching, towards Millie's diner. There was a big crowd there, from the number of cars. Maybe they were holding a town meeting as only the citizens of Unforgiven, Oklahoma could, around a pan of French fries.

"Hey. Hey, wait." A child's shout came from behind Jemma, but she ignored it, she'd learned her lesson before. Better to ignore children completely. "Wait!" he wailed. "Super girl, wait."

Jemma was unwillingly amused at the comment and stopped to see who was chasing her. Coyote Little, the boy she'd rescued from Clarissa's run away car.

"Super girl?" she asked, glancing around the street to see where his mother was. Seriously, did no one ever watch this boy?

The boy caught up with Jemma, throwing himself against her legs to hold her there and leaning over to pant. Jemma watched him, wondering at it. He was little for his age, had short legs, but he seemed as if he'd been running for miles. She knew she'd seen him on the steps of the library, no more than half a block up the street. He must not get much exercise.

"Mom said I could call you that. I asked if you were an angel, or a super, or like Peter Pan, but she didn't know."

"She didn't tell you I'm a witch?" Jemma asked with a smile. This boy had a way of calming her when she was spoiling for a fight.

"Witches have brooms," he said as if she was stupid. "Can I fly too?"

Jemma shrugged wanting to pull her leg away. Pretty soon, someone was going to start screaming, and today, she wasn't sure she could stop herself from cursing people.

"Can I?" he demanded. "I have a super cape, but you don't. You can borrow it."

Jemma crouched, shoving the pain to the back of her mind. "Everyone can fly. You see, we used to have wings, but we forgot about them, because we don't need them anymore."

"Oh." He nodded with wide, excited eyes. "Will I remember if I go up really high and —"

"NO!" Jemma grabbed his wrist, suddenly horrified. "You must never jump from some place high. Never. You have to start off on the ground and always with a grown-up."

"Will you teach me?" he said with a broad grin, as if he had planned this all along.

Jemma just stared.

"Pleeeeeease," he begged. "I'll be good, forever."

"Well," Inspiration struck her suddenly. "You have to ask your mother."

"Okay!" He turned and started running, right back out into the street.

"Stay out of the street," Jemma shouted. Oddly enough, he listened, veering into the crosswalk.

As he reached the other side of the street, Jemma noticed a girl slip out from behind a column in front of the court house. His sister. Had she been there the whole time? Hiding from Jemma, no doubt.

Jemma threw her a dark glare and turned towards the diner.

Wreckage

"Where's May Bell?" Allen shouted anxiously.

Kai and the rest of Jemma's magical guests came running out of the kitchen, where they were unpacking the groceries.

There was damage everywhere. Glass, broken windows, a little hole in the roof over the kitchen, and there was debris from the storm scattered all around, but the first thing Allen had done was yank up a stupid hoe and run outside with it. Kai took one look at the tatters of the yellow brick road and wanted to scrap the whole thing and start over.

After everything he'd heard today, Kai rather thought Jemma could use a fantasy where the witches weren't killed, and where tornados weren't vehicles to other realms. But he hadn't started painting yet. The wreck brought home to him just how unimportant his little contribution to her life was. So he was helping with the more important things: stocking her cupboards, cleaning up glass, putting boards over the windows.

Allen was standing in the doorway of May Bell's room when everyone got there.

"In the storm cellar," Nona said with a bite to her tone.

She wasn't now, nor had she ever been, a fan of Kai, but she seemed to no longer be taking Allen's side. Something about the baseball bat seemed to have pissed her off. She kept shooting bat-shaped little fire daggers at him.

Kai got singed by fireballs himself once every few seconds. And Hippa still followed him in the eye shape. Only Woolworth and Tangerine seemed not to despise him. Both were disappointed, and made a point of letting him see it in their stares, but they did nothing else. It was better than he deserved.

"Why is she in the storm cellar? Did Jemma do that alone?"

"We helped her. Storm's coming. She didn't think the house would survive, but the cellar should."

"But…" Allen shook his head looking around the house. "She doesn't think the house will survive? Is she even coming back?"

"Of course she is," Woolworth snapped turning away. "We have things to prepare. I suggest you take the extra supplies into the storm cellar with the mother."

He and Nona left, off to do whatever chore Jemma had left for them. Kai looked around the room in much the same way Allen had. She didn't think her home would survive. Her mother was in a coma and she was banishing her father.

"She didn't put anything of hers down there, did she?" Kai asked. Nona turned to look at Kai and shook herself back and forth for half a second. She seemed almost not to hate him. "What are her favorite things?" Kai demanded of Allen.

"A few books, and there's a photo, of her with her mother and Esther."

"Get them. And let's take the bench too, or the chair. She'll need something comfortable," Kai instructed and ran to get the journal he'd hidden in a pile with his dirty clothes.

"Don't think she plans to be in the cellar," Nona commented.

"Doesn't matter, these things are for after," Kai said over his shoulder. "Here, put this down there too."

"I'm not your servant," Allen snapped. "What is it?"

Kai flipped it open to reveal the first page, with his drawing of Jemma over a boiling caldron. He'd written a title above and a byline beneath the picture. *A Witch's Guide to Magical Creatures, by Jemima "Jemma" Tulip.*

"I was going to do drawings of us all, but I haven't gotten to it yet."

Tangerine ran up Allen's arm to peak over his shoulder. She looked up at Kai and smiled broadly.

Allen shut the cover and nodded. "Yeah, we'll add this to the other stuff."

Searching

"**I**f you're matron here, why can't you just call the stones?" Black Boot asked May Bell, as they searched yet another stretch of field.

"I don't know." May sounded frustrated. Her spirit lay against the ground, breathing in its scent, trying to feel the earth. "I don't understand any of it," she muttered. "I'm alive, I can control little things, but not nearly enough. We need to get into that house. I need to get the family tomes, and my body. We need to put me back."

"There are enough magical creatures in there to do it. If we could only get them back in the jars."

"Yes. But they aren't likely to fall for the same tricks again." She froze for a moment, silent, then she rolled over, lying on the ground and looking up at him. "Tom, all these years, and I didn't even know I was alive. She resents me, I could hear it when she called to me. How much more will she hate me once I'm back in my body? Once she knows I've been with you all this time?"

Black Boot shook his head, looking off the direction Jemma had flown. With the boots restored, and the knowledge that May was alive, he felt so many different ways at once. He had no idea what Jemma would come to feel, but he knew the first thing she would feel.

He returned his eyes to May Bell, the love of his life. He'd never imagined loving someone so much. So much it reached beyond reason and death. He had carried her spirit with him in the wind, and just now, he liked to think that was the reason she was still alive. Because he simply could not let her go.

"She will be happy to have you back," Black Boot assured her. He opened the hand where he still grasped the watch and held it out to his wife. "She hates me, but some part of her doesn't want me hurt. She can only love you a hundred times more than that. We both do."

Some of the fear slipped off May's face. But not all.

Black Boot suppressed his annoyance. She should just believe in him, as he did in her, but he would let it go this time. She was overwrought. He looked away.

"There's something wrong with how we're searching, or the way she hid the stones," he said looking off into the distance. "May…" he said slowly, tilting his head to the side.

Off in the distance, right along the horizon, were two small tornados, tearing across the land, heading their way—tornados he hadn't made.

"What is it?" May said distracted, leaning against the earth.

"You need to hurry, love. We have company."

"And for the Jessup's, wicked all, cursed be his sons to be cowards, cursed be her daughters to drown in their tears. Cursed are they all to be ours, called to my daughters forever in fear. And when comes the heir to my power, know her by the fire on her head, then shall all fates be decided, justice met out, for our sorrows and our dead." From the journals of Sarah Anne Smith, 2nd matron of the Women of Terra.

Half the town was indeed crammed into the diner, but no one was talking, or eating. They were staring at the television—an emergency weather report.

Jemma watched silently from the doorway, holding the door open, so it wouldn't ring and disrupt the room. The weatherman was showing four stormfronts converging over a tiny corner of Oklahoma. He looked completely baffled.

"It's unprecedented," the weatherman went on. "For four such strong storms to meet in one place."

"Well, Ed," the female anchor commented. "Unforgiven, Oklahoma is no stranger to freaky weather. Back in 2004, they had more tornados in that one town in a period of three months than the rest of the country had in the whole year."

"Oh, I remember, Connie. And I bet the citizens of Unforgiven remember too. But when you have four storm systems like this converging on one location, chances are you're going to have an even worse week. They are likely to experience hurricane weather, tornados, and freak blizzards. Unforgiven is a very dangerous place to be this week. That's why the state of Oklahoma is issuing a category 7 storm warning and suggesting the evacuation of the entire county.

"We'll be keeping you updated as the storm unfolds in Oklahoma. To all of you in Unforgiven, good luck; our prayers are with you."

The waitress muted the television as the commercials came on. The room hung on an uneasy silence.

"They're right," Jemma said, all eyes turning her way. "You need to leave while you can." She was more nervous than she expected, with all eyes on her. "Don't bother taking anything, just get your families and leave. I didn't kill my father. Gran cursed him, and now he's back… It's too much to explain. If there is anything I can do to protect the town, I will. But leaving is the safest course."

"Why isn't Esther here warning us?" Sheriff Hicks asked, moving around the waitress and a few customers to stand in front of Jemma.

Jemma drew in a deep breath, feeling the tears beat against her eyes to get out. "She's dead. Goin' on three months now." There were several startled gasps from around the room, but Sheriff Hicks looked unsurprised.

"I didn't kill her either." Jemma could barely restrain the tears, but the sound of them filled her voice. "But there'll be time to explain later, if anyone survives."

One woman grabbed her child's hand and started yanking him towards the door. The waitress set down the remote and began untying her apron. After another moment of staring at Jemma, the sheriff turned back to face the patrons.

"I suggest we take Miss Franklin's and the great state of Oklahoma's advice and evacuate the city. Any of you who has them should go stay with family as far away as you can get without heading east out of town, as that's where the worst of it seems to be. The emergency system will text the locations of state safety stations. If you aren't enrolled —"

Jemma didn't wait around, just headed out of the diner. She'd done her part.

"Jemima?" A teary-voiced woman in the back of the restaurant called out. Jemma looked over and recognized Mrs. Berttie, the librarian. She was one of Gran's closest friends. She had tears running down her face as she made her way through the crowd to stand before Jemma, and there was anger in her eyes.

"For shame, child. Your grandmother deserved to be sent off proper, with her family and friends. Does her brother even know?"

Jemma shook her head. No, Uncle Joseph was one of the few people Jemma felt truly bad for deceiving.

Mrs. Berttie stared at Jemma half angry and half sad for the longest time, then out of nowhere, she leaned forward and wrapped Jemma in an unyielding hug. Jemma hiccupped, and began to sob, reaching out to hold onto this woman she barely knew.

"It's okay, child. It's okay." She rubbed a hand down the back of Jemma's head soothingly, just like Gran would. "You're too much like her, is all. Contrary, and solitary."

Through her tears, Jemma choked out a laugh. "No one ever thinks I'm like her."

"You don't talk to enough people." She drew away from Jemma but kept hold of her shoulders. "Every time I'd come over for lunch and you'd give me that glare, like I was there to trick her—looked just exactly like she did at your age."

"You were friends that long?"

"Lord no, we were enemies," Mrs. Berttie said with a broad, almost proud smile. "A better enemy I've never found; it really was too bad I had to like her. Life was more exciting when she hated me, more dangerous."

Jemma smiled and reached up to wipe her tears away. "I'm sorry I didn't tell. I…I just couldn't risk someone taking me from Mama."

"Uh-huh," she grunted. "Just like Esther." She sighed, patting Jemma on the shoulder. "I've a big van. I'll come and take you and your ma along with me."

Jemma shook her head. "I have to stay and finish this. I have to fix it."

"You're just a little girl. I know you've powers, but they didn't do much good for your leg."

Jemma didn't exactly expect to survive this. It started with a sacrifice: one sister for another. And it would end in a similar way: one witch to save the town her ancestors cursed.

"I was little then," Jemma said, not exactly a lie, but nowhere near the full truth. "I know what's coming this time."

"I don't think Esther would forgive me for leaving you here."

"Then it's a good thing she isn't here to say a word."

"For shame." She slapped Jemma none too lightly on the shoulder. "Your grandmother is watching you right now, young lady. Don't you go shaming your upbringing just to save face."

Jemma's eyes snapped into narrow lines. "Are you one of the girls who said they would drown Gran?"

Mrs. Berttie startled. "Yes."

"Then it's you who should be ashamed."

Her eyes darkened with sadness, and she nodded gently. "To my dyin' day."

Jemma's anger slipped completely away, and she felt like crying again. "I can't come with you," Jemma said, biting her cheek. "Only I can unmake the boots and send Pa away. It has to be me."

Mrs. Berttie nodded slowly, just nodded. "Alright." She said nothing more. Turning away, she rushed out of the diner faster than Jemma could move.

The Road

Kai boarded the broken window in the living room and swept up the mess of glass, paper, leaves and dirt. Who knew what else.

The others were off doing their own tasks, but he stood now, staring down at the yellow brick road and thinking about *shallow little water ponies.* He was rather shallow when it came down to it. Even his reasoning behind the road was entirely without depth. It was a joke, comparing her to Dorothy because of their colorless worlds. But Jemma's world wasn't colorless; her walls were. Teasing a girl whose whole life was defined by tornados, about a story that centered around one, was the height of insensitivity.

He'd thought of momentary amusement instead of lingering happiness.

Kai bent down and began prying the lid off one of the paint can's he'd brought back: green. He'd cover the floor with it and start over.

Hippa popped up before him and began flashing over and over until he stopped.

"What?" he demanded of the pixie, grinding his teeth, and refusing to look directly at her. He couldn't, not after everything that had happened today; couldn't see a pixie without seeing the one Lypsy sold him for.

She was shifting through a million different shapes in a matter of seconds, but Kai didn't really see any of them.

"She deserves something better than one more reminder of how crappy her life is," Kai snarled, his eyes for the road not the fairy. "She's never going to forgive me anyway, but I have to get rid of this road."

"No, you don't." Woolworth came up alongside them. "You just have to make it hers. She likes the road, kelpie."

"I…" Kai stared at the gripie. He'd never spent much time with other magical creatures, at least not the ones unconnected with the sea. He was as much a believer in the old myths of monsters as any human. A week ago, had he seen a gripie, he would have walked to the other side of the street and made sure not to meet its eyes, for fear of being turned into stone so it could steal his soul and decorate its garden.

Jemma must have known the stories about all of them, but not for a moment did she believe the bad. Or at least she didn't let it influence her, as it did the rest of the world. The way it infected Kai.

"I kept seeing Lypsy. My cousin," Kai explained. "And thinking how it was all my fault. I'd asked to go to the dark market, knowing it was bad. She was sad, and I couldn't figure out how to help her. We're supposed to make people's lives lighter, happier, but I couldn't make hers happier. Then…that tractor was on top of Jemma, I thought she was dead, and…"

"And you thought you'd failed again," Woolworth said. "I have two sons, strong men, I always say, like their father. But they don't like me. I wasn't a good father when they were boys, and now I never see them. Black Boot caught me because I was spying on my family like a thief, trying to steal into their lives. My youngest, he saw me taken, I know he did. And I didn't want him to try and save me. He might have been hurt, but," Woolworth nodded almost to himself. "I wanted him to want to help. And I don't think he did. We're none of us perfect." He laid a hand on Kai, patting him.

"The only thing you're to blame for are the words you said and where you go from here. Knowing Jemma, you won't even have to work hard for her forgiveness. Don't destroy your gift because it has uncomfortable associations. I think she liked that you thought she was strong enough to take it."

He walked away, leaving Kai alone with Hippa. She was sitting on the edge of the paint can, in a nearly human shape. A tiny girl with large eyes, and hair like Jemma's, and a pair of thin, webbed wings, made entirely of light. He wondered if this was her real form, or if she was modeling herself on Jemma.

Kai stared at her for the longest time. Jemma wasn't the one too cowardly to face uncomfortable things. It was Kai.

"I'm sorry," he said to her.

She just smiled and shrugged, swinging her leg back and forth as she sat there watching him.

Kai smiled at her. "I have an idea."

My Other Girl

It was well and truly dark now, though it was only mid-day, and a dusting of rain dampened the earth. Black Boot watched the sky, turning around again and again. It was coming from every direction, this storm, and right in its center was Dust House.

"I've wondered why they never came for me," Black Boot said, almost to himself, turning around again. May Bell was crawling along the ground waiting for the voice of some ancestor to call out to her and tell her where their stone was hidden.

"But why now?"

"They must have made a deal with Ma, and now she's dead," May Bell said casually.

"She was the one who made the boots, not me!" Black Boot shouted, and the wind he carried flapped against his coat, angrily.

"I know," May muttered. "But it's the only thing that makes sense. What can they do to you?"

"Alone, nothing. I'm stronger than them. But together, a great deal and with Jemma's help, anything."

"Jemma didn't call them." May stopped. She pushed to her feet looking into the darkening sky and to the cyclones in the distance. Their voices were raised, to be heard above the thundering clouds and the screeching winds. Why was the world always threatening his happiness? "She wouldn't. Just earlier, you said…"

"I know what I said," Black Boot snapped. "And I know what I see. That's not just wind guardians coming. She's called someone else as well. We need to get into that house. We need to find the stones; that's the only way we're going to make her our little girl again. 'Cause right now, she's treating us like enemies."

May nodded. "It's just, so hard. She used to be such a happy little thing. Do you remember the little stump out in the back, where she would have her pretend feasts? How she would smile up at us as she mimicked Ma giving the blessing for the harvest."

"The stump." Black Boot spun, whipping out his coat in the air. In a swirl of wind, they vanished from the field to stand beside the old stump, only a foot outside the shield's perimeter.

Black Boot knelt in the dirt and lay his hand against it. "Clever girl."

"What?"

He stood, smiling at his wife. A single tiny cyclone went spinning around the old stump, throwing away dirt and roots until it came to the stones, buried in a ring around the stump.

"She buried them all in one place. Made them harder to find. Still in the circle and around the symbol of the first house." Black Boot crouched down to retrieve the headstones, but he paused. There was a shoe box with a name scribbled on the top buried beside them.

"Kadawada Traveler," Black Boot read off the box. Thrown off course, he reached down and lifted the box free. He cradled it carefully and removed the lid.

May Bell let out a tiny shocked gasp at the sight of the doll with its head ripped off. There were bits of fluff littering the box and a tiny bouquet of yellow flowers beside her.

Black Boot ran a hand along the doll's head. He had always hated this thing. It was hideous. But he leaned in and kissed her head, like Jemma always made him. His other little girl. She'd wanted a sister so badly.

Black Boot replaced the lid and returned the box to the ground.

"She buried the doll," May said in a teary voice. "Buried it, when Mama could easily have fixed it."

"Real people don't survive decapitation," Black Boot said flatly. Oddly, in this moment, he understood his daughter better than ever before. He knew without doubt that she understood the difference between a real sister and an imaginary one. But she had loved Kadawada, so she must be mourned.

"She was so little," May said, brushing her intangible hands across the box. "There was so much she will never understand."

"No, May. It's worse than that. She understands, she believes, and she's powerful." He lifted the stones one by one into his arms. Even now he'd found them, they fought him, growing heavier, trying to drag him to the ground. "She's the one we should fear."

"What? Why?"

For all May's worldliness, she fell back on her old naivety to lead her through things she didn't *want* to understand.

"May, she's Sarah's heir. And you mean to defy all the family traditions, to truly rope the wind, and give over the land to me: a male outsider. We're planning to go against everything she was raised to believe in. And I killed her sister. Let's hurry. I don't plan to be cursed for a hundred years."

"Jemima, half the times I felt hated, the feelings were my own. I just knew from the way they looked at me that it was hate. And I was wrong. Mostly, it was curiosity. Give people a chance to prove you wrong." From the journals of Esther Lynn Franklin, 6ᵗʰ matron of the Women of Terra.

*L*oose the wind.

The words struck out at Jemma as she walked out the door of the diner, nearly knocking her back inside. She glared up at the sky, half tempted to start yelling at it. Instead, she bent forward and walked against the wind.

Jemma kneaded her thigh as she walked. The pain was getting worse. She should have taken more than half a pill this morning.

Ha. Jemma scoffed at herself. This morning—when she'd woken with a smile. This morning when she knew without a doubt that this would be a good day. Yeah, she had the sight alright, and it made her an idiot.

"She says if you can teach her too," Coyote chirped from beside her, just skipping along next to her as though the wind wasn't bearing down on him.

Maybe it wasn't. Jemma cast another dark look at the sky. Maybe it only bore down on her. As if she wasn't the one about to help.

"What?" Jemma said after a second, returning her attention to the boy. "Doesn't anyone ever watch you?" she asked.

"Yes."

Jemma startled, nearly swung around but caught herself. She couldn't afford to do that to her leg twice in one week. Coyote's mother and sister were walking along behind her. His mother was smiling broadly, but his sister just watched, with wide curious eyes like Jemma was a circus sideshow. Jemma was tempted to jump at the girl and shout "boo!" But she refrained.

"I said you could teach him to fly, if and only if you taught me as well," Mrs. Little said.

Jemma stared at the woman, utterly lost. "Why?" Was the best response she could muster.

"It's always been a favorite fantasy of mine. And if you hadn't noticed, Cyo can be a bit reckless."

Jemma just nodded. They were supposed to be evacuating town, but she was standing here on the sidewalk asking for flying lessons.

"You know you're supposed to be fleeing, right?"

"Yes. That's why we came after you. We won't be able to make it out to the farm tomorrow because of the storm. I hope you won't mind rescheduling."

"Rescheduling? Why is everyone acting so weird all of a sudden."

"We've always been weird," the sister said. Jemma couldn't remember her name; was it a plant or an animal? All of the Little's had names like that. "Did Kai give it to you yet?"

Jemma shook her head slowly from side to side. So that was it; he'd put a spell on them.

"Oh," the girl said after a second. "Well, it's a great surprise. He thinks you'll like it."

"Look, if you were coming by to see Kai than you're gonna have to cancel your plans. I kicked him out."

"We were coming to see you," Mrs. Little remarked thoughtfully. "Jemma, do you have a ride out of town?"

"I'm not leaving. I have to stop Pa. If you want more details, ask Mrs. Berttie. I have to go."

"Wait. I wanna fly." Coyote grabbed Jemma's hand when she would have turned away, his eyes begging.

Jemma looked from son to mother to sister. Mrs. Little's eyes were soft and patient, but her daughter stared Jemma down like a fighter, ready to take off her head if she disappointed her brother. Coyote slid his hand down Jemma's wrist, into her hand.

The moment his little fingers closed around hers, Jemma's mind raced away. She saw him stretched out on a hospital bed, maybe a few years older, with tubes in his arms and a hollow look to his skin. She could see his parents on either side of the bed, smiling down at him and talking, and his sister lying beside him, running a hand through his hair to rough it up. Then all she saw was the sister, much older, maybe thirty, with her head thrown back and the pride of all her heritage shining in her eyes as she battled in a courtroom. But Jemma felt her, not just saw her, felt the way she carried her brother in her heart.

Jemma came back to the here and now, staring at the sister. But she nodded returning her gaze to Coyote. "When the storm is gone, you can all come over, Mr. Little too if he wants, and I'll give lessons."

"Ow ow owooooo!" Coyote shouted, startling a laugh out of Jemma and smiles from his mother and sister.

"That's what he does when he's happy," the sister explained with a shrug. "You know, because he's a coyote."

Jemma nodded. They were weird. Jemma might just come to like them.

Mrs. Little was watching Jemma similarly to how her daughter had earlier, warily. And Jemma wondered if they didn't already know that something was wrong with Cyo.

"We'll see you after the storm," Mrs. Little said. "Jemma, whatever it is Kai did, he likes you a great deal, and he seems like a nice boy. Maybe you should forgive him."

"You only think that because he made you. He's not normal. He only stayed with me because I saved his life, and now he owes it to me. It's weird…"

"It's not weird. It's an old idea, not a bad one. And I know he isn't normal. For goodness sakes, the boy twinkles."

"Sparkles," the sister corrected, and her eyes got a misty quality. At least one of them was under Kai's spell.

"Ugh." Coyote swung Jemma's arm back and forth, clearly bored. Mrs. Little rolled her eyes at her daughter and focused on Jemma.

"Life tends to steal people from us. Don't you think it's best not to throw any away?"

Jemma's hand tightened involuntarily around Coyote's.

"I have to go." She released the boy's hand and turned, but caught herself suddenly. "I don't remember your name, sorry," Jemma said to the sister.

"Oh, that's okay. Most people forget it. I'm Fern. I guess I'm a bit forgettable."

"No." Jemma shook her head. "I won't forget again. And someday, no one will." With that little curiosity, Jemma hurried away. When she was a block from them, she whistled, and took off into the air, only realizing once she was airborne, she hadn't used the flying powder once today.

The Wind Walked In

"Why are you painting when Jemma doesn't expect the house to survive?"

"What can I say?" Kai continued painting the wall to the left of the fireplace, beside the kitchen entrance. He infused each painting with as much of his magic as he could. He had no real understanding of how a protection spell worked, but he imagined it had something to do with putting all your energy behind something, so that's what he did.

"Kelpies are naturally hopeful creatures. Do you know if there's a copy of *Peter Pan* or *Jemima Puddle Duck* around here?"

"Well, definitely *Jemima Puddle Duck*. Why?"

Kai indicated the little painting he was doing. It was of a baby Jemma held in her mother's arms, laughing, and Hippa fluttering out of the sound. Hippa showed him the image of Jemma the day she was born, held in her mother's arms, and Kai imagined the rest. He used to love *Peter Pan*. Mom read it to him every night for a year after Lypsy left. He couldn't sleep otherwise, imagining all the horrible things the fairy might do to Lypsy, but Mom assured him that she was like Peter Pan and ran off to live with the fairies because she didn't want to grow up.

"There's this line in *Peter Pan* about the first baby laughing and the beginning of fairies." Kai said after a second. "But I can't remember it exactly. I want to paint it above this. And I'll need the other when I get around to Jemima Puddle Duck. I've never read it, but there must be something usable in it."

Allen nodded. "I'll look."

Kai watched the man head off towards Jemma's room. He caught sight of Hippa. She was in the hummingbird shape again, dragging the can of varnish Kai bought in town, over the patch of green by the benches. She just sort of shook the can and the varnish fell out, glossing the surface of the floor. Woolworth came along behind her with a rolling brush to make it smooth and even.

Maybe the house would survive, maybe it wouldn't, but if it did, they were going to do their best to make sure it was beautiful for Jemma.

Nona had been rushing around the house for a while now, yanking up everything she could tell Jemma touched frequently and rushing it down to the cellar. Tangerine was busy making lunch and writing out a hundred recipes for Jemma to try.

When he heard the squeak of the screen door and felt the rush of wet wind, Kai held his breath and looked up. He had to find a way to make it right.

"Jemm…" Kai's voice fell away. Black Boot walked into the house with his arms weighted with headstones and his wife's spirit at his side.

"Well." Black Boot sounded impressed as he looked around the room, but his expression was derisive. "How pretty."

His wife's spirit didn't remain at his side but rushed off into the rooms, searching. "Where am I?"

As if the words snapped him back into reality, Kai jumped to his feet. "Hippa, find Jemma," Kai shouted.

Black Boot darted forward towards the fairy but he was too slow. She sped around him and out of the house. Very carefully, Black Boot set the stones aside and advanced on Kai. He didn't care, Hippa was the most powerful creature in the house, and now Black Boot couldn't lay a hand on her. Woolworth was edging carefully from the room. Allen came down the hallway and stopped short seeing Black Boot.

"Shit," Allen muttered.

"Language, Allen," Kai teased, and bent back down to return to his work. He could leave, he was certain of it. His life debt to Jemma meant he could return to her unless they had actual chains to hold him. But he didn't even try.

The longer he distracted her parents, the more likely the others would get away.

"Where am I?" the mother shouted again. Kai cast a look at her over his shoulder.

"A nursing home in Tulsa," Kai commented, startling Allen, who searched the room to see who Kai was talking to, apparently he could not see the spirit. Jemma's mother covered her mouth, anxiously.

Black Boot just shook his head slowly. He wasn't fooled. Together, Tangerine, Woolworth and Nona went inching across the floor towards the front door. Kai opened his mouth to make another off-hand comment.

"No." Black Boot threw up his hand and the wind rushed out from under his coat tails, slamming the front door shut and grabbing onto the escaping creatures in a leash of air. "No one's leaving just yet."

"Sisika was the daughter of a shaman, had a great place among her people, but for the sin of her love, she was shunned. As was I, by my father's people, for the same sin. Their people it seems are not so different as they believe." From the journals of Sarah Anne Smith, 2ⁿᵈ matron of the Women of Terra.

The winds tossed Jemma back and forth like a baseball. She was exhausted from the sheer force of will it took to keep on course. And she wasn't even sure she *was* on course. The world was so dark. She flew low for fear of the lightning, striking not at the earth, but into the heart of the clouds. It was terrifyingly beautiful, but Jemma couldn't appreciate it, because she needed to get home, and she couldn't see the way, could barely force her wings to cooperate, couldn't shake all the voices in her head.

Loose the wind.

Free them.

SET ME FREE.

End this.

They pounded in her head and before her eyes. Though she felt like crying for the pain and the fear, she fought the tears. Somehow, she was certain despite what she'd said and asked the others to do, and despite the fact that he clearly had no respect for her, Kai would still be there. She knew it. He wouldn't leave her, even if he wanted to. So she fought the tears. Jemma wouldn't let him glimpse her feelings again.

When she thought she was home, or nearly there, Jemma flew even lower, mere feet above the ground. But she couldn't see past a foot in front of her face, and Pa had cleared the fields. For the first time in her life, she had no idea where she was, and it terrified her.

She couldn't be far from home. Could she? The wind had been known to toss ships hundreds of miles off course, but that was on the sea, in hurricanes. And what use would she be to the wind if she was a hundred miles away?

Jemma kept flying, even lower. Her feet brushed the ground, but all she could see was tilled earth and darkness. Her breathing grew fast and painful. Where the hell was she?

Jemma's left foot struck something hard and solid sticking up out of the earth and she went tumbling through the air. She tried to right herself, tried to steady her tumble, but her head struck something and she fell face first to the ground. Her left knee struck a rock as she landed, shooting pain up her good leg.

"*Shit!*" Jemma rolled over, pained in both legs now, and cradled her left knee between both hands. She lay on her back, panting, and staring up at the sky, as she fought to hold in the tears.

Loose the wind.

"I can't do that if I can't even find my way home," Jemma shouted at the sky.

She shut her eyes, cradling the knee. She rocked from side to side fighting the pain. It all hurt so much, every move, every muscle, every breath.

"I can show you home, little girl." A man's deep, thickly accented voice startled Jemma's eyes open. She dropped her leg. "But I do not think you mean to loose the wind."

A man stood above Jemma. As tall as he was and dressed all in dark clothing, he looked precisely like a shadow. His voice was lovely and deep, and seemed to meander through the air, almost heavy, no—rich. It was a very foreign accent, maybe Russian, but not like bad guys on spy shows. His voice didn't sound silly or sinister. It sounded warm and rich and curious.

For a moment, Jemma completely forgot the pain with the sudden desire to ask where he was from and what it was like there. To ask him to say "she sells seashells by the seashore" just to hear it in his accent.

"Little girl?" he asked, leaning down to check on her. Jemma remembered suddenly that she had just taken a tumble from the sky, yelled at the wind, and had no idea who this man was, though he apparently knew her. She should be cautious.

"Who are you?" Jemma demanded, using her hands to push up to a sitting position. Both of her legs sent stabbing pains running up her bones, but she ignored it.

He chuckled. "I am Ilya, guardian of the north wind."

"Oh." Jemma nodded, not looking at the man. She could barely make out his face anyway. Her mind went racing away. "I'd never thought of their being others, but it makes sense. That's why the three different types of handwriting. Where are the others?"

"Behind you."

Jemma threw a glance over her shoulder and saw two more shadowy figures a few feet from her, and the unmistakable shape of Sotsona's tree. They were by the old lake. She'd probably hit one of the wall rocks when she fell.

Claim your stone. Claim your place.

"We are sorry you fell." Another interesting accent came from one of the figures behind Jemma. Some kind of Spanish she guessed; but with a lower tone than she was used to hearing, warm. Even though he spoke slowly, his voice hurried across the air. He was the taller of the two behind her, but still a bit shorter than Ilya. Jemma wanted to say that name, it sounded like it would feel fun on the tongue. She hoped the man behind her had a fun name too.

Jemma pushed slowly to her feet, peering into the darkness at the shadows of the three wind guardians. The shortest one stood a little differently. Jemma didn't know exactly what made her think it, because she could only see the barest outline of shape, but she rather thought the third one was a girl.

"So…if you're guardian of the north wind, Pa must be guardian of the west wind."

Ilya nodded, as the other two shadows approached. Even on her feet, Jemma was a good foot and a half shorter than Ilya.

"I am Luciano."

"Luciano." It was a fun name. "Is that Spanish? Are you from Mexico?"

He laughed. "Argentina."

"Ohhh," Jemma said gleefully. What fun she could have questioning them all. "And you are?"

"Nsombi." The girl had a young voice, very quiet. She said nothing else. She was nearer Jemma's height than the others, maybe even the same height.

"Pa ages," Jemma said thinking about the young girl before her. "So you must too." Luciano nodded, with his head tilted to the side.

Jemma got the distinct impression he was amused by her excitement. But she didn't care. She had three people from all across the world, with lovely names and beautiful accents, and for a moment, she didn't care that her legs hurt, or that the wind wanted free, or that Pa needed to be banished, or that Kai was a jerk, or anything at all except that this might be her only opportunity to ever learn firsthand about the rest of the world.

"So, you must change guardians once in a while."

"Of course," Ilya scoffed. "Did you think your father the first?"

"Suppose not." Jemma shrugged taking no offense. "I just never thought of it. So, are the guardians always from the same countries?"

"An old guardian is tired, he picks a new one—"

"Or she," Jemma interrupted excitedly, indicating Nsombi—such a quiet, strong name.

"Yes, or she," Luciano went on with a chuckle in his voice. "Not always the same country, but always the same hemisphere."

"So, you would be guardian of the southern wind. And Nsombi the east. Where are you from?" Jemma demanded of the girl excitedly.

"Kenya," the girl replied and looked off at the sky. Clearly, she had better things to do than stand around answering Jemma's questions.

And Ilya too. "If we show you home, you will loose the wind?"

Jemma nodded slowly. "Why are you here? Why now?" Jemma asked looking from one of them to the next. "Surely you could have… done something before."

Ilya nodded. But it was Luciano who spoke. "We bargained with your grandmother. When you were in the hospital, we came one at a time; it is safer that way."

"The wind was growing restless long before. But we delayed. He should have known better. Always before the wind we go, but where the wind chooses," Illya added.

"We came when it was too dangerous to stay away," Luciano spoke up again. "To stop the witch who cursed the wind."

"She didn't curse the wind," Jemma snapped. "She helped Pa resist it. What do you mean you came to stop her? To kill her?"

"Yes." Ilya said it so matter-of-factly, like he wasn't talking about killing her grandmother. "But we did not. She begged us not to leave you orphaned."

"Well, parentless maybe, but both of them are alive, so I wouldn't have been orphaned."

"Is the same," Nsombi said softly, sympathetically, giving Jemma the first real exposure to her accent. It was musical, not like Irish or Jamaican accents but like…dancing slowly beneath the moon. In no rush.

The same. Was it? Wouldn't that make her an orphan now?

"Wait. Are you here to kill Pa?"

Memories of Unfamiliar Rooms

*B*lack Boot's coat tails flapped from the wind he was using to hold the littlest of the magical creatures to the wall. The kelpie seemed to have no desire to run. Despite the chaos of fluttering papers and broken floors Black Boot took in the house thoughtfully. Esther had rebuilt differently, harshly, and the boy was softening it with his paintings. They were actually quite beautiful, Black Boot took another step towards the boy. He stiffened a bit, but continued to paint. It was a portrait of Jemma as a baby. She was so alive in the painting, she seemed almost to reach out to him.

She used to reach out to him. Whenever he passed her crib, or later when she could walk, her arms were always in the air, begging him to lift her up. To hold her.

She was almost more alive in the painting than she was when she stood before him.

Black Boot jerked away, to the man his daughter obeyed, the man she hugged.

"Where's May's body?"

"Like he said, nursing home." The man was a poor liar. He looked everywhere but Black Boot and his voice went up at the end of his sentence questioningly.

"You're here, May," Black Boot said over his shoulder. "Just have a look, and see if you can find the jars."

"Jemma broke them," the gripie called out cheerfully, pinioned to the wall. "Called them evil."

Black Boot struck out against the little creature with a gust of wind, and felt a tingling leash of fire go racing through his nerves. It wasn't nearly as bad as it had been when he choked the boy, but Black Boot clenched his teeth and fought against the urge to scream.

"Tom," May Bell called out from the kitchen. "Tom you have to see this. I told you she'd heard me."

Black Boot started off towards the kitchen and noticed the man beginning to inch towards the door.

"In a minute. I have to take care of our guests." He looked around the room for something to bind the man with. It might not work for long with the creatures but it was better than nothing.

"Who is he talking to?" the man Jemma hugged hissed at the kelpie but was ignored

The room was so bare, the best thing Black Boot saw to bind the man was his shoe laces. Did his daughter actually live here?

"Kelpie, get me some rope."

"Name's Kai, and," he said without looking away from the wall, "I really doubt she has any."

"Tom!" May called, again. She sounded half excited, half scared. She always sounded just a bit scared; it was under everything, her fear. Strange, he hadn't noticed before now. Trailing him in the wind, she had seemed fearless, but looking back, it was always there. "Tom."

"You know you don't have the magic to hold them, so why bother?" the kelpie said, painting what looked like a twinkle beside Jemma's mouth.

"Oh, I can hold them. I can hold you all." Black Boot glanced at the stones. It worked for Jemma, and she wasn't matron. May was matron.

"May, come here. I need you to bless the stones."

"You need to see this, Tom," May Bell said walking obediently to the bench to bless the stones.

"We need to trap them first. Bless the stones, and I'll have the wind bury them."

"The table is all scratched up with different writing. I knew Jemma had the sight."

"Then why didn't it warn her about us?" Black Boot scoffed. There were many magical things he believed in, but the sight wasn't one of them. No prediction he'd heard about his life had come true.

You will travel the world, but never know home.

No. He would prove that one wrong too. He was going to have a home here, he, Jemma, and May Bell. They would be happy, and powerful, and no one would ever come between them again.

"It warned her about you," the kelpie said, and this time his eyes rose to meet Black Boot's, showing his insolence. "Did you find those books, Allen?"

"What? Here." The man tossed the books at the kelpie without looking, his eyes riveted on Black Boot.

He could feel them, see them out of the corner of his eye. But Black Boot didn't look away from the kelpie. After a moment, the boy winked, laying aside his paint brush. He grabbed the books off the floor and began flipping through.

"Done." May stole Black Boot's attention. "Do you think they will truly keep her out? She is a descendant of Sarah. She can call on the stones."

"We don't need it to work forever," Black Boot said, and as he did, a tiny whirlwind swept through the house, lifting the stones, sweeping open the door and rushing out. Papers, and books fluttered around the room. Black Boot and May walked into the kitchen.

"That will hold you," he sneered, releasing the magical creatures from the ropes of wind.

"I am worried for Sarah. She wants so much to be loved by these people. She would be happier far away. But she will not leave. She still believes our father will return." From the journals of Sotsona, Sacrifice of the Women of Terra.

Jemma looked from one shadowed face to the next, but no one spoke. It was one thing to unmake the boots, to send Pa away forever, but it was another thing entirely to allow him to be killed.

"Answer me. Are you here to kill him?" Jemma repeated.

"Only if you fail," Illya answered.

"What exactly was the deal you made with my grandmother?" Jemma asked, suddenly not so interested in their stories.

"She said you would be the one to free the wind," Luciano said. "That you had been trying for some time, but always your father caught you."

The words seemed to tickle something in the back of Jemma's mind, but she couldn't say what. She didn't remember trying to free the wind.

"The boots," Ilya said, as if understanding Jemma's thought process. "You tried to take them."

As he said it, a giggling Jemma ran through her mind, yanking at the ties of Pa's boots, but he lifted her into the air, away from them.

"She promised when she died, you would know how to stop him, and you would do so."

"That isn't a deal," Jemma hissed. "What's your part? And how did she convince you?"

It was Ilya's turn to laugh now, and though it was a deep thing, seeming to come from the very center of his being, it was full of joyful amusement. "She did not convince us; you did. We hear your voice in the wind, little girl, always the same word."

"Stop," they all said as one. Jemma took an involuntary step backwards. It was all so strange.

"We stop for you," Nsombi spoke hesitantly, tilting her head to the side to study Jemma as if she should know this.

"No other guardian has ever had a child," Luciano said. "Somehow, you are not just the child of your mother and father but of the wind as well."

Jemma didn't particularly like the sound of that. It sounded like what Gran said at the ceremony of the stone.

Jemima Tulip Franklin, eighth daughter of Sarah's line. You are a child of the earth. We take the name Terra because that is what we are, the earth of this spot where our first sister died. Take up your stone, and join the sisterhood. Today, you are Terra.

She hadn't wanted to take the stone then, and she didn't want to accept the wind now. Why couldn't she just be plain old Jemima Tulip Franklin, a no one, from nowhere, who read as much as she breathed and just happened to fly.

"I still don't know your part of the deal," Jemma said rather than asking the myriad of questions jumbling around her head.

"We agreed not to harm her and not to kill him, if you could loose the wind," Luciano explained.

Jemma nodded and paced away from the little group, into the darkness. Both her legs screamed against the exercise, but she could barely feel it. First the wind threatened her mother, and now its guardians were threatening her father, and all the deaths would be on her hands. Maybe she really was Sarah's heir. Maybe she would be responsible for just as much pain and heartache.

"You said," Jemma said, turning slowly to face the guardians, "that when a guardian grows old, he can stop being one. Does he die then? Or does he, sort of, retire?"

"Your father cannot stop," Ilya said firmly.

"Why? You said…"

"If he had stopped before, even after what had happened to your mother, the wind might have released him. But no more," Luciano explained.

"He must repay the years he trapped the wind." Ilya's voice was uncompromising, but beneath the harsh certainty, Jemma thought she heard a bit of sympathy. "Twenty-six years of faithful service. Two for each year he wore the shoes. Then he may stop."

Jemma shuddered a bit as she walked away. It wasn't that she wouldn't do it, but if there was another way, she wanted it. Was that so bad?

The punishment wasn't horrible. Pa chose this life, but then he saw something else he wanted. Equally, maybe, but not more. No one else could have everything they wanted.

Jemma looked at the people who must hate her father, must not like her much either.

We stop for you.

"The wind is quite wild. Is there any way to…" Jemma waved her hands uselessly.

"This is why we are here," Ilya said. "To limit the destruction. And to do what must be done, if you will not."

Jemma nodded. "I'll do it."

Literary Heritage

The moment Black Boot and his wife's spirit left the room, Tangerine, who was by far the fastest of the creatures, ran out the door to test the barrier. Woolworth simply slumped against the wall.

"What's going on?" Allen asked. Kai only looked over at him, lifting the books from the ground. "He said May, and you were talking to someone else. Is she….here?"

"Yes."

"I can't escape." Tangerine's voice preceded her into the room as she came rushing back. "I don't understand. Jemma's barrier didn't hold things in."

"It wasn't meant to," Nona said and her cloud began to grow red with fire. "We should just overpower them. If we kill…"

"The mother," Woolworth interrupted. "It would mean killing the mother. She blessed the stones, and…" He looked from one of them to the next, "I do not think any of us is ready to explain that."

Kai nodded morosely. They should have told Jemma they'd seen her mother's spirit helping Black Boot, as soon as they realized. Maybe she would have seen this coming. But then again, she wanted to trust her father. How much more would she want to trust her mother.

"Do you suppose she's only doing bad because she's been stuck with Black Boot so long that he's rubbed off on her?" Kai asked. He didn't look up, just opened the tiny little copy of *Jemima Puddle Duck* and flipped through the pages. "I mean, she doesn't seem evil, just wrong."

"Few people are evil," Woolworth commented, sounding as defeated as Kai felt.

"So….her mother is here? Like a ghost…but she isn't dead." Allen spoke but was generally ignored.

"You should try the barrier, Kai," Tangerine suggested. It was the first time she called him by his name, not just *you*. "Your life debt should ensure you can reach her."

Kai shook his head. "I'm more use here. Jemma's too angry with me right now to accept my help."

"So, you all see her? May Bell?" Allen asked when the room descended into silence.

"When she wants us to," Nona offered. "She is a spirit, not a ghost, like a projection of her conscious mind."

"But she doesn't want Jemma to see her?" Allen asked. "That doesn't fit with the woman Esther described. She said once she was born, Jemma was her whole world; she wouldn't be helping Jemma's father."

Tangerine shrugged. "People change. She's been with Black Boot all this time. He is her whole world now. And if I don't miss my guess, she thought she was dead."

"Yes," Nona agreed. "She seemed just as shocked as Black Boot when Jemma said she was alive."

Kai heard it all washing around him, but he was caught up in the little story. The depressing little story that Jemma was named for. He didn't think he would paint the damned duck; the narrator of the story didn't even seem to like it. It was…beaten and belittled and ignored by everyone. And even her ending wasn't terribly happy.

Jemma was nothing like that. She was…awesome.

Her face…when she called the earth around his legs, the air itself had been charged. And her eyes were full of dancing sparks of power, as if she simply couldn't hold it all in. She was awesome. There was no other word for it. But not the casual sort of awesome that was thrown around at skate parks; the sort that was made up of its roots. She was the awe-striking, awe-inspiring, awful, fear-of-God sort of awesome. The kind that left you frightened, speechless, and magnetically, reverently drawn to that person forever.

"What do we do about this? Jemma's spells are in here—that is, if she'll even be willing to use them, once she finds out," Allen said heavily. "This is her mother we're talking about. Jemma's practically lived in her room for years."

"She doesn't need the spells." Kai came out of his stupor, dropping the book to the floor, and opened *Peter Pan* instead, searching for the quote. "She's going to come back and send him away, send them both if that's what it takes, with just…herself. So, what was this plan of Jemma's?"

"Nothing complicated: show her father her mother's body, unmake the shoes, and banish him forever from the town," Nona whispered floating next to Kai's ear.

He found the quote he was looking for and lay the book open on the floor. Standing, he used a pencil to begin lettering the wall.

"So, what was it she needed your help for?"

"Protecting the town from the wind," Nona replied. "We were to help her make a barrier, similar to the one with the stones, but with our magic, so it would be more powerful."

Kai nodded. "Alright, who thinks they can perform a life-force swap?"

Most Beloved of the Wind

Black Boot ran a finger across the coarse scars of the messages gouged into the table. The violence of it crawled under his skin, unsettling him. The knife lay there with bits of wood caught on it. Spirits had *taken* her. His little girl. They used her to scratch out angry messages she couldn't help but feel. They tried to control her. Did control her, as the wind had once controlled him.

He'd seen something like this only once, at a fair with May. She always loved fairs, loved running into the fortuneteller's tent. He knew it was a sham. The woman said they would have the binding love of matched souls and remake the world with it. May smiled up at Tom, insisting he leave more money than the woman asked for.

And he'd done it, of course he had. He'd known May for less than a week then, and the prediction made her cling to his arm and rub her head against his shoulder. It was worth the extra money. But the woman knew he didn't believe, and as he left, she grabbed his arm, threw back her head, and with her left hand, she began scratching words into the black cloth over her table, with the nail on her pointer finger.

Most beloved of the wind, you will travel the world, but never know home.

He didn't like the idea of Jemma having the sight, the idea of something beyond her control taking her body for its own ends.

"We have to find a spell for Jemma too," he said absently.

"To do what to her?" May accused, as if she wasn't as much a part of locking their daughter out. As if she hadn't intended to steal her magic for their ends.

He hated that. Hated it when May looked at him like a monster but wanted the results his methods produced. She wanted the creatures captured as much as he did but had lectured for days after he bought the vessels to store them.

"To free her from the spirits, to let her control them, instead of the other way around." He snarled the words and papers flew up off the floor, floating before his face.

Black Boot yanked the paper out of the air so he could glare at his wife.

"But…the sight is a powerful gift. Ruth had the sight." May sounded thrilled, covetous even. She'd always loved the little bits of power the land gave her, loved her own magnetic quality.

"And it did nothing to stop her from being stoned," Black Boot snapped, trying to drag her back to reality.

May shook her head, sighing at him as if he were a stupid child she simply couldn't explain some concept to. If she had a body, he would reach out for her, make her face him with her insults.

"My daughter will not be controlled."

May spun around to face him, her eyes burning. "She isn't you. When will you learn? There is nothing wrong with being led."

Black Boot scowled, running his hand across the table. "Led? This…it takes you over, you are not yourself, out of control. Jemma shouldn't suffer anymore. You've never been controlled; you wouldn't understand."

"Never been controlled!" She shouted so loud the house shook with it, the ground rolled. In the cupboards, the sound of clashing dishes jangled, and the hanging pots collided, ringing like gongs. "Have I been anywhere but by your side these eight years, my love? Have I failed to do something you wanted?"

The odd thing was, she had. She might trail him, fixed to his side for eternity, but she was not his to control, and she didn't see it.

"Well then," he sighed, for once her anger completely relieving him of his own, "is that a fate you want for your girl?"

She only stared at him, unable to answer.

Black Boot looked away. Straightening the paper in his hands, he read the spell written on it twice before it sunk in.

She would banish him forever, and free the wind, with no regard to the destruction it would cause.

Black Boot looked up suddenly. May was now as much a part of him as any organ or limb. He'd never known such love for another thing. It must be something about May Bell, because he simply didn't have such powerful feelings for other things. He would break the world apart to be with her, destroy it to make her smile, and he was not alone. Esther would have done anything for her, and Sy, everyone who knew her loved her. Even the wind.

Black Boot stared down at the page again.

"I know where she put your body," he said after a moment.

"Where?"

"Where you're safe from me," Black Boot said bitterly. "You're in the storm cellar."

"Esther Lynn won't be home before I pass. But I know, I know she'll break the curse. She was always the best of us, even leavin', she sends money home like a good girl. She'll do what's right when her time comes." From the journals of Belle Dade, 5th matron of the Women of Terra.

O nly Nsombi was leading Jemma home. All three guardians staying together for long caused all sorts of trouble. The other two were going to different points around the farm to hold off the wind when it came. As it was, Jemma could barely fly through the tossing and turning of the current. She didn't see Nsombi; it was as though her body just faded away to allow the wind to push her on ahead.

Jemma wanted to ask if it had been like that for Pa. Wanted to ask why a person would choose to spend their life of serving a faceless, formless force, moving across the earth; willing to give up family, and friends and a home. What could the wind possibly offer that would stave off the loneliness? But she didn't ask. She felt the wind guiding her along, taking over for her tired wings, almost as if it was holding her up, like a friend, like family.

She should have known really, that somehow, she was a part of the wind. No other witch in their family had ever been able to fly as Jemma had. They could make themselves weightless with the powder and levitate, but Jemma could truly fly. She could be one with the sky or stand on the ground and be one with that.

"You are of the earth, I am of the sky, I don't even know what the hell that means," Jemma spoke the lyrics of a song Allen introduced her to: "Farther." Gran hated that song, and the band, so Jemma would only play it louder, just to get Gran to come and yell at her.

Jemma giggled. It was the oddest thing, she should feel like crying, and maybe she did, but Mrs. Berttie was right, she was contrary. Just like Gran.

It was beginning to rain in earnest now. Jemma couldn't see, but she felt safe with the wind at her back. With Nsombi guiding her. Wasn't that odd?

"Did you meet her?" Jemma asked. It was the only question important enough to ask of the girl in the wind.

One syllable. "No." She wasn't much of a talker.

"Gran was of the earth, wholly and completely. But…I kind of think she liked that I wasn't. She'd yell and nag and lecture about my responsibilities to the earth, to the family, and to the curse. But she liked it when I fought her, even better when I won, I think. She liked me." A tear ran away down Jemma's face and fell off to join the rain, but it didn't leave her sad. In fact, it seemed almost to open her up with a tiny bit of joy.

It felt as if the girl was about to say something when a tiny ball of light came hurtling through the sky and knocked Jemma to the ground for the second time today.

She landed on her ass this time, but it was no less painful.

"Damn," Jemma groaned. "I'm gonna be sore forever."

Hippa flashed before Jemma, darting from one shape to the next. It was too much to keep up with. She saw the headstones and the jars and a man, maybe a woman. She just moved so quickly.

"Hippa, slow down. I don't understand, slow down."

Jemma glanced to her side. With Hippa here, she could make out Nsombi's face. She was pretty and even younger than Jemma had assumed, maybe nine. And she was smiling up at Hippa delighted. She looked unfettered, like a flower drifting along with the current of a stream. Perhaps traveling with the wind was a good thing.

Hippa popped into the hummingbird form and pressed the tip of her beak to the bridge of Jemma's nose. This Jemma understood fine. *Pay attention*, the fairy was saying.

The pixie moved back from Jemma's face, and shifting more slowly this time, showed Jemma the stones, a pair of boots and the door of her house. That was all Jemma needed to see. She shoved past the pain suffusing her body and stood.

Pa found the stones.

Jemma whistled, and her feet came off the ground. Nsombi rose off her feet, watching Jemma much the same way she had watched the pixie and sweeping her arm before her. She dissolved into the wind and a draft pushed Jemma forward.

Into Action

Another time, there might have been arguing over who was to do what, but there wasn't time now. Everyone just did as Kai suggested. Jemma's plan was to move her family stones to strategic spots around the town, and by adding Nona's and Woolworth's magic to it, create a burning vacuous shield that at the very least should stop the destruction from going beyond Unforgiven.

It was actually kind of genius. No one but Jemma would think of something like that. Probably because while magical beings should all have a sense of kinship, what with all the secrets they shared, the truth was, different species tended to keep to themselves. Witches had been using bits of different dead magical creatures for centuries, but no one ever considered actually combining their living powers. Nona's fire to burn away the debris, and Woolworth's ability to cleanse the air as a sort of filter, to let the air through but slower.

Black Boot had royally screwed that plan by taking the stones. And Kai was going to have to seriously consider what a bad influence Jemma was having on him. He never cursed this much, even in his head. But that could wait until later. Right now, they had to come up with something to use to form the barrier, something magical. They also needed to swap enough of Kai's life force with Allen so he could get the job done. And they needed to do it all before Black Boot and May Bell finished their umpteenth fight and came back out here. Plus, there was the small matter of the growing storm outside. The door wasn't open, but Kai felt the rain. It was infusing him with power, but also with a sense of foreboding. That was no natural storm. Something was coming and it was angry.

"So…will I basically be you?"

"No." Kai scoffed as if this was utter nonsense. "This isn't *Freaky Friday*. You are in your body and I'm in mine; otherwise, what's the point of the swap? I'm just giving you enough of my magic to fool the barrier because I can leave."

"Okay, but...do I, will I have magic?"

Kai considered this. His brush paused halfway through the letter S of *skipping*. He supposed so. That would be the only way to give over enough life force. He would have to give Allen his powers, his sparkle. Kai's brush was midway to the wall when a horrible thought struck him. Could he paint without the magic? He never considered them separately. Why would he? They were all parts of him. But what if one was irrevocably linked to the other? What if he became like the hollow creatures in the corners of the dark markets, nothing but empty vessels where magic used to live?

That deep all-consuming fear that overcame him when the vendor looked his way, and asked, "What about him?" rose up in Kai. A yawning need for more power, more sparkle. If he could have more, ever more, he would never be vulnerable again. He could sparkle so brightly, he'd repulse all the darkness in the world.

If he gave that away, what was he?

Maybe it would be better if he just went himself. That way, he still had the magic, could keep himself safe.

His eyes fell on the baby Jemma in his painting, with her laughter bringing forth the first fairies. Another thought came along to chase the last away.

Would he have given it all up, would he have become one of the hollow creatures, if it would have helped Lypsy?

Yes.

Wasn't that exactly the reason he didn't run, even when he felt the madness of grief, and the desperation for something to fill up her emptiness, settle inside his cousin's heart? He would have done it for her, and she didn't even know it. But Jemma would.

"Yep," Kai said lightly and got back to work on the painting. "You're going to sparkle and finally see what it's like to be this good-looking. Careful you don't get a big head though, I'll be taking the magic back."

Allen didn't say anything, but Kai knew he had noticed the hesitation. A minute later, Nona, Tangerine, and Woolworth came out of Jemma's room dragging her set of encyclopedias. Kai did a double-take looking at the book titles.

"*Encyclopedia Mythical: The Definitive Reference on All Creatures of Legend, Myth, and Fantasy.*" Kai laughed as he read. "Only Jemma. Okay. You've blessed them?"

All three creatures nodded. Tangerine was not about to be left out, and she pointed out that adding her magic meant bending plants to her will and they could push against the wind.

"Time to go, Doc." Kai untied his bag of treasures from his belt loop. "Careful with these. There's some pretty powerful stuff in here."

Allen reached out to take the bag and Tangerine hopped up onto it. For a moment, both men had a hand on the bag and Tangerine had a hand on each man. The room grew still as she whispered, and she glowed a brighter orange than any one of her blushes.

When the moment passed, and Kai's hand fell away, no one spoke. Allen was sparkling, and the light threw all of his best features into flattering relief. Kai stepped back, feeling weighted as never before. Worse even than when he had walked under the weight of Black Boot's chains. At least then, he felt his magic, felt the hope so innately rooted in what kelpies were. But he couldn't feel any of it. Couldn't hide from the deep dark.

Allen didn't say a thing. As if the magic filled him with a sense of purpose and confidence, he yanked up the mesh bag of Jemma's encyclopedias, flashed a quick grin and slipped out the door, taking the sparkle with him.

Strange, it wasn't until he had to confront it that Kai realized how completely frightened he was of the dark.

Waking Kisses

"*I* have no idea what I'm doing," May Bell shouted in frustration and stormed away from her body.

They found the storm cellar easily and stood staring at her body with all its machines, and emptiness for the better part of five minutes before either was willing to approach it.

Being near her body was doing nothing for May Bell's temperament. She was so angry at the wasted time that more than once now, she turned to yell at the bodies buried in the ground.

Black Boot didn't think that was a good idea. They were the ones whose headstones were guarding the house. If they turned on May Bell, things would not go well. But he didn't say anything.

He didn't know what the sight of her body was doing to him, but it wasn't making him angrier. He sat beside her body—held her hand.

She didn't hold him back, but it was so much more than he'd felt in years. But May couldn't feel it, and he saw how that ate at her. So when she paced away, he stood as well.

Down here it was like they were in their own world. He knew a storm raged outside, but they could barely hear it. Even the bodies in the ground didn't disturb them. They'd traveled together for years but were never so completely connected as in this moment.

"We should bring down one of the creatures, see what they can do."

"They don't want to help us, and without the jars, we have no way to make them."

"They might do it for Jemma, so she can speak to you." He wandered around the only space of the cellar that wasn't crowded with the dead. Just the perimeter, maybe three feet wide, around the whole of the cellar in a circle. Witches and their circles—he would never understand what they thought was so special about them. Someone had brought down a bench, with pillows for cushions and paintings of flowers all over it. The kelpie's work, Black Boot imagined. There was a stack of books on it, and beside the books lay a photo: Jemma, her grandmother and May Bell. He lifted it, wondering at the stark difference between Jemma's smile in the photo and all the expressions he'd seen on her face since he returned.

"She said we would remake the world with our love," he said in a near whisper. "But she never said we would make it better."

"Don't remind me." May was so angry. As angry as he was when his parents died. "Sometimes I fantasize about finding her and killing her."

"Do you?" The words shocked him. Shocked him straight out the haze he lived in and into reality. He had done this to her, even she no longer bared much resemblance to the woman in the photo.

"Don't you?" May demanded. "Look at us, look at what we did. What if we just had a lovely little romance that ended when you moved on, as it should have? It could have been perfect."

"I know I said my life was better before, but…"

"What? You didn't mean it? Don't lie to me, I know you too well."

"I meant it. But, I would do it again. I love you too much to have never been with you, even knowing what would come."

May Bell closed her eyes and lay her spirit along the bed beside her body. "Even knowing what would happen to Jemma?"

He shrugged, even as he was shaking his head. But the truth was yes, he would.

"When my parents died, I stood in the yard, with the house still burning and the smell still singeing my nose, having to answer the sheriff's questions. He looked at me like I'd done it—killed my parents in their sleep, because they grounded me. He thought I would kill for something so small. All I thought, all I felt was anger, so much anger I wanted to kill him, kill everyone. And Dax found me, showed me how the wind could free me from all the anger and sadness. As I traveled with him, I truly left all of it behind. There were so many things to see and explore that I thought I was happy. Until I met you." He walked over to the bed where his wife lay. He ran a finger across her face, his own softening into a younger man's smile.

"I was with you five minutes and it was already clear I'd never been happy, and never would be without you. When I said I was better off before, I meant it, but I meant I was better off from now. But those first years with you, and the first few with Jemma—they were the best of my entire life. I could never give them up."

May Bell's spirit reached out for him, her eyes glowing warm and amber with her love. She reached for him and as she did, she vanished, leaving him bereft for the touch of her, as always.

"May." Black Boot shuddered leaning towards his sleeping wife. His eyes closed, wishing just this once they could feel one another. He settled his lips against hers.

A shock of breath and electricity rushed over him, and lashes fluttered against his cheek. Tom Traveler froze, unwilling even to breathe for the hope that filled his chest.

May Bell blinked, once twice, and life returned to her cheeks.

"T –"

The door to the cellar slammed open, and a great rush of wind startled Tom away from his wife. He peered up the stairs as the clatter of the storm invaded this little sanctuary.

"Nooooooo!"

Black Boot spun around, nearly falling to his knees as the ground beneath him shook and the house tilted before his eyes. May Bell's spirit was back, floating beside her empty body. He'd only been distracted from her for a moment, but apparently it was a moment too long for her spirt to bear. Was she so dependent on him now? Could she not even inhabit her own body without him holding her there?

Black Boot's heart broke as he watched her. With burning eyes, and surging power May Bell bellowed out her rage.

"Mother's Farm is thriving, but lonely without her. When Sarah isn't working, she spends most her time at the mission, but that place only reminds me of Mama's pain. I feel better among her people. They have wonderful stories of her as a child. They make her feel alive again." From the journals of Sotsona, Sacrifice of the Women of Terra.

Jemma, Hippa, and Nsombi arrived at the house, bringing the east wind with them. It met with the west wind that always surrounded Pa, and the pair tussled, shaking the house, the barn and everything in sight. Jemma stood in the center of the melee and hesitated. If she stepped forward, out of the eye and into the storm, would she survive?

Behind her, Nsombi must have sensed her fear. She lay a hand on Jemma's arm and nodded. Jemma looked away, towards her house as the door banged open. She took one step, then another.

She was nearly to the house when she felt the shove of what must be a hundred hands reach up to block her way.

What?

She shoved forward, against the hands, but they would not budge, would not let her through.

"Gran?" Jemma whispered, shoving against the shield. It shouldn't work for Pa. How was the shield working for him?

"You can't come in just now, Jemma," Pa's voice rang out from the doorway.

Jemma looked up at her father's looming shadow blocking the light's escape from the house. He took a step towards her, but his eyes were gazing past her to Nsombi.

"Making friends are you?"

"I told you I would let you see Mama. All you had to do was wait." Jemma shook her head slowly.

As he walked, she saw into the house. Kai and the other creatures stood together, but she didn't see Allen. She caught Kai's stare and willed him to understand what she couldn't shout. She needed them to run, needed them to get into the storm cellar, because as soon as Pa's feet touched the earth, she was going to release the wind.

Woolworth seemed to catch Jemma's meaning before the rest. Tugging on the others, he set off towards the kitchen. But Kai stayed. Not just stayed, he walked forward, towards the night and the storm. Towards Jemma.

She heard the sound of Pa's boots crushing the dust at the base of the steps and tore her eyes away from the inside of the house.

"You'll understand soon, Jem Beam. We're doing this for you."

"We—your boots!" Jemma shouted aghast, cutting her own question off in shock as she stared at the perfectly pristine black boots on Pa's feet. They'd been scuffed and encrusted with dirt earlier, returning to the earth, and now they were like new. And the shield was working for Pa. "How…who would help you?"

"I'm not so evil as that," he laughed.

Jemma launched herself at him, but the shield held her back. She beat at the shield as she wanted to beat at him to make him feel just a fraction of the pain she felt. He laughed at her. Stole her home, turned the earth against her and locked her out like she was the evil threatening her family line and he would laugh at her.

She heard Kai calling out, but it barely registered. There was only rage. Jemma's fists fell against the shield again, and she felt the brush of familiar fingers. Gran. Her fingers brushed across Jemma's apologetically.

Pa had roped Gran's magic, just like he'd roped the wind. Jemma let her hands drop slowly to her side and the rage within her settled into a quiet, seething power. He couldn't have her family's magic. He couldn't taint and destroy Jemma's heritage; she wouldn't let him.

Jemma drew herself up and stared at her father, with all her anger and hatred rolling around in her eyes and in her heart. Even the rain falling around them wasn't safe from the electricity singing in the air. The droplets flashed with it, striking the ground with tinkling sparks.

She knew why the spell Gran banished him with wasn't in any of her spell books, or her journals, because it was a curse. It came out of rage and hatred and magic, and she didn't want that for Jemma. But just now, Jemma didn't care and she didn't need anyone's help to find the words.

"Black Boot, curse upon this land." Jemma snarled a curse of her own making. "Bain of my family, leave this—"

"NO!" A wispy figure, near translucent, slipped between Jemma and her father, frozen in the dust, and stared into Jemma's eyes pleading. "We only need a little more time, Jemma."

"Mama," Jemma gasped. The electricity, the magic, everything deserted her. Jemma fought even to draw breath.

Mama.

"Yes, Jemma mine." She tilted her head to the side, gazing at her as if she loved her above everything. As if she waited her whole life for this moment, as Jemma had.

Joy and hope rushed up to fill the places where Jemma's hatred had been. All her life she had waited for her mother to come home, to speak. At last, she was home.

"Mama." Jemma reached out for her mother but the shield rose up to block her.

The shuddering cold of a hundred hands met Jemma's and her hand curled away, though she could feel Gran trying to cling on. Jemma looked from one parent to the next. From the corner of her eye, she saw something move on the porch. Kai was walking towards them, his eyes sympathetic. He knew.

Jemma swung her gaze back to the ghostly form of her mother, and as she did, the dream that warmed her heart last night flashed through Jemma's mind.

They all knew Mama's spirit was helping Pa. And Hippa tried to show her.

"You did this?" Jemma asked in a whisper, her eyes filling with betrayal. She could barely hear herself over the thunder and wind, over the pounding of water against the earth, but she saw her mother understand.

"We are trying to unite me, soul and body." Her mother pled understanding. "We couldn't risk that you would banish us first."

Jemma nodded. No, she supposed they couldn't risk that. "All this time, you followed him? Did you even look back?"

"He pulled me along in the wind, Jemma," her mother explained.

She had such a soft voice, like music. It was the hum that filled her mind, when she allowed it to wander into her second sight. The voice she longed for all these years. But as her words slipped over Jemma and the rain pounded the ground between them, Jemma felt as though that voice might kill her.

"How hard did you fight?" Jemma asked, in a small voice, but growing larger. "How hard did you fight to leave him, and *come to me*? When I was laying on your bed clinging to you, and forgetting how to pray, because no matter how good I was, or how much I begged, you never came back. He called me a heathen," Jemma said, with tears in her voice, but steel beneath them. "He shattered everything that we were, but he could call me names and convince you to bar me from my home."

"Jemma mine."

"Don't call me that," Jemma snapped as she felt something break inside her. "Don't you dare call me that."

Jemma Mine, No More

Black Boot couldn't move. Couldn't get between his wife and daughter as he watched Jemma's heart break again.

"Answer the question," Jemma ordered. "How hard did you try? Because I don't think you worked very hard at it. That would mean leaving him. I read Gran's journals, and yours; you would follow him anywhere."

"And what wouldn't I do for you, Jemma? We could have wandered forever, but when you were born, we came back here—for you."

Jemma nodded, and Black Boot saw at once that was the wrong thing to say. Her anger he could handle, he deserved her anger, but he watched her innocence and the last vestiges of hope vanishing from her face, and his heart broke as well. He'd done this to her. Tears rolled off his face to join the relentless rain, but as always happened when his feelings rose up, the wind rose with it.

It rushed from his coat and shoved at the little wind guardian behind Jemma and the pixie at her side. But Jemma was unmoved, as heavy as the stone remaking her heart.

"Well, I am so sorry." Jemma spat the words at her mother. "I ruined your life, didn't I? You would have much preferred to turn your back on your heritage and give yourself entirely to him, because you were stupid."

"You will not speak to me that way," May Bell snarled, as if she had the right of a mother, but Jemma clearly didn't see it that way.

"I just did." Jemma raised a bitter challenging eyebrow. "You were too stupid to see that he never loved you the way you loved him. You would give up everything for him, but he will give up nothing!"

"Shut up!" May Bell bellowed, and the earth rolled beneath Jemma's feet. "You don't know what your father's been through. You don't understand what he needs."

Jemma laughed, really laughed. Leaning forward, she braced herself on her knees as the apparent hilarity took her over. And when she looked back up, her electric charge was back, making her eyes sizzle.

"I don't give a pigs stinkin' shit." Jemma said each word with slow precision, and the rolling of the earth changed directions, racing out towards them and setting even the house trembling. "He had his chance. He could have given all of it up, let go of the wind and chose us, but he wouldn't. And now, I will never choose him."

"You don't mean that," May said slowly, her calm returning. "I've watched you these past few days; you want him here. You want his love. You want us to be a family. And you can have it all, Jem Beam. We just need a little time to fix things, and we can all be together again. Doesn't that sound lovely?"

Jemma just stared at her mother, but the earth shook harder. Black Boot shuddered; he could feel it cracking beneath his feet. It would swallow him whole.

The wind rushed out from his coat, flying at Jemma like a pair of fists, and shoved her into the air.

"Jemma!" the kelpie shouted, running from the porch to catch her, but the shield stopped him.

He needn't have tried to save her; the little wind guardian was after her in seconds, shooting into the air, but even she was unnecessary. Jemma righted herself as if she had wings, and dirt leapt up beneath her feet forming steps. She walked down them slowly, her eyes all for her father now.

"How many times was I thrown by you, before that last storm? 'Cause I truly can't remember. I thought we were happy, but I read those journals, and it seems like maybe I was wrong."

When her foot touched the last layer of earth, Black Boot shook in earnest. He'd known she was powerful, but even Esther couldn't command the earth so casually.

"I never meant to hurt you," Black Boot said in a low voice, frightened.

"You keep sayin' that. But you know what you don't say, Black Boot?" She held his eyes as she said it, as she cut her ties with him, snarling the name the world had given him. "You don't say you're sorry. You don't say you love me. You haven't laid eyes on me for eight years and you haven't a kind word for me. Do you know what I think?" She looked at May too as she asked this, looked between them, tilting her head like she was imparting a slightly funny secret. "I think you can't love. I think neither of you even remembers how. You're too caught up in each other to ever give love to anyone else."

"Jemma, we do love you." May pled, and Black Boot heard it in her voice as well: fear of Jemma's power, and desire for it.

With such power, they could do anything.

"We're doing this for you."

Then, She Smiled

"Well, thank you, Mama," Jemma said with a sweet slice of a smile, but her eyes sparked so she didn't appear entirely human any longer.

Kai marveled at her, even as his heart broke for her. This was just what he'd wanted to spare her from, by not telling her of her mother the moment he'd recognized her as the body in the bed. But he should have told her. Should have given her the chance to be prepared for it, instead of letting her parents ambush her.

"Now's time I return the favor. You love each other so much, this should be a treat. I want you to stay together, for always. Black Boot —"

They all heard the revving engine and the swish of tires at the same moment.

"Damn it! What now?"Jemma threw up her hands and pivoted towards the approaching vehicle.

A pair of headlights cut through the darkness and rain, only just managing to screech to a halt in time to avoid hitting Jemma and the little girl beside, who'd flown a moment before. Jemma truly was a … strange attractor of all that was magical in the world.

The new arrival wasn't Allen, which was a good sign. He hadn't been gone nearly long enough to complete his task. He might not even have made it to town yet.

It was a van, and the moment it stopped, the front passenger door screamed open and a man jumped out with a shotgun trained on Black Boot.

"Sheriff Hicks?" Jemma asked, completely thrown.

"Get in the car, Jemma," the sheriff ordered.

"I already told—"

"Get off our property," Black Boot shouted and the wind picked up the sheriff, shotgun and all, and threw him into the sky.

The little girl Kai didn't recognize shot into the air after the man. The driver's door banged open, and Mrs. Berttie jumped out.

"We're not letting you hurt this girl," Mrs. Berttie shouted advancing on Jemma's parents. And it was all Kai could do not to laugh.

"Mrs. Berttie, get in the van. I can handle this," Jemma shouted.

On the other side of the van, the girl returned a still sputtering sheriff to the ground. She gave a little tug and yanked the gun free of his hands and opened the chamber, dropping the bullets to the ground. She threw it into the back of the van, shaking her head.

"Jemima Franklin, I made your gran a promise to see you safe. I'm keepin' it."

The wind was rushing all around them, and the rain was coming down in buckets. Kai watched Jemma turn from one person to the next, her eyes chaotic with indecision. She didn't know what to do. She couldn't keep everyone safe and banish her father all at once.

"Just go, Jemma," Kai shouted, holding her eyes firmly. "Give them a little time."

Jemma stared at him across the distance unmoving even as Mrs. Berttie tugged at her elbow. Jemma's expression shifted between heartache, and fear, anger and confusion, maybe even slight hope.

"You come too, boy," Mrs. Berttie called out.

Before Black Boot could answer, or Jemma could insist and the rest of the plan fell apart, Kai just shook his head.

"I have a painting of Jemima Puddle Duck to finish," he said with a broad grin. "Don't worry. I'm safe here."

Jemma shook her head. But she stepped towards the van, haltingly.

"You haven't been taking your pills, have you?" Kai shouted after her, stepping forward involuntarily, as if to prolong her parting. He was rewarded with the barest flash of her smile, her real smile, the one that woke the world.

"Haven't had a chance yet, nurse."

Kai smiled after her. The adults shoved Jemma into the van, and Hippa darted in after. The sheriff tried to grab the other girl, but she backed away and vanished like so much air.

As the van pulled away, Kai let his smile fall, and he walked slowly back into the house. He was soaked through and through, but he felt nothing from it. And Jemma was crushed. Her parents had the upper hand, for the moment. Allen better do his damned job.

Kai smiled faintly; there really was something fun about cursing even if only in his mind. He might start doing it more often. If he survived.

"Sometimes, I close my eyes and wrap my arms across each other, and whisper, 'Jemma mine,' like you used to. It feels better for a moment, then I open my eyes and you're still asleep." From the Journals of Jemima Tulip Franklin, heir of Sarah, and 8th generation daughter of Terra.

There were more people in the van besides Mrs. Berttie and Sheriff Hicks. Jemma saw them but her mind didn't exactly register who they were. She couldn't even speak as the van sped away. *Mama.* She couldn't get past that. Mama was a spirit, walking and talking, and helping Pa. She had repaired the shoes, blessed the stones to keep Jemma out. To keep her own daughter out. And now she had everything she needed: the family stones, the power of the matron bones, and all the spells. No wonder Gran had said Jemma must perform the matron services as soon as she passed.

"Stop!" The van screeched to a halt at Jemma's shout.

"What, what is it?" Mrs. Berttie exclaimed.

"This is far enough. They can't see us now. I have to go back."

"Jemma, I don't think that's such a good idea." Sheriff Hicks turned around in his seat to look at Jemma, but he kept being distracted by Hippa and staring her way instead. "We know you can fly, but even birds don't fly in this kind of storm."

"I know," Jemma muttered, amused at the way his eyes stayed only on Hippa. He was making the poor pixie uncomfortable. After a second, she darted under Jemma's soaking hair to hide. "It's only going to get worse. Look, I already have magical help from three very angry wind guardians, a pixie, and what I think are a pair of kelpies bringing this lovely tropical storm. But I cannot protect you and banish Pa."

"Jemima, just what is it that makes you think you have to be the one to send him away?"

To begin with she was the only member of Sarah's line left, with any loyalty. And in the past few days Jemma had done so many things that she didn't know she could do. And just at this moment, with all the anger and hurt and power rushing through her, she felt strong enough to lift the entire state of Oklahoma and move it to another realm. Jemma shrugged.

"Everything." Jemma couldn't explain half of what she was thinking, so she didn't even bother to try. She felt warmth suffuse her neck. Steam rose from her hair; it fluffed out around her neck in light dry curls. Jemma smiled. Apparently, Hippa didn't like hiding in damp hair.

Everyone in the van just stared. There were six of them, including the sheriff and Mrs. Berttie. Linda Blake sat against the window in Jemma's row, Mr. Lewis was beside her, and in the back row, Mr. Little was shoved in next to Minnie Marsh.

"It was really nice of you to come for me like this, but you can't help."

"But we brought a coven," Minnie exclaimed.

Jemma spun around in her seat to face Minnie Marsh, the girl who pretended to be her friend for a whole summer just so she could get Jemma to use magic and have her real friends film it. The only thing Jemma felt looking at the girl she once wanted to kill was amusement.

"It doesn't work like that. This isn't wicca or TV magic. We don't stand in circles chanting words in ancient languages. And a coven is thirteen; you're six, about half shy." Mr. Little smiled at Jemma's condescension with deep understanding.

"You use the power over locations where your ancestors suffered, or did great deeds. You even use their bones and burial sites, like a shaman," Mr. Little offered, and Jemma nodded. "But it can't hurt to have people around you offering you their strength. That's the idea of a coven — people coming together supporting each other."

"But Pa has the house." Jemma shook her head. "My mother is helping him, she's…the oldest living woman in Sarah's line. And for some reason, the spirits of my ancestors are helping her."

He shrugged as if this was nothing. "Your home isn't the most powerful place on your property." Mr. Little nodded at Jemma as if waiting for her to supply the answer.

"The wall," Jemma said after a moment. Then she shook her head. "Sotsona's spirit may not even let you set foot there."

"But you will." Mrs. Berttie faced forward and slammed the wheel of the car in the opposite direction, speeding off into the darkness as if possessed.

"What makes you think I'm more powerful than a hundred-and-fifty-year curse against the town and all its people?" Jemma demanded.

"Well, Esther was certain you would be," Mr. Lewis spoke for the first time. "After that day in town when Clarissa called you a witch, she came back to town with the earth rumbling and called us cowards."

"She said it would serve us right if we were cursed another hundred and fifty years," Linda put in. "Asked us if we hadn't learned our lesson yet."

"She said you were the most powerful witch in your entire family's history," Sheriff Hicks added, rubbing his wrist. "Said you kept waiting for us to be better people; said you kept on saving us, even from yourself."

"You can do this," Mrs. Berttie finished. "She believed in you, and so do we."

Jemma couldn't say a word. She'd had no idea Gran defended her that way. Had no idea Gran thought that highly of her. Gran insisted Jemma was Sarah's heir, but she never seemed to think that made Jemma more powerful.

The day of the ceremony of the stone, when Gran called Jemma forward to choose her stone and take her place among the sisters of her family, Gran had given her this look, like she knew Jemma didn't mean a word of what she said, but she hadn't pressed. Why? If she thought Jemma so powerful, why wouldn't she want to force her to mean every word of the oath?

"Jemma." Minnie's small voice emerged from behind her. "I wanted to say…."

"Look." Jemma's eyes pierced her into place. "It's really sweet and all that you want to have an epiphany moment right now and try to apologize. But frankly, I have bigger problems than you, so save it."

In the front seat, Mrs. Berttie gave a loud snort. Hippa flew out from under Jemma's hair to stick out her tongue at Minnie. The pixie settled on Jemma's shoulder and rubbed her little hummingbird head against her neck soothingly. No one spoke. And in the silence, Jemma couldn't seem to shake Mama's face, Mama's voice.

Mama. It was a dream come true and a nightmare all at once.

Mama had the power to stop Jemma from doing what was right. Was that why Gran wanted to send her away? Did the creatures know she was working with Pa? Why didn't anyone trust Jemma with the truth, with the task?

Claim your stone, claim your place.

Such Power

There was something odd about the way the kelpie just gave in, about the way he went along with them. It was raining, he had his trinkets back, and he owed Jemma a life debt. Shouldn't he be fighting to fulfill it?

"She hates us," May Bell said in a flat, toneless voice as she preceded Black Boot into the house. "She would have banished us both."

"She was angry," Black Boot said casually. He could no more blame Jemma for her rage than he could take responsibility for the wind shoving her into the air when he grew afraid. They were so alike, he and his daughter.

"Angry? She would have cursed you, like Mama did. She's willing to let the land suck her dry, and die here, to make sure you leave," May shouted.

"May, she'll calm down, and she'll see things our way. We just have to wake you. Where's the doctor?" he demanded of the kelpie, ignoring May Bell for the moment.

The boy shrugged and walked over to the wall. But Black Boot knew that look; he was hiding something.

"Where are the others?" he snarled, advancing on the boy. He was sopping wet. The water fell off him and pooled on the floor, as if he were nothing but human. "What did you do?"

Black Boot yanked the boy up by the shoulders and slammed him against the wall. "Where are the others?" Black Boot felt the sting of fire shooting out of the boy's skin and into his hands. He felt the burn of it, but would not let go. "Tell me what you did."

He just shrugged, looking slightly bored. "I sent him for more paint. I wanted something darker."

"Argh!" Black Boot shouted out his rage and his pain, throwing the boy across the room as his hands began to blister.

"Tom." May Bell rushed to his side and stared down at his blistering palms. "Hold the watch; it worked before, maybe it will again."

Black Boot was panting against the pain, but he watched the kelpie crawl over to the wall beneath the broken window. He began prying the lid off a paint can. He was planning something. That's why he sent Jemma away; they had some plan. His daughter he could forgive, but this boy was another matter.

Black Boot reached into his pocket for the watch. As before, the moment it touched his skin, he felt relief. But this time, it didn't take the pain away completely or the blisters at all. His hands were bubbled up and stinging, and they would stay that way, unless he could convince Jemma to heal him.

"She shouldn't have that kind of power," Black Boot said. The kelpie did not look up, just moved about as though he wasn't listening to him. "You're matron here."

"I know," May Bell said slowly. "But, I'm also a spirit. Maybe the fact that I'm divided is confusing the ancestor spirits. We need to fix me, maybe then…"

Her voice trailed away, and she walked towards the kitchen with a hungry look in her eye. Black Boot watched the kelpie. The doctor was gone; it was part of some plan, and the other creatures were nowhere in sight, but they couldn't all have left. Why did he want the doctor gone? "What is it you know, boy? You don't have any magic left to defend yourself, and while I may not be able to touch you, I'd bet my boot can."

Spitting into the Wind

Kai shook his head and smiled. "So, it's true what everyone says about southerners and corporal punishment?" Kai's joke didn't have his usual pithy charm, but he didn't relish the idea of being tortured. He should have gone to the cellar with the others. But he couldn't leave Jemma to face it all alone. It had been too gut-wrenching watching her beat at the shield helplessly. How was it her parents failed to feel that?

"We aren't southerners," May Bell corrected from the doorway of the kitchen, staring between her husband and Kai. "This is the Midwest. What is it, Tom?"

"He didn't give away his magic without reason. And he chose the doctor with a purpose too. You know something about May, don't you? Something you don't want us to know."

"I know she's a crappy mother." Kai pushed to his feet. If he was going to be tortured, he would prefer start out looking his enemy in the eye. "There were signs long before this. I mean, you named your daughter after a duck that the narration calls a simpleton."

Black Boot was glaring at him, but at the comment, there was the barest flash of amusement in his eyes. Then the glare returned. If Kai could only distract them for a little while, Allen could protect the town, and Jemma would come back to finish the job.

"It's a beautiful book. I love that story," her mother exclaimed.

"Why?" Kai was surprised to find that distracting people was something he was very gifted at, even without the sparkle to draw their eyes.

"She's a sweet little duck. All she really wants is to raise her own babies. And she never gives up." May Bell shouted the last bit, as if defending herself.

As far as Kai could see, she just came up with that last trait in the moment. It was the only decent thing about the book, but even that didn't bring it up to par with Jemma.

Kai shrugged, staring at the mother, pretending he didn't understand. "I don't know. I just think it's no wonder she hates the name."

"She hates it?" May asked, and seemed to shrink.

"Yep." Kai turned slightly, lifting a can of paint onto the desk and peering at its label for something to do. "Won't let anyone call her that."

"She really won't forgive us, will she?" May Bell asked her husband, looking lost. "I thought, I hoped that she would just be so happy to see us…"

"We just have to show her how it can be," Black Boot reassured his wife, but he was beginning to show signs of doubt. "Once you're whole, once she sees we can fix her too, that it won't be like before, then she'll come around."

"Won't be like before." May Bell nodded and then she begged. "Are you sure we can do it?"

"You remade the boots without even having a body. Only think how powerful you will be once you have it. And we have that book of spells; we'll break the wind's hold on me and the land's hold on you. We'll remake the world together. I promise," Black Boot said fiercely.

They didn't really make sense, Jemma's parents. One moment they were cold and calculating, and the next they were like desperate children who'd never grown up.

"We almost had it before," May said. "We don't need the others, just you and me."

She spun around to leave the room, but her eyes fell on Kai and narrowed, flashing gold with power. "I want you to paint Jemima Puddle Duck right there." She indicated the wall above the desk. "I'm going to teach my daughter to love her name. Just you wait and see."

Black Boot followed his wife from the room, his original question forgotten. Kai stared after them. It was as though each was a child, completely filled with selfish desires, but with none of the innocence that made children precious. How had Jemma turned out so well? It must be something to do with the grandmother, or with Jemma herself.

Kai stared at the wall before him. The spirit of Jemma's mother wanted a duck above the desk. It wasn't a bad idea, but he wasn't about to paint the sweet little doormat duck from the story, no matter how much it persevered. He'd paint a Jemma Puddle Duck.

"Dragged my children to the wall, where their aunt died. Made 'em swear loyalty to each other, made Mary bleed into the earth, as Mother's journal said. I'd thought to feel closer to her. Don't. We're only closer to the land."

From the journals of Josephine Ness, 2nd matron of the Women of Terra.

 rs. Berttie slammed to a stop about a foot short of the wall, and Jemma thanked her lucky stars for the van's seat belts. Jemma went out first—alone. Even Hippa waited inside the van. Jemma limped over to the wall, in so much pain it began to feel like she was supposed to hurt.

The van's headlights lit the wall and the tree, but the rest of the world was a blank expanse of pouring rain. It beat her down heavily as she walked, soaking her hair in seconds. At the wall, she stopped and lay her hand over Gran's stone. She wasn't sure she could pick out her own from the wall, but Gran's she knew.

"Why is it you thought I could do so much, and told everyone but me?" Jemma whispered. Shaking her head, she replaced the stone on the wall, and walked slowly along it, feeling each one, waiting for something to strike her, something to spark her inside. Halfway along the wall, she saw a stone sticking up out of the ground, pointy, with a little bit of red staining it.

It must have been what tripped her earlier as she flew.

Jemma bent down and yanked at the stone. It wouldn't budge. She yanked harder, certain now this was her stone. More certain than she'd ever been of anything. She'd found it for a reason.

She yanked and heard the groaning twist of tree branches moving. She looked up. The tree was turning, a huge hand, twisting towards Jemma. Before she had time to really think about it, her apparent rescuers rushed out and formed a little half circle behind her.

The tree twisted more, pulling itself up by its roots to reach towards them. Jemma yanked harder. This was her stone, and she had to claim it.

"Let it go," she whispered. Not even bothering to look at the tree, or the people behind her, she just stared at the stone. "It's mine. I'm gonna do what you should have, long ago," Jemma shouted yanking all the harder. "I'm gonna tell my mother no, like you should have told your sister. I'm gonna protect the town, not just what's mine. Like you were supposed to." Jemma tugged with her feet braced alongside it, leaning away, but it wouldn't budge. She glanced back as two pairs of hands closed around her shoulders.

On her right, Mr. Little had her by the shoulder, with Mr. Lewis, and Minnie making a chain behind. On her left, Mrs. Berttie had Jemma's shoulder with Sheriff Hicks and Linda finishing out that chain. Jemma returned her attention to the ground, to her stone.

"I'm gonna do what you should have. And what your sister should have, and every generation that came after. I'm going to live up to that oath they make us take. I'm going to serve the land, and the people. I'm going to put what I want after what they need." She gave a mighty tug; the people on either side of her shoulders gave a mighty tug. The tree twisted, spun around in the earth, and the ground split at its feet, running off in a little fissure straight for Jemma. The stone flew free, and with the *half* coven at her back, Jemma went tumbling backwards. The tree settled back to its original position. Jemma held tightly to a long pointed rock with bloodstains all up and down it.

It wasn't her blood from tripping; this was Sotsona's blood. Jemma lay on her back in the pile of people who helped her free the stone and stared open-mouthed, letting the rain pour in. This was the stone that killed Sotsona. And she released it, let Jemma have it. And not just Jemma; she'd let the town have it.

Amidst laughter and groaning, Jemma rolled onto her knees and forced herself painfully to her feet. The others did as well, most of them smiling in the aftermath of the power flooding them. Jemma looked between them, and her eyes came to rest on Minnie, the girl she thought she would never forgive.

Jemma held the stone out to her.

"Sotsona is cool with you being here," Jemma said.

"Cool?" Mrs. Berttie questioned. "When did you start talking like that?"

Jemma shrugged, nodding for the others to reach out too. After everyone had laid hands on it, Jemma lifted the stone and limped over to the wall, placing it beside Gran's. She cast a glance over her shoulder at her coven and nodded towards the wall.

"You wanna' stand over here," she said, waiting until they all came near her. Jemma cast a glance into the sky, into the torrents of rain. "You're here for your son," she shouted. "Why not come and claim him?"

A bright bolt of lightning hit the ground mere inches from Jemma's feet. And a curtain of lighting followed, shuddering across the ground, sizzling and crackling, and a fanfare of thunder drowned out the din of the rain.

When the lighting cleared, two figures stood before Jemma sparkling like the sunlight across the water.

"Are all kelpies so dramatic?" Jemma asked dryly.

Kai's rather austere-looking father rolled his eyes and shook his head.

Seven

"Kelpie!" Black Boot shouted, yanking with all his might at the door to the storm cellar. It wouldn't budge, and the blisters on his hands had popped so the handle was eating into his flesh.

"It won't budge, May. Who knows what they are doing to you down there."

"Use the wind," May ordered.

Black Boot shot her a killing glare, as if he hadn't already thought of that. "It's a storm cellar, and its locked from the inside. I'd need to clear away the house to even reach it."

"So do it!" she shouted, and the house shook. "Do you think I care about a house? You promised me my daughter. You promised me a family. Open that cellar!"

Black Boot yanked harder. He gathered the wind around him, letting it twist and pull at the house, forming a cyclone in the midst of the kitchen. And an empty paint can came shooting through the air to hit him in the back of the head.

Black Boot spun away, dropping the handle. The cyclone only grew. There were pans and cupboard doors flying around the room. The kelpie was on the ground, clinging to the wall of the entryway, with his feet flying out behind him, dragged towards the cyclone.

"You'll kill her for real this time," he shouted.

A frying pan went hurtling out of the cyclone, barely missing the boy's head and struck his hand. It popped open, releasing the wall only to be yanked out behind him from the force of the wind. But he clung on with the one hand, fighting to avoid the suction. "You can't control it. She'll be sucked up and die."

How many times was I thrown by you?

Black Boot cast the winds of the cyclone apart, flinging out everything. The kelpie got caught up in the rush of air, and flung into the other room, striking his head on the wall, and getting slightly pummeled by kitchenware. He slumped against the wall, likely unconscious.

Seven.

The leash of wind had lifted Jemma and cast her into the air seven times before the cyclone. She nearly died from a fall twice. The other times, he caught her as she rose. But those two times, when she was flung away, as he bent to repair whatever damage she was doing to his shoes. Those times it was May to save her. The last was the day of the cyclone, only hours before. He hadn't meant to throw her, not that it seemed to matter to anyone else. It hadn't been on purpose, but…he hadn't meant not to throw her either. He'd only meant to protect the boots. And now he only meant to open the cellar.

What if the kelpie was right? He didn't have that sort of control. He could lose May Bell forever.

Black Boot stood, shuddering in the mess of the room. The window was broken open, had taken part of the wall with it as the kitchen table flew through. There were pans, and knives and broken dishes everywhere. May stood in the center of the mess, untouched. But all he saw was her bloody body on the day of the cyclone.

He saw Jemma, with her twisted, useless leg and the blood on her forehead. And the tractor upside down, with its blades in the air, and the truck and all the tools littered about, the house all but obliterated.

Kadawada Traveler. The daughter who wasn't real, and the one he'd surely never wanted, was buried in the ground behind this house, and he couldn't help but mourn her too. His other girl, and how easily it could have been Jemma.

"I can't, May." Black Boot dropped his face. "I can't risk it. Can't you…try to go to your body without me?"

May Bell stared at him as if he was a stranger. Her eyes were full of tears and terror, and she shrunk before him.

"But what if, what if it means I have to be without you? You woke me before; I know you did. I can't do it without you. The second you let me go, I was pulled from my body."

Black Boot shuddered and collapsed onto the floor. "But if I try to open it, I might kill you. He's right; I don't have that sort of control."

May nodded. A firm snap of the head and she spun away from him, walking to the hole in the wall.

"I'll have to give you complete control over the wind first, and reunite with my body later."

"Gran is dead. Buried in the cellar, because we put what we love in the ground. When I close my eyes, I see the dirt like I'm her, raining over my eyes, suppressing the world, suffocating life. I wish it would." From the journals of Jemima Tulip Franklin, Sarah's heir, and 8th generation daughter of Terra.

"*I* tend to respond to drama with drama." Kai's mother had a silky voice yet somehow threatening. Jemma watched as she reached under the strap of her long sundress and pulled out a scrap of paper.

It seemed ever so slightly like an affectation, the way she shook it, the way her gaze seemed to take in Jemma and only Jemma. As she gave the paper a firm little snap, lightning crashed directly behind her and Kai's father, illuminating the pair, like they were members of the Adam's family. Jemma smiled despite herself; clearly, Kai got his flair entirely from his mother.

Jemma cast a quick glance at Kai's father to find him looking resigned, if slightly annoyed.

"The world is a dangerous place for one alone," Kai's mother began reading from the page, her eyes darting repeatedly to Jemma. "It's eight o'clock in Oklahoma. Do you know where your son is? Would you know if he died?"

"Jemma," Mrs. Berttie gasped her name, half laugh, half rebuke.

Jemma pulled her shoulders back. "It wasn't drama. They were pointed questions designed specifically to make you feel guilty." As she said the last, Jemma's eyes shifted straight for Kai's father. She didn't know precisely what went on between them, but she knew he and Kai were not on the best of terms. "He's been missing from his home at least four days, probably more, Pa had to drag him from California to

Oklahoma, so it must have taken time. When did you know he was missing?"

"Who are you, little witch? And what have you done with my son?" Kai's mother demanded, and the clouds were painted with flashes of light.

"Am I really all that short?" Jemma demanded of her *coven*. She nearly laughed; she wasn't going to stop calling them that any time soon. "Everyone keeps calling me little."

"You will answer my wife." His voice was quiet and firm. Jemma faced Kai's father, wondering what had drawn these two to one another. He didn't sparkle nearly as much as her, or Kai.

Kai's parents stood in the downpour but the rain did not wet them; it fell on them, and made them sparkle more, but it neither slid away nor made them wet. Jemma was tempted to walk up and feel their skin, see if it was cold or warm, to see if it felt damp at least. She wanted to know if they simply absorbed the water or if they only looked dry.

"Little witch."

"Jemma," she snapped returning her attention to the man's face. Why was everyone so insistent she stay focused. She would much rather stand here chatting for a while longer. "My name is Jemma, and I rescued your son from my father."

"Is he…was he hurt?" his mother asked, breathlessly. "We went to where we felt his magic but it wasn't him."

Jemma shook her head confused. "He was nearly starved of water when they got here. I saved him, and he swore me a life debt. What do you mean it wasn't him? You are Kai's parents, aren't you?"

"Yes," his father snapped. "But the man we saw was not him, and what's more, we couldn't touch him because of some elf enchantment."

"That must be Allen," Jemma said, looking at Hippa who hovered just inside the cover of the van. "But I don't understand why he would have…" Jemma's words drifted to a stop as she put the pieces together. "That's what he meant. Kai said to give them time, but he didn't mean my parents; he meant Allen, to give him time to protect the town."

"From what exactly?" Kai's father asked. The mother was silent, but her eyes bit into Jemma.

Jemma looked at the man in front of her—another father who'd failed his child. "He's been here three days and he didn't even ask to use the phone. I think that's because of you. Do you ever tell him you love him? He deserves to hear it. He's a…" Jemma thought of everything he said today, and how much it hurt, then she thought of what she'd seen in his eyes back at the house, how he'd given his magic to Allen. "He's a nice boy. And he tries to take care of me, even though he only met me a few days ago. He tried to make me friends, and…he painted me a yellow brick road." Kai's father seemed to have no expression, but his mother had her hands clinched and tears running down her face.

"Whatever it is that happened between you, Kai is a good boy. A lot damn nicer than me. It wasn't his fault, and you need to tell him that. Before he gets like me and is willing to curse himself just to curse you."

"Who is it you're going to curse?" his mother demanded.

"No matter, it isn't any of you. I wanna offer you a trade. Kai's debt for a flood."

There were several exclamations from behind her.

"What?"

"Jemma, you can't do that."

"Think about this."

But Jemma ignored them all. Kai's mother caught her eyes, wouldn't release them; she stepped closer. She seemed somehow softer the closer she grew. When she stood just before Jemma, she bent low so their eyes were level. Apparently, Jemma was shorter than she felt.

"It is dark magic to trade a life debt," she said slowly. "Your life will never know joy if you turn on something so pure."

Jemma gave one sharp nod, wanting to laugh. Her life would never know joy anyway; at least if she did this, she could see Kai safe.

"What is your deal precisely?" She kept her face close. Jemma found it oddly uncomfortable to meet this woman's eyes; that usually wasn't a problem for her.

"I will give you his debt, so you can take him away, but first you will flood this basin." Jemma nodded behind her. "It used to be a lake; I need it to be a lake again."

The woman stared into Jemma's eyes a moment longer. "Are you quite certain this is what you want? You have not perhaps been wandering around with the words 'only you' in your mind, have you?"

Jemma's eyelids thinned into tiny slivers and her voice took on a bit of a bite. "I can't say I much like your son when he puts an effort into sparkling," Jemma snapped. "This is all my doing."

"Fine." She spun away so quickly, Jemma nearly slipped on the wet ground from the shock of it. "We will flood the lake, and you will keep our son safe."

"That wasn't the deal." Both Jemma and Kai's father snapped at the same moment, casting distrustful looks at one another.

"No, it wasn't," Kai's mother said with a sharp smile. "But I don't participate in dark magic, or interfere with my son's debts. If he offered you his life, it's yours. We'll discuss his coming home after you finish with your cursing, *little* witch."

Curtains of lightning fell between the kelpies and Jemma. When it cleared, the couple was gone. The rain that pelted Jemma and her coven shifted suddenly, pouring directly into the basin where the lake used to be. It came down in waves, more like the spill of a waterfall than rain pour.

Hippa flew out of the van and straight up to Jemma. Jemma stared at the fluttering hummingbird and her eyes grew wet. She shivered as the wind hit her soaking body. It was almost over now.

Odd, she always imagined that breaking the curse would entail a moment of all-encompassing power and a great shower of light or the songs of angels. Not this odd step-by-step acceptance that it wasn't so much about her. Allen was protecting the town, Sotsona had accepted Jemma's coven, representatives of the town had accepted and forgiven them. And the lake was being filled. Everything in place, and none of it by her, none but the last step. All that was required was the sacrifice: her life for the town, as Sotsona had been sacrificed for her sister.

"Jemma," Minnie called from behind her, but Jemma didn't turn.

"I can't curse them," Jemma whispered to the pixie. "It will taint the sacrifice, and some of the stain will linger. But…I can't let them stay. And I don't have the spells I wrote."

Just let go, Jem beam, let it come to you. Magic 'aint about thinking. It's feeling.

"All I feel is anger," Jemma answered the Gran in her mind, aloud.

No, not you. Look down deeper, girl. Deep in your heart where no one can see. What is it you hide away? That's where magic dwells. It ain't history, or inheritance, it ain't even power really. It's what you have that the rest of us lacked. A soul wantin' not but to forgive. Let loose your soul, Jemima Tulip. Free it from the chains you've made in fear. Then you can claim your place.

Jemma bent forward, bracing herself on her aching knees. She was cold and wet, shivering a bit, and she ached all over, but all she felt was sorrow. All her life it seemed she wanted one thing: Ma back. And now she had it, and with everything inside her, she wanted Gran instead. She wanted to lay down on the ground and sob until her tears and not the rain refilled the basin.

Slowly, she felt several pairs of arms closing around her as she cried. Jemma wanted to fight, wanted to shove them all away and never let them see her like this. But at the same time, she wanted to reach out and cling to them, so she stood still and let their arms enfold her.

Skewered

Kai regained consciousness slowly. His head was pounding, his whole body ached, and there was a sharp stinging pain in his side. He didn't want to open his eyes. The hiss and scream of the wind was louder, but he couldn't hear the rain any longer.

There was a warm wet stream of something running down his abdomen, from his left side, exactly where his side stung. He didn't want to look. It wasn't going to be good. Maybe if he kept his eyes closed, he would pass out again, and wake up somewhere nicer, like a hospital or contested gang turf. Some place where dying really was the worst thing he had to worry about.

That wasn't the case here. He had Jemma to worry about. Kai pried one eye open, only to squeeze it shut again as the bright yellow lights from the house hit his eyes. How were the lights even staying on in this mess of a storm? The wind should have knocked out power lines long before now. Maybe they had a generator, maybe power lines were underground in Oklahoma. Maybe Kai was wondering about nonsense so he wouldn't have to open his eyes.

He shifted his legs, and little things went tumbling off. He shoved to a seated position, and the sharp stab in his side had his eyes popping open involuntarily. There was a serving fork sticking out of his side. A serving fork!

Kai laughed. Midwest kitchens were more dangerous than he'd thought. Kai only laughed harder and watched the fork shake.

"Aaahhaahaaa," he groaned as the jiggling fork stabbed into more of his flesh. It wasn't in very deep, just enough to make him bleed and ache. He should yank it out, right?

Kai looked around the rest of the room, and all his humor vanished. The kitchen, or what was left of it, was nearly without an outside wall. Its ceiling was completely destroyed, and there were bits of broken glass, utensils, and pans scattered everywhere. The living room was barely better. The wall between it and the kitchen had a giant crack running up it, slicing between the giggling baby Jemma and her mother. The second bench was embedded in a wall two feet to Kai's left, the wall of May Bell's room, leaving a huge gouge in it. And there was a whole in the ceiling near the doorway, or maybe a more accurate description would be a bit of ceiling in the hole where the roof used to be. Half of the yellow brick road was sticking up out of the floor.

All things considered, a fork in the side and an aching head weren't so bad. Kai looked at the room, not his side, as he gave the fork a quick hard yank.

"Aaaaaaa." Kai bit down on his lip. This was so much worse. His side started throbbing in earnest now, and the blood slid out faster, not to mention how badly the air stung his wound.

"Skewered? Gotta' be a fish's worst fear." Black Boot laughed, coming up on Kai's right, from the bathroom. "Wouldn't make much of a soldier, would you?" He held out a first aid kit in his own bandaged hands, seeming to wait for Kai's response. He could keep waiting. "You do decent work with a bit of paint though. The bathroom your work too?"

Kai yanked the first aid kit away from the man. Refusing to remain so far below him, Kai shoved to his feet, clinching his teeth to avoid making any noise.

You're too soft.

And so what if he was? Where was it written that every boy in the world had to want scars from kitchen utensils and never acknowledge pain?

"I've never had any interest in being a soldier," Kai snapped, trying to pull open a band-aid while holding onto his bleeding wound.

"Here, it's too big for that." Black Boot yanked the first aid kit back and found gauze pads. He pulled Kai to face him none to gently, yanking Kai's hand away so he could look at the wound. He used a bit of gauze to clear away the extra blood, careful not to let it get on his own bandages, and yanked out another piece. "So…she doesn't like her name?" he asked hesitantly, as he shoved the gauze against the wound and pressed Kai's hand to it, digging around in the first aid kit for tape.

Kai just stared at the man for a second. He thought of what he had seen of this man's memories and what he'd felt. All regret and fear, this man. Kai nodded. "She won't let Allen call her that."

Black Boot wouldn't meet Kai's eyes as he applied the tape. "Is he…like a…."

Kai knew what Black Boot couldn't get out, and would have shrugged his shoulder but for the pain that shot across his side. "More like a brother from what I've seen. But he's doing his best to do a father's job."

Black Boot stepped away and gave Kai a mocking smile. "I think you'll live."

Kai let his bloody shirt fall back over the wound. "Do you even see this place? Your daughter's home," he snapped. While he would take his father's comments without a word, Kai wouldn't be mocked by this man who was still half monster. It made him angry, and the fact that he thought he had a right to knowledge of Jemma's life made him even angrier.

Black Boot shrugged. "This is Oklahoma, tornados happen. And May's working on a solution. It won't happen anymore."

Kai shook his head, walked to the bench sticking out of the wall and began tugging. "You want to be free, to have control over yourself. Why don't you think the wind deserves the same?"

All around him, the wind picked up, and Kai had a second's fear over agitating this man. He had no defenses. But he only yanked harder on the bench and gritted his teeth against the pain, and the fear.

"The wind is just going to keep fighting you, and one day, Jemma or her mother are going to get well and truly caught in the crossfire and die." He shouted the last, giving the bench a hard tug. It came out with a loud whining crack and sent Kai stumbling backwards with the bench in his hands. He managed to catch himself before he fell, the front end of the bench landing with a loud thwack on the floor.

"Jemma can handle herself," Black Boot said in a sort of dazed voice. Kai dropped the bench. Walking right up to the man, he glared him in the eye.

"Do you hear yourself? Jemma can handle herself," Kai snarled the words. "Like she should have to. But that isn't even what you're thinking about, is it? I heard you earlier when you said she shouldn't have that much power. You weren't worried for her, or scared of her. You were jealous."

Black Boot startled, knocked out of his contemplations by the words. But Kai wasn't done.

"You're jealous of your daughter's power. How jealous? Which do you love more, honestly, Jemma or her power?" Kai wouldn't let the man have space, staring into his eyes so he couldn't escape the assault of the words. The wind grew around them, and little things began to move. "Because if you don't have the right answer, and I think we both know you don't, than the best thing, the most fatherly thing you can do for her is leave."

"We both love our daughter," May Bell interrupted, but Black Boot didn't seem to hear her, he was staring straight ahead.

Kai slowly faced the woman. More than anything, he wanted her to be right. But Jemma seemed to have them both pegged. They didn't know how.

"You should go see what she painted for you," Kai said nodding into her room. "When she was nine."

She glared between him and Black Boot a moment longer then walked through the door, and turned around as if looking for the trap.

"On the ceiling, so you'd see it if you woke and she wasn't there." He watched her look up, saw her face shut down, wiped clean of all emotion.

Black Boot came out of his stupor and walked over to the whole in the wall, peering through. The wind grew even stronger in the house, shoving the bench into Kai's legs. Black Boot yanked his head out of the wall suddenly and went storming from the house, carrying the wind with him. After a moment of hesitation, staring at the ceiling, May Bell ran out close on his heels. Waiting only a moment longer to see they didn't notice him, Kai rushed to the kitchen to check on the others.

Tied Down

*B*lack Boot stood panting amidst the rage of four winds. The other guardians beat at him as if they thought they could tear the boots apart with their gusts. But they couldn't; they couldn't stop him.

"No one can stop me!" he shouted. "Nothing can hold me. I am my own man."

"Tom." She came rushing after him, and just now, she was the last person he wanted to see.

"What are you waiting for?" he shouted into the sky. "Don't you want to kill me? Are you afraid?"

"Tom, stop it." She reached out to grab his arm but her hand slid through him and it was more than he could take. Tom turned on the shadowy spirit of his wife, swiping at her and yanking at her arms, willing her to be before him, whole and real so he could kill her and have done with this.

He swiped and he swung and the wind swirled around them, but she stood untouched before him, with tears streaking her face. Her ghostly form was so much less of her than he wanted but still so much more than their Jemma had—because of him.

"ARGHHHHHHH! I wish she had never been born," he cried out anguished, and all at once, the wind died around him and he collapsed, yanking clumps of the wet dirt in his hands and slamming them again and again back down. "I wish she had never been born."

"No you don't," she hissed, and the earth shuddered beneath him. "Don't talk about her that way. You love her."

Black Boot heard from the hiss of her words that her teeth were clamped tight around them.

"I can't do this anymore, May. I'm sorry. I can't do it."

"Yes you can. I am going to break the wind for you, and bend the earth to your will, and you are going to give me what I was promised!" Her voice rose with each word, and the ground cracked where he was kneeling, splitting between his hands and knees so he had to roll backwards to keep from being swallowed up. She stood above him, alight with anger in this dark night. "We are Terra, daughters of the earth! We can belong to no other. But *I* do. I chose you, and you will do this *one* thing for me. I don't care if she does hate us now. I don't care if she thinks we're monsters, and we have to lock her in the cellar until she loves us again. We are going to be a family, and you are going to be a man for once in your life and hold onto your *temper*."

"May." The word was torn from him as tears began running down his cheek. "The dress she's wearing, you wore that the day you told me you were pregnant."

She just stared at him, unable to see the significance.

"I never knew fear like that day. Not when my house was burning around me, or when I thought you had died."

"You were afraid for her."

He shook his head. "I was afraid for me." He panted. "I felt… further away from the wind, and the peace, and the power it gave me than ever before. It was the first time I used the wind for something other than it wanted. When I left that day, and I said I had to, I said I was being torn from you. It wasn't true. And not two days later, before I even had time to regret leaving, you followed me, swore to follow me anywhere."

She stared at him for a moment. Silent. Then a hand rose to cover her mouth, as if her whole world would escape from between her lips with the sob.

"It isn't because I don't love her. Or you." Tom shoved to his feet. "That's just it, I love you too much. I love her too much. You pull me away from the wind, and make me feel all these things I can't control. I keep fighting against the wind like it's the problem. So sure, if I can only control it, then everything will be better. But…it never will be. I should have died with my parents. You should have had a happy life here. And she—"

"Don't. Don't say it again," she begged through her tears. "Just… stop."

Her hand reached out, just a breath from his chest, and they stared at each other, always one breath apart.

347

"Love and family, mothers and daughters, self-sacrifice. There is so much more to this family than just the curse. Why is that all we ever speak of?"

From the journals of Belle Dade, 5th matron of the Women of Terra.

When Jemma's tears faded and the others stepped slowly away, she didn't know what to do. She wanted to say something rude, to get back on steady ground, with them tolerating her begrudgingly and her just slightly outside. But she couldn't. Nor could she bring herself to thank them or truly acknowledge what they'd done.

Mrs. Berttie seemed to understand and saved Jemma from the decision. She shouted to be heard over the wind and the downpour behind them, "So what now? How does having the lake help you?"

"That's more about the curse than anything else. Sarah's curse," she explained, realizing the boots were a curse as well. "Now I have to bring Pa here, somehow."

"And how do you propose to do that? A high-speed chase?" Sheriff Hicks asked.

Jemma shook her head. Lifting her face to the sky, she felt the cold wind, nearly frosty.

"Ilya," she called out, hoping he was paying attention.

The man materialized out of the wind before her. "I've seen no results yet," he commented looking unimpressed, then he leaned towards her and she could see the warmth in his eyes. "It need not be on your hands, little girl. We can handle it."

Jemma shook her head. "Nsombi is a little girl, too."

"He is not her father."

Jemma nodded. "I only need you to bring him here; the three of you. Bring him here and hold him, while I work a spell. Can you?"

"We can, if we can get through the shield."

Jemma nodded. "It'll take a moment, but you'll be able to."

Without a word, Ilya was gone. Jemma was startled by the speed of it. She always wanted more time. She always put things off, always begged for five more minutes reading, or sleeping, or flying. But her time was up.

She returned to the wall, the others stepping out of her way. Jemma lifted Gran's stone.

"None of this could've happened if I'd done the matron service like Gran wanted." Jemma spoke mostly to herself and Hippa. "But I didn't see the point. The only reason to do it was to make Gran proud, and she never could've seen it."

Shaking her head, Jemma held out her left hand and stabbed it with the stone. Her audience gasped at the sight, her blood dripping down onto the stone, into the wet earth. Jemma crouched, oblivious to the pain, and gathered bits of bloody earth into her hand, rubbing it across the wound. She stood.

"Blood of my ancestors," Jemma intoned with her eyes shut and her fist wrapped tight around Gran's stone, and the dirt on her palm. "Earth of my history. Everything that I am, I offer to you. From this day on, your willing guardian. Today, I, Jemima Tulip Franklin, eighth daughter of Sisika's line, offer my oath and take up your name. I am Terra."

Sparks of light popped in Jemma's palm, and the dirt slid over her softly, healing the wound. She replaced Gran's stone reverently, willing her tears away. There wasn't time.

She turned to her coven. "You'll need to get behind the tree, hold onto it and to each other," Jemma ordered.

"What about you?" Minnie asked.

Jemma said not a word; all around her the earth rose up, holding onto her.

"Damn," Linda Blake exclaimed, awed. But in short order, everyone obeyed, running to the tree to hold on tight.

"Hippa, you should fly away now. I can't keep you safe from the wind."

Hippa wasn't listening. She flew under Jemma's hair, warming her whole body, drying it. Jemma wanted Hippa with her, the warmth alone made her feel better. But —

"My hair isn't going to keep you safe," she whispered. "This kind of wind reshapes worlds. Please."

Hippa darted in front of Jemma's eyes and shifted into the shape of a little girl with fluttering wings and her hands braced on her hips as she glared.

"Please," Jemma repeated. Hippa stuck out her tongue and rolled her eyes. Then she flew over to the tree with Jemma's coven and darted into Mr. Little's pocket.

Jemma shut her eyes, raised one heavy, earth-encrusted leg and slammed it against the ground. She felt her magic rushing out from the spot, seeking other matrons. She opened her mouth, ready to say something she would never remember, when she felt it. *Gran.* She felt Gran's spirit settling at her back to defend Jemma in her hour of need like an avenging angel.

Jemma released the tears, couldn't stop them. All this time, Gran said they put what they loved into the earth, and the earth returned the love, but Jemma never understood. It was the love, not the ground, that gave her power. Gran's love. She felt Gran's hands settling on her shoulders, proud and loving.

With a suddenness that sent the top half of Jemma's body flying out behind her, held up only by her legs of earth, the wind and the earth split the shield wide, sending out a giant shockwave. Behind the tree, her coven clung on for dear life, the wind lifting their legs from the ground.

But at her back, Gran held Jemma in her arms. Gran's magic and Sotsona's and every matron back to Sisika gripped Jemma's legs tight and offered her the strength of their love. They held her—safe and beloved. Jemma had never understood until this exact moment, but she had never been alone. She was Terra.

Thrown

Kai made sure the others were secure in the cellar. Their magic was holding the cellar shut tight. They had to keep May Bell away from her body. In her body, she might win the struggle for control of the land. Nona offered to open the storm door and let Kai in, but he refused. That was just the sort of opening Black Boot needed.

No, he was more use to Jemma here. For half a second earlier, it seemed like he was getting through to Black Boot. He'd looked into his eyes and for the barest of instants, he'd seen a man. Once Kai was certain the others were safe, he ran outside to try again.

He was just in time to watch as three figures materialized out of the wind around Black Boot, then all was chaos. A blast of wind sent Kai flying into the porch beam, and another pushed at him from the side, shoving him towards the broken kitchen window. He fought against it wrapping both his arms around the beam, but still the wind pulled at him.

There was a loud, violent scuffle out in the battle of meeting winds, but he couldn't see a thing for the darkness and the swirl of dirt and mulch. There were shouts and profanity, and over and over the squish and plop of bodies striking mud. Then suddenly all the wind rose up, dragging Kai's body up along with it.

Just as suddenly, it slammed down, sending shockwaves out across the land. Kai lost his hold and was flung backwards into the wall of the house. He struck the porch with a thud he felt throughout his body, but he charged to his feet, ignoring the pain, and rushed out into the yard.

Black Boot was gone, and his wife, and the ground was split open. He glanced back at the house, and even that seemed slightly off-kilter. Headstones lay littered across the ground.

Kai had no idea where he was going, but the moment he saw the stones scattered about, he set off running. Something was about to happen, and he needed to be with Jemma when it did.

"Jemma," he shouted charging into the darkness. "Jemma." He should feel her, but he'd given his magic away.

"Kai." He heard perhaps the last voice he wanted to hear and saw his father appear in a stream of lightning.

"Not now," Kai shouted barely registering the man. He ran around his father. "I need to get to Jemma."

"Kai, that girl can handle herself."

"Well, she shouldn't have to!" he shouted, but he didn't slow down. "Everyone keeps saying that, but I'm not leaving her alone. Maybe I can't save her home, or her, or bring back the family she wanted, but I'm not leaving her alone."

He didn't hear a thing from his father, and that was fine with him. Let him be disappointed if he wanted, Kai didn't care. He ran on, until his father's hand on his elbow pulled him up short.

"Fine." Dad said only that and his hand was gone. Kai fell through the air with a deluge of water and wind and landed with a splash in a wide lake. He went under, battered by the rainfall.

"The town adopted the name Unforgiven after I shared my grandmother's journals with the town council. Rather suits them, but then, who don't it suit? Everyone's sinned against someone." From the journals of Mary Croger, 4ᵗʰ matron of the Women of Terra.

The rush of wind shoved the top half of Jemma's body this way and that. Slowly, she grew the dirt higher, past her knees, all the way to her waist, holding her to the ground like a tree with roots a hundred miles deep. She saw Sotsona's hand bend around her coven like a cage, saving them from blowing away. And in the distance, the barest light of day invaded the storm clouds.

Was it tomorrow already?

The wind rushed back and forth in every direction as each force battled to control the current. She felt like she was in a wind tunnel with the air shoving her skin back into the spaces of her jaw, and her hair all but pulled out. Every so often, the current would shift direction and she was shoved to the side.

She heard the battle as it raged towards her, the fight for supremacy, the fight for freedom. And as the storm of air approached, Jemma fought for breath. For strength.

As if they knew she needed it, Jemma heard the voices rising up behind her. Three words repeated over and over. Perhaps there was power in numbers, in voices rising together for a common cause, because as she heard the words, Jemma felt infused with the strength of their belief:

"Hold on, Jemma. Hold on, Jemma. Hold on, Jemma."

She wasn't alone.

The air around Jemma went completely still. She was in the eye of the storm. The wind rushed around outside, but nothing touched her. And in center of the eye, just feet before her, the guardians of the four winds appeared, with three holding one in place, though he kicked and fought like a wild thing.

"Pa, stop," Jemma ordered.

He stilled, and with him the battling winds. His eyes found Jemma.

Her Heart Breaks in My Hands

Black Boot felt all his power drain away at the sound of her voice, and he fell completely still. It had always been so, always but when he had walked away. When he fled her voice as it chased him around the world. His little girl, and he had failed her, again and again, but still she loved him.

Would she love him unto death? Death at his hands.

He looked up, forgetting the hands locked tight around his arms, or the small arm around his throat. He looked up and found her eyes.

She was magnificent, standing all but stone for the earth wrapped around her waist high, with her hair a wild cloud of fire billowing behind her, and her eyes so sad and quiet, they had no business in this chaos.

"I am so sorry." The words were ripped from him as he met her eyes. How was it he'd not once said that to her? Not once held her, or told her how truly he loved her?

She watched him for the longest time, and he thought his heart would break. She could not forgive him. How could she, after all he had done?

"I forgive you," she said, barely more than a whisper, but it washed through the burning fires of his soul and soothed him.

May Bell appeared beside him, but her eyes were all for Jemma. Jemma observed her mother, and a tear slipped free of her eye.

"Would you have come back…" Jemma began, and her eyes returned to him. "Would you have stayed if you knew she was alive?"

Her question startled him so much, he glanced between wife and daughter, not even sure if he understood a difference. But Jemma did. And they both knew his answer. She nodded once, then shook her head as if shaking off tears.

"That's fine. That's good," she muttered.

"Jem Beam, your Pa had his good points. He was a hard worker, and at times, a sweet if lonely soul. And he loved your Mama like I've never seen anyone love. Made him powerful, and powerful afraid. Like nothing but their love mattered, a Romeo and Juliet, epic-type love. Suppose I didn't quite understand a love that consuming, might even have gotten in its way, but that's another matter." From the journals of Esther Lynn Franklin, 6th matron of the Women Terra.

Of course he would stay for May Bell. Jemma had overheard Gran on the phone once with a friend. It was long past Jemma's bedtime and she should have been sleeping, but she snuck out to go sit by Ma, and she'd heard Gran talking.

"I oughtta give up," she'd said. "Don't know who I'm tryin' to fool thinking she'll wake. She never did want to live without 'im. That's what got us into this mess."

Jemma regarded her mother now and wondered what could make a being so connected to another that their life had no meaning without them. But she rather thought Gran was right.

"Jemma, we love you. So much. Please, let us stay and fix this."

Jemma noticed Pa didn't beg, didn't even look as though he cared to stay any longer. But Ma would fight for him.

"I've wanted to hear your voice so badly," Jemma whispered.

"Let us stay, Jemma mine," Ma whispered hesitantly, a soft entreaty. And Jemma wanted to shout that she wasn't hers. That she was Gran's, and that Ma had the only thing that really mattered to her: Pa. But the words caught in her throat and she longed more than ever to feel her mother's arms close tight around her.

Beyond Mama, she saw the other guardians growing restless. Pa was still, but he wouldn't be for long. He always wanted to do what was right, but he never did have the strength.

"I used to dream that you would wake up, and you'd wrap me in your arms and we'd go out together and find Pa, and we'd smile and hug, and it would be perfect," Jemma said looking tearily between them.

"We can have that," Mama said. Jemma smiled at her sadly.

"No we can't, Mama. That's a fantasy. It stops right there, when the moment is perfect, before I remember that he left me bleeding and screaming by what he thought was your corpse. Before I have to recognize that you never loved me as much as him. And just before he starts to feel tied down again and tries to be rid of us."

Pa jerked involuntarily in the arms of the guardians, and the wind picked up beyond the eye. But Jemma needed to have her say.

"I don't think you ever wanted us dead, Pa. Just…gone. Out of your way, maybe even hating you, enough so we'd never let you back again."

His breathing grew heavy, and he couldn't look her in the eye any longer.

"Gran made it easy on you with the curse. You could say she was stopping you, pretend she'd poisoned your memory so much that I'd rather pluck out my eyes than see you. But it wasn't true." He looked up and his eyes pierced her, tried to intimidate her, but Jemma knew fear when she looked it in the face.

"I should have seen you coming long before I did. Would have had the time to prepare for you. It never should have come to this. But I didn't want to be ready. I wanted you to win, to say just once that you loved me so I could let you stay."

In the eye of the storm, there was utter silence. Nsombi was on Pa's back, holding him with an arm wrapped around his throat; she stared at him for a moment, then her eyes found Jemma, full of sympathy. The other guardians looked away, almost in shame. Pa returned Jemma's stare, always frozen. Mama jerked her head back and forth between them, finally diving in front of Pa so her face was level with his.

"*Say it!*" Ma shouted and all around the earth shook.

The clay encasing Jemma's legs began to crack.

Dragged to Her Side

Kai swam to the edge of the lake. He had no idea where he was, and the wind was so strong, he had to crawl up the shore with his head down. He barely made it. He didn't know where he was going, but the wind was worse up ahead, so he headed there.

He made it to the crest of a small slope, still on his hands and knees, and Kai saw the rush and whirl of a tornado cyclone held exactly in place. Just past it, trapped beneath a tree, were several people huddled together chanting something Kai couldn't make out as the wind battered them with whatever it could yank from the ground.

Kai crawled closer, digging his fingers deep into the dirt as though that would hold him. The closer he got, the more the wind pulled at him. He wasn't sure what he meant to do, but he had to try. Kai raised his head, to peer into the tumult, but there was too much flying around to make anything out. But he knew Jemma was in there.

He came up against a wall as he crawled. Loosely piled stone but not one budged despite the wild winds. Kai was a person who easily accepted a sign. He reached up carefully laying his hand over one long pointed stone, and lifted it free. He expected a bit of resistance from the stone, so steadfastly resistant to the wind, but it slid free.

Kai jabbed it into the ground to help his journey towards the funnel. It clung to the ground as it had the wall. A touchstone he could leverage himself against.

He was nearly upon the winds when the ground began to shake and a great scream rose up over the den of clashing forces. The quaking ground slowly loosened the stone's hold on the earth, and Kai felt the winds pulling at him.

My Rage Drags the Wind

*B*lack Boot felt rage growing in him like never before. It rose with the wind and did battle. May Bell's voice echoed around the stillness of the eye, but he couldn't see her, couldn't hear her. Jemma was all there was.

He wished she had never been born. Wished he could never have failed her, could not fail her now. But he would, he would fail her if he stayed, he would fail her if he spoke, he would fail her if she made him go.

It was all he ever did. Failed the people he loved. He couldn't save his parents. Couldn't face the questions and be the man they raised. He failed to serve the wind, after everything it had given him. He even failed May. May whose love was so completely incorruptible, that she loved him even as she hated him. He failed her.

"Tell her," May begged. "I know you love her, please. Why won't you speak?"

No. She couldn't understand, her love was too simple, too certain. But he saw Jemma's eyes across the space. She understood. Her mother was cracking the ground around her with her frustrations, and the wind was piercing its way back into the eye to pull at her, but Jemma's eyes held his. She knew what would come now.

Black Boot breathed slowly, taking her in as though this would be his last sight of her. Her eyes flashed with power, and the earth fell away from her legs.

Which do you love more?

"Tell her," May continued to beg, then spun around, rushing to Jemma. "He loves you, he does. He was so scared and alone when I met him, and he didn't think he could love. But he loves you."

"I know, Mama," Jemma said softly.

Black Boot couldn't stand it. Why did she have to say that? With more force than he should possess, Black Boot threw himself backwards, knocking aside his captors. His wind charged in, knocking aside every other force to rush at Jemma.

She didn't know. How could she know what even he wasn't sure of?

The wind rushed at her like an army of a thousand men charging a wall. But she didn't shift her gaze from his. Black Boot regained his feet, and almost at once, the others were on him. It didn't matter, he was more powerful than a thousand wind guardians right now. He cast them aside with a gust and advanced on his daughter.

Her eyes flashed again, and she took a step towards him. The force of her step reverberated around the clearing. He glanced down; on Jemma's feet were a pair of gleaming black boots, just like his, only—*stronger*. He froze, mesmerized by the boots as Jemma made her way towards him.

You're jealous of your daughter's power. Which do you love more: Jemma or the power?

She Quiets the Wind

Kai lifted the rock high, as the wind yanked at him and slammed it towards the ground. It barely skimmed the surface, but it caught hold. He clung to it, dragging his body closer to the stone, to the center of the chaos.

He was nearly there when all the wind that had been swirling ever upwards was pummeled by a stronger force and collapsed inwards on itself.

The fog of flying debris cleared and Kai just had time enough to see all the wind rush in at Jemma, but it couldn't touch her. She stood firm and electrically charged as the wind rushed around her. She lifted her face high, and raised a finger to her lips, and though it rushed and grabbed for her, the wind was quiet.

He heard the people chanting, "Hold on, Jemma," heard the downpour, and he heard Jemma, calm amidst the slash and swing of wind.

"Gran isn't the only one with power over the clay, Pa. And you aren't the only one with sway on the wind." Jemma advanced on Black Boot. But he didn't watch his daughter; his eyes were all for her feet, and the shiny bright boots she wore.

"Jemma mine. Please," her mother begged coming up beside her. "I'm so sorry I left you. I always wanted you with me. Please, let us stay."

"I asked Gran if I could take Grandpa's name, be a Franklin. She said no at first, said I was only angry with Pa. I am, sort of. He left me here, bleeding and crying and begging him to stay. Why should he get to claim me? But I also asked because of all the things you wrote, and Gran tells me, about Grandpa Sy. I want to be his girl, a good soul." From the journals of Jemima Tulip Franklin, Sarah's heir, 8th generation daughter of Terra.

Jemma looked at her mother and smiled, slowly shaking her head. Would she fight this way just for herself, Jemma wondered, but it didn't matter. May Bell was as much a part of Pa now as she was a part of herself. "It has to end, Mama. No more ripping the earth apart chasing what just can't be."

"No. Please." She reached out for Jemma, and Jemma reached out in return, but they just slipped through each other. "It can be."

Jemma stared at her empty hand for a moment. The wind was everywhere, growing stronger, and she was forgetting the others, in favor of wishing for her mother. She shut her fingers into a fist, and dropped it to her side.

"You know you're alive now," Jemma said. Her mother's eyes filled, darting between Pa and Jemma.

"Don't send us away."

"I think this time it's a choice. For you," Jemma said, and her gaze shifted back to Pa, so intent on her shoes that he could not even see her. "But not for him."

"But…you have to understand, Jemma. He's always so alone, but you…." Mama waved her arm behind Jemma and Jemma followed the motion. Huddled under the tree, her six-member coven were clinging together and chanting for her, and crawling on the ground beneath the wind, Kai was making his way to her side.

"You are surrounded by love," Mama finished.

Jemma's eyes returned to her mother's face, and a shudder slipped through her. Yes. She was surrounded by love, just not the love she wanted. No more forever wishing, and waiting, and hoping.

"I love you, Mama. I love you too, Pa. But it's time to say goodbye." Jemma shifted her gaze his way, and took a deep breath. He did not even seem to hear her. "Black boots—"

"No, Jemma, you'll curse yourself too!"

"Of this soil were you grown, and of this soil am I keeper," she spoke ignoring her mother's cries. This was no curse. It was only an end. "Return to the earth from which you sprung, and let loose the wind."

For a moment, nothing happened. Then Pa's eyes flew to Jemma's, and the boots began to dissolve. With every bit of dust that fell away, the wind rose higher, tugging and shoving at everything around. Jemma stumbled back a step, and glanced down; her boots were dissolving as well.

"I love you." The gruff words were torn from Pa, and he reached forward suddenly, grabbed hold of Jemma's fingers, clinging to them for dear life. "Jemima Tulip, I love you."

Jemma opened her mouth to respond, but the boots fell away completely. The wind rushed out at once in all directions. Jemma flew into the air, pulled away from Pa and the clearing. She fought the wind, searching for Pa, and saw him slowly dissolve into dust, carried away.

Jemma reached for him and Mama as she vanished as well, but the wind pulled them further and further apart. She was too caught up in her parents even to make her wings work and the wind threw her off with all its pent-up rage. She landed like a boulder in the midst of the lake and the pouring rain and struggled against the water.

She kicked out, and flapped her arms wildly, trying to stay up as the water closed in around her. Water flew up into her nose and mouth and eyes, and she coughed sputtering. She floundered wildly. She'd never learned to swim.

Jemma kicked out against the water. It was pulling her down, and a jagged cramp shot straight up her leg and all the way to her right shoulder. Jemma screamed out against the shock of it, both hands flying to her leg, and she went under.

Bright purple lights flashed before her eyes, and she saw stones, so many stones raining down on her, pummeling her body. Blood falling on soil. Rage, such rage, and so much pain, attacking her, pulling her down. The final sacrifice.

Freed

T he west wind swept out across the world heedless of any obstacle. It slammed against mountains and buildings, shuddered over lakes and rivers, and carried its servant caught up in its flow. *Free.*

At the little town of Unforgiven, it met with a barrier, fire and cool air, and braced flora, but nothing could hold the wind now. It rushed on, into the barrier, and the air caught fire, burning away all the debris it carried in its wake, slowing its progress across the town. It rushed through the deserted streets, upsetting trashcans and signs, and shaking the buildings but freed of debris and slowed, it did little damage.

To the east of the town, it met with a warm steady breeze that made no move to shove it back, but would neither yield its place. The currents met and skirmished a bit, shuffling up the dust of the earth and playing among the trees. But after a while, the west wind moved on.

In the south, it clashed with a hot current. They met, vying for might, and the southern wind warmed the west wind so it was nearly tired from the encounter and moved along in another direction.

When it met with the north wind, as frigid and solid as a wall of ice, the west wind did not even stop to play, moving westward where it was most at home.

It swept across a little home, sitting lopsided on the ground. The home where it was first bound. And a rage filled the wind so it would wipe the home away. But from within the walls, the voices of the liberated rose up, and from outside, the voice of a debtor, and all called on the wind to pass. To let go of vengeance, and pass in gratitude for its freedom. The wind moved on.

After Her

The stone held Kai in place as the wind lifted Jemma into the air and threw her. He saw her rise, her eyes locked with her father's, saw her pulled away by the current. He waited for her to fly, or calm the wind, or pull herself to the earth with an arm of clay. But nothing happened, she was falling fast.

Kai didn't think, he opened his fingers, releasing the stone and let the wind carry him after her.

He saw her hit the water, splash around for a moment then go under. He hit the ground a bit further off and crawled into the lake. The wind swept across the lake, carrying everything it could get hold of. As Kai dove under, searching for Jemma, he saw a van hurtling through the sky towards them.

He dove. He couldn't see Jemma anywhere. Kai swam deeper and deeper into the dark lake, searching for her. He breathed her name into the water and swam deeper.

The van hit the lake and sent out huge rippling shock waves. Kai rode the flow of the wave letting it drive him faster forward. Then he saw her, sinking, fighting to swim with one arm, with the other clenched around her right leg.

He shot out towards her, swimming with all his might. She was floundering, sputtering and fighting for breath. When Kai reached her, he wrapped an arm around her waist and struck out for the surface. Jemma flapped out her left arm with him, but there wasn't much strength behind it, as she fought for air.

He pulled her head to his, fitting his mouth over hers, and blew air back into her lungs. He felt them swell against him, but Jemma went completely still in his arms. Kai pulled away enough to see her shocked face. He smiled, shaking his head at her and pumped his legs harder, dragging them to the surface of the lake.

"Your grandpa wasn't the first man to turn my head. Tommy Lewis in town had the loveliest smile and sparkly eyes. Still does. But he never came close to Sy. Because Sy made me feel free to be myself. And loved, even when I was a bit of a witch." From the journals of Esther Lynn Franklin, 6ᵗʰ matron of the Women of Terra.

Jemma and Kai broke the surface of the lake, and he immediately began paddling for the nearest shore. Jemma helped weakly. Everything ached, she was tired, and she couldn't work up the energy to think beyond this second. When they finally dragged themselves up to the edge of the lake and lay under the light misting of rain, Jemma closed her eyes, coughing out the remains of the water from her lungs.

Her eyes popped open and a hand flew up to cover her lips. Kai was sitting beside her staring with a patiently amused smile.

She knew what he was thinking. What he saw. But she wasn't about to let him have that satisfaction.

"I thought you gave away your magic," she blurted out to change the direction of his thoughts, and hers. It wasn't a kiss. It wasn't a kiss. It was CPR.

Kai nodded, smiling, still not distracted it seemed. "Sure, I can't sparkle, but I'm still a kelpie. We're water creatures, I can breathe under water."

"Really?" Jemma tilted her head to the side thinking it over. "I'll have to…"

"Make a note of that." Kai finished with her, a broad grin painting his features. Jemma fought the urge to sigh. He was beautiful, with or without the magic.

"Are you sure you can't sparkle?"

Kai laughed but made no response.

"Are you laughing at me?" Jemma asked annoyed.

"I wouldn't dream of it," Kai lied with another laugh. Jemma humphed and looked away.

The air was so still and quiet. She searched the banks of the lake, morning light steamed in through the slowly dissipating clouds, but she didn't find what she was looking for. Her parents were gone.

"Is that Mrs. Berttie's van?" Jemma asked staring off across the lake. "Oh! My coven." Jemma shoved to her feet, biting down hard on her tongue to keep from shouting against the pain in her side.

Kai was up, and looping her arm around his shoulder to support her before she was even fully up. "You really need to start taking your pills," he muttered.

"Yes, nurse."

"You think I'm kidding, but I'm not. Maybe I should hire you a nurse." Kai helped her slowly up the hill. Jemma closed her eyes and just let his voice wash over her. "Coven, hm? I didn't peg you for a team player."

"Hey." Jemma smacked him in the side.

"Argh," Kai let out an involuntary groan and a hand shot out to cover his side.

"You're hurt. Oh shit, I'm so sorry."

Kai just laughed as Jemma shoved away his hand to look. "What happened to you?"

But he wouldn't answer, just kept laughing.

"What's so damned funny?" she shouted as they made it to the crest of the hill, but Kai only laughed harder.

"Jemma!" Minnie Marsh rushed forward, followed closely by Mr. Little, Linda Blake and Mrs. Berttie. The others hung back and just watched.

"Are you hurt?" Linda called out.

"He is," Jemma muttered. "But he won't stop laughing long enough to tell me how the hell it happened."

Kai threw his head back and laughed a bit more.

"Quit that," Jemma hissed between her teeth.

"Are you alright, Jemma?" Mr. Little stepped up and took Kai's arm from Jemma, holding it up, so Linda who was a nurse could get a look at Kai's side.

Jemma nodded. She wanted to yell at Kai some more, or do just about anything other than talk about what happened, but she looked up at Mr. Little and the words slipped out.

"Thank you, for…" She waved her hand towards the tree. "It helped."

He nodded back, smiling. "I had to," he said with a shrug. "Coyote never would have let me hear the end of it, if I had let something happen to Super Girl."

"You'll want to be careful about having your kid around Jemma," Kai commented, with one arm over his head while Linda poked at his wound. He chuckled at his own joke before he even got it out. "She has the biggest potty-mouth of any fourteen-year-old I've ever met."

Jemma narrowed her eyes at him. "I thought you were from California."

"We're easy-going people."

Minnie Marsh giggled, but as soon as Jemma's eyes fell on her, she thought better of it and sucked the laughter back in.

In Her Eyes, I Sparkle

"Hey," Kai said to the strange woman examining him. "You want to check on Jemma when you're done? She hasn't taken her pills, and her leg is really hurting."

"Ha," Jemma scoffed. "My eyelids hurt. Hell, my eyelashes hurt. Everything hurts."

Kai couldn't resist teasing her just a bit more. "I bet your lips feel pretty good though."

Her eyes flashed and the air crackled, but before Kai could even laugh, a hand flew out and smacked him upside the head.

"Hey," Kai started, then his tone shifted dramatically. "Mom! What are you doing here?"

"The girl you're teasing called your father and I here to rescue you."

"You did what?"

Jemma shrugged, looking superior, then he watched as a cold mask of disinterest settled over her. "I figured someone's parents ought to do their job."

Everyone was silent for a moment staring at Jemma. It was so much easier to just pretend nothing happened than to actually talk about it. Kai saw her standing there, so alone, even with everyone around her.

He pulled her into a tight hug, like he should have done two days ago, and just let her be for a moment.

"I think they really do love you, Jemma."

"Just not enough."

Kai didn't know what to say. So he shrugged. "My father threw me into a lake. I said I needed to get to you, and he just threw me into the lake with all the rain they were bringing."

Jemma giggled "What are you complaining about? You're a water horse, you can swim."

"Yeah," Mrs. Berttie called. "Not like my van."

Everybody laughed for a moment, and Jemma slowly pushed out of Kai's hug, with an embarrassed half smile. But before anyone spoke, Hippa flew out in front of the group shaking her little girl's head and with a pop of bright light, the van was out of the lake and dripping onto the dirt road just past the tree.

"Wow," Minnie breathed. "Your life is so exciting."

"I wasn't the first Terra to rebuild her home. Storms have been sweeping across us long before your Pa, and they'll do so long after. The trick is to learn to see the fun of it, making something old new again." From the journals of Esther Lynn Franklin, 6th matron of the Women of Terra.

It took a while to get home. The van was probably fine, but apparently, submerging a combustion engine made it a bit hard to start. In the end, it was Hippa who brought them. In a bright flash of light, they appeared in the dirt before the house.

The ground was cracked open, with fissures bisecting little areas around the different headstones on the ground. And the house itself didn't look very good. It was lopsided, with the kitchen and that entire side of the house sticking up out of the ground while the other half seemed intent on sinking into it. The wall of the kitchen had a huge hole in it, and its roof was all but gone. The kitchen table lay in the dirt several feet away. And even the living room had very little wall left.

"There wasn't much house to save," Kai's father said. He was standing at the foot of the porch steps. "But I did my best."

Jemma gave him a brief smile. "Thank you." With a nod to Mr. Little, who was holding her arm, Jemma reclaimed her arm and limped painfully forward.

Gran's headstone was on the ground a few feet away. She reached into the dirt and dragged it up against her chest. She hated the idea of Pa using this stone to help keep her out of her own home. Hated the idea of him touching it when he had so much hate for Gran. Slowly, carefully, Jemma stood back up and brushed the loose dirt off the stone.

Esther Lynn Franklin
Terra
You are daughter of the earth and her guardian

April 3,1953- April 28, 2012

Jemma closed her eyes, laying her hand on Gran's name as if it could call her spirit to her, but nothing happened.

You are daughter of the earth and her guardian.

The words were carved into the stone of every single matron. It was what took Jemma the longest, when she buried Gran, carving in these words. She'd wanted to put something else—beloved Grandmother, or maybe even just Gran. But at the time, it seemed to Jemma that being matron was the thing that made Gran proudest, so that was how future generations should remember her.

Smiling now, Jemma lay the stone on the ground and looked up at Kai's father.

"You'll wanna stand over here now."

He gave her a pompous look and walked slowly over to join the group. Jemma let her hands fall to her sides and rolled her shoulders. She raised her eyes to the house and shook out her body like she was doing the hokey-pokey. As she did, the house picked itself up from the ground, following Jemma's motion, shaking off loose boards, and broken glass, which joined the dirt, as yet more dust. Even the debris from the house that already lay on the ground dissolved, returning to the earth Gran grew it from.

When Jemma fell still, the house settled slowly back into its rightful place on the ground, and the fissures in the ground sealed themselves together. But Jemma wasn't quite finished. The ground around Gran's stone sparked with electricity and a tiny shift of wind brushed across it. Jemma whistled a low, long cry like an egret swooping across a lake and little sparks followed the song. When she stopped, there was a new stone lying where the last had been. Jemma bent to retrieve it and started heavily towards her slightly broken house.

"We've a fully packed pantry for once. Who wants something to eat?"

Dust House

So, that's why they called it Dust House. Kai couldn't get over it. He had a million ideas for paintings now, but was too exhausted to start any of them. He caught his parents exchanging uncomfortable looks as they followed along with the rest of Jemma's guests into the house. He didn't think they were overly fond of her. But they hadn't known her long. Soon enough, they'd like her better than him.

The inside of the house wasn't so easily repaired. Jemma stopped in the center of the living room and looked around with something halfway between resignation and horror, then she hobbled off to check on the bathroom.

Kai heard the toilet flush and the shower come on at the same time and smiled. She came out and nodded to all her guests.

"It's working." Then without waiting to see if anyone would speak, she limped towards the kitchen. She was probably off to let the others out of the storm cellar—as usual, worrying about everyone else first.

Kai went the opposite way, searching under the mess on the floor for her pills and straightening things as he went. The others began to follow suit, with the exception of his parents.

"When the first baby laughed for the first time, its laugh broke into a thousand pieces, and they all went skipping about, and that was the beginning of fairies," Mrs. Berttie read the quote off the wall. *"Peter Pan.* A good choice. You do beautiful work."

"Thanks," he said, his head next to the ground, searching beneath a bookshelf.

After a moment, Kai saw his mother begin to gather up the papers scattered across the ground and stack them on the desk.

"Oh, Kai," Linda called out. "Here's a first aid kit. We really should put a fresh bandage on your stab wound."

"Stab wound?" Mom exclaimed rushing over.

"It was only a fork, Mom. I'll live. Anyway, I need to find Jemma's pills."

"Over here," Mr. Lewis called out. "In the fireplace."

"Great." Kai held up his hands. Mr. Lewis tossed the bottle like a football.

Kai caught sight of Dad from the corner of his eye walking around looking at Kai's paintings. Silent and withdrawn, as always.

Jemma came limping out of the kitchen with Woolworth, Nona, and Tangerine behind her. She carried a bunch of water bottles in her arms.

"Storm got most of the dishes, and I shut off the gas just in case. But the generator's working."

"Come sit down and have your pills," Kai ordered. Unsurprisingly, she ignored him and walked around to give everyone a water bottle.

Kai shook his head and walked into her mother's room. He tossed the pill bottle onto the recliner so he could drag it out. Kai nearly had it out the door when his father came up behind him and started pulling as well. He didn't say anything, just helped Kai to lift it off the ground so it wouldn't scratch the yellow brick road.

They settled it next to the one bench in the living room and Kai didn't even bother asking. He just walked up behind Jemma, grabbed her on either side of her waist and carried her over to the chair. He shoved her into the seat and nodded to her.

"You're sitting on your pills. Take them."

"Yes, nurse," she sighed and a pouty look came over her features. "I really am small, aren't I?"

"It will come to no good, this lie, but I cannot abandon my sister. Still, I have such visions when I sleep, of lonely women as the years pass, and such pain suffered to right our mistakes. Such a heavy price love requires."

From the journals of Sotsona, Sacrifice of the Women of Terra.

Jemma was exhausted, and she hadn't had this many people in her house, ever, that she could remember. She made a point of introducing everyone and passing out drinks, then she sat around wondering how exactly she was supposed to kick people out who had no transportation.

There were new paintings on the wall, but she couldn't bring herself to look closer. A giant piece of her yellow brick road was sticking up out of the floor. She probably needed to call the insurance people. There was no ceiling in the kitchen. And May Bell's body was still in the cellar, down there with all the dead.

Jemma was half tempted to leave her there. But she knew she wouldn't. Even if she hadn't already liked Kai, she would love him now. She kept giving him dirty looks and pretending to be annoyed with him, but really it was nice that he shoved her into a seat, because her leg was killing her. And she was glad he forced the pills on her. But more than that, even without his sparkling, he had a way with people; he was putting everyone at ease. All Jemma had to do was sit there and doze.

Hippa settled back on her shoulder in the hummingbird form and her wings beat a steady rhythm against Jemma's cheek. She could barely keep her eyes open. She just lay there, letting them drift shut, and listened to the various discussions flying around the room.

"This house is going to cost quite a pretty penny to fix," Sheriff Hicks commented.

"Maybe not. You saw what she did before," Mrs. Berttie commented.

"Do you suppose Esther had the forethought to put Jemma's name on the policy?" Linda asked.

"Can you even put a fourteen-year-old on an insurance policy?" Mrs. Berttie asked.

Off in another corner, Kai was arguing ever so subtly with his parents.

"As I see it, she saved you and you returned the favor pulling her from the lake," his father snapped. "You may stay long enough to say goodbye, then we're getting out of here."

"I don't see it that way," Kai countered. "And I'll stay until I feel my debt is fulfilled."

"Kai. No one is forcing you to leave today," his mother said with a voice of steel. "Clearly, your little friend needs someone around, and it's nice that you want to take care of her. But…this isn't a place you can stay indefinitely, and I imagine Jemma wouldn't want you suffering from staying here."

Woolworth and Tangerine were talking with Mr. Little about Jemma's terrible eating habits and how someone would have to see to them once they were gone. And Nona was entertaining Minnie and Mr. Lewis with fire tricks.

Jemma had a soft smile on her face and wanted to drift to sleep, but she resisted. She was waiting for something.

When she heard the familiar screech of the truck's breaks she sighed and settled more comfortably into the chair.

"Jemma?" Allen came rushing into the house shouting her name. "Jemma, are you alright?"

Jemma waved her arm but didn't bother to get up. He rushed over and pulled her into a tight hug.

"Thank God! I was so worried."

"I'm fine. Just tired. You alright?"

"Yeah, I'm good. The town's good. Is…are you sure you're alright?"

"I didn't curse him," Jemma said softly, rolling her head to the side, half asleep. "Just unmade the boots, so he can't control the wind. Oh, May Bell's body's in the cellar. Check on it, will you?"

She didn't notice the silence that fell over the room. Just drifted to sleep unable to hold it off any longer.

Dim Light in the Deep Dark

Jemma slept for a few days. It worried Kai a great deal, but Allen was unconcerned. He kept saying "acute exhaustion" as if that was good. Kai refused to leave until she was awake and sent him away herself, as did the rest of her magical creatures.

Hippa perched herself on the post of Jemma's bed and refused to leave her side. Kai rather doubted Jemma would ever be rid of that particular pixie. Not that she wanted to be.

The town was so well protected from the worst of the storm that the nation's news stations didn't know what to make of it. But the weather still hadn't settled entirely back to normal. There was an unseasonably cold wind hanging around Oklahoma that no one could explain, and there were intermittent showers and lightning storms due to the fact that Kai's parents insisted on staying in town until this was all sorted out.

"You should paint an open gateway that looks somewhat overgrown and hidden on the arch from the kitchen." Kai rolled his eyes at his mother's comment. The renovations on the house were going oddly quick since half the town had shown up to offer help, or money, or supplies. Jemma was suddenly a local hero.

Kai had only one job: painting. And everyone and their cousin seemed to have an opinion about what he should paint.

"You know, like *The Secret Garden*," she added when Kai didn't respond.

He was wearing headphones so he could pretend not to hear, but his mother knew him better than that. "Look, Mom, I have a very specific vision for this place."

"And constructive criticism never hurt anyone."

"So, that's why Dad slept on the couch for a month after he said the lead in your play couldn't be named after a candy bar?"

Mom laughed, shaking her head. "No sweetie, he slept on the couch because I felt like torturing him, and because he said Hershey sounded like a good name for a transvestite."

Kai chuckled, "*Him*shey would be better." Mom slapped Kai lightly on the shoulder and he went back to work on his dark forest.

"I wanted to tell you…" Mom let the words drift off the way she did when she was waiting for him to look at her. Kai lay the paint brush on his drop sheet and turned to face her. She smiled; reaching out a hand, she lifted his chin. "I'm very proud of you, and the way you look after that girl, all this you're giving her. No matter what happens in the future with your friendship, she's never going to forget you, or stop loving what you gave her."

Kai nodded. "Thanks," he choked out, turning around so he wouldn't have to look at her. "I said some pretty awful things to her before, and I didn't exactly get a chance to apologize yet."

"You will." She ran a hand over his hair and ruffled it up a bit. She stepped closer and peered into the dark forest Kai was painting, at the woman in the distance, following a tiny orb of light. She gave a large sigh, and pulled Kai back against her, wrapping her arms around him. "It was never your fault that she ran away," she whispered. "You know that, don't you?"

Kai nodded. He did know, but there was a difference between knowing and believing.

"I just…I can't shake the feeling that I should have been able to help her."

"There's a rainbow in every storm. Not after, you mind; in. And I dare you to find it, Jem beam, I dare you." From the journals of Esther Lynn Franklin, 6th matron of the Women of Terra.

Jemma woke up in her room with the light streaming in and the faint sound of hammers and saws outside. She rolled onto her side and stared at her alarm clock. It was nearly noon. How late was Gran going to let her sleep? Jemma shoved up in bed, it wasn't like Gran to…

Her feet hit the floor and it all came rushing back. Gran, dead. Pa returning. May Bell in the wind, with him. Freeing the wind, essentially enslaving Pa, and May Bell going with him.

Hippa came flitting over to Jemma and popped into little fireworks again and again as she had when Jemma freed her. Jemma smiled and reached out a hand to rub over the pixie's head as she shifted back into her favorite shape.

"I'm glad you're here." Jemma coughed; her throat was so dry. "Come on."

Together, they made their way out into the main part of the house. But it wasn't the same house at all. No one was around as she emerged, so Jemma had a chance to just look. It truly felt as though she had stepped out of her room and into another world.

The yellow brick road at her door led out into the rest of the house, by way of a little cove painted on the floor and the bottom half of the wall by the bathroom. There were mermaids and mermen, and singing girls that Jemma could only assume were sirens, and in the distance, a little ship flying a pirate flag. There was even a little group of water horses, some shaped like horses, others like people, all sparkling. Jemma bent close, searching the crowd, but there was no Kai among them.

Leading up from the beach were a set of rolling hills. Atop the highest hill sat the ruins of a beautiful castle. It should seem lonely sitting there facing the sea, but there were vines of roses growing up over it, making it look more like Sleeping Beauty's castle than the ruins of a great nation. It looked hopeful—waiting to be reawakened.

Her bench was back, and the other bench was padded and painted as well. This one looked like a hollowed-out tree trunk; it had moss growing on different spots and a little woodpecker poking at it.

Across the room, where there used to be a wall, there wasn't. Someone must have decided it was easier to simply get rid of the wall to May Bell's room. There was an arch there now, with a curtained partition but no doors. Someone had brought May up from the cellar. She lay with her bed facing into the living room.

Jemma turned away to look at happier things.

Along the main wall of the living room, Kai had painted three very different worlds, but they all seemed to blend from one to the next seamlessly. The first was a dark forest, with a dark dreamy figure wandering through. She was all in shadows but for her face, cast in the light by the little fairy she followed. A beautiful girl, with slightly round features and queenly stature; her eyes though—they were so sad, and so…intent. She was seeking something. But she was at the far edge of the forest, almost off the wall completely, and the forest led away. There were tiny little frightening creatures peering out, sometimes just eyes in the darkness.

The forest led to a dark cave, overlooking a wide field. From inside the cave, little puffs of smoke were rising, and the faintest hint of a sleeping dragon could be seen, all but camouflaged to his surroundings. Just outside the cave were scattered remains of knights, or at least their armor. And crossing the field was a small army of soldiers.

The further across the field she looked, the lighter it became, until it looked like midday and the field gave way into farmland. There were crops that looked remarkably like her own, and a smattering of animals, but in the center, on top of a rock with her head thrown back, was Jemma's namesake. Only she didn't look much like herself. This Jemima Puddle Duck had her wings braced on her hips and sparks of electricity popping out of her eyes. She still wore her bonnet and shawl, but the shawl was purple, and from the way it flapped in the wind, it looked more like a cape. She had a small army of tiny magical creatures spread out behind her with capes of their own.

"Super duck."

Jemma jerked her head to the side and beamed at Kai. But before she even opened her mouth to say something, she saw the wall behind him. The wall surrounding the fireplace. It was the only wall not covered with fantasy creatures. Jemma approached it slowly. He'd painted the photo from Pa's watch, though she'd never shown it to him. It was a little different; she was laughing, and Hippa was flying out of the laugh, but…now she had it, even though Pa had carried it away with him. And above it was a painting of Jemma with Pa. He was holding her by the hands and swinging her around, when she was just about five. She didn't even have a picture of something like that.

But the very best part, the part that had Jemma reaching out to touch it, was the painting of her and Gran, scrunched together in the recliner, with Gran running a hand down Jemma's hair.

"How did you even…"

"Hippa," Kai answered coming up to stand beside her. "She shows me what you dream."

"*Thank you.*"

"You're welcome." He stared at her for a moment as if trying to read her mind. "Jemma, about what I said to you —"

"It's cool."

"No," Kai said forcefully. "It's not alright, Jemma. I don't know what came over me. Well, I do. But it's no excuse. I should never have spoken to you like that, no one should. You deserve better. And I'm more sorry than I can say."

Jemma nodded and felt her eyes fill. Would she ever stop crying?

"I forgive you."

Kai smiled and nodded to the bench. "Sit down, I'll get you some water and your pills."

Jemma laughed but said nothing, turning to look closer at the wall. She followed the images up to where they vanished into a bit of painted mist that tied the whole room together. There were little shapes in the clouds and Jemma looked up higher and nearly fell backwards. He was painting the ceiling. That wasn't finished; there were mostly sketches of what was to come. The only bit he had painted was Jemma, flying with an open smile on her face and butterfly wings.

"I don't have butterfly wings," she said looking over to catch Kai's eye as he walked back into the room.

"How do you know? They're invisible. Careful." Kai nodded behind her. "You'll fall into crocodile river."

Jemma glanced down at what looked like a little rushing river. At the edge was a cartoonish, slightly familiar-looking crocodile. She leaned closer to get a better look; it seemed to have a lollypop in its mouth.

"Aaa!" Jemma jumped back, startled when the crocodile suddenly opened its jaw to show her its rainbow lollypop, and snapped it shut again.

"How did you do that?" Jemma demanded, half breathless from fear, half from giggles.

"Magic," he whispered and winked at her.

Jemma couldn't say a word. Reaching out, she took the glass he offered and swallowed half a pill. She wasn't about to be bullied into more when she felt fine.

"You are Terra. Daughter of the earth and her keeper. No other love may claim you, and no other duty pull you from her arms. Claim your stone, and take your place amongst your sisters. Terra evermore." Oath of the Stone.

Jemma found out where everyone else was a while later when she went into the kitchen and found the source of the hammering. Apparently not content to just rebuild, the town of Unforgiven had pooled their resources and were building a fourth bedroom, a guest bedroom they said, because it was about time she had more guests. Woolworth and Nona were supervising. Apparently, the time locked together in the cellar had given them a better appreciation of one another. And Tangerine was supervising improvements to the kitchen.

She forced two plates of leftovers down Jemma, certain she must be hungry. Then she started talking about the book of recipes she'd made for her, and how they would have a cooking lesson later in the day.

There was so much noise and activity it didn't really feel like her house anymore. But then it wasn't, was it? She'd broken the curse, saved the town, and now everyone thought they had a right to some say in her life. She should really stay, talk to the people rebuilding her home, thank them maybe. But Jemma slipped out of the house and started walking.

The fields would need planting soon, but she supposed that wasn't going to be up to her either.

"Jemma. Wait up," Allen called out from behind her. "You're up! Where are you going?"

"Oh, you know, running away to join the circus. Figure it will have less activity than the house."

"They're only trying to show how grateful they are, Jemma. It'll die down in a few days."

And go back to just us. Jemma thought morosely. *Damn, I'm hard to please.*

"You going to talk to me, or just yourself?" Allen asked after a second. "Look, I know this isn't ideal, but you're stuck with me, kid. Is that really so bad?"

Jemma shook her head. Then she came to a sudden stop and faced Allen with her hands on her hips.

"Yes. Because you're not being yourself. You used to consult me, and encourage me to do my own thing, and listen when I wanted to bitch about Gran. Now all of a sudden you are just in charge and I have to go along with you. With everyone!"

"Jemma." Allen laughed. "Your being a bit dramatic. You've just woken up. What are we forcing on you?"

"Oh, I don't know: no cussing, food, pills, the house. It's a different house from when I fell asleep, and no one asked me anything. But why should they? It's not mine, is it? Gran left it to you, didn't she?"

Allen looked away hesitantly. "No, Jemma, the house is yours, but it's in a trust that I control, until your twenty-fifth birthday."

"Twenty-fifth?" Jemma laughed angrily and spun away. "Well, then it's basically your house. I don't know why I'm complaining, you should get to do what you want with it."

"Jemma, I'm sorry. I should have consulted you, but…I thought it was best to get moving on things."

"Well, if you'd asked me, I would have told you to fix May Bell's wall. It's a hell of a lot easier than making a new room."

"I thought you might like opening it up a bit, so she's part of the house."

"Well, I don't want her to be!" Jemma shouted and felt like collapsing even though she knew she'd slept for days. "I want her in a 'home' or in a corner or somewhere the hell away from me."

Allen drew himself up and nodded. "I know."

"But it doesn't matter what I want, because you're in charge."

"It matters. And I'll make you a deal. In a few months, when you aren't so angry, if you still feel the same, I'll find a new setting for her."

Jemma was near panting, and there was a loud angry pounding behind her eyes. She thought maybe she could see her pulse. And all she could think was, she chose him. May Bell chose Pa, over her own daughter. So why should Jemma give a shit about her anymore? Jemma didn't want to care, but the more she tried not to, the angrier she grew.

"I understand why you're angry with her, I do. Kai told me what happened. But…I think you need to give it time, so you don't do something you regret later, okay?"

Jemma bit her cheek and shrugged, not sure at the moment what she wanted. She wanted to run away, but she wanted everyone to be here when she got back. She wanted to sob, and scream, and laugh all at once. She wanted May Bell gone, because what she really wanted to do was run in there and shake her body, and yell at her, and make her *come back*. She wanted some control in her life, but she didn't want to lose Allen. He was all she had left.

"Will you be listening to me about other things?" Jemma bit out. "Or do you know and control everything?"

Allen laughed. "You've got a wide, evil streak in you, kid. What is it you want me to hear?"

"I want to have a funeral for Gran—"

"Of course," he interrupted, looking magnanimous.

"I'M NOT DAMNED FINISHED!" Jemma shouted at the top of her lungs waving her arms in his face.

Allen raised a hand to the bridge of his nose and rubbed it, closing his eyes. When he opened them, there was a tight smile on his face. He waved an arm for Jemma to continue.

Jemma knew she was being awful. But she had a screaming voice in her head. And she was about to suggest something that went against every family tradition. And she was scared and lost and so much angrier than she had been last week, but she shouldn't be, and she couldn't make it stop.

"I want to burry Gran next to Grandpa. And I either want to move the house, or move the bodies in the cellar. I don't like living in a tomb. And I want…I want. Well, I guess that's it. NO! I want to finish school my way." She saw him open his mouth to argue so she rushed on, afraid if he pushed her too much, she might go back to her old plan and run away. "I'll make friends and have people over. But I'm already enough of a freak with the limp and the magic. Being years ahead of everyone won't make me any friends. I want to finish with home schooling, and I'll go away to college."

"Are you finished now?" Allen asked sarcastically.

"For the moment."

"I will consider and discuss each one of those things, and any others you bring up, on a few conditions."

Jemma drew herself up and held her breath, waiting for the worst.

"You can't just scream at the top of your lungs or set off an earthquake every time I don't respond just how you want."

"Do you feel an earthquake?"

"I'm not damned finished." Allen cracked a half smile. "I'm not trying to be your father, Jemma. But I need to look after you. Not because you can't, or because you shouldn't have to, but because I love you, kid. Quit acting like you don't know that. We may not always have been family, but we are now, and you know it. Life sucks right now, so I'll give you a little rope, but sometimes I am going to make decisions for your best interest that you don't love, and I need you not to blow up at me, or try to…" He waved his arms around helplessly, "bamboozle me."

Jemma smiled and shrugged.

"That wasn't an answer."

"Neither was 'I'll think about it,'" Jemma pointed out, and started back towards the house. She felt immensely more comforted by his flapping useless arms than by anything he'd said. He was still Allen, slightly stupid, silly, afraid of magic, and her friend.

"I mean it, Jemma. I'm gonna need your word on this." Allen started after her.

"Were you and Gran lovers?" Jemma asked casually. Allen's response was not so calm.

"Hell no! That's disgusting. Where did you get that idea?"

"Pa."

"That man has a sick mind."

"He didn't know we were talking about you at the time." Jemma shrugged. "He thought because she let you win a fight now and then."

Allen shook his head, still clearly disgusted. "Jemma." He took her elbow and drew her to a stop. "There's something I need to tell you. I've been avoiding it because I knew how you felt about the curse, but…it's broken now. You believe that, right."

"Sure." Jemma watched him cautiously.

"I'm…Gil Jessup was my great, great, great grandfather," he said dramatically as if he expected the sky to fall in. Jemma thought back to how they met in the hospital. He'd been the night doctor after she had one of her surgeries and he came to check on her expecting her to be asleep, but she was sitting in bed, glaring at the cage around her leg, holding all the pins in place.

"Those make excellent weapons, you know." he'd said in that cutesie little voice everyone used with children.

Jemma regarded him with contempt; she wasn't a baby. And this wasn't her first cage. She knew perfectly well what it was for.

"Then I'd just have to wear it a third time, when I broke my leg again."

"Well, you don't actually have to use it. Just threaten. Most of the school kids will run."

"They already run."

"Oh, a real badass, are you?"

That was the exact moment Jemma decided to like him: when he cussed with a nine-year-old little girl like she was a grown-up.

Jemma looked at Allen now and shrugged. "Can't be. You're too smart to have been inbred. You must be adopted."

"You are so mean," Allen said through a helpless laugh. "My family has no history of inbreeding."

Jemma patted him on the shoulder and continued walking. "No, of course not."

"Jemma- small, redheaded witch from the tiny, almost nonexistent town of Unforgiven, Oklahoma. Guardian to a plot of long-cursed land and the last of a powerful line of witches. Spell breaker. Liberator of the west wind. All winds stop for her. Why?" From A Witch's Guide to Magical Creatures *by Jemima Tulip Franklin.*

Allen agreed to have all the bodies removed from the cellar and planted by Sotsona's tree. After the storm passed, people noticed the tree was flowering for the first time since the curse. The stones from the wall had all flown away and littered the bottom of the lake. The town council got together and decided to make a little cemetery out of the land, a memorial to the influential women of Dust House. It gave them a local legend to tout out for tourists, and a chance to make up for the mistakes of the past.

Jemma, Allen, and few others were the only ones present when the bodies were laid to rest there, but Jemma rather liked the new home for her ancestors. It was beautiful, overlooking the lake, and it was so much more alive than when they were hidden in the cellar.

The funeral for Gran was held several days later. Relatives from all over the country came to pay their respects, and a large portion of the town. Everyone of Jemma's magical guests insisted on staying to support her. Even the three wind guardians.

Jemma listened to one person after another come up and say something kind about her grandmother, or funny, or frankly sad. But by the end of it, she felt oddly happy. So many people loved Gran. She'd been cantankerous, pushy, a bit of a know-it-all, a witch, and not a little bit smug, but she'd touched a lot of lives. If she was lucky, Jemma just might grow up to be something like her.

At the end of the service, Jemma brought forward the new headstone she'd made.

ESTHER LYNN FRANKLIN
Born for the earth, died for love
Wife, mother, grandmother, friend,
and a better enemy you'll never find.

Jemma couldn't quite force words past her lips but the stone said what she wanted people to remember: the woman beyond the witch.

*

There were so many people in the house after the service, so many people talking to her, and she couldn't say she remembered a word of it. But she remembered what happened after, when one after another of her friends left.

The three guardians were the first to go. They had stayed around, not together but close enough so they could be sure Jemma came out of the struggle alright.

"You are everything your grandmother promised," Lucianno said clasping Jemma's hand between both of his. "She would be most proud."

"Thank you."

"We are in your debt, little witch," Ilya said with an uncharacteristically broad smile. "All winds are lighter now. If you have need of us, only call."

Jemma shook her head, unsure what to say. She didn't like having people in her debt. But before she could speak, Nsombi walked over with a bright smile and hugged Jemma.

"Sisters now?"

It took Jemma until just that moment to figure out why such a gregarious-looking little girl spoke so little. But she threw her arms around the girl as well, giving her a tight hug. She would like to have a sister.

"What language do you speak?" she asked when she pulled away.

"Swahili," she said with a wide smile.

"I'll have to learn some."

Nsombi smiled.

Ilya began laughing. "And Russian, little witch."

Jemma nodded.

"And Spanish."

"I already know a little Spanish," Jemma said. "But it would be fun to learn some more."

"Adios, brujita."

"Kwaheri, dada."

"Das, vidanya."

Jemma felt a little left out with her ordinary goodbye, so she just waved and promised herself she would learn at least a few phrases in all three languages. Maybe even more.

When they were gone, Tangerine announced that she was ready to leave. Now that none of them had any great fear of Pa, Tangerine said she would use her own magic to get home and save Jemma the trouble. It wasn't any trouble, but Tangerine insisted; she didn't like to be taken care of.

But she very much enjoyed taking care of others. Before she left, she pulled Jemma into her mother's room, where she hadn't been since unmaking the boots.

"Now I need a few promises from you."

Jemma nodded and smiled, even though her whole body felt stiff; she didn't want to be in here. If Tangerine made her promise to forgive her mother, she would agree, but it would be a lie.

"I need you to cook at least one meal for yourself a week. Something that excites you, and you take your time with. I promise it will taste better if it excites you." Jemma nodded. "And you must promise to come visit me in Colorado. And last of all," she paused here, and just stared at Jemma for a moment, "you must smile a bit more."

Jemma nodded. Tangerine hopped off the headboard and ran up Jemma's arm, squeezing her neck as best as her little arms could.

"It was my honor to meet you," she said and vanished, leaving Jemma alone in her mother's room.

Jemma looked at her mother and waited for all the anger to come. After a few seconds, it seemed like it wouldn't come at all. That nothing would. May looked like an empty shell. As tears began to crowd Jemma's eyes, she felt her anger wanting to creep back in. She left the room, pulling the curtains together as she went.

When it came time for Woolworth to leave, Jemma felt like trapping him in one of the magic jars hidden beneath her bed, just to have his snarling, grouchy presence. It was almost like saying goodbye to Gran again.

"You will not cry over me," he snapped, noting the redness in Jemma's eyes. "The kelpie can feel, remember."

Jemma smiled. "I'm going to miss you most of all."

"Nonsense, no one misses a gripie."

"I will. Woolworth," Jemma said intensely bending down so her face was level with him. "When you get home…tell your sons you love them, tell them you're sorry for whatever it is you did. Maybe they want to forgive you but they're waiting for you to want them badly enough to risk being hurt."

He nodded over and over, and suddenly swiped his face and stomped his foot. "See what you've made me do. The kelpie will never let me hear the end of this."

Jemma laughed, swiping away a few tears herself. "Well, what do you care what he thinks? Kelpies eat their young, you know."

Woolworth threw back his head, his entire body, and rolled around laughing on the table.

Nona asked for a private word in Jemma's room after she said her goodbyes to everyone else. She floated around the room, looking at Jemma's different books and the notes she had pinned to her wall.

"I did something without your permission, and I want to explain it to you," she said out of nowhere, spinning to face Jemma. "I believe things happen for a reason. Not everyone does, and that suits me fine, because I like convincing people."

Jemma rolled her eyes and smiled. She was going to miss Nona.

"I think your father found the five of us because we needed something you had, or you needed something we had. It had to be us five. No others. And it took me a while to see why. But I realized why at your grandmother's funeral. You aren't a witch, Jemma. Or at least you aren't only a witch. You are a liberator. It's a much higher calling. You released the wind, and all of us, and this town. You even released your Gran from her heritage to just be a woman."

Jemma was stunned. Had she done all that? It didn't really seem like it. All she'd really done for Pa's captives was open a few jars and gave them food to eat. Nona was blowing this way out of proportion.

"Nona, thank you. But…"

"You're young yet, so you haven't the perspective to see it. But you will. You are a different breed of woman."

"What is it you did?" Jemma asked beginning to feel a bit afraid.

Nona smiled, and her body shook, shifting between grey and red like she couldn't make up her mind how to feel.

"I named you a contact, in a network of women, protectors scattered across the globe. We help women, and the occasional man, from things that would threaten their lives, or those of their children. We help women like your mother. For now, all you are is a contact. If a woman is in danger and comes to you, you call me, and I will tell you where to send her. But I hope one day you will decide to be a full member."

They hugged and Jemma said she would consider, but what she thought most about after Nona left was one sentence. *Women like your mother.* Was her mother like that? Did she need help?

Jemima Tulip, the Witch Who Loosed the

Wind

K ai was actually dreading leaving this place. He'd hated it in the beginning, but now, he might just miss the dry air and the accents that seemed to get only so much more pronounced when he walked into a room. Or someone or other instructing him on his artistic choices, even the general store. But most of all, he'd miss the funny little witch who'd saved his life, twice.

"You know, I still owe you a life debt. I don't think I should leave until I've repaid it, or at least taught you to swim." Kai was standing on the porch with his parents waiting in the dusty driveway.

"Yeah, I've been thinking about that," Jemma said with a coy smile. The girl just wouldn't stop flirting with him. "I was talking with Doe, and she said there are a few schools of thought on life debts. One says I saved you, so you owe me. Another says I saved you, so for the rest of your life, I'm responsible for the things you do, because you wouldn't be around if it weren't for me."

Kai laughed. She would go that way. "Let's not be dramatic. You gave me a glass of water."

"Bucket," Jemma corrected. "And you'd best be rememberin' that the next time you do something stupid, because it's gonna be half my fault."

"Alright." Kai chuckled. "I got you something."

"Yeah, a house full of paintings that come to life at odd moments. And the most beautiful journal in the world."

"This is better. I know how much you wanted a picture of me. So here." Kai reached into his back pocket for the rolled up tee shirt Fern had given him that day in the general store. He shook it open in front of Jemma, with a playful grin on his face.

Jemma stared at it confused for half a second then burst out laughing, laying her head against his chest as she giggled.

"*I heart boys who sparkle*," she read with a broad smile, taking the *Twilight* tee-shirt from his hands to look at it closer. But he could feel the tears gathering in her eyes. She was going to miss him. "He doesn't look a thing like you." Jemma complained staring at the *Twilight* star. "He's so pale."

"Kelpies get more sun than vampires; it's not his fault."

"This isn't a picture of you," Jemma said, balling up the shirt in her hand and bracing it on her hip.

"Well, then I guess you're just going to have to Skype with me or come and visit sunny California."

Jemma nodded and threw her arms around him. "I'm gonna miss you."

Kai hugged her back, briefly. Then pulled her away. "I've gotta be serious for a minute, Jemma. The reason your father caught me, aside from the obvious I-was-a-sucker part, is that your mother was standing there in the wind, telling me only I could save you."

Jemma drew away, staring at him like she wanted to run. He wasn't sure if he should leave with her so clearly conflicted. It wasn't like the girl who'd tossed him the bucket of water to turn her back on anyone, even someone who'd broken her heart.

"I should have told you about her when I realized who she was, but I worried she was bad."

"She is," Jemma snapped.

"She said only I could save you, but I don't think she meant it literally, Jemma. I think…she thought she was dead, but she felt you out here calling to her, so sad, and angry and she wanted to help."

"So, she brought me you," Jemma said falling back on sarcasm as was so frequently her way. "Awfully fond of yourself, aren't you?"

"Awfully," Kai agreed with a wink. "Just think about it, will you? Not everyone gets a chance to talk with their comatose parent, but you did. So, she wasn't perfect, who is? I think if you give her a chance again, she may come back." She only glared at him, not that he'd expected much else from her. "Alright, see you soon, Jemima Tulip, the witch who *loosed the wind*."

He ran down the steps to his parents and was nearly gone in a flash of lightning when he turned around with a broad grin. "Don't forget to take your pills."

"Kelpie A.K.A. Waterhorse- close relative of both the siren and the mermaid, maybe others. Water dependent creatures need not live in water, but must be near it. Sparkle drawing in humans, the contact feeds their magic. As yet unspecified powers over water. Generally regarded as shallow, in constant need of affirmation, seems more like boundless curiosity. Kai wants to know everyone, and everything. If you hear the words 'only you' when you see one, smack it upside the head." From A Witch's Guide to Magical Creatures *by Jemima Tulip Franklin.*

"Yes nurse," Jemma whispered as Kai vanished. Jemma unrolled the shirt and pulled it over her head. Why was everyone determined to make her forgive May Bell?

The only truly good news Jemma could think of was that Hippa was going to stay. She'd explained, through her charades, that her parents were dead and she would much prefer to live with Jemma. She supposed that wasn't exactly good news. Hippa had no parents, but then neither did anyone else living here.

Maybe she should get the townies to call it Orphan House instead of Dust House. Jemma giggled at the thought and walked back along her yellow brick road, passing the quick-sand-dunes of time, Kai painted on the floor next to the doorway. Every so often, the dunes would flip upside down, like they were in an hourglass, and as they fell, they would turn into a beautiful Arabian palace, with a girl in long, flowing clothes crouched in its shadow scribbling away on a scroll, glancing every so often at the setting sun. Kai hadn't said, but Jemma was sure she must be Scheherazade. It made her desperate to run out and buy a copy of *The Thousand and One Nights*.

Jemma didn't think she'd ever get over this place. Kai only painted the living room and bathroom, but every single corner had some hidden treasure in it. And he'd left a shit-load of magic, enchanting each thing to come to life when Jemma least expected it. But there was one painting in particular that drew her attention just now.

The girl following a pixie into the dark forest. Jemma had pried most of Calypso's story out of Kai's mother when she caught her staring at the painting. It explained a lot about Kai. He'd seemed, when she first met him, sort of... shallow, but that wasn't it at all.

Hippa flew up next to Jemma and automatically began shifting from one shape to the next, the first, a flapping tongue stuck between two lips. Hippa's way of indicating Allen; she felt he talked too much and didn't pay attention to her attempts to communicate with him.

Jemma smiled and let Hippa have her tirade. Apparently, Allen swatted at her, nearly hit her, just because she was watching him talk on the phone.

"I know, he's a shit head," Jemma said absently. Apparently, that was an image Hippa hadn't thought of because she shifted into Allen's head with a giant turd on it and back into a hummingbird rolling through the air, laughing her wings off. Jemma giggled, Allen was going to be seeing that a lot now.

Hippa glanced at the painting and back at Jemma shifting into the little fairy girl she chose from time to time and tilting her head to the side questioningly.

"It's Kai's cousin," Jemma responded. "They were out one day, and she left him alone to follow a pixie. Left him all alone, but he feels to blame because she never came home."

Hippa flew up close to the picture, staring at it. She shifted into a hummingbird again and began poking the pixie in the painting with her beak.

"Hippa," Jemma laughed, and lifted a hand to pull the fairy gently away. "It could be a bad pixie or not. She left Kai, so she can't be very good."

At this, Hippa shifted into a rolling eye. She liked Kai better than she had at first but he was by no means her favorite person.

"I want to find her. You wanna' help?"

Hippa nodded happily and flew off towards the door. Jemma laughed. "We have to do research first. Figure out where to start looking, come up with a grid maybe and start blocking off sections when we search them."

Hippa hummingbird flopped down on the couch and rolled over onto her back with an open beak and closed eyes.

"I know, I'm a dead bore. Will you help me anyway?"

Hippa fluttered up to land on Jemma's shoulder, flapping her little wings constantly.

"Pixie-(Hippa) smallest of all fairy creatures, grows no bigger than two inches. Most powerful of any magical creature yet discovered. In constant motion. Can travel through time and magical dimensions because they are made of the light energy between them. Telepathic and telekinetic. Immeasurably strong, age for centuries, but have offspring just before dying, like stars. They are all orphans. Always seeking beings to connect with." From A Witch's Guide to Magical Creatures *by Jemima Tulip Franklin.*

Two weeks later, a few days before Jemma's birthday, Allen knocked on her door and stood in the doorway hesitantly.

"What?" Jemma demanded. "Do you have cancer or something?"

Allen rolled his eyes. And Jemma released the breath she'd been holding. He thought she was only sarcastic, but the truth was she couldn't handle any more bad news.

Things were getting back to normal, but Allen never spent this much time with her and every so often, they had large blow-up fights. Their tempers blew up, nothing magical.

The Little family were coming over for her birthday. Jemma was going to give them all flying lessons. Allen wanted a party, but Jemma didn't feel quite in the mood, but she liked being around the Littles, a real family. A loving one. She should be jealous, but when she was with them, for a little while, she felt like one of them.

"You really are the most ornery female in all of Oklahoma, you know that?"

"Only because Gran's dead," Jemma replied with a sweet smile. She actually liked his insults better than when he was solicitous.

"This came for you in the mail." He held out a postcard. "If you want to talk, you know where to find me."

He tossed the postcard on her bed and walked out. Jemma stared at it, across the room on her bed for the better part of a minute. He wouldn't say that if it was from someone he thought she'd like to hear from. Before she could go crazy wondering, Jemma walked over to snatch it off the bed.

Hippa flew down from the little swinging perch Jemma had installed for her to peer at the postcard over her shoulder.

The picture was of a UFO flying by a sign that said Welcome to New Mexico. Jemma flipped it over;

Jemma,

I've always loved you. More than I can say. Happy Birthday.

Love,

Pa

Below his note was another note, clearly still in his writing, from her mother.

Jemma mine,

I will always love you. I only wish you could believe me.

You are such a beautiful, strong, young woman,

Mama would be proud. I am proud too.

Loving you always,

Mama

Jemma sat down on the edge of her bed with the postcard between her thumb and fingers. Hippa settled on her shoulder and rubbed her head against Jemma's cheek as she did when it was clear she needed comfort.

"He never sent a card before. They never did," Jemma scoffed and tossed it onto the bed.

Jemma stood up and went back to her computer wanting to think of something else. But as soon as she sat down, Hippa began poking her in the ear with her little beak.

"Hippa, quit that. Hippa!"

Hippa flew in front of Jemma and popped into a wide bright light. Jemma saw, as if in a dream, her mother and father reaching out for her, as Jemma unmade the boots, both of them crying. It was before her for a moment, then it vanished and she saw Hippa again, in the little fairy girl shape. She gave Jemma a sad sympathetic look then flew over and kissed her softly on the cheek.

"Fine," Jemma said with a shuddering sigh. A few tears slid down her cheek. "Because you want to." Standing, Jemma lifted her computer into her arms and walked from the room, grabbing the postcard as she went.

Allen was in the living room, facing the TV he'd set up in the entertainment center he shoved where her bookshelf used to be. He looked up and watched Jemma walk to her mother's room without a word.

Jemma settled into the chair not looking her mother's way, and leaned back with the laptop on her knees. She continued her search for hard-to-reach bodies of water, good places for a kelpie on the run to hide. She let the postcard fall to the side of the chair as she searched. Hippa settled on her shoulder, rubbing her head against Jemma's cheek and beating her wings constantly.

She'd made a list of about ten places before she got up a few hours later. As she shut her laptop and shoved it under her arm, Jemma turned and faced her mother for the first time in weeks. She leaned down and kissed her mother's forehead, spinning away quickly.

May Bell's lips shifted into a soft smile and her fingers curled in around the sheet.

Jemma walked away with her back to the bed. "Night, Mama."

*D*alila Caryn is the author of fantasy novels *The Forgotten Sister* and *Future Queen.* She holds a bachelor's degree in creative writing from the University of California–Riverside. Her love of poetry and epic fantasies influenced her unique writing style. Family provides her with constant inspiration for creating genuine stories of love and redemption. In her free time, she can be found in corners reading about magical worlds or creating them, always with far more coffee than mere mortals can stand.

Yenthe Joline is a freelance character designer and illustrator living in the Netherlands. She is passionate about telling stories with her art and uses flowing, energetic lines to make her pirates, superheroes, and fairies seem to leap right off the page. She is home- schooled and comes from a big happy family where she is the oldest of seven siblings. When she is not creating worlds and characters with her art, she loves to read, watch movies, and spend time with her family.